MW01503520

Hugo Richard Meyer

The British State Telegraphs

Hugo Richard Meyer

The British State Telegraphs

1st Edition | ISBN: 978-3-75244-339-4

Place of Publication: Frankfurt am Main, Germany

Year of Publication: 2020

Outlook Verlag GmbH, Germany.

Reproduction of the original.

THE BRITISH STATE
TELEGRAPHS

BY

HUGO RICHARD MEYER

CHAPTER I
INTRODUCTION

SCOPE OF THE INQUIRY

The story of the British State Telegraphs divides itself into two parts: the purchase of the telegraphs, in 1870, from the companies that had established the industry of telegraphy; and the subsequent conduct of the business of telegraphy by the Government. The first part is covered by Chapters II to VI; the second part by the remaining chapters. Both parts contain a record of fact and experience that should be of service to the American public at the present moment, when there is before them the proposal to embark upon the policy of the municipal ownership and operation of the so-called municipal public service industries. The second part, however, will interest a wider body of readers than the first part; for it deals with a question that is of profound interest and importance at all times—the problem of a large body of civil servants in a Democracy.

Chapters II to VI tell of the demand of the British Chambers of Commerce, under the leadership of the Chamber of Commerce of Edinburgh, for lower charges on telegraphic messages; the appointment by the Government of Mr. Scudamore, Second Secretary of the Post Office, to report upon the relative merits of private telegraphs and State telegraphs; the character of the report submitted by Mr. Scudamore; and the reasons why that report—upon which rested the whole argument for nationalization—was not adequately considered either by the Select Committee of the House of Commons, to whom the Bill for the purchase of the telegraphs was referred, or by the House of Commons itself. The principal reason was that the agitation carried on by the Chambers of Commerce and the newspaper press[1] proved so successful that both political parties committed themselves to nationalization before Mr. Scudamore's report had been submitted to searching criticism. Under the circumstances, the Disraeli Ministry was unwilling to go into the general election of 1868 without having made substantial progress toward the nationalization of the telegraphs. In order to remove opposition to its Bill in the House of Commons, the Disraeli Ministry conceded practically everything asked by the telegraph companies, the railway companies and the newspaper press.[2] The result was that the Government paid a high price absolutely for the telegraphs. Whether the price was too high, relatively speaking, is difficult to say. In the first place, the price paid—about $40,000,000—was well within the sum which the Government had said it could afford to pay, to wit, $40,000,000 to $50,000,000. In the second place, the Government acquired an industry "ready-made," with an established staff of highly trained men educated in the school of competition—the only school that thus far has proved itself capable of bringing out the highest efficiency that is in men. In the second place, the Government acquired the sole right to transmit messages by electricity—a right which subsequent events have proved to cover all future inventions, such as the transmission of messages by means of the telephone and of wireless telegraphy. Finally, in spite of the wastefulness that characterized the Government's operation of the telegraphs from the day the telegraphs were taken over, the Telegraph Department in the year 1880-81 became able to earn more than the interest upon the large capital invested in the telegraphs. But from that year on the Government not only became more and more wasteful, but also lost control over the charges made to the public for the transmission of messages. It is instructive to note, in this latter connection, that the control over the rates to be charged to the public was taken out of the hands of the Government by Dr. Cameron, who represented in the House of Commons the people of Glasgow, and that another Scotch city, Edinburgh, had initiated and maintained the campaign for the nationalization of the telegraphs.

One of the most extraordinary of the astounding incidents of the campaign and negotiations that resulted in the purchase of the telegraphs, was the fact that in the debates in the House of Commons was not even raised the question of the possibility of complications and dangers arising out of the multiplication of the civil servants. That fact is the more remarkable, since the leaders of both political parties at the time apprehended so much danger from the existing civil servants that they refused to take active steps to enfranchise the civil servants employed in the so-called revenue departments—the customs, inland revenue and Post Office departments—who had been disfranchised since the close of the Eighteenth Century. The Bill of 1868, which gave the franchise to the civil servants in question, was a Private Bill, introduced by Mr. Monk, a private Member of the House of Commons; and it was carried against the protest of the Disraeli Ministry, and without the active support of the leading men in the Opposition.

In the debates upon Mr. Monk's Bill, Mr. Gladstone, sitting in Opposition, said he was not afraid that either political party ever would try to use the votes of the civil servants for the purpose of promoting its political fortunes, "but he owned that he had some apprehension of what might be called class influence in the House of Commons, which in his opinion was the great reproach of the Reformed Parliament, as he believed history would record. Whether they were going to emerge into a new state of things in which class influence would be weaker, he knew not; but that class influence had been in many things evil and a scandal to them, especially for the last fifteen or twenty years [since the Reform of Parliament]; and he was fearful of its increase in consequence of the possession of the franchise, through the power which men who, as members of a regular service, were already organized, might bring to bear on Members of Parliament."

Chapters VII and following show that Mr. Gladstone's apprehensions were well-founded; that the civil servants have become a class by themselves, with interests so widely divergent from the interests of the rest of the community that they do not distribute their allegiance between the two great political parties on the merits of the respective policies of those parties, as do an equal number of voters taken at random. The civil servants have organized themselves in great civil service unions, for the purpose of promoting their class interests by bringing pressure to bear upon the House of Commons. At the parliamentary elections they tend to vote solidly for the candidate who promises them most. In one constituency they will vote for the Liberal candidate, in another for the Conservative candidate.

Thus far neither Party appears to have made an open or definite alliance with the civil servants. But in the recent years in which the Conservative Party was in power, and year after year denied—"on principle" of public policy—certain requests of the civil servants, the rank and file, as well as some of the minor leaders of the Liberal, or Opposition Party, evinced a strong tendency to vote rather solidly in the House of Commons in support of those demands of the civil servants.[3] At the same time the chiefs of the Liberal, or Opposition Party, refrained from the debate as well as from the vote. It may be that the Opposition Party discipline was not strong enough to enable the Opposition chiefs to prevent the votes on the momentous issue raised in the House of Commons by the civil servants from becoming for all practical purposes Party votes; or, it may be that the Liberal Party leaders did not deem it expedient to seek to control the voting of their followers. Be that as it may, the fact remains that the Conservative Ministry that was in power, repeatedly called in vain upon the House of Commons to take out of the field of Party politics the issue raised by the civil servants in the period from 1890 to 1905. The Conservative Ministry year after year denied the request of the Post Office employees for a House of Commons Select Committee on the pay and position of the Post Office employees. On the other hand, the support of that request came steadily from the Liberal Opposition. In the General Election of January, 1906, the Post Office employees threw their weight overwhelmingly on the side of the Liberal Party; and immediately after the opening of the new Parliament, the newly established Liberal Government announced that it would give the Post Office employees the House of Commons Select Committee which the late Conservative Ministry had "on principle" of public policy refused to grant.

Shortly after the General Election of January, 1906, the President of the Postal Telegraph Clerks' Association, a powerful political organization, stated that nearly 450 of the 670 Members of the House of Commons had pledged themselves, in the course of the campaign, to vote for a House of Commons Select Committee. At about the same time, Lord Balcarres, a Conservative whip in the late Balfour ministry, speaking of the 281 members who entered Parliament for the first time in 1906, said "he thought he was fairly accurate when he said that they had given pretty specific pledges upon this matter [of a Select Committee] to those who had sent them to the House." Sir Acland-Hood, chief whip in the late Balfour Ministry, added: "...nearly the whole of the supporters of the then [1905] Government voted against the appointment of the Select Committee [in July, 1905]. No doubt many of them suffered for it at the general election; they either lost their seats or had their majorities reduced in consequence of the vote." And the new Prime Minister, Sir H. Campbell-Bannerman, spoke of the "retroactive effect of old promises extracted in moments of agony from candidates at the general election." And finally, at the annual conference of the Postal Telegraph Clerks' Association, held in March, 1906, Mr. R. S. Davis, the representative of the Metropolitan London Telegraph Clerks, said: "The new Postmaster General had made concessions which had almost taken them [the postal clerks] off their feet by the rapidity with which one had succeeded another and the manner in which they were granted."

Chapters XIV to XVII describe the efforts made by the civil servants to secure exemption from the ordinary vicissitudes of life, as well as exemption from the necessity of submitting to those standards of efficiency and those rules of discipline which prevail in private employment. They show the hopelessly unbusinesslike spirit of the rank and file of the public servants, a spirit fostered by the practice of members of the House of Commons intervening, from the floor of the House as well as behind the scenes, on behalf of public servants who have not been promoted, have been disciplined or dismissed, or, have failed to persuade the executive officers to observe one or more of the peculiar claims of "implied contract" and "vested right" which make the British public service so attractive to those men whose object in life is not to secure full and untrammeled scope for their abilities and ambitions, but a haven of refuge from the ordinary vicissitudes of life. Members of the House of Commons intervene, in the manner indicated, in mere matters of detail of administration, because they have not the courage to refuse to obey the behests of the political leaders of the civil service unions; they do not so interfere from the mere desire to promote their political fortunes by championing the interests of a class. They recognize the fact that the art of government is the art of log-rolling, of effecting the best compromise possible, under the given conditions of political intelligence and public spirit, between the interests of a class and the interests of the country as a whole. Their views were forcibly expressed, on a recent occasion, by Captain

Norton, who long has been one of the most aggressive champions in the House of Commons, of the civil servants, and who, at present, is a Junior Lord of the Treasury, in the Sir H. Campbell-Bannerman Liberal Ministry. Said Captain Norton: "As regarded what had been said about undue influence [being exercised by the civil servants], his contention was that so long as the postal officials ... were allowed to maintain a vote, they had precisely the same rights as all other voters in the country to exercise their fullest influence in the defense of their rights, privileges and interests. He might mention that all classes of all communities, of all professions, all trades, all combinations of individuals, such as anti-vaccinationists and so forth, had invariably used their utmost pressure in defense of their interests and views upon members of the House...."

The problem of government in every country—irrespectively of the form which the political institutions may take in any given country—is to avoid class legislation, and to make it impossible for any one class to exploit the others. Some of us—who are old-fashioned and at present in the minority—believe that the solution of that problem is to be found only in the upbuilding of the character and the intelligence of the individual citizen. Others believe that it is to be found largely, if not mainly, in extending the functions of the State and the City. To the writer, the experience of Great Britain under the experiment of the extension of the functions of the State and the City, seems to teach once more the essential soundness of the doctrine that the nation that seeks refuge from the ills that appear under the policy of *laissez-faire*, seeks refuge from such ills in the apparently easy, and therefore tempting, device of merely changing the form of its political institutions and political ideals, will but change the form of the ills from which it suffers.

FOOTNOTES:

1 The reason for the opposition of the newspaper press to the telegraph companies is discussed in Chapter VIII.

2 The concession made to the newspaper press is described in Chapter VIII.

3 The efforts of the civil servants culminated in the debate and vote of July 5, 1905. Upon that occasion there voted for the demands of the civil servants eighteen Liberalists who, in 1905-6, became Members of the Sir H. Campbell-Bannerman Liberal Ministry. Two of them, Mr. Herbert Gladstone and Mr. Lloyd George, became Members of the Cabinet, or inner circle of the Ministry.

CHAPTER II
THE ARGUMENT FOR THE NATIONALIZATION OF THE TELEGRAPHS

The indictment of the telegraph companies. The argument
from foreign experience. The promise of reduced tariffs and
increased facilities. The alleged financial success of foreign
State telegraphs: Belgium, Switzerland and France. The
argument from British company experience.

In 1856 the Chambers of Commerce of Great Britain, under the leadership
of the Chamber of Commerce of Edinburgh, began an agitation for the
purchase by the Government of the properties of the several British telegraph
companies. In 1865, the telegraph companies, acting in unison, withdrew the
reduced rate of twenty-four cents for twenty words, address free, that had
been in force, since 1861, between certain large cities. That action, which will
be described further on, caused the Chambers of Commerce to increase the
agitation for State purchase. In September, 1865, Lord Stanley of Alderley,
Postmaster General, commissioned Mr. F. I. Scudamore, Second Secretary of
the Post Office, "to inquire and report whether, in his opinion, the electric
telegraph service might be beneficially worked by the Post Office—whether,
if so worked, it would possess any advantages over a system worked by
private companies—and whether it would entail any very large expenditure
on the Post Office Department beyond the purchase of existing rights."

In July, 1866, Mr. Scudamore reported, recommending the purchase of the
telegraphs. In February, 1868, he submitted a supplementary report; and in
1868 and 1869, he acted as the chief witness for the Government before the
Parliamentary Committees appointed to report on the Government's Bills
proposing to authorize the State to acquire and operate the telegraphs.[4] The
extent to which the Government, throughout the considerations and
negotiations which finally ended in the nationalization of the telegraphs,
relied almost exclusively upon evidence supplied by Mr. Scudamore, is

indicated in the statement made by the Chancellor of the Exchequer, Mr. G. W. Hunt, on July 21, 1868, that Mr. Scudamore "might be said to be the author of the Bill to acquire the telegraphs."[5]

Mr. Scudamore reported that the Chambers of Commerce, and the various writers in the periodical and newspaper press who had supported the proposal of State purchase, had concurred in the following general propositions: "that the charges made by the telegraph companies were too high, and tended to check the growth of telegraphic correspondence; that there were frequent delays of messages; that many important districts were unprovided with telegraphic facilities; that in many places the telegraph office was inconveniently remote from the centre of business, and was open for too small a portion of the day; that little or no improvement could be expected so long as the working of the telegraphs was conducted by commercial companies striving chiefly to earn a dividend and engaged in wasteful competition with each other; and, finally, that the growth of telegraphic correspondence had been greatly stimulated in Belgium and Switzerland by the annexation of the telegraphs to the Post Offices of those countries, and the consequent adoption of a low scale of charges; and that in Great Britain like results would follow the adoption of like means, and that from the annexation of the British telegraphs to the British Post Office there would accrue great advantage to the public, and ultimately a large revenue to the State." Subsequently, before the Select Committees of Parliament, Mr. Scudamore maintained that in the hands of the State the telegraphs would pay from the start.

Mr. Scudamore continued his report with the statement that he had satisfied himself that in Great Britain the telegraph was not in such general use as upon the Continent; that "the class who used the telegraphs most freely were stock brokers, mining agents, ship brokers, Colonial brokers, racing and betting men, fruit merchants and others engaged in business of a speculative character, or who deal in articles of a perishable nature. Even general merchants used the telegraphs comparatively little, compared with those engaged in the more speculative branches of commerce." He added that from 1862 to 1868 the annual increase in the number of telegraphic messages had ranged pretty evenly from 25 per cent. to 30 per cent., indicating merely a gradual increase in the telegraphic correspondence of those classes who had been the first to use the telegraphs. He said there had been none of those "sudden and prodigious jumps" that had occurred on the Continent after each reduction in the charges for telegraphic messages, or after each extension of the telegraph system to the smaller towns.

Mr. Scudamore held that it was a serious indictment of the manner in which the telegraph companies had discharged their duties to the public, that the small tradesman had not learned to order goods by telegraph, and had not thereby enabled himself to get along with a smaller stock of goods kept constantly on hand; that the fishing villages on the remote coasts of Scotland that had no railways, had no telegraphs; that the public did not send "millions of messages" of this kind: "I shall not be home to dinner;" "I will bring down some fish;" "You can meet me at four;" and that the wife and children, away from their home in the country village, did not telegraph to the husband and father: "Send me a money order." Mr. Scudamore's notions of the uses to which the telegraphs ought to be put were shared by the Chancellor of the Exchequer, Mr. Hunt, who looked forward to the day when "persons who have a difficulty in writing letters will have less difficulty in going to a telegraph office and sending a message to a friend than writing a letter."[6]

Mr. Scudamore supported his position with the subjoined reports from countries in which the State operated the telegraphs. The Danish Government had reported that the telegraph was used by merchants generally and for social and domestic purposes. Prussia had reported that in the early days, when the charges had been high, the use of the telegraph had been confined almost exclusively to bankers, brokers, large commercial houses and newspaper correspondents, but that with each reduction in the charges, or extension of the telegraphs to small towns, the number of those who regularly sent out and received messages had increased considerably. Switzerland had reported that messages relating to personal business and family affairs formed as important a part of the whole traffic as the messages of banking interests and other trading interests.

France had reported that 38 per cent. of the messages related to personal business and family affairs; and Belgium had reported that nearly 59 per cent. of the messages related to personal business and family affairs.

To indicate the manner in which the use of the telegraph increased with reductions in the charges made, Mr. Scudamore reported that in Belgium, in 1863, a reduction of 33 per cent. in the charge had been followed by an increase of 80 per cent. in the number of telegrams; and that, in 1866, a reduction of 50 per cent. in the charges had been followed by an increase of 85 per cent. in the traffic. In France, in 1862, a reduction of 35 per cent. in the charge, had led to an increase of 64 per cent. in the number of messages. In Switzerland, in 1868, a reduction of 50 per cent. in the charge had been followed, in the next three months, by an increase in business of 90 per cent. In Prussia, in 1867, a reduction of the charge by 33 per cent. had, in the first month, increased the number of messages by 70 per cent. The increase in business always had followed immediately, said Mr. Scudamore, showing that new classes of people took up the use of the telegraphs.

Finally, Mr. Scudamore stated that in 1866, the proportion borne by the total of telegrams sent to the aggregate of letters sent, had been: in Belgium, one telegram for every 37 letters; in Switzerland, one telegram for every 69 letters; and in the United Kingdom, one telegram for every 121 letters. The relative failure of the people of the United Kingdom to use the telegraph freely, Mr. Scudamore ascribed to the high charges made by the telegraph companies, and to the restricted facilities offered by the companies.

In 1868, the British companies were charging 24 cents for a twenty-word message, over distances not exceeding 100 miles; 36 cents for distances between 100 and 200 miles; and 48 cents for distances exceeding 200 miles. For messages passing between Great Britain and Ireland, the charge ranged from $0.72 to $1.44. In all cases the addresses of the sender and of the sendee were carried free.

Promise of Lower Charges and Better Service

The Government proposed to make a uniform charge of 24 cents for twenty words, irrespective of distance. Mr. Scudamore stated that he fully expected that in two or three years the Government would reduce its charge to 12 cents. The only reason why the Government did not propose to adopt immediately the last mentioned rate, was the desire not to overcrowd the telegraphs at the start before there had been the chance to learn with what volume of traffic the existing plant and staff could cope.[7]

In 1868 there was in the United Kingdom one telegraph office for every 13,000 people. The Government promised to inaugurate the nationalization of the telegraphs by giving one office for every 6,000 people.[8] In the shortest time possible, the Government would open a telegraph office at every money order issuing Post Office. At that time the practice was to establish a money order office wherever there was the prospect of two money orders being issued a day; and in some instances such offices were established on the prospect of one order a day.

The contention that the public interest demanded a great increase in the number of telegraph offices, Mr. Scudamore supported by citing the number of offices in Belgium and France. In the former country there were upward of 125 telegraph offices which despatched less than one telegram a day. In fact, some offices despatched less than one a month. The Belgium Government, in figuring the cost of the Telegraph Department, charged that Department nothing whatever for office rent, or for fire, light and office fittings; nor did it

12

charge the smaller offices anything for the time given by the State Railway employees and the postal employees to the Telegraph Department. In France there were 301 telegraph offices that took in less than $40 a year; 179 offices that took in from $40 to $100; and 185 offices that took in from $100 to $200.

Mr. Scudamore over and again assured the Parliamentary Select Committee of 1868 that the telegraphs in the hands of the State would be self-supporting from the start, and that ultimately they would be a considerable source of revenue. But he supported his indictment of the telegraph companies of the United Kingdom by drawing upon the experience of the State telegraphs of Belgium, Switzerland, and France, under very low rates on inland telegrams, as distinguished from telegrams in transit, or telegrams to and from foreign countries. In taking that course, Mr. Scudamore ignored the fact that the inland rates in question were not remunerative.

Belgium's Experience

The Belgium State telegraphs had been opened in 1850. In the years 1850 to 1856, they had earned, upon an average, 36.8 per cent. a year upon their cost. In the period 1857 to 1862, they had earned, upon an average, 24.3 per cent. In 1863 to 1865, the annual earnings fell to an average of 13.5 per cent.; and in 1866 to 1869, they reached an average of 2.8 per cent. only. The reasons for that rapid and steady decline of the net earnings were: the opening of relatively unprofitable lines and offices; increases in wages which the Government could not withhold; a slackening in the rate of growth of the profits on the so-called foreign messages and transit messages; and a rapid increase in the losses upon the inland messages, which were carried at low rates for the purpose of stimulating traffic.

At an early date the Belgium Government concluded that the first three of the four factors just enumerated were beyond the control of the State, and therefore permanent. It resolved, therefore, to attempt to neutralize them by developing the inland traffic to such proportions that it should become a source of profit, that traffic having been, up to that time, a source of loss. Accordingly, on January 1st, 1863, the Government lowered the charge on inland messages from 30 cents for 20 words, addresses included, to 20 cents. As that reduction did not prove sufficiently effective, the charge on inland messages was reduced, on December 1st, 1865, to 10 cents for 20 words. Under that reduction the loss incurred upon the inland messages rose from an annual average of $13,800 in 1863 to 1865, to an annual average of $59,500 in 1866 to 1869; and the average annual return upon the capital invested fell to 2.8 per cent. This evidence was before Mr. Scudamore when he argued from the experience of Belgium in favor of a uniform rate, irrespective of distance, of 24 cents for 20 words, not counting the addresses. Mr. Scudamore shared the opinion of the Belgium Government that the rate of 10 cents would so stimulate the traffic as to become very profitable. As a matter of fact, things went from bad to worse in Belgium, and for many years the Belgian State telegraphs failed to earn operating expenses.[2]

By way of explanation it should be added that the so-called transit messages and foreign messages were profitable for two reasons. In the first place, the Belgian Government kept high the rates on those messages. In the second place, those messages are carried much more cheaply than inland messages. The transit messages, say from Germany to England, have only to be retransmitted; they are not received across the counter, nor are they delivered across the counter and by messenger. The foreign messages are burdened with only one of the two foregoing relatively costly operations. In 1866 the Belgian Government stated that, if the cost to the Telegraph Department of a given number of words transmitted as a message in transit be represented by two, the corresponding cost of the same number of words received and transmitted as a foreign message would be represented by three, while the cost of the same number of words received and transmitted as an inland message would be represented by five.

Swiss Experience

The Swiss State telegraphs, the experience of which Mr. Scudamore also cited in support of his Report, were opened in 1852; and in the period from 1854 to 1866 they earned, on an average, 18 per cent. upon their cost. Throughout that period the average receipts per inland messages were 21 cents, and the average receipts per foreign message were 39 cents. In the year 1865 the average receipts per message were 21 cents for inland messages, and 30 cents for foreign and transit messages, which constituted 39 per cent. of

14

the traffic. In the following year, 1866, the average receipts upon the inland traffic remained unchanged; while those upon the foreign and transit traffic, 43 per cent. of the total traffic, fell to 20 cents. This reduction of 33 per cent. in the average receipts upon the foreign and transit traffic, caused a decline of 45 per cent. in the total net receipts, and reduced the earnings upon the capital from 15.2 per cent. in 1865, to 7.5 per cent. in 1866.

Thus far the receipts from the inland messages had not covered the operating expenses incurred on account of those messages. The profits, which had been very large, had come from the foreign messages and messages in transit.[10] The Government, alarmed at the decline in profits resulting from the fall in the average receipts per message in the foreign and transit traffic, resolved upon a special effort to stimulate the growth of the inland traffic. Accordingly, on January 1st, 1868, it lowered the rates on inland messages of 20 words, address counted, from 20 cents to 10 cents. The inland traffic immediately doubled; but the cost of handling it more than doubled. The increase in the traffic necessitated the stringing of additional wires, and the employment of more instruments, linemen, telegraphers and office clerks. At the same time the Government was obliged to concede all round increases of wages and salaries, in consequence of the general increase in the cost of living which accompanied the world-wide revival of trade ushered in by the discovery of gold in California and Australia, the introduction of steamships upon the high seas, and the building of railways in all parts of the world.

The inland messages increased by leaps and bounds from 397,289 in 1867 to 2,118,373 in 1876; and still the receipts from them did not cover the operating expenses. In 1874 and 1875, for example, those expenses averaged 14 cents per message. Accordingly, in 1877, the Government adopted a new scale of charges on inland messages, to wit: an initial charge of 6 cents per message, to which was added 0.5 cent for every word transmitted. The Government assumed that the average length of the inland messages would be 14 words; and that the average receipts per message would be 13 cents. It hoped soon to reduce the average cost per message below 13 cents, and hoped thus to make the inland traffic remunerative. But those expectations never were realized; and to this day the inland messages have been carried at a loss.[11]

In 1861, the French State telegraphs reduced the rate for messages of 20 words, counting the address, to 20 cents for intradepartmental[12] messages, and to 40 cents for interdepartmental messages. In 1866 the average receipts per message were: 38 cents on the inland traffic; $1.38 on the foreign traffic; and 55.8 cents on the traffic as a whole. With these average receipts per message, the earnings were $1,541,519; while the operating expenses were $1,796,692. In other words, the State telegraphs lost $255,173 on the working, besides failing to earn any interest on the capital invested in them, $4,760,000.

In making the foregoing statement, no allowance is made for the value of the messages sent "on public service," messages for which the State would have been obliged to pay, had the telegraphs been owned or operated by companies. No such allowance can be made, because the several official French statements submitted by Mr. Scudamore as to the number of messages sent "on public service" applied to the years 1865 and 1867, years for which the operating expenses were not given. Furthermore, the messages sent on public service in 1865 and 1867 were so numerous as to indicate so loose a construction of the term "on public service" as to make the returns worthless for the purpose of determining the commercial value of the saving resulting to the State from the public ownership of the telegraphs. For 1865, the number of messages "on public service" was returned as 568,647, the equivalent of 23 per cent. of the number of messages sent by the public. For 1867, the number was returned as 168,999, the equivalent of 5.94 per cent. of the messages sent by the public. That those figures represented an unreasonable resource to the telegraph for the transaction of the State's business, is proved by the fact that in the United Kingdom, in the period 1871 to 1890, the value of the messages sent "on public service" was equivalent to less than 2 per cent. of the sums paid by the public for the transmission of telegraphic messages. On the basis of any reasonable use of the telegraphs "on public service," the financial results of the French State telegraphs would not have been altered materially. The deficit, in 1866, on account of operating expenses, $255,173, was sufficient to permit of the sending of 457,300 messages "on public service," the equivalent of 16 per cent. of the messages sent by the public. It would be unreasonable to assume that the State could have need of such recourse to the telegraphs.

Summary of Foreign Experience

To sum up the evidence from Belgium, Switzerland, and France, submitted by Mr. Scudamore in 1866 to 1869: This evidence was that rates of 20 cents and 10 cents for 20 words, applied to inland messages, developed an enormous inland traffic, but that that traffic was unremunerative. So long as the rates on foreign messages and transit messages had remained very much higher than the rates on inland messages, the Belgian and Swiss State telegraphs had paid handsomely. But as soon as the latter rates had approached the level of the former rates, the net revenue had tumbled headlong; and there was, in 1868 and 1869, no certainty that it would not disappear entirely, or be reduced to such proportions as no longer to afford an adequate return upon the capital invested in the telegraphs. In the case of France, no evidence was presented that the State telegraphs ever had paid their way, though the prices obtained for the transmission of foreign messages and transit messages were between three and four times the returns obtained from the transmission of inland messages.

English Companies' Experience

While the evidence from Belgium, Switzerland and France, presented by Mr. Scudamore, did not support the proposition of a low uniform rate, irrespective of distance, the evidence furnished by the experience of the telegraph companies of the United Kingdom pointed strongly to the conclusion that a uniform rate, irrespective of distance, of 24 cents for 20 words, addresses not counted, was not remunerative in the then state of efficiency of the telegraph. In this connection it must be borne in mind that at this time messages had to be retransmitted at intervals of 200 or 300 miles; and that, while the maximum distance a message could travel was only 160 miles in Belgium, and 200 miles in Switzerland, it was 600 miles in the United Kingdom.

In 1861 the telegraph business of the United Kingdom was in the hands of two companies which had been organized in 1846 and 1852 respectively: the Electric and International Telegraph Company, and the British and Irish Magnetic Telegraph Company. In that year, 1861, a new company, the United Kingdom Electric Telegraph Company, invaded the field with a uniform tariff, irrespective of distance, of 24 cents for 20 words, addresses free. The established companies had been charging 24 cents for distances up to 25 miles; 36 cents for distances up to 50 miles; 48 cents for distances up to 100 miles; 60 cents for distances up to 200 miles; 96 cents for distances up to 300 miles; and $1.20 for distances up to 400 miles.[13]

The United Kingdom Company began operations in 1861 with a trunk line between London, Birmingham, Manchester, Liverpool and intermediate and neighboring towns. Shortly afterward it opened a second trunk line from London to Northampton, Leicester, Nottingham, Sheffield, Barnsley, Wakefield, Leeds and Hull; and across through Bradford, Halifax, Rochdale, and Huddersfield to Manchester and Liverpool. Subsequently the company extended its line to Edinburgh and Glasgow, thus lengthening to upward of 500 miles, the distance over which messages were transmitted for 24 cents.[14]

In July 1865, the Board of Directors reported as follows to the stockholders: "The Directors much regret to state that, notwithstanding their earnest efforts to develop telegraphic communication so as to render the shilling [24 cent] rate remunerative, the company has been unable to earn a dividend. The system of the company consists of trunk lines almost exclusively embracing nearly all the main centres of business, telegraphically speaking, of the country. Seeing that the company was working under the greatest possible advantages, and that upward of four years had elapsed since the formation of the company without the payment of any dividend to the proprietary, the directors conceived that they would not be justified in continuing the shilling [24 cent] system, and arrangements were therefore agreed to for its alteration. The directors waited until the last moment before reluctantly adopting this step, but having sought publicity in every way, having persistently canvassed in every department of business, and having endeavored by personal solicitations of numerous active agents to attract trade, they at last saw themselves compelled to agree to a measure that was greatly antagonistic to their personal wishes, but absolutely essential for the well-being of the company, and requisite, as they believe, for the permanent interests of the telegraphing community."

In 1865, the United Kingdom Telegraph Company joined with its competitors, the Electric and International Telegraph Company, and the British and Irish Magnetic Telegraph Company, in the following rates for 20 words, addresses free: 24 cents for distances up to 100 miles; 36 cents for distances between 100 and 200 miles; and 48 cents for distances beyond 200 miles.

In July, 1866, the directors of the United Kingdom Telegraph Company reported that in the last half-year "the company earned an amount of profit equal to 6 per cent. dividend over the whole of its share capital."

When the United Kingdom Company had entered the field, in 1861, with the 24 cent rate, the old established companies, the Electric and International and the British and Irish Magnetic, had been compelled to adopt the 24 cent rate between all points reached by the United Kingdom Company. In February, 1863, the directors of the Electric and International Company reported that the 24 cent circuit between London, Liverpool, Manchester and Birmingham still was unremunerative. The company was losing money on every message transmitted, though the 24 cent rate had increased business to such an extent that the company had been obliged to add two wires to the circuit in question. Since the business done by means of the additional wires did not pay, the directors had charged the cost of those wires to operating expenses, not to capital account. The company did not care for the business, but could not refuse to take it. In July, 1865, the directors reported: "After a trial of four years, the experiment of a uniform shilling rate [on certain circuits] irrespective of distance, has not justified itself."

The half yearly reports of the British and Irish Magnetic Company from 1862 to 1865 reported that "for any but very short distances," the 24 cent tariff was "utterly unremunerative." The effect of the rate was to absorb in unavoidable additional expenses a very large portion of the increase in revenue coming from the increase in business.

In 1859 the London District Telegraph Company was organized for the purpose of transmitting telegraph messages between points in Metropolitan London. In 1860 the company had 52 stations and 73.5 miles of line; and it carried 74,582 messages. In 1862 it had 84 offices and 103 miles of line, and it carried 243,849 messages. In 1865 the company reached its highest point, carrying 316,272 messages. The company at that time had 123 miles of line and 83 offices. The London District Telegraph Company began with a tariff of 8 cents for 10 words, and 12 cents for a message of 10 words with a reply message of 10 words. It soon changed its tariff to 12 cents for 15 words, experience having shown that 10 words was an insufficient allowance.[15] Subsequently the company added porterage charges for delivery beyond a certain distance. In 1866, the company raised its tariff to 24 cents. The company never earned operating expenses; and in November, 1867, its shares, upon which $25 had been paid in, fluctuated between $3.75 and $6.25.[16]

Mr. Robert Grimston, Chairman of the Electric and International Telegraph Company, in 1868 commented as follows upon the experience of the London District Telegraph Company. "A very strong argument against the popular fancy that the introduction of a low rate of charge in towns and country districts would induce the shopkeepers and the lower classes to use the telegraph is furnished by the example of the London District Telegraph Company. A better or a wider field than the metropolitan for an illustration of this theory could not surely be furnished. The facts, however, being, that after several years of struggling existence, the tariff being first fixed at 8 cents, and then at 12 cents, the company has never paid its way."

FOOTNOTES:

[4] *A Report to the Postmaster General upon Certain Proposals which have been made for transferring to the Post Office the Control and Management of the Electric Telegraphs throughout the United Kingdom, July, 1868*; *Supplementary Report to the Postmaster General upon the Proposal for transferring to the Post Office the Control and Management of the Electric Telegraphs, February, 1868*; *Special Report from the Select Committee on the Electric Telegraphs Bill, 1868*; and *Report from the Select Committee on the Telegraphic Bill, 1869.*

Unless otherwise stated, all the material statements made in this chapter are taken from the foregoing official documents.

[5] *Hansard's Parliamentary Debates*, July 21, 1868, p. 1,603.

6 *Special Report from the Select Committee on the Electric Telegraphs Bill, 1868*; q. 2549 and 1581.

7 *Special Report from the Select Committee on the Electric Telegraphs Bill, 1868*; q. 2508; and *Report from the Select Committee on the Telegraphic Bill, 1869*; q. 346.

8 *Report from the Select Committee on the Telegraphic Bill, 1869*; q. 327; and *Special Report from the Select Committee on the Electric Telegraphs Bill, 1868*; q. 88.

9 *Supplementary Report to the Postmaster General upon the Proposal for transferring to the Post Office the Control and Management of the Electric Telegraphs*, 1868; and Sir James Anderson, in *Journal of the Statistical Society*, September, 1872.

BELGIAN STATE TELEGRAPHS

	Inland messages			Foreign Messages			
	Cost per message	Receipts per message	Loss per message	Cost per message	Receipts per message	Gain per message	m
	CENTS						
1860	42.0	35.4	6.8	25.4	49.0	23.6	
1861	38.4	35.0	3.4	23.0	44.8	21.8	
1862	39.4	33.6	5.8	23.6	43.2	19.6	
1863	30.0	22.4	7.6	18.0	34.0	16.0	
1864	27.0	22.4	4.6	16.2	31.2	15.0	
1865	25.4	20.8	4.6	15.2	27.0	11.8	
1866	18.0	11.8	6.2	10.8	23.4	12.6	
1867	18.2	11.6	6.6	11.0	24.0	13.0	
1868	18.4	11.4	7.0	11.0	22.4	11.4	
1869	17.2	10.8	6.4	10.2	21.2	11.0	

10 *Archiv für Post und Telegraphie*, 1903, p. 577.

11 *Archiv für Post und Telegraphie*, 1903, p. 574.

12 For administrative purposes France is divided into so-called "Departments."

13 *Journal of the Statistical Society*, March, 1881.

The Tariff of the Electric and International Co., for 20 words (addresses not counted after 1854), was as follows:

In 1840, and for some years after, the charge was 2 cents a mile for the first 50 miles; 1

cent a mile for the second 50 miles; and 5 cents for each mile beyond 100 miles.

In 1850 the maximum charge for 20 words was reduced to $2.40; early in 1851 it was reduced to $2.04; and in November, 1851, it was reduced to 60 cents for 100 miles, and $1.20 for distances beyond 100 miles.

1855		1862		1864		1865	
Miles	**$**	**Miles**	**$**	**Miles**	**$**	**Miles**	**$**
50	0.36	25	0.24	50	0.24		
100	0.48	50	0.36				
150	0.72	100	0.48	100	0.48	100	0.24
151 and beyond	0.96	200	0.60	200	0.60	100 to 200	0.36
		300	0.96	300 and beyond	0.72	200 and beyond	0.36
		400 and beyond	1.20				

	1855	1865
To Ireland, by marine cable	1.20	0.72 to 0.96

In February, 1872, two years after the uniform rate of 24 cents, irrespective of distance, had been put in force by the Government, the Telegraph Department made a careful examination of 7,000 messages sent from the large cities to all parts of the United Kingdom. The average charge per message was found to be 27 cents; under the rates enforced by the telegraph companies in 1865, the average charge would have been 52 cents.—*Report of the Postmaster General* for 1872.

14

UNITED KINGDOM TELEGRAPH CO.

	Miles of line	**Miles of wire**	**Number of offices**	**Number of messages**
1861	305	1968	16	11,549
1862	372	2741	22	133,514
1863	831	5099	48	226,729
1864	1343	8096	100	518,651

1865	1672	9506	125	743,870

15 *Journal of Statistical Society*, March, 1881.

16 *Miscellaneous Statistics for the United Kingdom*, 1862, 1864, 1866 and 1868-9; *Parliamentary Paper* No. 416, Session of 1867-68; and *Journal of the Statistical Society*, March, 1881.

LONDON DISTRICT TELEGRAPH CO.

	Miles of line	Miles of wire	Number of offices	Number of messages
1860	73	335	52	74,582
1861	92	378	78	114,022
1862	103	401	84	243,849
1863	107	430	81	247,606
1864	115	454	80	308,032
1865	123	470	83	316,272
1866	150	495	80	214,496
1867	150	495	81	239,583
1868	163		82	

CHAPTER III
THE ALLEGED BREAK-DOWN OF *LAISSEZ-FAIRE*

Early history of telegraphy in Great Britain. The adequacy of private enterprise. Mr. Scudamore's loose use of statistics. Mr. Scudamore's test of adequacy of facilities. Telegraphic charges and growth of traffic in Great Britain. The alleged wastefulness of competition. The telegraph companies' proposal.

Upon the foregoing evidence, taken from the experience of the State telegraphs of Belgium, Switzerland, and France, and from the experience of the telegraph companies of the United Kingdom, Mr. Scudamore reached the conclusion that in telegraphy, in the United Kingdom, private enterprise had broken down. He stated his conclusion in these words: "It is clearly shown, I think, … that the cardinal distinction between the telegraph system of the United Kingdom and the systems of Belgium and Switzerland is this: that the latter have been framed and maintained solely with a view to the accommodation of the public, whilst the former has been devised and maintained mainly with a view to the interests of shareholders, and only indirectly for the benefit of the public." These words were intended to convey, and they did convey, the meaning that the policy of *laissez-faire* had broken down. That policy rests on the assumption that in the long run, and upon the whole, the public interest is conserved and promoted by the activities of the individual citizens who are seeking to promote their personal fortunes—by the activities of "the mere speculator and dividend seeker"—to employ the phrase that came into common use in 1866 to 1869, and ever since, has been made to do yeoman service.

Let us test by the evidence—of which a large part is to be found tucked away in the appendices to Mr. Scudamore's reports—this conclusion that in telegraphy, in the United Kingdom, private enterprise had broken down, and the policy of *laissez-faire* had been discredited.

The first thing to note in this connection is, that in the case of telegraphy, as in the case of so many other British industries, public ownership has been a parasite. It has been unwilling to assume the risk and burden of establishing the industry, and has contented itself with purchasing "ready-made" the industry after it had been developed by private enterprise. When Mr. Ronalds attempted to interest the British Government in telegraphy, he was told "that the telegraph was of no use in times of peace, and that the semaphore in time of war answered all the required purposes."[17]

In 1837, British individuals and companies began to stake their money upon the telegraph in Great Britain; and in 1854 they even carried the telegraph industry to continental Europe, notably to Belgium. In 1850 and 1851, the Governments of France, Belgium and Switzerland, profiting by the losses suffered, and the technical advances made, by British individuals and companies, appropriated, so far as their countries were concerned, the new industry.

The Electric and International Telegraph Company was formed in 1846, out of the reorganization of properties, that in 1837 had embarked in telegraphy in England, and in 1845 had carried the telegraph industry to Belgium.[18] At this time the use of the telegraph was confined almost exclusively to railway purposes, such as train signalling. The possibility of use for commercial purposes was so little appreciated by the public, that the Electric and International Company, after purchasing, in 1846, Messrs. Cooke and Wheatstone's inventions, was looked upon as a complete commercial failure. The shares of the company for several years were almost valueless; the chief source of revenue then being contracts obtained from railway companies for the construction and maintenance of railway telegraphs.

Between 1846 and 1851 great improvements were made in telegraphy, and the public gradually learned to use the telegraph. In 1849 the Electric and International declared its first dividend, mainly the result of the contracts with the railway companies. In November, 1851, a cable was laid between Dover and Calais; for the first time the prices of the stock exchange securities in Paris were known the same day within business hours on the London stock exchange; and the financial and trading interests became convinced of the value of the telegraph.[19]

The Electric and International Company began in 1846 with a capital, paid in, of $700,000, which had been increased, by the close of 1868, to $5,849,375. The company grew steadily, and in 1867 it had 10,000 miles of line, and 49,600 miles of wire. In March, 1856, when the company had a record of five years for dividends ranging from 6 to 6.5 per cent. on the capital paid in, the stock of the company was selling at 80, which showed that the investing public deemed the returns inadequate, considering the risks attaching to the business. In January, 1863, when the company had a record of three years as a 7 per cent. company, the stock still stood under par—at 99.5. In 1864 the company paid 8 per cent., in 1865 it paid 9 per cent., and in 1866 to 1868 it paid 10 per cent.[20]

The British and Irish Magnetic Telegraph Company was formed in 1857 by amalgamation of the Magnetic Telegraph Company, organized in 1851, and the British Telegraph Company, organized in 1852. In March, 1856, the Magnetic had a paid up capital of $1,500,000, which was worth 60 cents on the dollar; and the British Company had a paid up capital of $1,170,000, which was worth 47.5 cents on the dollar. In January, 1864, the amalgamated company was paying 4.5 per cent., and its shares were worth 62.5. In 1865 the British and Irish raised the dividend to 5 per cent.; in 1866 to 6 per cent., and in 1867 to 7.5 per cent. In 1866 the stock sold at 78 to 90; and in 1867 at 90 to 97. In 1867 the company had 4,696 miles of line, and 18,964 miles of wire.

The United Kingdom Telegraph Company was organized in 1860, and began operations in 1861. In November, 1867, its shares were worth from 25 cents to 35 cents on the dollar. At that time the company had 1,692 miles of line, and about 9,827 miles of wire.

The London District Telegraph Company, which subsequently became the London and Provincial, began business in 1860 with 52 offices in Metropolitan London. In 1862 it increased the number of its offices to 84; and at the time of its sale to the State, it had 95 offices. The company never earned operating expenses. It began by charging 8 cents for 10 words; later on it charged 12 cents for 15 words; and in 1866 it raised its charge to 24 cents.

Very little new capital was invested by the telegraph companies after 1865, because of "the very natural reluctance of the companies to extend the systems under their control so long as the proposal of the acquisition of those systems by the State was under consideration," to use the words of Mr. Scudamore.

| Adequate Results of Private Enterprise |

The foregoing facts show that private enterprise was ready throughout the period beginning with 1838 to incur considerable risks in establishing the new industry of telegraphy, and in giving to the public facilities for the use of that industry. Private enterprise did not at any time adopt the policy of exploiting the public by confining itself to operations involving little or no risk, while paying well. It is true that once a company had reached the position of paying 5, 6, 7, 8, or more, per cent., it tried to maintain that position, and refrained from making extensions at such a rate as to cause a decrease in the dividend. But that fact does not warrant the charge that the companies neglected their duty to the public. Until the threat of purchase by the State arrested extensions, and the dividends rose unusually rapidly, the earnings of the companies were moderate; and finally, though the companies tried to maintain whatever rate of dividend had once been attained, the investing public never believed that even the Electric and International would maintain indefinitely the 10 per cent. rate. That is shown by the fact that until the public began to speculate on the strength of the prospect of the State paying a big price for the property of the Electric and International, the stock of that company never sold for more than 14 years' purchase.[21] Had the public believed that the 10 per cent. dividend would be maintained indefinitely, the stock would have risen to 25 years' purchase, the price of the best railway shares.

| Mr. Scudamore's Statistics |

In order to show that the people of the United Kingdom suffered from a lack of telegraphic facilities, when compared with the people of Belgium and Switzerland, Mr. Scudamore stated in his reports of 1865 and 1866, that there were: in Belgium, 17.75 miles of telegraph line to every 100 square miles; in

Switzerland, 13.7; and in the United Kingdom, 11.3. He stated, also, that there were in Belgium 6.33 telegraph offices to every 100,000 people; in Switzerland, 9.9; and in the United Kingdom, 5.6.

Mr. Scudamore obtained the figures with regard to the United Kingdom from the Board of Trade returns.[22] For 1865 to 1867, those returns were very incomplete; but in 1868 they became very full. Mr. Scudamore's reports of 1865 and 1868 were not ordered, by the House of Commons, to be printed, until April, 1868, when the completed Board of Trade returns were available. But neither in the reports as laid before Parliament, nor in the testimony given before the Select Committee of Parliament in 1868, did Mr. Scudamore draw attention to the fact that the statement that the United Kingdom had only 11.3 miles of telegraph line to every 100 square miles of area, and 5.6 telegraph offices to every 100,000 people, was based on incomplete returns.

The Board of Trade return for 1868 stated that the Lancashire and Yorkshire Railway Company had 432 miles of telegraph lines and that various other companies not enumerated in 1865, had, in 1868, 3,665 miles of line. If it be assumed that in the period from 1865 to 1868 the Lancashire and the other railway companies not enumerated in 1865, increased their net at the same rate as did the three railway companies that were enumerated in 1865, namely, 11 per cent., there must have been, in 1865, not less than 3,825 miles of telegraph line of which Mr. Scudamore took no account in fixing the total mileage at 16,066 miles. If it be further assumed that one-third of the 3,825 miles in question paralleled telegraph lines of the telegraph companies, there were left out of account in 1865 by Mr. Scudamore 2,550 miles of telegraph line, the equivalent of 2.1 miles per 100 square miles of area. On the foregoing assumptions the mileage that should have been assigned to the United Kingdom in 1865 was not 11.3, but 13.4.

Considerations similar to the foregoing ones, when applied to Mr. Scudamore's statement that there were, in 1865, 2,040 telegraph stations, show that there probably were 2,680 telegraph stations in 1865, a full allowance being made for duplication. The last named figure would have been equivalent to 8.9 telegraph offices for every 100,000 people as against 5.6 reported by Mr. Scudamore.

The foregoing corrections probably err in the direction of understating the telegraph facilities existent in the United Kingdom in 1865. These corrected results show that in the matter of telegraph line per 100 square miles of area, the United Kingdom was abreast of Switzerland in 1865, though considerably behind Belgium; and that, in the matter of telegraph offices per 100,000 people, it was almost abreast of Switzerland, and considerably in advance of Belgium.

In this connection it is helpful to note that in 1875, after the British Government had spent about $12,500,000 in rearranging and extending the telegraph lines, as against Mr. Scudamore's estimate of 1868 that $1,500,000 would suffice for all rearrangements and extensions, the number of miles of telegraph line per 100 square miles of area was, 20 in the United Kingdom, and 27.4 in Belgium.[23]

Mr. Scudamore submitted several other arguments in support of the statement that private enterprise had failed to provide the public with sufficient telegraphic facilities. He submitted a list of 486 English and Welsh towns, ranging in population from 2,000 to 200,000, and stated in each case whether or not the town was a telegraph station; and if it was one, whether the telegraph office was, or was not, within the town limits. Mr. Scudamore summarized the facts elucidated, with the statement that 30 per cent. of the 486 towns were well served; that 40 per cent. were indifferently served; that 12 per cent. were badly served; that 18 per cent. were not served at all; and that the towns not served at all had an aggregate population of more than 500,000.[24]

Mr. Scudamore did not define his standards of good service, indifferent service, bad service, and absence of service; but examination of his data shows that his standards were so rigorous that the state of affairs revealed in his summary was by no means so bad as might appear at first sight. Mr. Scudamore took as the standard of good service, the presence of a telegraph office within the town limits. He characterized as indifferent the service of 98 towns in which the telegraph office was within one-quarter of a mile of the Post Office, though outside of the town limits; as well as the service of 88 towns in which the telegraph office was within one-half a mile of the Post Office, though outside of the town limits. He called the service bad in the case of 38 towns in which the telegraph office was within three-quarters of a mile of the Post Office; as well as in the case of 22 towns in which the telegraph office was one mile from the Post Office. He said there was no service whenever the distance of the telegraph office from the Post Office exceeded one mile. In this connection it should be added that the telegraph lines followed the railway; and that in consequence of the prejudice against railway companies in the early days, very many cities and towns refused to allow the railway to enter the city or town limits.

Mr. Scudamore's data showed that there had been in 1865 not less than 96 towns in which the distance between the Post Office and the nearest telegraph office exceeded one mile. In a foot-note, in the appendix, Mr. Scudamore stated that in 1868, not less than 25 of the 96 towns had been given a railway telegraph office; but no mention of that fact did he make in the main body of the report, the only part of the document likely to be read even by the comparatively small number of the Members of Parliament who took the trouble to read the document at all. As for the writers of the newspaper press, and the general public, they accepted without exception the statement that in 1868 not less than 18 per cent. of the towns in question, with an aggregate population of over 500,000, had no telegraphic service. As a matter of fact the statement applied only to 14.6 per cent. of the towns, with an aggregate population of 388,000;[25] and many of the towns that still were without service in 1868 would not have been in that condition, had not the agitation for the nationalization of the telegraphs arrested the investment of capital in telegraphs in the years 1865 to 1868.

Mr. Scudamore also submitted a table giving the total number of places with money order issuing Post Offices in England and Wales, Scotland and Ireland; and stated what number of those places had respectively perfect telegraph accommodation, imperfect telegraphic accommodation, and no telegraphic accommodation.[26] Mr. Scudamore contended that the public interest demanded that each one of those places should have at least one telegraph office, that office to be located as near the centre of population as was the Post Office. He submitted no argument in support of that proposition. But Parliament and the public accepted the proposition with avidity, since Mr. Scudamore promised that the extension required to give such a service would not cost more than $1,000,000, about 1/11 or 1/12 of the total sum invested by the several telegraph companies. Mr. Scudamore also promised that, after the service had been thus extended, the total operating expenses of the State telegraphs would be less than 45 per cent. of the gross receipts; that the State telegraphs would at least pay their way, and that they probably would yield a handsome profit. But when Mr. Scudamore came to extend the State telegraphs, he spent upon extensions, not $1,000,000, but about $8,500,000, and when the State came to operate the telegraphs, the operating expenses quickly ran up to 87 per cent. of the gross receipts in three years, 1874 to 1876. These errors of Mr. Scudamore justify the statement that he made no case whatever against the system of *laissez-faire*, or private ownership, on the ground of the extent of the facilities offered to the public, under the system of private ownership. For obviously it was one thing to condemn the telegraph companies for not building certain extensions, those extensions being estimated to cost only $1,000,000, and a different thing altogether to condemn the telegraph companies for refusing to build out of hand extensions that would cost $8,500,000 and would be relatively unremunerative, if not absolutely unprofitable.

Tariffs and Growth of Traffic

It remains to consider whether the facts as to the charges made by the telegraph companies for the transmission of messages, and the facts as to the rate of increase in the number of messages transmitted, supported Mr. Scudamore's contention that the system of private ownership of the telegraphs had failed to conserve and promote the public interest.

In 1851, the Electric and International Telegraph Company carried 99,216 messages, receiving on an average $2.41 per message. In 1856, the year in which the Scotch Chambers of Commerce began the agitation for nationalization, the company carried 812,323 messages, receiving on an average $0.99 per message. In 1865, the year in which the telegraph companies abolished the rate of 24 cents, irrespective of distance, that had been in force between the leading cities, and the Chambers of Commerce increased the agitation for purchase by the State, the Electric and International carried 2,971,084 messages, receiving on an average $0.49 a message. In the period from 1851 to 1867, the messages carried by the company increased on an average by 28.76 per cent. a year; the average receipts per message decreased on an average by 7.58 per cent. a year; and the gross receipts of the company increased on an average by 13.61 per cent. a year.

In the period 1855 to 1866, the messages carried annually by the British and Irish Magnetic Company grew from 264,727 to 1,520,640, an average annual growth of 17.58 per cent. At the same time the average receipts per message fell from $0.96 in 1855, to $0.48 in 1866.

In the period from 1855 to 1866, the number of messages carried annually by all of the telegraph companies of the United Kingdom increased from

1,017,529, to 5,781,989, an average annual increase of 16.36 per cent.

In the same period, from 1855 to 1866, the telegrams sent in Switzerland increased on an average by 13.14 per cent. each year; those sent in Belgium increased on an average by 31.45 per cent.; and those sent in France increased on an average by 25.40 per cent. When one takes into consideration that in Belgium, in 1867, only 38 per cent. of the messages transmitted related to stock exchange and commercial business, and that in France in the same year only 48 per cent. of the messages sent related to industrial, commercial, and stock exchange transactions, there is nothing in the comparison between the rate of growth in the United Kingdom on the one hand, and in the countries of Continental Europe on the other hand, to indicate that the use of the telegraphs for the purposes of trade and industry was held back in the United Kingdom by excessive charges or by lack of telegraphic facilities. So far as the United Kingdom lagged behind, it did so because the public had not learned to use the telegraphs freely for the transmission of personal and family news. And when, in 1875, under State owned telegraphs, the public of the United Kingdom had learned to use the telegraphs as freely as the public of Continental Europe used them, Mr. W. Stanley Jevons, the eminent British political economist, in the course of a review of the price paid for this free use of the telegraphs, said: "A large part of the increased traffic on the Government wires consists of complimentary messages, or other trifling matters, which we can have no sufficient motive for promoting. Men have been known to telegraph for a clean pocket handkerchief"—Mr. Jevons, in 1866 to 1869, had been an ardent advocate of nationalizing the telegraphs.[27]

Mr. Scudamore in 1866 to 1869 caused many people to believe that the United Kingdom was woefully behind the continental countries in the use of the telegraphs. He did so by publishing a table which showed that in 1866 there had been sent: in Belgium, 1 telegram to every 37 letters carried by the Post Office; in Switzerland, 1 telegram to every 69 letters; and in the United Kingdom, 1 telegram to every 121 letters. That table, however, really proved nothing; for in 1866, there were carried: in Belgium, 5 letters for every inhabitant; in Switzerland, 10 letters; and in the United Kingdom, 25 letters.

Had the people of Belgium and Switzerland written as many letters proportionately as the people of the United Kingdom, the table prepared by Mr. Scudamore would have read: Belgium, 1 telegram for every 185 letters; Switzerland, 1 telegram for every 172 letters; and the United Kingdom, 1 telegram for every 121 letters.

Mr. Scudamore could, however, have prepared a table showing that the people of Switzerland and Belgium used the telegraph more freely than did the people of the United Kingdom, but not so much more freely as to call for so drastic a remedy in the United Kingdom as the nationalization of the telegraphs. The table in question would have shown that in 1866, there was transmitted: in Switzerland, 1 telegram to every 3.75 inhabitants; in Belgium, 1 telegram to every 4.25 inhabitants; and in the United Kingdom, 1 telegram to every 5.3 inhabitants. The table in question would also have indicated the necessity of care in the use of the several kinds of statistics just put before the reader. The table placed Switzerland in advance of Belgium, while the other sets of statistics had placed Belgium in advance of Switzerland.

Alleged Wastefulness of Competition

Mr. Scudamore's concluding argument was that little or no relief from the evils from which the public was suffering could be expected "so long as the working of the telegraphs was conducted by commercial companies striving chiefly to earn a dividend, and engaged in wasteful competition." In support of the charge of wasteful competition he stated "that many large districts are provided with duplicate and triplicate lines, worked by different companies, but taking much the same course and serving precisely the same places; and that these duplicate or triplicate lines and duplicate or triplicate offices only divide the business without materially increasing the accommodation of the districts or towns which they serve." But when Mr. Scudamore sought to substantiate this charge of waste arising out of competition, he could do no more than state that not less than 2,000 miles of line in a total of 16,066 miles were redundant, and that perhaps 300 to 350 offices in a total of 2,040 offices were redundant.

The evidence presented by Mr. Scudamore failed to reveal a situation that called for so drastic a remedy as the nationalization of the telegraphs. It revealed no evils or shortcomings that it was unreasonable to expect would be sufficiently mitigated, if not entirely removed, by the measures proposed by the telegraph companies.

Mr. Robert Grimston, Chairman of the Electric and International Telegraph Company, stated that the telegraph companies long since would have asked Parliament to permit them to consolidate, had there been the least likelihood of Parliament granting the request. Consolidation would have made the resulting amalgamated company so strong that the company would have been justified in adopting a bolder policy in the matter of extending the telegraph lines to places remote from the railways. No single company could afford to assume too large a burden of lines that would begin as "suckers" rather than "feeders." A company with a large burden of that kind would be in a precarious position, because any of the other existing companies, or some new company, might take advantage of the situation and cut heavily into that part of the company's business that was carried on between the large cities and was bearing the burden of the non-paying extensions. But if the existing companies were to consolidate, the resulting company would become so strong that it need not fear such competition from any company newly to be organized. That there was much strength in that argument appears from the fact that, in 1869, Mr. Scudamore as well as the Government adopted it in support of the request that the State be given the monopoly of the business of transmitting messages by electricity. Mr. Scudamore argued that since the State was going to assume the burden of building and operating a large number of unprofitable, or relatively unprofitable, extensions, it should not be exposed to the possibility of competition from companies organized for the purpose of tapping the profitable traffic between the large cities, "the very cream of the business." Mr. Scudamore added that he had been told that a company was on the verge of being organized for the purpose of competing for the business between the large towns as soon as the properties of the existing companies should have been transferred to the State.[28]

The Companies' Proposal

The telegraph companies proposed to give the public substantial safeguards against the possibility of being exploited by the proposed amalgamated company. They proposed that Parliament should fix maximum charges for the transmission of messages, in conjunction with a limit on dividends that might be exceeded only on condition that the existing charges on messages be reduced by a stated amount every time that the dividend be raised a stated amount beyond the limit fixed. The companies proposed also that shares to be issued in the future should be sold at public auction, and that any premiums realized from such sales should be invested in the plant with the condition that they should not be entitled to any dividend. Provisions such as these, at the time, were in force in the case of certain gas companies and water companies. They have for years past been incorporated in all gas company charters; and they have worked well. There was no reason, in 1866 to 1869, why the proposals of the telegraph companies should not be accepted; that is, no reason from the view-point of the man who hesitated to exchange the evils and shortcomings incident to private ownership for the evils and shortcomings incident to public ownership.

FOOTNOTES:

17 *The Edinburgh Review*, July, 1870.

18 *Annales télégraphiques*, 1860, p. 547.

The company obtained a concession covering the whole of Belgium. In September, 1846, it opened a line between Brussels and Antwerpen. The tariff charged was low, but the line was so unprofitable that, in 1847, the company declined to build from Brussels to Quiévrain, where connection was to be made with a proposed French telegraph line.

19 *Journal of Statistical Society*, March, 1881.

20 *Statistical Journal*, September, 1876, and current issues of *The Economist* (London).

21 *Journal of the Statistical Society*, September, 1872.

22 *Miscellaneous Statistics for the United Kingdom*, 1868-9, and *Parliamentary Paper*, No. 416, Session 1867-68.

Length of electric telegraphs belonging to railway companies and telegraph companies respectively.

In placing the total mileage of telegraph line at 16,066, in 1865, Mr. Scudamore excluded the mileage of the London, Chatham, and Dover Railway Company.

Railway Companies:	1865	1866	1867	1868

Lancashire & Yorkshire	Not	stated	430	432
London, Brighton & South Coast	241	266	284	284
London, Chatham & Dover	134	134	134	140
South Eastern Railway	324	333	351	351
Other Railway Companies	Not	stated	...	3,665
Total returned	699	733	1,199	4,872
Electric Telegraph Companies:				
Electric & International	9,306	9,740	10,007	10,007
British & Irish Magnetic	4,401	4,464	4,696	4,696
The United Kingdom	1,672	1,676	1,692	1,692
The London District	123	150	150	163
So. Western of Ireland	Not	stated	...	85
Total of Companies	15,502	16,030	16,545	16,643
Grand Total returned	16,201	16,763	17,744	21,515

23 In the *Fortnightly Review*, December, 1875, Mr. W. S. Jevons, the eminent British statistician and economist, stated that the telegraph mileage was 24,000 miles. This statement is accepted in the absence of any official information. From 1870 to 1895 neither the *Reports of the Postmaster General*, nor the *Statistical Abstracts*, nor the *Board of Trade Returns* stated the mileage of telegraph lines; only the total mileage of telegraph wires was published.

24 Mr. Scudamore's percentage figures, in some instances, were only roughly correct.

25

Distance of the Telegraph Station from the Post Office, miles	Number of Towns	Range of Population	Aggregate Population
1.25	7	2,000 to 16,000	43,000
1.50	7	2,000 to 65,000	84,000
1.75	2	2,000 to 4,000	6,000

2.00	6	2,000 to 15,000	23,000
2.50	3	3,000 to 5,000	11,000
3.00	6	2,000 to 8,000	23,000
3.25	1	4,000	4,000
3.50	4	2,000 to 4,000	11,000
3.75	1	3,000	3,000
4.00	3	4,000	12,000
4.50	2	3,000	6,000
4.75	2	3,000 to 5,000	8,000
5.00	7	2,000 to 37,000	62,000
5.50	1	5,000	5,000
6.00	4	2,000 to 4,000	12,000
6.75	1	4,000	4,000
7.00	5	4,000 to 7,000	27,000
9.00	2	3,000 to 6,000	9,000
9.25	1	3,000	3,000
10.00	2	3,000 to 6,000	9,000
12.50	1	14,000	14,000
14.00	1	4,000	4,000
17.75	1	3,000	3,000

?	1	2,000	2,000
	71		388,000

26

	England and Wales	Scotland	Ireland
Number of places having Post Offices that issued money orders	2,056	385	509
Number of such places having: Perfect telegraph accommodation	648	91	109
Imperfect accommodation	567	92	33
No accommodation	850	196	367

27 *The Fortnightly Review*, December, 1875; and *Transactions of the Manchester Statistical Society*, 1866-67.

28 *Report from the Select Committee on the Telegraphic Bill*, 1869: q. 321 to 329. In 1868, Mr. Scudamore and the Government had said that the State ought not to be given the monopoly of the telegraph business. *Special Report from the Select Committee on the Telegraphs Bill*, 1868; q. 124 and following, 319 and 320, and 2,464 and following.

CHAPTER IV
THE PURCHASE OF THE TELEGRAPHS

Upon inadequate consideration the Disraeli Ministry
estimated at $15,000,000 to $20,000,000 the cost of
nationalization. Political expediency responsible for
Government's inadequate investigation. The Government
raises its estimate to $30,000,000; adding that it could afford
to pay $40,000,000 to $50,000,000. Mr. Goschen, M. P., and
Mr. Leeman, M. P., warn the House of Commons against the
Government's estimates, which had been prepared by Mr.
Scudamore. The Gladstone Ministry, relying on Mr.
Scudamore, estimates at $3,500,000 the "reversionary rights"
of the railway companies, for which rights the State ultimately
paid $10,000,000 to $11,000,000.

On April 1, 1868, the Disraeli Government brought into Parliament a "Bill
to enable the Postmaster General to acquire, work, and maintain Electric
Telegraphs in the United Kingdom."[29] At this time the Government still was
ignorant of the precise relations existing between the telegraph companies and
the railways; and it did not foresee that the purchase of the assets of the
telegraph companies would lead to the purchase of the reversionary rights of
the railways in the telegraphs, the telegraphs having been, for the most part,
erected on the lands of the railways, under leases of way-leaves that still had
to run, on an average, 23.7 years. At this time, therefore, the Government
contemplated only the purchase of the Electric and International Company,
the British and Irish Company, the United Kingdom Company, and the
London and Provincial, the successor of the London District Telegraph
Company.

Purchase Price estimated at $15,000,000 to $20,000,000

In the course of the debate upon the order for the Second Reading of the
Bill, the Chancellor of the Exchequer, Mr. G. W. Hunt, said that "if the House

would excuse him, he would rather not enter fully into details with respect to the purchase at present. But he would say that, speaking roughly, it would take something near $20,000,000, or, at all events, between $15,000,000 and $20,000,000 for the purchase and the necessary extensions of the lines." He added that if the purchase should be made, the telegraphs would yield a net revenue of $1,050,000 a year; and that sum would suffice to pay the interest on the debt to be contracted, and to clear off that debt in twenty-nine years.[30]

Parliament was to be prorogued in August; and a General Election was to follow prorogation. The Government naturally was anxious to avoid having to go into the General Election without having achieved the nationalization of the telegraphs; particularly, since the opposition party also had committed itself to State purchase. Then again, the Government believed that the value of the telegraphs was increasing so rapidly that the State would lose money by any postponement of the act of purchase. For these reasons the Government entered into negotiations with the various interests that evinced a disposition to oppose in Parliament the Government's Bill, until finally all opposition was removed.

Politics forces Government's Hand

The Bill, as introduced, proposed that the State pay the four telegraph companies enumerated, the money actually invested by them—about $11,500,000—together with an allowance for the prospective increase of the earnings of the companies, and an additional allowance for compulsory sale. The last two items were to be fixed by an arbitrator who was to be appointed by the Board of Trade. The companies flatly rejected this offer, pointing, by way of precedent, to the Act of 1844, which fixed the terms to be given to the railways, should the State at any time resolve upon the compulsory purchase of the railways. The Act in question prescribed: "twenty-five years' purchase of the average annual divisible profits for three years before such purchase, provided these profits shall equal or exceed 10 per cent. on the capital; and, if not, the railway company shall be at liberty to claim any further sum for anticipated profits, to be fixed by arbitration."

The Government next offered the companies the highest market price reached by the stock of the companies on the London Stock Exchange up to

May 28, 1868, plus an allowance for prospective profits, to be fixed by arbitration. The companies rejected that offer, but accepted the next one, namely, twenty years' purchase of the profits of the year that was to end with June 30, 1868.[31] Mr. W. H. Smith, one of the most highly esteemed Members of the House of Commons, who was himself a director in the Electric and International, subsequently spoke as follows of these negotiations: "In 1868 the telegraph companies were by no means desirous to part with their property, but the question whether the Government should be in possession of the telegraphs having been forced on their consideration, the three principal companies very reluctantly came to an arrangement with the Government of the day. He did not wish to express any opinion on the bargain which had been made, and would only say for himself and those with whom he was associated, that they very deeply regretted to be obliged to part with property which had been profitable, and which they had great pleasure in managing."[32] Mr. Smith added that the net earnings of the Electric and International had increased from $336,815 in 1862, to $859,215 in 1868; and that the average annual increase per cent. had been 17.2 per cent.

The state of the public mind at the time when the Government introduced its Bill, was indicated in the issue of April 11, 1868, of *The Economist*, the leading financial newspaper of Great Britain. Said the journal in question: "Even if the companies resist, they will not be very powerful opponents— firstly, because the leaders of both parties have already sanctioned the scheme; and, secondly, because the companies are exceptionally unpopular. There is, probably, no interest in the Kingdom which is so cordially disliked by the press, which, when united, is stronger than any interest, and which has suffered for years under the shortcomings of the private companies. The real discussion in Parliament, should there be any, will turn upon a very different point, and it will be not a little interesting to observe how far the current of opinion on the subject of State interference with private enterprise, has really ebbed within the last few years. Twelve or fourteen years ago it would have been useless for any Chancellor of the Exchequer to propose such an operation…. It was [at that time] believed on all sides that State interference was wrong, because it shut out the private speculators from the natural reward of their energy and labor."

Before the Select Committee of the House of Commons to which was referred the Government's Bill, Mr. Scudamore argued that if Parliament could not make a reasonable bargain with the telegraph companies, it could authorize the Post Office to build a system of telegraphs. But that measure ought to be adopted only as a last resource. It was of paramount importance to avoid shaking the confidence of the investors that private enterprise would be allowed to reap the full benefits of its enterprise, and that it would be exposed to nothing more than the ordinary vicissitudes of trade. That the possibility of competition by the State, by means of money taken from the people by taxation, never had been included within the ordinary vicissitudes of trade. Coming to the question of paying twenty years' purchase of the profits of the year 1867-1868, Mr. Scudamore said: "The telegraphs are so much more valuable a property than we originally believed, that if you do not buy them this year, you unquestionably will have to pay $2,500,000 more for them next year.... Their [average] annual growth of profit is certainly not less than ten per cent. at present. If you wait till next year and only give them nineteen years' purchase, you will give them more than you will now give. If you wait two years, and give them eighteen years' purchase, you will still give them more than you will now give, assuming the annual growth of profit to be the same. If you wait four years, and give them sixteen years' purchase, you will again give them more, and in addition you will have lost the benefit accruing in the four years, which would have gone into their pockets instead of coming into the pockets of the nation."[33]

Purchase price estimated at $30,000,000

In the House of Commons, the Chancellor of the Exchequer, Mr. G. W. Hunt, said: "The terms agreed upon, although very liberal, were not more liberal than they should be under the circumstances, and did not offer more than an arbitrator would have given. The companies had agreed to sell at twenty years' purchase of present net profits, although those profits were increasing at the rate of 10 per cent. a year. He was satisfied the more the House looked into the matter, the more they would be satisfied with the bargain made."[34] The Chancellor of the Exchequer continued with the statement that Mr. Scudamore estimated that the Postmaster General would obtain from the telegraphs a net revenue of $1,015,000 at the minimum, and $1,790,000 at the maximum. The mean of those estimates was $1,402,500, which sum would pay the interest and sinking fund payments—3.5 per cent. in all—on $40,000,000. The Government, therefore, could afford to pay $40,000,000 for the telegraphs. Indeed, on the basis of the maximum estimate of net revenue, it could pay $50,000,000. But Mr. Scudamore confidently fixed at $30,000,000 at the maximum, the price that the Government would have to pay. Mr. Scudamore's estimates of net revenue "would stand any amount of examination by the House, as they had stood very careful scrutiny by the Select Committee, and for the Government to carry out the scheme would not only prove safe but profitable."

By this time the Government had learned that it would be necessary to purchase the reversionary rights of the railway companies in the business of the telegraph companies. The Government had agreed with the railway companies upon the terms under which it was to be left to arbitration how much should be paid for those reversionary rights. The Chancellor of the Exchequer stated that he was unwilling to divulge the Government's estimates of what sums would be awarded under the arbitration; for, if he did divulge them, they might be used against the Government before the arbitrators. "But Mr. Scudamore, whose ability with regard not only to this matter, but also to other matters, had been of great service to the Government, had given considerable attention to the matter, and Mr. Scudamore believed that $30,000,000 would be the outside figure" to be paid to the telegraph companies and the railway companies. The Chancellor of the Exchequer added that Mr. Scudamore's "calculations had been submitted to and approved by Mr. Foster, the principal finance officer of the Treasury."

In passing, it may be stated that Mr. Foster had stated before the Select Committee of the House of Commons that he had given only "two or three days" to the consideration of the extremely difficult question of the value that the arbitrators would be likely to put upon the railway companies' reversionary rights.[35]

Parliament warned against Government's Estimates

Mr. Goschen, of the banking firm of Frühling and Goschen, who had been a member of the Select Committee, and had taken an active part in its proceedings, replied that "the inquiry [by the committee] had been carried on under great disadvantages. An opposition, organized by private interests [the telegraph companies and the railway companies], had been changed into an organization of warm supporters of the Bill pending the inquiry. Before the Committee there appeared Counsel representing the promoters [*i. e.*, the Government], and, at first, counsel representing the original opposition to the Bill [*i. e.* the telegraph and railway companies]; but in consequence of the change in the views of the opposition, who during the proceedings became friendly to the Bill, there was no counsel present to cross-examine the witnesses. Consequently, in the interests of the public, and in order that all the facts might be brought to light, members of the committee [chiefly Mr. Goschen and Mr. Leeman] had to discharge the duty of cross-examining the witnesses. The same causes led to the result that the witnesses produced were all on one side...."[36]

Mr. Goschen emphasized the fact that upon the expiring of the telegraph companies' leases of rights of way over the railways, the reversionary rights of the railways would come into play, and that the Government, after having paid twenty years' purchase to the telegraph companies, "would probably have to pay half as much again to the railways." "The railways had felt the strength of their position so much, that they had pointed out to the committee that they would not only be entitled to an increase in the rate which they now received [as rent from the telegraph companies] as soon as the leases expired, but they would also be entitled to an indemnification [from the State] for the loss they would sustain in not being allowed [in consequence of the nationalization of the telegraphs] to put the screw on the telegraph companies." Mr. Goschen said "he felt very strongly on this point because he was convinced that it was impossible to find an instance of any private enterprise which, while it returned a profit of 15 per cent. to its shareholders, enjoyed a monopoly for any great length of time." If the Government purchased the assets of the telegraph companies, the railway companies would succeed in compelling the State to share with them the great profits to be obtained from the business of telegraphy. They would do so by compelling the Government to pay a big sum for their reversionary rights in the telegraph companies, as the price for abstaining from building up a telegraph business of their own, upon the expiry of the telegraph companies' leases. No business that yielded a return of 15 per cent. could be worth twenty years' purchase, for such returns were very insecure, because of the certainty that competition would arise from persons who would be content with ten per cent., or less.[37]

Mr. Leeman, who had sat on the Select Committee, and had, with Mr. Goschen, done all of the cross-examining directed to bring out the points that told against the Government's proposal, followed Mr. Goschen in the debate. He began by stating that he spoke with "twenty years' experience as a railway man;" and he directed his argument especially against the terms of the agreements made by the Government to purchase the reversionary rights of the railways in the telegraph companies' businesses. "Mr. Scudamore, who was what he had already been described to be—a most able man—had not known, up to the time of the second reading of the Bill [June 8, 1868], what were the existing arrangements between the telegraph companies and the railway companies; and, subsequently, while still without the requisite knowledge on that point,[38] he went and agreed on the part of the Government to buy the interest of the telegraph companies at 20 years' purchase of their profits. In addition it was to be remembered that the railway companies had reversionary interests which would come into operation after comparatively short time for which their arrangements with the telegraph companies were to continue. In July, 1866, Mr. Scudamore estimated the necessary outlay on the part of the Government at $12,000,000. In February, 1868, another officer of the Government raised the estimate to $15,000,000; but it was not until the Bill came before the committee [July, 1868], that Mr. Scudamore said that $30,000,000 would be required.... He [Mr. Leeman] undertook to say that Mr. Scudamore was as wide of the mark in his estimate of $30,000,000, as he had been in his estimate of $12,000,000. At the expiration of their agreements with the telegraph companies, several [all] of the railway companies would have it in their power to compete with the Post Office in the transmission of telegraphic messages. No doubt this fact would be brought under the notice of the arbitrators when the value of their reversion was being considered, and at what price would the arbitrators value this reversionary power of competition? Had Mr. Scudamore made any estimate on the subject? Owing to the position in which Mr. Scudamore had placed the Government, the railway companies had demanded and had been promised terms in respect of their reversions, which he, as a railway man, now said it was the duty of any Government to have resisted...."[39]

Railway Companies' Reversionary Rights

For the better understanding of this question of reversions, it must be stated that the telegraph companies, for the most part, had erected their poles and wires on the permanent way of the railway companies, under leases of way-leaves, which, in 1868, still had 23.7 years to run, on the average.[40] As the leases should expire, the railway companies would have an opportunity to try to obtain better terms, or to order the companies to remove their plant, and then to erect their own plant, and themselves engage in the telegraph business. But the railway companies were handicapped by the fact that the leases did not expire together, and that it would be difficult to build up a new telegraph system piecemeal out of the parts of line that would become free in the next three years to twenty-nine years. There was, therefore, much room for difference of opinion on the question how far the railway companies would be able "to put the screw" on the telegraph companies upon the successive expirations of leases. The Stock Exchange doubtless took the contingency into consideration, that being one reason why the Electric and International shares did not rise above fourteen years' purchase of the annual dividends. Mr. Scudamore, before the Select Committee, expressed the opinion that the railway companies could force the telegraph companies "to give them somewhat better terms; that would be the extreme result of any negotiations between the telegraph companies and the railway companies." To Mr. Foster, principal officer of the Finance Division of the Treasury, whom the Government called to support Mr. Scudamore's evidence, Mr. Leeman put the question: "Looking at it as a financial question, do you suppose all the railways in the country, having power to work their telegraphs at the end of ten years, but for this Bill, will not put in a claim for a very large sum in respect of that reversion?" The witness replied: "I do not think it would be of very great value in the first place, and in the next place it would be a value deferred for ten years, which would very much diminish it." To the further query: "You do not take the view that we shall have to pay the railway companies and also the telegraph companies for the same thing," he replied in the negative.[41]

Shortly after the Government's Bill had been referred to the Select Committee, the Government made the railway companies this proposition, which was accepted. The Government was to acquire perpetual and exclusive way-leaves for telegraph lines over the railways, and the price to be paid therefor was to be left to arbitration. The railway companies were to have the choice of presenting their claims either under the head of payment for the cession of perpetual and exclusive way-leaves to the Government; or, under the head of compensation for the loss of right to grant way-leaves to any one other than the Government, as well as for the loss of right themselves to transmit messages, except on their own railway business. The Government was of the opinion that the sums to be paid to the railways under this agreement would not be large enough to raise above $30,000,000, the total sum to be paid to the telegraph companies and the railways.

Parliament enacted the Bill of 1868 authorizing the Government to purchase the property of the telegraph companies and the rights of the railways; but it provided that the resulting Act of 1868 should not take effect, unless, in the Session of 1869, Parliament should put at the disposal of the Postmaster General such monies as were required to carry out the provisions of the Act of 1868.

The Government immediately appointed a committee to ascertain the profits earned by the telegraph companies in the year that had ended with June, 1868. The committee, which consisted of the Receiver and Accountant General of the Post Office, and other gentlemen selected from the Post Office for their general ability, but especially for their knowledge of accounts, in June and July, 1869, reported that the aggregate of the sums to be paid to the six telegraph companies was $28,575,235,[42] the companies having put in claims aggregating $35,180,185.

While the Bill had been before the Select Committee, the Government had agreed to purchase the properties of Reuters Telegram Company (Norderney Cable), as well as of the Universal Private Company. The price paid for those properties absorbed the margin on which Mr. Scudamore and the Government had counted for the purchase of the reversionary rights of the railways.

In the meantime, the Disraeli Ministry, which had carried the measure of 1868, had been replaced, on December 9, 1868, by the Gladstone Ministry. On July 5, 1869, the Marquis of Hartington, Postmaster General, laid before Parliament a Bill authorizing the Post Office Department to spend $35,000,000 for the purpose of carrying out the act of 1868. The Marquis of Hartington said that $28,575,000 would be required for the purchase of the assets of the telegraph companies; that $3,500,000 would cover the claims of the railways, which had not yet been adjusted; and that $1,500,000 would suffice to rearrange the telegraph lines and to make such extensions as would be required to give Government telegraph offices to 3,776 places, towns, and cities, the present number of places having telegraph offices being 1,882.

The Marquis of Hartington stated that Parliament "was quite competent to repudiate the bargain of 1868, if they thought it a bad one…. Having given the subject his best consideration, he must say, without expressing any opinion as to the terms of the bargain, that if they were to begin afresh, he did not think they could get the property on better terms." He added that the "Government would take over the telegraphs of the companies on January 1, 1870, on the basis of paying twenty times the profits of the year 1867-68. But that in consequence of the increase of the business since 1867-68, the $28,575,000 which the State would pay the telegraph companies, would represent, not twenty years' purchase of the profits in 1870, but considerably under seventeen years' purchase of those profits. The trade of the Electric and International had been found to be growing at the rate of 18 per cent. a year; that of the British and Irish at the rate of 32 per cent."[43]

The Chancellor of the Exchequer, Mr. Robert Lowe, was by no means so sanguine. He spoke of the "immense price" which the Government was asked to pay, "a price of which he, at all events, washed his hands altogether. The Right Honorable Gentlemen opposite [Mr. Hunt, Chancellor of the Exchequer

49

in 1868], had accused them of appropriating the honor of this measure. He had not the slightest desire to contest the point with the Right Honorable Gentleman, who was welcome to it all. The matter was found by the present Government in so complicated a state that it was impossible for them to recede; but unless the House was prepared to grant that [*i. e.* a government monopoly] without which they believed it would be impossible to carry on the business effectively, it would be better that they should reject the Bill altogether."[44]

Mr. Torrens moved an amendment adverse to the Bill, but his motion was defeated by a vote of 148 to 23. Before the vote was taken, Mr. W. Fowler, of the firm of Alexander & Company, Lombard Street, speaking of the reversionary rights of the railway companies, had said: "Therefore, for what the House knew, there might be contingent liabilities for hundreds of thousands or millions of pounds sterling more."[45]

The measure became a law in August, 1869; and on February 5, 1870, the telegraphs of the United Kingdom were transferred to the Post Office Department. In the course of the year 1870, the Government bought the properties of the Jersey and Guernsey Company and of the Isle of Man Company. Those purchases, together with a large number of minor purchases made in 1869, but not previously mentioned, raised the total sum paid to the telegraph companies to $29,236,735.

Not until 1879 were the last of the claims of the railway companies adjusted. The writer has not succeeded in finding a specific official statement of the aggregate sum paid to the railway companies for their reversionary rights and for the grant to the Post Office of perpetual and exclusive way-leaves over their properties, but he infers that that sum was $10,000,000 or $11,000,000. That inference is based on testimony given in 1888 by Mr. C. H. B. Patey,[46] Third Secretary to the Post Office, and on information given by the Postmaster General in 1895.[47] It will be recalled, that in 1869, the Marquis of Hartington, Postmaster General, had told the House of Commons that the payments for the rights in question would not exceed $3,500,000. The Postmaster General doubtless spoke on the strength of assurances given by Mr. Scudamore. It will be remembered also that Mr. Leeman, in 1868, had warned the House in strong terms that Mr. Scudamore's estimates were not to be trusted. Finally, it will be remembered that in 1869, Mr. W. Fowler, a financier of high standing, had warned the House of Commons that "there might be contingent liabilities of thousands or millions of pounds sterling more."

FOOTNOTES:

[29] *Hansard's Parliamentary Debates*, April 1, 1868, p. 678, the Chancellor of the Exchequer.

[30] *Hansard's Parliamentary Debates*, June 9, 1868, p. 1,305.

[31] *Special Report from the Select Committee on the Electric Telegraphs Bill*, 1868. Mr. Scudamore: q. 3,477 and following, 3,352 to 3,364, 172, and 3,379 to 3,386.

[32] *Hansard's Parliamentary Debates*, July 26, 1869, p. 755.

[33] *Special Report from the Select Committee on the Electric Telegraphs Bill*, 1868; q. 3,366 and following, 3,484 and following, and 2,204 to 2,226.

[34] *Hansard's Parliamentary Debates*, July 21, 1868, p. 1,557 and following.

[35] *Special Report from the Select Committee on the Electric Telegraphs Bill*, 1868; Mr. Foster, q. 2,857, *et passim*.

[36] *Special Report from the Select Committee on the Electric Telegraphs Bill*, 1868.

Mr. Leeman cross-questions Mr. Scudamore.

2,331. "Did you agree with the Telegraph Companies till after this Bill was sent to the Select Committee?"—"No."

2,332. "At the time this Bill was sent to this Committee you had petitions against you, had you not, from 25 or 30 different interests?"—"Yes; quite that."

2,333. "Since that time, have you, with the exception of the interest which Mr. Merewether now represents [Universal Private Telegraph Co.], bought up every interest, or contracted to buy up every interest, which was represented by those petitioners?"—"Yes, subject to arbitration and the approval of the committee."

2,334. "They had largely, upon the face of their petitions, controverted the views you have been expressing to this Committee?"—"They had endeavored to do so."

2,335. "They had in fact?"—"They had endeavored to put forward a case against me. I do not say it was a good case."

2,336. "In direct opposition to the information you have been supplying to the Committee?"—"Undoubtedly."

2,337. "The Electric and International Telegraph Company was the company most largely interested, was it not?"—"Yes."

2,338. "That company had put forth its views controverting in detail what you have been stating to the Committee in the course of your examination?"—"Attempting to controvert it."

2,339. "By your arrangements, since the time at which this Bill was submitted to this Select Committee to inquire into, you have in truth shut the mouths of all these parties?"—"They are perfectly welcome to speak; I am not shutting their mouths."

2,340. "Do you propose to call them?"—"No, but they are here to be called."

2,341. "You do not propose to call them. This is the fact, is it not, that this Bill was sent to the Select Committee, with special instructions to make inquiries into various matters raised by petitions from 25 to 30 different interests, and you have, since that time, subsidized every interest that could give any information to this Committee; is not that the fact?"—"Not quite."

37 *Hansard's Parliamentary Debates*, July 21, 1868, p. 1,568 and following.

38 *Special Report from the Select Committee on the Electric Telegraphs Bill*, 1868.

Mr. Leeman examines Mr. Scudamore.

Question 2,330. "When the Bill was read a second time in the House of Commons, had you knowledge of the contents of the terms of the agreement between the Telegraph Companies and the Railway Companies, which enabled you to form any judgment financially as to what you might ultimately have to pay in respect of the Railway Companies?"—"No, I had not."

39 *Hansard's Parliamentary Debates*, July 21, 1868, p. 1,578 and following.

40 *Special Report from the Select Committee on the Electric Telegraphs Bill*, 1868; Appendix, No. 7.

Leases to expire in:	Number of miles of telegraph line

3 to 6 years	1,280
7 " 10	4,046
11 " 20	3,211
20 " 99	4,927
Average unexpired length of all leases:	23.67 years.

41 Special *Report from the Select Committee on the Electric Telegraphs Bill*, 1868; q. 2,980, 3,023, and 1,132.

42 *Parliamentary Paper*, No. 316, Session 1873.

	Sums to be Paid	Capitalization
Electric and International Co	14,694,130	6,200,000
British and Irish Magnetic Co	6,217,680	2,670,000
United Kingdom Co	2,811,320	1,750,000
A London and Provincial Co	300,000	325,000
Reuter's Telegram Co. (Norderney Cable)	3,630,000	1,330,000
Universal Private Co	922,105	?

A This Company was paid the highest market value of its shares on the Stock Exchange in the first week of June, 1868, plus an allowance for prospective profits.

43 *Hansard's Parliamentary Debates*, July 5, 1869, p. 1,216 and following, and July 26, p. 759 and following.

44 *Hunsard's Parliamentary Debates*, July 26, 1869, p. 767.

45 *Hansard's Parliamentary Debates*, July 26, 1869, p. 747.

46 *Report from the Select Committee on Revenue Department Estimates*, 1888; q. 1,984.

47 *Report of the Postmaster General*, 1895, p. 37.

CHAPTER V
NONE OF MR. SCUDAMORE'S FINANCIAL FORECASTS WERE REALIZED

The completion of the telegraph system cost $8,500,000; Mr. Scudamore's successive estimates had been respectively $1,000,000 and $1,500,000. Mr. Scudamore's brilliant forecast of the increase of traffic under public ownership. Mr. Scudamore's appalling blunder in predicting that the State telegraphs would be self-supporting. Operating expenses on the average exceed 92.5% of the gross earnings, in contrast to Mr. Scudamore's estimate of 51% to 56%. The annual telegraph deficits aggregate 26.5% of the capital invested in the plant. The financial failure of the State telegraphs is not due to the large price paid to the telegraph companies and railway companies. The disillusionment of an eminent advocate of nationalization, Mr. W. Stanley Jevons.

Estimated Expenditure versus *Actual Expenditure*

As soon as the telegraphs had been transferred to the Government, the Post Office Department set to work to rearrange the wires wherever competition had caused duplication or triplication; to extend the wires into the centre of each town or place "imperfectly" served; to build lines to all places with money order issuing Post Offices that had no telegraphic service; to enlarge the local telegraph system of Metropolitan London from 95 telegraph offices in 1869, to 334 offices at the close of 1870; to give cities like Birmingham, Leeds, Edinburgh, Glasgow and Manchester, from 14 to 32 telegraph offices each;[48] to provide additional wires to meet the anticipated growth of traffic; and to release some 5,000 or 6,000 miles of wire for the exclusive use of the railway companies in the conduct of transportation. For these several purposes the Post Office Department, in the course of the three years ending with September, 1873, erected 8,000 miles of posts, and 46,000 miles of wire;

strengthened 8,500 miles of line; laid 192 miles of underground pipes and 23 miles of pneumatic pipes; and laid 248 miles of submarine cable. By September, 1873, the Post Office Department had spent upon the rearrangement and extension of the telegraphs, the sum of $11,041,000.[49] Something over $2,500,000[50] of that sum represented the cost of repairing the depreciation suffered by the plant in the years 1868 and 1869, a depreciation for which full allowance had been made in fixing the purchase price. The balance, $8,500,000, represented new capital outlay.

In 1868 Mr. Scudamore had stated before the Select Committee of the House of Commons that it would cost $1,000,000 to rearrange the telegraphs and give perfect telegraphic service to 2,950 places.[51] In 1869, the Postmaster General, the Marquis of Hartington, had told the House of Commons that $1,500,000 would cover the cost of rearranging the telegraphs and giving perfect accommodation to 3,776 places.[52] In April, 1867, on the other hand, Mr. W. Stanley Jevons, an eminent economist, had estimated at $12,500,000 the cost of "the improvement of the present telegraphs, and their extension to many villages which do not at present possess a telegraph station."[53]

Mr. Scudamore's estimate of the cost of extending the telegraphs to 841 places that had no telegraphic accommodation, was based on the assumption that each such extension would require, on the average, the erection of three-quarters of a mile of telegraph line. But when the Post Office Department came to build to "new" places, it found that "the opening of upward of 1,000 additional telegraph offices necessitated the erection of not less than 3,000 miles of telegraph line."[54]

The results have shown that Mr. Scudamore's other estimates of the cost of rearranging and extending the telegraphs, presented by himself in 1868, and by the Postmaster General, the Marquis of Hartington, in 1869, were equally wide of the mark. Numerous *Committees on the Public Accounts* sitting in the years 1871 to 1876, together with the *Committee on Post Office Telegraph Department*, 1876, attempted to inquire into the enormous discrepancy between the estimated cost and the actual cost of rearranging and extending the telegraphs. But none of those attempts were rewarded with any success whatever.[55] The representatives of the Post Office and of the Treasury always attributed the discrepancy "to the purchase of undertakings which were not contemplated at the time when the original measures were submitted to the House, and to unforeseen expenses for extensions." But the State, as a matter of fact, made no purchases beyond those contemplated in 1869—excepting the purchase of the Jersey and Guernsey cable for $286,750, and the purchase of the Isle of Man cable for $80,680. As for unforeseen extensions, in 1869, the Marquis of Hartington had counted on carrying the telegraphs to 3,776 places, and in 1878 there were but 3,761 postal telegraph offices, counting the 300 offices in London, and the numerous offices in the several large principal cities.[56]

Mr. Scudamore, aided by the state of public opinion created by the agitation of the British Chambers of Commerce under the leadership of the Chamber of Commerce of Edinburgh, carried away the Disraeli Ministry and the Gladstone Ministry. Even more powerful than Mr. Scudamore's argument from the extensive use made of the telegraphs on the Continent of Europe, was Mr. Scudamore's promise that the State telegraphs should begin by paying a profit sufficient to cover the interest on $30,000,000 at the lowest estimate, and $50,000,000 at the highest estimate; and that the profit should increase with the advancing years.

Penny Postage Precedent

Before examining the evidence upon which Mr. Scudamore predicted such large profits, it will be well to consider briefly the nature of the evidence afforded to Mr. Scudamore by Sir Rowland Hill's epoch-making "invention of penny postage." This is the more necessary, since Mr. Scudamore himself cited the success of penny postage in support of his proposal for a uniform rate of 24 cents for telegraph messages. Upon the introduction of the penny postage, the letters carried by the Post Office of the United Kingdom jumped from 76,000,000 in 1839 to 169,000,000 in 1840, and to 271,000,000 in 1845. But the net revenue obtained by the Post Office Department from the carriage of letters fell from $8,170,000 in 1839 to $2,505,000 in 1840. Though the net revenue increased each year beginning with 1841, not until 1863 did it again reach the point at which it had been in 1839. In 1863, the number of letters carried was 642,000,000—almost four times the number carried in 1840, and eight times the number carried in 1839.[57] In short, the evidence from the penny postage was, that care must be used in arguing from an increase of business to an increase of net revenue; and that the prospect of a great increase in business did not necessarily justify the incurrence of indefinitely large charges on account of interest on capital invested.

Mr. Scudamore's Revenue Forecasts

Mr. Scudamore began by assuming that the Post Office would take charge of the telegraphs on July 1, 1869; and that by that time the telegraph companies would have developed a business of 7,500,000 messages a year. On the basis of the traffic of 1866, and under the companies' charges, 55 per cent. of the business would consist of messages carried 100 miles or less, which would be charged 24 cents each; 30 per cent. would be messages carried from 100 to 200 miles, being charged 36 cents each; 10 per cent. would be messages carried beyond 200 miles, which would be charged 48 cents; and, finally, 5 per cent. would consist of messages to and from Ireland, which would be charged from 72 cents to 96 cents. The adoption of the uniform rate of 24 cents, irrespective of distance, would reduce by 33 per cent. the charge on the messages sent from 100 to 200 miles, and would increase those messages by 90 per cent.; it would reduce by 50 per cent. the charge on the messages carried more than 200 miles, and would increase those messages by 90 per cent.; and, finally, it would increase by 150 per cent. the number of messages between Great Britain and Ireland. The introduction of the uniform 24 cent rate, therefore, would increase the total number of messages from 7,500,000 to 10,612,500. That last number would be further increased by 10 per cent. in consequence of the general increase of facilities, and a material reduction in the charges made for the delivery of messages to points outside of the free delivery areas. Thus the total number of messages that the Post Office telegraphs would carry in the first year would be 11,673,000, or, say, in round numbers, 11,650,000.

Since the average message would be somewhat over 20 words in length, one might count on average receipts per message of 28 cents; so that the

11,650,000 messages in question would bring the Post Office a gross revenue of $3,400,000.

Mr. Scudamore next proceeded to estimate what it would cost to earn the $3,400,000 just mentioned. He began with the total working expenses, in 1866, of the four leading companies, namely $1,650,000. He stated that the companies had said that if permitted to consolidate, they could reduce expenses by $275,000 a year. But if the Post Office were to take over the telegraphs, it would reduce the expenses by more than the last mentioned sum, for it could use the existing Post Office buildings, the existing staff, and so forth. Deducting numerous other items representing expenses that the companies had incurred on account of the operation of foreign cables and the conduct of other forms of business that the Post Office would discontinue, Mr. Scudamore reached the conclusion that the Post Office, in 1866, could have operated at a total cost of $1,325,000 the plants of the four telegraph companies.

Mr. Scudamore added 10 per cent. to the last mentioned sum, in order to cover the cost of maintaining and operating the extensions that the State proposed to make at a cost of $1,000,000. He took 10 per cent. because $1,000,000 was 1/11 or 1/12 of the capital invested in the plants of the telegraph companies. That raised to $1,457,500 Mr. Scudamore's estimate of the cost of operating the telegraphs on the supposition of a business of 7,500,000 messages.

Mr. Scudamore then allowed 33 per cent. or $437,250, for the assumed increase in the number of messages from 7,500,000 to 11,650,000. He said the Post Office might safely assume that it could increase its business by 55 per cent. at an increase of 33 per cent. in the operating expenses, since the Electric and International Telegraph Company recently had increased its business by 105 per cent. at an increase of 33 per cent. in the operating expenses. Mr. Scudamore's conclusion was that the Post Office could carry 11,650,000 messages, yielding an income of $3,400,000, at a cost of $1,895,000, thus obtaining a net revenue of $1,505,000.

To that sum must be added the net revenue to be obtained from the carriage of messages for the newspaper press, $60,000; and $225,000 to be obtained from the rental of the State's cables to the several foreign cable companies. Thus Mr. Scudamore counted on a maximum net revenue of $1,790,000.

By similar reasoning, under the supposition that the total number of messages should not exceed 7,500,000, Mr. Scudamore arrived at a minimum estimated net revenue of $1,015,000. Taking the average of the two foregoing estimates, he said the Government "might with almost entire certainty rely upon a net revenue within a range of from $1,000,000 to $1,800,000, the mean of which was $1,400,000." That was for the first year; in the subsequent years the net revenue would increase rapidly. He said: "It is the experience of all people who have worked a large business of this kind that the cost does not by any means increase in proportion to the increase of business; you can always do a greater amount of business at a less proportionate cost than you can do a smaller amount."

Mr. Goschen repeatedly asked Mr. Scudamore whether he would stand by his estimates, and whether he deemed them moderate, adding that the Select Committee was taking the matter almost exclusively on his [Mr. Scudamore's] evidence. Mr. Goschen always received the strongest assurances that the Committee might rely on the estimates submitted.[58]

Mr. Scudamore's predictions as to the growth of traffic that might be expected from the great increase in the facilities for telegraphing, and from the reduction of the charges by fully one-half, turned out to be brilliant indeed. They were fully realized. The number of messages increased from about 6,500,000 in 1869, to 9,850,000 in 1870-71, to 19,253,000 in 1874-75, and to 26,547,000 in 1879-1880.[59]

But Mr. Scudamore's predictions as to the net revenue to be obtained from the State telegraphs turned out to be appalling blunders. In only thirteen out of thirty-six years, from 1870-71 to 1905-06, did the net revenue reach Mr. Scudamore's minimum estimate; in only two of those thirteen years did it reach the maximum estimate; and in only seven of the thirteen years did it reach the average estimate. In the period 1892-93 to 1905-06, the operating expenses aggregated $231,196,000, while the gross receipts aggregated $229,761,000. In the latter sum are included $8,552,000, the proceeds of the royalties paid the Government by the British National Telephone Company for the privilege of conducting the telephone business in competition with the State telegraphs.[60] If that sum be excluded from the postal telegraph gross revenues, as not having been earned by the telegraphs, it will be found that in the period, 1892-93 to 1905-06, the operating expenses exceeded the gross revenue by $9,987,000.

Operating Expenses under-estimated by one-half

Mr. Scudamore, in 1869, predicted that the operating expenses would be 51 per cent. to 56 per cent. of the gross revenue, in the first year of the working of the telegraphs by the Post Office; and that they would continue to be correspondingly low. In 1875, a Committee appointed by the Treasury reported that in consequence of the great extension of facilities effected since 1870, "it would be difficult for the Government to work the Telegraph Service as cheaply as did the Companies, but a reasonable expectation might be entertained that the expenses might be kept within 70 per cent. or 75 per cent. of the gross revenue. That would leave a margin sufficient to pay the interest on the debt incurred in purchasing the telegraphs."[61] As a matter of fact, the operating expenses only once have come within the limits fixed by the Committee of 1875; and at the close of 1900-01, they had averaged 92.5 per cent.[62] Here again, the telephone royalties are included in the gross receipts.

On March 31, 1906, the capital invested in the telegraphs was $84,812,000.[63] To raise that capital, the Government had sold $54,300,000 three per cent. bonds at an average price of about 92.3;[64] and for the rest, the Government had drawn upon the current revenue raised by taxation.

Aggregate Telegraph Deficit

The net revenue earned by the telegraphs covered the interest on the bonds outstanding, in 1870-71, and in the years 1879-80 to 1883-84. On March 31, 1906, the sums annually paid by the Government by way of interest that had not been earned by the telegraphs, had aggregated $22,530,000, or 26.5 per cent. of the capital invested in the telegraphs.[65] Upon the sums invested since 1874, aggregating $34,534,000, the Government has received no interest.

Parliament Responsible for Deficits

The statement is commonly made, and widely accepted, that the financial failure of the State telegraphs is due to the excessive price paid for the plant. But that statement overlooks two facts: that since 1892-93 the telegraphs have not earned operating expenses; and that in 1880-81 the telegraphs became abundantly able to earn the interest even upon their immoderate capitalization.[66] The statement in question also overlooks the fact that the telegraphs easily could have maintained the position reached in 1880-81, had not the House of Commons taken the reins out of the hands of the successive Governments of the day. The House of Commons after 1881 fixed the wages and salaries to be paid the Government telegraph employees in accordance with the political pressure those employees were able to bring, not in accordance with the market value of the services rendered by the employees. The House of Commons also reduced the tariff on telegrams from 24 cents for 20 words, to 12 cents for 12 words. It took that course against the protests of the Government of the day, and cut deep into the margin of profit of the telegraph department.

The fact that the House of Commons after 1880-81 took the reins out of the hands of the successive Governments of the day, in no way diminished Mr. Scudamore's responsibility for the appalling errors into which he fell when he forecast the financial outcome of the nationalization of the telegraphs. Mr. Leeman, of the Parliamentary Select Committee of 1868, expressly asked Mr. Scudamore: "You do not think there is any fear of the cost being increased by the salaries being much increased under the management of the Post Office?" Mr. Scudamore without hesitation replied in the negative, though he had just stated that in the Post Office and in all Government departments the pay of the lower grades of employees was somewhat higher than it was in commercial and industrial life.[67] Moreover, Mr. Scudamore, as one of the two chief executive officers of the Post Office, must have been aware that the Government was neither perfectly free to promote men according to their merit, and irrespective of length of service, nor free to discharge men who were comparatively inefficient and lax in the discharge of their duties. He must have known that those disabilities made it impossible for the Post Office to work as cheaply as private enterprise worked.

As for the House of Commons forcing on the Government the 12 cent rate for messages of 12 words, that action was due largely to the expectations raised by Mr. Scudamore himself in 1868 and 1869, that the nationalization of the telegraphs would soon give the public a twelve cent rate.

Mr. W. Stanley Jevons, the eminent statistician and economist, who, in 1866 to 1869, had warmly supported the proposal to nationalize the telegraphs, in 1875 pointed out that while the postal telegraph traffic had increased 81 per cent. in the period 1870 to 1874, the operating expenses had increased 110 per cent. He said: "The case is all the more hopeless, since the introduction of the wonderful invention of duplex telegraphy has doubled at a stroke, and with very little cost, the carrying power of many of the wires."[68]

In 1870 each wire afforded one channel for communication; in 1895 it afforded two channels under the Duplex system, four channels under the Quadruplex system, and six channels under the Multiplex system. In 1870 the maximum speed per minute was 60 to 80 words. In 1895 the fixed standard of speed for certain circuits was 400 words, while a speed of 600 words was possible of attainment. The "repeaters" used for strengthening the current on long circuits also were greatly improved after 1870.[69]

FOOTNOTES:

[48] *Report by Mr. Scudamore on the Reorganization of the Telegraph System of the United Kingdom,* January, 1871.

Number of telegraph offices before and after the transfer of the telegraphs to the State:

	1869	1870
London	95	334
Birmingham	10	14
Edinburgh	9	15
Leeds	10	18
Glasgow	13	19
Manchester	21	32

This table does not indicate fully the expense incurred by the State in providing local telegraph systems. Under the companies the offices were all concentrated in the heart of the city; under the Post Office administration the offices were spread throughout the city and suburbs.

49 First Report from the Committee on Public Accounts, 1873; Appendix, p. 118; and Report from the Committee on Public Accounts, 1874; Appendix, p. 159 and following.

50 Report by Mr. Scudamore on the Reorganization of the Telegraph System of the United Kingdom, January, 1871, p. 43.

51 Special Report from the Select Committee on the Electric Telegraphs Bill, 1868; q. 1,864 and 1,922.

52 Hansard's Parliamentary Debates, July 5, 1869, p. 1,217.

53 Transactions of the Manchester Statistical Society, Session 1866-67.

54 Special Report from the Select Committee on the Electric Telegraphs Bill, 1868; q. 1,922 and 94; and First Report from the Committee on Public Accounts, 1873; Appendix, p. 96.

55 Report from the Select Committee on Post Office (Telegraph Department), 1876, p. xi. "The Committee have not received any full and satisfactory explanation of these great differences between the estimated expenditure of 1869 and the actual expenditure incurred up to 1876."

56 Miscellaneous Statistics of the United Kingdom, current issues from 1872 to 1882.

TELEGRAPH STATIONS OPEN TO THE PUBLIC:

	1869	1871	1872	1873	1874	1878	1
Telegraph Companies	A2,155	0	0	0	0	0	
Post Office Telegraphs	0	2,441	3,369	3,659	3,756	3,761	
BRailway Stations	1,226	1,833	1,804	1,815	1,816	1,555	
	3,381	4,274	5,173	4,474	5,572	5,316	
Miles of Line	21,751	?	C22,000	?	D24,000	?	E
Miles of Wire	90,668	68,998	91,093	104,292	106,730	114,902	1

A In 1,882 places.

B For the benefit of the traveling public, and of persons residing in the immediate vicinity of railway stations, the Post Office made arrangem whereby the railway companies received messages from the public for transmission to the postal telegraphs, and received messages from the postal telegraphs for delivery to the public.

C *Report of the Postmaster General*, 1895, p. 36.

D *The Fortnightly Review*, December, 1875, W. S. Jevons.

E *Report of the Postmaster General*, 1880, p. 16.

57

THE PENNY POSTAGE WAS INTRODUCED ON DECEMBER 5, 1839.

	Letters Carried	Gross Revenue	Net Revenue[A]
1839	76,000,000	11,955,000	8,170,000
1840	169,000,000	6,795,000	2,505,000
1845	271,000,000	9,440,000	3,810,000
1850	347,000,000	11,325,000	4,020,000
1859	545,000,000	16,150,000	7,230,000
1863	642,000,000	19,350,000	8,950,000

A The British Post Office does not charge itself with interest upon the capital invested in the postal business; it charges itself only with interest upon the capital borrowed on account of the telegraphic business.

58 *Special Report from the Select Committee on the Electric Telegraphs Bill*, 1868; Appendix, pp. 27 and 28; and q. 1,813 and following, and 2,439 and following. Compare: *Hansard's Parliamentary Debates*, July 5, 1869, p. 1,219 and following, the Marquis of Hartington, Postmaster General.

59

Number of messages.

1869	6,500,000 (estimated)
1870-71	9,850,000

1871-72	12,474,000
1874-75	19,253,000
1879-80	26,547,000
1884-85	33,278,000
1889-90	62,403,000
1894-95	71,589,000
1899-1900	90,415,000
1905-1906	89,478,000

In 1869 Mr. Scudamore revised his estimate of the number of messages in 1870-71, reducing it to 8,815,400. *Hansard's Parliamentary Debates*, July 5, 1869, p. 1,219, the Marquis of Hartington, Postmaster General.

60 Garcke: *Manual of Electrical Undertakings*. The current issues report the amount of these royalties. *The Report of the Postmaster General*, 1885, p. 9, and *Parliamentary Paper*, No. 34, Session of 1901, state that these royalties are included in the gross revenue of the telegraphs.

61 *Report of a Committee appointed by the Treasury to investigate the causes of the increased Cost of the Telegraphic Service since the Acquisition of the Telegraphs by the State*, 1875, p. 6.

62 *Parliamentary Paper*, No. 295, Session of 1902.

Proportion borne by operating expenses to gross revenue, after excluding from operating expenses all expenses properly chargeable to capital account. The capital account of the telegraphs having been closed in September, 1873, the Post Office, since that date, has charged to operating expenses all expenditures on account of extensions, the purchase of sites, and the erection of buildings.

	Average percentage of operating expenses	Range
1870-71	57.24	
1871-72	78.94	
1872-73 to 1874-75	88.77	85.13 to 92.40
1875-76 to 1884-85	79.34	72.27 to 85.50
1885-86 to 1891-	91.31	87.72 to 95.30

1892-93 to 1900-01	98.30	95.43 to 101.07
1901-02 to 1905-06	100.38	99.69 to 108.06

Parliamentary Paper, No. 34, Session of 1876. Lord John Manners, Postmaster General: "In the first two years after the transfer the expenditure was kept down, because no charge was raised for maintenance, as it took the form of renewal of the plant of the late companies, which, between 1868 and 1870, had, in some instances, been allowed to fall into decay, and was therefore considered properly chargeable against capital."

63 That sum was made up as follows:

Telegraph companies	$29,237,000
Railway companies	10,000,000
Extensions: 1870 to 1873	11,041,000
Extensions: 1874 to 1906	34,534,000
	$84,812,000

64 *Parliamentary Paper*, No. 267, Session of 1870.

65 The subjoined table gives, for successive periods, the average capital sums upon which the net revenue earned by the telegraphs would have paid the interest; and also the average sums actually invested in the telegraphs in those periods. The first column of the table is constructed on the assumption that the interest paid by the State for borrowed money was 3.25 per cent. from 1870-71 to 1883-84; 3 per cent. from 1884-85 to 1888-89; and 2.75 per cent. from 1889-90 to 1900-01.

The ten million dollars paid to the railway companies some time between 1873 and 1879 are not included in the sum put down for the average capital investment in 1875-76 to 1877-78, since it has been impossible to assign that payment to specific years.

The results of the year 1870-71 should be ignored, since the cost of the maintenance of the telegraphs was charged to capital account in the year in question.

	The net revenue sufficed to pay interest on:	**The average capital actually invested was:**
1870-71	52,710,500	33,790,000
1871-72 to 1874-75	20,090,000	40,045,000

1875-76 to 1877-78	31,305,000	41,715,000
1878-79 to 1884-85	52,785,000	54,510,000
1885-86 to 1888-89	24,646,000	60,545,000
1889-90 to 1891-92	44,033,000	63,446,000
1892-93 to 1905-06	Nil	74,243,000

66 The net revenue sufficed to pay the interest on:

	$
1877-78	30,165,000
1878-79	41,190,000
1879-80	51,310,000
1880-81	69,455,000
1881-82	55,055,000
1886-87	14,745,000

67 *Special Report from the Select Committee on the Electric Telegraphs Bill*, 1868; q. 3,296 to 3,302.

68 *The Fortnightly Review*, December, 1875.

69 *Report of the Postmaster General* for 1895; Historical Outline of the Telegraph Service since 1870.

CHAPTER VI
THE PARTY LEADERS IGNORE THEIR FEAR OF AN ORGANIZED CIVIL SERVICE

Mr. Disraeli, Chancellor of the Exchequer, opposes the enfranchisement of the civil servants. Mr. Gladstone, Leader of the Opposition, assents to enfranchisement, but expresses grave apprehensions of evil results.

One of the most extraordinary of the numerous astounding episodes in connection with the nationalization of the telegraphs was the fact that in the debates in the House of Commons was not even raised the question of possible danger arising from increasing enormously the number of civil servants. That is the more astounding, since, in 1867 and 1868, prominent men in both political parties had grave misgivings as to the future relations between the State and its employees, even though those employees who were in the Customs Department, the Inland Revenue Department, and the Post Office were at the time disfranchised.

Mr. Disraeli on Civil Servants

In July, 1867, while the House of Commons was passing the "Representation of the People Bill," Sir Harry Verney, a private member, moved the addition of a clause to enable public officers connected with the collection of the revenue to vote at elections.[70] The Chancellor of the Exchequer, Mr. Disraeli, asked the House not to accept the Amendment. He said: "He wished also to recall to the recollection of the committee a Treasury Minute which had been placed on the table, in which Minute the Government had drawn attention to the impropriety and impolicy of officers in those branches of the public service to which the honorable baronet [Sir Harry Verney] had referred, exercising their influence over Members of Parliament, in order to urge upon the Government an increase of their salaries. Even at the present time an influence was exerted which must be viewed with great jealousy, and every Government, however constituted, would find it necessary to use its utmost influence in restricting overtures of that description. But what would be the position of affairs if these persons—so numerous a body— were invested with the franchise. From the experience of what was passing in this city—and he wished merely to intimate, and not to dwell upon the circumstance—he was led to believe the result would be that there would be an organization illegitimately to increase the remuneration they received for their services—a remuneration which, in his opinion, was based upon a just estimate. He did not deny that the class referred to by the honorable baronet were entirely worthy of public confidence, but the conferring the franchise upon them would place them in a new position, and would introduce into public life new influences which would not be of a beneficial character. He trusted therefore that the committee would not sanction the proposal of the honorable baronet."

The amendment was lost; and in the following year, 1868, Mr. Monk, a private member, carried against the Government of the day, a bill to enfranchise the revenue officers.[71]

The Chancellor of the Exchequer on Civil Servants

The Chancellor of the Exchequer, Mr. G. W. Hunt, said he felt bound to move that the bill be committed this day three months—*i. e.*, be rejected. He said it was an anomaly in the laws that the dockyard laborers were not disfranchised. "If the matter were inquired into calmly and dispassionately, he was not at all sure that a good case might not be made out for affixing to them the same disability that is now attached to the revenue officers. The fact did not at all tend to the purity or the impartiality of electors in places where many of these men were employed, and strenuous efforts were made by members representing them to increase the privileges of the dockyard men and the number of persons employed, which did not tend to economy or the proper husbanding of the national resources. Continual applications were made by these gentlemen [the employees in the Revenue Departments] respecting their position and salaries, and these applications had of late years taken a very peculiar form, being not merely made through the heads of departments, or by simple memorial to the treasury, but in the form of resolutions at public meetings held by them, and communications to Members of Parliament by delegates appointed to represent their interests. He put it to the House, whether, in the circumstances supposed, the influence possessed by them would not be very considerably increased, and whether the Government of the day would not have far greater difficulty in administering these departments with respect to the position and salaries of the officers concerned, if the measure were carried."[72]

Mr. Gladstone's Warning

Mr. Gladstone said: "The suggestion he would make would be that Parliament should give the vote, and, at the same time, leave it in the discretion of the Government of the day to inhibit any of these officers from taking any part in politics beyond giving their simple vote.... Again, before they proceeded to lay down the principle of general enfranchisement, one thing to be considered was the very peculiar relations between the revenue officers and the Members of that House. There it was necessary to speak plainly. He was not afraid of Government influence in that matter, nor of an influence in favor of one political party or another; but he owned that he had some apprehension of what might be called class influence in that House, which in his opinion was the great reproach of the Reformed Parliament, as he believed history would record. Whether they were going to emerge into a new state of things in which class influence would be weaker he knew not; but that class influence had been in many things evil and a scandal to them, especially for the last fifteen or twenty years; and he was fearful of its increase in consequence of the possession of the franchise, through the power which men who, as members of a regular service, were already organized, might bring to bear on Members of Parliament. What, he asked, was the Civil Service of this country? It was a service in which there was a great deal of complaint of inadequate pay, of slow promotion, and all the rest of it. But, at the same time, it was a service which there was an extraordinary desire to get into. And whose privilege was it to regulate that desire? That of the Members of that House...."

FOOTNOTES:

[70] *Hansard's Parliamentary Debates*, July 4, 1867, p. 1,032 and following.

[71] *Hansard's Parliamentary Debates*, June 10, 1868, p. 1,352 and following; June 12, p. 1,533 and following; and June 30, 1,868, p. 390 and following. Compare also: *Parliamentary Paper*, No. 325, Session 1867-68: *Copy of Report to the Treasury by the Commissioners of Customs and Inland Revenue upon the Revenue Officers' Disabilities Bill.*

[72] The measure was carried against the Government by a vote of 79 to 47.

CHAPTER VII
The House of Commons Is Responsible for the Financial Failure of the State Telegraphs

Sir S. Northcote, Chancellor of the Exchequer in Mr. Disraeli's Ministry of 1874 to 1880, is disillusioned. The State telegraphs become self-supporting in 1879-80. The House of Commons, under the leadership of Dr. Cameron, M. P. for Glasgow, overrides the Ministry and cuts the tariff almost in two. In 1890-91 the State telegraphs would again have become self-supporting, had not the House of Commons, under pressure from the civil service unions, increased wages and salaries. The necessity of making money is the only effective incentive to sound management.

The consideration of the reasons for the financial failure of the State telegraphs may begin with the discussion of the effect of the building of unremunerative extensions. In 1873 the Treasury Department forced the Post Office Department to abandon the doctrine that every place with a money order issuing post office was of right entitled to a telegraph office. The treasury in that year adopted the policy of demanding a guarantee from private individuals whenever it did not care to assume the risk of a telegraph office failing to be self-supporting.[73] The new policy, of course, applied only to places not yet provided with telegraphic service, for the withdrawal of an established service would have led "to an immense amount of public inconvenience and agitation that the Government would have been unable to resist."[74]

In speaking of the policy of requiring guarantees in order to check the pressure brought by the House of Commons for additional telegraphic services, the Chancellor of the Exchequer, Sir Stafford Northcote, in 1875, said: "The Government cannot give the answer that private companies could, and I am sure did, give. This is a point worthy of consideration, not so much in regard to the telegraph service itself, in which we are now fairly embarked, and of which we must make the best we can, as in reference to suggestions of acquisitions of other forms of property, and the conduct of other kinds of business, in which I hope the House will never be led to embark without very carefully weighing the results of this remarkable experiment."[75]

The guarantee in question, which had to be given by private individuals, covered: the annual working expenses; interest on the capital investment; sinking fund payments which should repay in seven years the capital invested; and a margin for certain contingencies.[76] In August, 1891, was abolished the provision requiring a guarantee of the repayment of the capital in seven years.[77] At the same time, the local governments were authorized to give the guarantee that continued to be required.[78] In 1897, upon the occasion of Her late Majesty's Diamond Jubilee, the Treasury authorized the Post Office to assume one-half of the burden of non-paying telegraphic services; and since May 1, 1906, the Post Office assumes two-thirds of that burden.[79]

The guarantees demanded after 1873 proved an effective check upon log-rolling. For example, in 1876, Catrine, in Ayrshire, with a population of 2,000, still was without telegraph service, while Tarbolton, in Ayrshire, population 500, had acquired such service previous to 1873.[80] In the period from 1874 to 1878 the number of postal telegraph offices increased only from 3,756 to 3,761.

Before leaving this subject, it is necessary to warn the reader against misleading tables published in several official documents, and purporting to show that non-paying offices rapidly became self-supporting.[81]

Those tables are constructed on the basis of including in the cost of telegraph offices only the allowance to the local postmaster for telegraph work, and the cost of maintaining the instruments in the office, and of excluding the cost of maintaining the wire, the cost of additional force required at the central station in London and at the district centres because of the large number of outlying branches, as well as the interest on the capital invested. Those omissions led the Treasury Committee of 1875 to say: "We fear the full cost of working these numerous and unremunerative offices is not realized [appreciated]." In 1888, Mr. C. H. B. Patey, Third Secretary to the Post Office, was asked by a Select Committee of Parliament: "Where you have established telegraph offices at money order offices under guarantee from individuals interested, do you find that eventually these offices pay?" He replied: "No; in exceedingly few instances do they pay. The guarantee has continued, and after seven years we have got a fresh guarantee in order to continue the office."[82] Mr. Patey's testimony is corroborated by the continued, and successful, agitation of the House of Commons for the reduction of the guarantee demanded by the Treasury.

The second reason for the financial failure of the State telegraphs is, that while the precipitate reductions made in the rates charged to the public led to a great increase in the number of messages transmitted, that very increase of business was accompanied by such augmented operating expenses, that some years elapsed before the reduced average margin of profit per message carried sufficed to pay the interest on the immoderate capitalization of the State telegraphs. The increase in the operating expenses was in part inevitable; in part it was due to the waste inherent in all business operations conducted by executive officers who hold office, either at the pleasure of legislative bodies elected by manhood suffrage, or at the pleasure of large bodies of voters.

In 1876, Mr. C. H. B. Patey, Principal Clerk in the Post Office Department, stated that the average of the operating expenses per telegraphic message transmitted was 16 cents to 18 cents.[83] At that time, with a traffic of 21,000,000 messages a year, and average receipts per message of 28 cents, the net revenue of the telegraphs was $1,060,000, while the interest on the bonds outstanding was $1,475,000. In 1879-80, with a traffic of 24,500,000 messages, average receipts per message of 26 cents, the telegraphs yielded a net revenue of $1,667,000, while the interest on the bonds outstanding was $1,632,000. And in 1880-81, with a traffic of 27,300,000 messages, the net revenue rose to $2,257,000, while the interest on the bonds outstanding remained at $1,632,000. A large part of that improvement was due to a diminution in the waste with which the telegraphs had been conducted in

1874 to 1878. The nature and the extent of that waste are indicated in the fact that the number of clerks, telegraphists, and subordinate engineers was reduced from 6,783 in 1876, to 6,220 in 1880,[84] at the same time that the number of telegraph offices was increased from 3,741 to 3,929, and the number of messages was increased from 21,000,000 to 24,500,000.

The Telegraphs become self-supporting

In 1880-81, the telegraphs earned 3.25 per cent. on $69,455,000,[85] which was $16,180,000 in excess of the total capital invested in them. Under conditions which shall be described on a subsequent page, the Government, "very much at the instance of the House of Commons,"[86] raised wages and salaries, so that, in the period from 1880-81 to 1884-85, the expenses on account of salaries and wages increased $1,100,325, while the gross receipts increased only $752,635. In 1884-85, the net revenue sufficed to pay the interest at 3.25 per cent. on $45,710,000 only.

In the meantime, on March 29, 1883, the House of Commons had carried against the Government of the day, the resolution of Dr. Cameron, Member of Parliament from Glasgow: "That the time has arrived when the minimum charge for Inland Postal Telegrams should be reduced to 12 cents."[87] Dr. Cameron said: "He brought forward the motion—and he did so last year[88]—because he was absolutely opposed to the taxation of telegrams [*i. e.*, to raising more revenue from the telegraphs than was requisite to paying the interest on the bonds outstanding]; and he believed that taxation could be levied in no other manner that would be so prejudicial to the commerce, intercourse, and convenience of the country. At the present moment there was practically no taxation of telegrams, or, at all events, the principle of the taxation of telegrams had not been affirmed. The surplus revenue [above the interest on the debt outstanding] earned up to the present time had been so small that it was impossible by sacrificing it to confer any substantial advantage upon the public. But the telegraph revenue was increasing; and it appeared to him that they had now arrived at a point where a remission of taxation must be made in the shape of extra facilities [*i. e.*, reduced charges] for the public, or the vicious principle of the taxation of telegrams for the purpose of revenue must be affirmed. They had, it might be contended, not

74

yet exactly arrived at that point, but they were remarkably near it; and his object in bringing forward the motion from year to year had been to afford the Government no excuse for allowing the point to be passed, but to bring up the subject every year; and the moment it was admitted that a change could be made without loss to the taxpayers he should ask the House to indicate its opinions that the change might be made.... He maintained that the principle of taxing telegrams was most erroneous. It was one of the worst taxes on knowledge[89]—a tax on economy, on time, and on the production of wealth. Instead of maintaining a price which was prohibitory not only to the working classes but also to the middle classes, they ought to take every means to encourage telegraphy. They ought to educate the rising generation to it; and he would suggest to the Government that the composing of telegrams would form a useful part of the education in our board schools."

The Chancellor of the Exchequer, Mr. Childers, "hoped the House would not agree to the motion" even if it were ready to accept Dr. Cameron's estimate that the immediate reduction in the net revenue would not exceed $850,000. "He had heard with surprise in the course of the debate some of the statements which had been made in regard to the unimportance of large items of expenditure [and of revenue]; and he was all the more surprised when he remembered the great anxiety which had been expressed during the present session in regard to the Public Expenditure, and the care which ought to be taken over it."[90]

Dr. Cameron, in the course of his speech in 1882, quoted a statement recently made by Mr. Fawcett, Postmaster General, to the effect that there was an average of 80,000 telegrams a day for 5,600 offices, or 14 telegrams per office. The representative from Glasgow added: "The state of things which they now had, therefore amounted to this—that from each telegraph office was sent a number of messages which afforded a little over half an hour's work per day for the operator. It would, therefore, at once be seen that there was ample room for increased business, without any increase of expenditure."[91] The foregoing argument overlooked the fact that the wires between the large cities were being worked to something like their full capacity; and that the low average of 14 messages per office was due solely to the existence of hundreds of offices in small places that had very little traffic. And shortly after the House of Commons had passed Dr. Cameron's resolution, in 1883, against the protest of the Government, the Treasury authorized the Post Office to spend $2,500,000 in putting up 15,000 miles of additional wires, and in otherwise preparing for the great increase in business that would arise between the larger towns in consequence of the reduction of the tariff.[92] And by July 5, 1885, three months before the date set for putting into force the reduced rate, the Post Office had engaged 1,202 additional telegraphists and learners,[93] to assist in doing the business which Dr. Cameron in 1882, had said could be done "without any great increase of expenditure."

Tariff is cut almost in two

On March 30, 1885, Mr. Shaw-Lefevre, Postmaster General, brought in a bill to give effect to Dr. Cameron's resolution of March 29, 1883.[94] The measure provided for a rate of 12 cents for not exceeding 12 words, address to be counted, and one cent for each additional word. The Postmaster General began by reminding the House of Commons that Dr. Cameron's resolution had been carried against the Government, and by a considerable majority. That the Post Office has spent $2,500,000 in preparing for the increase of business anticipated from the 12 cent tariff. That the loss of net revenue was estimated at $900,000 for the first year; and that it would take four years to recover that loss. That since Dr. Cameron's resolution had been passed, the financial position of the telegraph department had grown "decidedly worse," the net revenue having fallen from $2,200,000 to $1,275,000, the latter sum yielding barely 2.5 per cent. on the capital invested in the telegraphs, $55,000,000. Mr. Shaw-Lefevre said the decrease in the net revenue had been due "to the very considerable additions to the salaries of the telegraphists and other officers made two or three years ago very much at the instance of honorable Members of the House, and which Mr. Fawcett [the then Postmaster General] considered to be absolutely necessary," and also to increased cost of maintenance[95] arising from the necessity of replacing worn-out plant. The Postmaster General also drew attention to the fact that a new and dangerous factor had appeared: the competition of the telephone.[96]

The Bill became law; and the 12 cent tariff went into effect on October 1, 1885, the close of the first half of the fiscal year 1885-86. The number of messages jumped from 33,000,000 to 50,000,000, while the net revenue dropped from $1,370,000 to $440,000. In the next three years, 1887-88 to 1889-90, the number of messages increased to 62,400,000, and the net revenue rose to $1,451,000, or within $431,000 of the interest on the capital invested, $62,748,000. In the following year, 1890-91, the messages continued to increase at the rate at which they had increased in the three preceding years, and the net revenue would once more have sufficed to pay the interest on the capital invested, had the operating expenses not been swollen by increases in wages and salaries granted under pressure brought by the telegraph employees upon the House of Commons. The raising of salaries and wages continued through the subsequent years; and in the thirteen years 1893-94 to 1905-06, the State telegraphs have earned the operating expenses in five years only.[97]

In 1888, the *Select Committee on Revenue Departments Estimates* reported as follows: "Your Committee are of the opinion that the reasons urged against treating the Post Office as a commercial business are not applicable in anything like the same degree to the Telegraph Department; and that the increasing annual deficit in the accounts of the latter cannot be viewed otherwise than with grave concern. Looking to the increasing costliness of the service as a whole, and to the constant pressure upon it of demands for increased and unprofitable expenditure, your committee deem it their duty to call attention to the fact that the Department of the Postmaster General, in all its branches, is a vast Government business, which is most likely to continue to be conducted satisfactorily, if it should also continue to be conducted with a view to profit [beyond the payment of interest on the debt outstanding], as one of the revenue yielding departments of the State. Excessive expenditure appears to your committee to be sooner or later inevitable in a great Government business which is not administered with a view to an ultimate profit to the State."

Had the House of Commons permitted the successive Governments of the day to act upon the doctrine contained in the foregoing quotation, the State telegraphs would have been self-supporting ever since the year 1880-81. They would have paid the full interest upon the whole capital invested in them; in spite of the high prices paid to the telegraph companies and the railway companies for the sale of those companies' plants and rights.

FOOTNOTES:

73 *Report from the Select Committee on Revenue Estimates*, 1888; q. 2,396, Mr. C. H. B. Patey, Third Secretary to the Post Office.

74 *Report from the Select Committee on Revenue Estimates*, 1888; q. 950, Sir S. A. Blackwood, Secretary to the Post Office.

75 *Hansard's Parliamentary Debates*, April 15, 1875, p. 1,025.

76 *Hansard's Parliamentary Debates*, August 4, 1887, p. 1,126, the Marquis of Salisbury, Prime Minister.

77 *Hansard's Parliamentary Debates*, August 31, 1893, p. 1,580, Mr. A. Morley, Postmaster General.

78 *Hansard's Parliamentary Debates*, May 27, 1892, p. 134, Sir James Fergusson, Postmaster General.

79 *Hansard's Parliamentary Debates*, August 9, 1901, p. 289, Mr. Austen Chamberlain, Postmaster General; and May 9, 1906, p. 1,294, Mr. Sydney Buxton, Postmaster General.

80 *Report from the Select Committee on Post Office* (*Telegraph Department*), 1876, Mr. C. H. B. Patey, Principal Clerk in the Post Office; q. 3,705 and following, and 2,021.

81 *Report of a Committee appointed by the Treasury to investigate the Causes of the Increased Cost of the Telegraph Service since the Acquisition of the Telegraphs by the State*, 1875, p. 8; and *Parliamentary Paper*, No. 34, Session of 1876, p. 6.

NON-PAYING TELEGRAPH OFFICES

	London	The rest of England and Wales	Scotland	Ireland	Total
1872	10	417	40	261	728
1874	7	303	28	111	440
1875	0	150	6	72	228

82 *Report from the Select Committee on Revenue Departments Estimates*, 1888; q. 2,621.

83 *Report from the Select Committee on Post Office* (*Telegraph Department*), 1876; q. 2,712, 2,713 and 3,734.

Average operating expenses per telegram:

	Cents
At office where handed in	2
For receipt at transmitting office	3
For forwarding from transmitting office	3
For receipt at delivery office	3
For delivery to addressee	2
Stationery forms used	1
Rent of offices, way-leaves, and maintenance of wires and instruments	2 to 4
	16 to 18

84 *Miscellaneous Statistics of the United Kingdom*, current issues.

85

	Messages	The net revenue paid 3.25 per cent. interest on: $
1875-76	20,974,000	32,600,000
1877-78	22,172,000	30,165,000
1878-79	22,490,000	41,190,000
1879-80	24,500,000	51,310,000
1880-81	27,300,000	69,455,000
1884-85	33,300,000	45,710,000

86 *Hansard's Parliamentary Debates*, March 30, 1885, p. 1,072 and following, Mr. Shaw-Lefevre, Postmaster General, 1883-84.

87 *Hansard's Parliamentary Debates*, March 29, 1883, p. 995 and following.

88 *Hansard's Parliamentary Debates*, June 26, 1882, p. 422, Dr. Cameron moves the resolution: "That the working of the Postal Telegraph Service, with a view to the realization of profit, involves a Tax upon the use of Telegrams; that any such Tax is inexpedient, and that the profits derived from the service is now such that the charges for Inland Telegrams should be reduced."

89 Ever since the nationalization of the telegraphs the newspaper press messages had been carried at special rates which did not cover operating expenses.

90 *Hansard's Parliamentary Debates*, March 29, 1883, p. 1,018 and following.

91 *Hansard's Parliamentary Debates*, June 26, 1882, p. 427.

92 *Treasury Minute*, June 14, 1883, *with Regard to Reduction of the Minimum charge for Post Office Telegrams*; and *Hansard's Parliamentary Debates*, April 24, 1884, p. 499, the Chancellor of the Exchequer; and April 24, p. 569, and August 7, p. 138, Mr. Fawcett, Postmaster General.

93 *Hansard's Parliamentary Debates*, July 5, 1885, p. 1,825, Lord John Manners, Postmaster General.

94 *Hansard's Parliamentary Debates*, March 30, 1885, p. 1,072 and following.

95 The increase in salaries and wages in 1880-81 to 1884-85 was $1,100,000, and the increase in the cost of maintenance was $538,000.

96 Compare also *Hansard's Parliamentary Debates*, June 6, 1887, p. 1,180, Mr. Shaw-Lefevre.

97

Year	Number of Messages	Net Revenue, $	Year	Number of Messages	Net Revenue, $
1884-85	33,278,000	1,371,000	1894-95	71,589,000	-50,000
1885-86	39,146,000	839,000	1895-96	78,840,000	646,000
1886-87	50,244,000	442,000	1896-97	79,423,000	678,000
1887-88	53,403,000	614,000	1899-00	90,415,000	326,000
1888-89	57,765,000	1,061,000	1901-02	90,432,000	-848,000
1889-90	62,403,000	1,451,000	1902-03	92,471,000	-548,000
1890-91	66,409,000	1,259,000	1903-04	89,997,000	-1,530,000
1891-92	69,685,000	922,000	1904-05	88,969,000	-917,000
1892-			1905-		

| 93 | 69,908,000 | 94,000 | | 06 | 89,478,000 | -63,500 |

The minus sign denotes an excess of operating expenses over receipts.

CHAPTER VIII
THE STATE TELEGRAPHS SUBSIDIZE THE NEWSPAPER PRESS

Why the newspaper press demanded nationalization. Mr. Scudamore gives the newspaper press a tariff which he deems unprofitable. Estimates of the loss involved in transmitting press messages, made by responsible persons in the period from 1876 to 1900. The State telegraphs subsidize betting on horse races.

Before proceeding with the further discussion of the intervention of the House of Commons in the details of the administration of the State telegraphs, it is necessary to review briefly the tariff on messages for the newspaper press.

Before the telegraphs had been acquired by the State, the telegraph companies maintained a press bureau which supplied the newspapers with reports of the debates in Parliament, foreign news, general news, a certain amount of London financial and commercial intelligence, and the more important sporting news. While Parliament was in session, the messages in question averaged about 6,000 words a day; during the remainder of the year they averaged about 4,000 words daily. The annual subscription charges for the aforesaid services ranged from $750 to $1,250. Before the Select Committee of 1868, the representatives of the newspapers asserted that those subscription charges yielded the telegraph companies, on an average, 8 cents per 100 words. They further asserted that the telegraph companies ascribed 62.5 per cent. of the cost of the press bureau to the transmission of the news; and 37.5 per cent. to the collecting and editing of the news.[98] But neither the representatives of the press, nor the Select Committee itself, called any representatives of the telegraph companies to testify upon these latter points.

The subscribers to the companies' press bureau service also were allowed to send messages at one-half the rate charged to the general public; and in case the same newspaper message was sent to several newspapers in the same town, the charge for each address after the first one was 25 per cent. of the sum charged the first addressee. By coöperation, therefore, the newspapers in the larger towns were able to obtain considerable reductions from the initial charge, which, as already stated, was 50 per cent. of the tariff charged the general public.[99] Apparently, however, little use was made of these privileges. In 1868, for instance, the subscriptions to the press bureau aggregated $150,000, whereas the sums paid for messages to individual newspapers aggregated only $10,000.[100]

The Newspapers' Grievance

The newspaper proprietors admitted that the charges for the press bureau service were entirely reasonable; but they desired to organize their own press bureaux on the ground that they were the better judges of what news the public wanted. Since the telegraph companies would not give up their press bureau, the newspaper proprietors joined in the agitation for the nationalization of the telegraphs.[101]

As soon as the Government began to negotiate with the telegraph companies for the purchase of their plants, the newspaper proprietors organized a committee to protect their interests and to represent them before the Select Committee to which had been referred the Electric Telegraphs Bill of 1868. That Bill had said that the tariff was to be uniform, irrespective of distance, and was not to exceed 24 cents for 20 words, address not to be counted. It had said nothing on the subject of the tariff to be charged to the newspaper press.

On May 15, 1868, Mr. Scudamore had written the Committee of the newspaper proprietors: "As a matter of course the Post Office would not undertake to collect news any more than it would undertake to write letters for the public, but the news being collected, it could, and I submit, ought, to transmit it at rates at least as low as those now charged, and which though they are unquestionably low, are still believed to yield the companies a considerable profit.... It seems to me, indeed, that the transmission of news to the press throughout the United Kingdom should be regarded as a matter of national importance and that the charge of such transmission should include no greater margin of profit than would suffice to make the service fairly self-supporting."[102]

Thereupon the newspaper proprietors demanded: "That the maximum rate for the transmission of telegraphic messages [for newspapers] should not exceed that which is now paid by each individual proprietor [as a subscriber to the companies' press bureau], which is, for transmission, exclusive of the cost of collection, 4 cents per 100 words."[103] This demand assumed that the companies' charge of 8 cents per 100 words was remunerative; that it was made up of two separable parts: a charge for transmission, and a charge for collecting and editing; and that the charge ascribed to transmission still would remain remunerative even after the charge ascribed to collecting and editing had been withdrawn. Upon none of these several points were the officers of the telegraph companies asked to testify, the statements of the newspaper proprietors being allowed to stand unsupported.

In order to insure the payment of an average sum of 4 cents or 5 cents per 100 words, the newspaper proprietors proposed that messages be transmitted for the newspapers "at rates not exceeding 24 cents for every 100 words transmitted at night, and at rates not exceeding 24 cents for every 75 words transmitted by day, to a single address, with an additional charge of 4 cents for every 100 words, or for every 75 words, as the case may be, of the same telegram so transmitted to every additional address." By way of compromise, Mr. Scudamore proposed a charge of 24 cents for 75 words or 100 words for each separate town to which each message might be sent, and the limitation of the 4 cent copy rate to copies delivered by hand in the same town. Mr. Scudamore, however, withdrew that proposal, and accepted the proposition of the newspaper proprietors, which became the law. It is needless to add that the opposition of the newspaper press to the Bill of 1868 would have delayed the passage of that Bill even more than any opposition on the part of the telegraph companies and railway companies could have done. Indeed, it is probable, that the newspaper press could have defeated the Bill.

In 1875 the Treasury appointed a *"Committee to investigate the Causes of the Increased Cost of the Telegraphic Service since the Acquisition of the Telegraphs by the State."* That committee consisted of three prominent officers taken from the Post Office Department and other departments of State. Upon the newspaper tariff fixed by the Act of 1868, the Committee reported: "The consequences of such a system must be obvious to every one. Even at ordinary times the wires are always largely occupied with press work, and at extraordinary times they are absolutely flooded with this most unremunerative traffic, which not only fills the wires unduly to the exclusion of better paying matter, but necessitates a much larger staff than would be necessary with a more reasonable system [of charges].[104] After very careful consideration of these points, Mr. Weaver [one of the members of the committee, and the former Secretary of the Electric and International Telegraph Company], has no hesitation in expressing his opinion that the principle of the stipulations of the tariff authorized by the Telegraph Act, 1868, both as regards messages transmitted for the public, and those forwarded for the press, is essentially unsound, and has been the main cause of the large percentage of expenditure as compared with the gross revenue. In order to provide for the prompt and efficient transmission of the vast amount of matter produced by such a system, a considerable extension of plant was necessary, involving a large original cost, besides a regular yearly outlay for maintenance and renewal, and not only so, but a large and constantly increasing staff had to be provided to work lines, which, if taken separately, would not be found to produce anything approaching to the cost entailed for erecting, working, and maintaining them. It will be obvious, therefore, that, unless a retrograde step be taken in order to amend the principles upon which the stipulations of the tariff are made up, it would be unreasonable to expect that the revenue derived for telegraph messages under the present system can ever be made to cover the expenses of working, the interest upon capital, and the ultimate extinction of the debt."[105]

In May, 1876, Mr. C. H. B. Patey, Principal Clerk in the Post Office Department, testified that the Post Office was losing $100,000 a year by transmitting 220,000,000 words for the newspaper press at an average price of 8 cents per 100 words. Mr. Patey said 180,000,000 words were being carried at the rate of 4 cents per 100 words, or for $74,180 in the aggregate; and 40,000,000 were being transmitted at the rate of 24 cents per 100 words, or, for $109,795 in the aggregate.[106] Mr. Patey submitted no calculations in support of his statement that there had been a loss of $100,000 on newspaper messages yielding $183,975. But he cited two illustrations from Hull and the Nottingham-Sheffield-Leeds-Bradford group of towns. He stated that the Post Office received $1,600 a year for messages transmitted to six newspapers in Hull, and spent $5,275 on the transmission of those messages. He added that the service supplied to nineteen towns included in the Nottingham-Sheffield-Leeds-Bradford group of towns yielded $21,760, and cost the Post Office $38,270.[107]

In 1876, the Postmaster General, through Mr. S. A. Blackwood, Financial Secretary to the Post Office,[108] asked the Select Committee on the Post Office (Telegraph Department) to recommend to Parliament that the tariff on newspaper press messages be made "24 cents for 75 words or 100 words for each separate town to which each message may be sent, and that the 4 cent copy rate be limited to copies delivered by hand in the same town." That, it will be remembered, was the proposal made and withdrawn in 1868 by Mr. Scudamore. The Select Committee recommended that the amount of the loss on the newspaper press messages be clearly ascertained, and that the copy rates be raised sufficiently to cover that loss. But Parliament failed to act on the recommendation.

Mr. Patey had supported Mr. Blackwood's request with the statement, based upon inquiry of postmasters throughout the United Kingdom, that "in a very large number of towns only a small part of the telegraphic news transmitted was inserted in the newspapers. In many cases, on inquiry of the proprietors, it was stated that it was not inserted inasmuch as it was not of interest to the readers. In other cases, because the amount of local news was more than would admit of the special telegraphic news being inserted." Mr. Patey also had quoted from a recent issue of the *Glasgow Herald* the statement, that "there was not a leading provincial paper in the Kingdom, the sub-editorial room of which was not littered in the small hours of the morning ankle deep with rejected telegraph flimsy;" and from a recent issue of the *Freeman's Journal*: "The fact is, that the Post Office, and the better class of papers as well, are both over-pressed with these cheap duplicate telegrams. We suppose we pay for about ten times as many as we print. Though we get them, and pay for them, so as to insure having the best news from every quarter, we regard them rather as a nuisance, and would be glad to have them reduced in quantity." And finally, Mr. Patey had argued that the newspaper press was able to pay much more than it did pay, "inasmuch as there had been a tendency on the part of the papers generally, not confined only to the large papers," to get their news by special messages prepared by their own agents and not sent in duplicate to any extent.[109]

Before the *Select Committee on the Revenue Departments Estimates*, 1888, Mr. C. H. B. Patey, Third Secretary to the Post Office, stated: "We believe that the tariff under which the press messages are sent in this country causes a loss amounting to nearly $1,000,000 a year."[110] In August, 1888, in the House of Commons, Mr. Cochrane-Baillie asked the Postmaster General "whether in view of the *Report of the Committee on the Revenue Departments Estimates*, he could state that the Government would bring in further legislation to relieve the country from the loss incurred by the present arrangement in connection with press telegrams?" The Postmaster General replied that "he was quite in accord with the Committee on Revenue Departments but he feared it would be difficult to effect any change, since the newspaper press tariff was fixed by the Act of 1868, and had been in force for upward of eighteen years."[111]

Annual loss on Newspaper Messages estimated at $1,500,000

In November, 1893, Mr. Arnold Morley, Postmaster General, stated in the House of Commons that "the best estimate that can be formed by the officials at the Post Office points to the loss on the newspaper press telegrams being at least $1,500,000 a year; and it probably is still more."[112] In April, 1895, Mr. Arnold Morley, Postmaster General, repeated the foregoing statement, and "maintained it in spite of various statements to the contrary in the newspapers." He added: "and I should be quite willing to arrange for an impartial investigation such as is suggested by the Right Honorable Gentleman, if I were to receive satisfactory assurances that the press would abide by the result of an inquiry, and would undertake not to oppose the passage of the necessary legislation for a corresponding revision in the charges, if it should be shown that they are insufficient to provide for the cost of the service."[113] The assurances were not forthcoming; and the newspaper press tariff remained unchanged.

In April, 1900, Mr. R. W. Hanbury, Financial Secretary to the Treasury, and representative in the House of Commons of the Postmaster General, a member of the House of Lords, said: "The penny postage realizes an enormous revenue and brings in a profit, but every other part of the Post Office work is carried on at a loss. The whole profit is on the penny letter."[114]

Betting on Horse Races subsidized

The Telegraph Act of 1868 provided that newspaper rates should be given to "the proprietor or occupier of any news room, club, or exchange room."[115] The clubs or exchange rooms in question are largely what we should term "pool-rooms," places maintained for the purpose of affording the public facilities for betting on horse races.[116] In 1876 Mr. Saunders, proprietor of the Central News Press Association, testified that his association would send in the course of a day to the same list of addressees the results of a number of races. The words in the several messages might not aggregate 75 words, and thus his association would be charged for the transmission of one message only. In that way a number of messages would be transmitted "gratuitously." Mr. Saunders added that, in 1875, the Post Office had transmitted gratuitously for his association 446,000 sporting messages. Mr. Patey, Third Clerk in the Post Office, added that while the Post Office received 4 cents for transmitting from 8 to 10 sporting messages, it had to make 8 to 10 separate deliveries, by messenger boy, on account of those messages which were counted as one; and that each such delivery cost the Post Office on an average two cents. Thus, on a recent date, the Post Office had delivered the results of the Lichfield races to 205 addressees by means of 1,640 separate deliveries, and had received for the service, on an average, one-half a cent per separate message.[117]

In January, 1876, the Post Office discontinued the "continuous counting" of sporting messages.[118] It took the Department six years to summon the courage to make this change whereby was effected some diminution of the burden cast upon the general body of taxpayers for the benefit of the sporting element among the voters of the United Kingdom.

It would seem, however, that the practice of "continuous counting" had been resumed at some subsequent date. For, in March, 1906, in reply to a question from Mr. Sloan, M. P., the Postmaster General, Mr. Sydney Buxton, said: "Clubs are, under section 16 of the Telegraph Act of 1868, entitled to the benefit of the very low telegraph rates accorded to press messages; and I have no power to discriminate against a legitimate club because it is used for betting purposes. I propose to consider whether the section ought not to be amended in certain respects."[119]

On December 31, 1875, the Post Office discontinued entirely the practice —voluntarily assumed—of transmitting sporting messages to so-called hotels, in reality saloons. The waste of the public funds that the Post Office had incurred in response to pressure from the publicans, is illustrated in Mr. Patey's statement that the Post Office had received from a certain Liverpool hotel $0.82 a week for messages which had entailed a weekly expenditure of $2.50 for messenger service alone.

FOOTNOTES:

98 *Report from the Select Committee on the Post Office (Telegraph Department)*, 1876, J. E. Taylor, Proprietor of the *Manchester Guardian*; q. 3,835 to 3,849, and 1,246; and C. H. B. Patey, Principal Clerk in the Post Office Department; q. 3,452 and following, 3,845, 3,377, and 3,383; and *Report by Mr. Scudamore on the Re-organization of the Telegraph System of the United Kingdom*, 1871, pp. 31 and 32.

99 *Special Report from the Select Committee on the Electric Telegraphs Bill*, 1868; Dr. Cameron, Editor and Manager of the *North British Daily Mail*; q. 1,430 and following.

100 *Report from the Select Committee on the Post Office (Telegraph Department)*, 1876, C. H. B. Patey, Principal Clerk in the Post Office Department; q. 4,900 and 4,901.

101 *Special Report from the Select Committee on the Electric Telegraphs Bill*, 1868; J. E. Taylor, Proprietor of the *Manchester Guardian*; Wm. Saunders, Proprietor of the *Western Morning News*; Dr. Cameron, Proprietor of the *North British Daily Mail*; and F. D. Finlay, Proprietor of the *Northern Whig*.

102 *Report from the Select Committee on the Post Office (Telegraph Department)*, 1876; J. E. Taylor, Proprietor of the *Manchester Guardian*; q. 3,854 to 3,862.

103 *Report from the Select Committee on the Post Office (Telegraph Department)*, 1876; G. Harper, Editor *Huddersfield Chronicle*, and representative of the Provincial Newspaper Society, which embraced about 300 newspapers.

104 Compare: *Report by Mr. Scudamore on the Re-organization of the Telegraph System of the United Kingdom*, 1871, pp. 31 and 32.

Daily number of words transmitted
for the newspapers:

	Parliament in session	**Parliament not in session**
1868	6,000	4,000
1870	20,000	15,000

105 *Report from the Select Committee on the Post Office (Telegraph Department)*, 1876; J. E. Taylor, Proprietor of the *Manchester Guardian*; q. 3,854 and 3,900; and G. Harper, Editor *Huddersfield Daily Chronicle*, and Representative of the Provincial Newspaper Society; q. 4,157 to 4,162.

106 *Report from the Select Committee on the Post Office (Telegraph Department)*, 1876; q. 5,057 to 5,074, 3,360, 3,377, 3,383, and 4,934 to 4,942; and Jno. Lovell, Manager of

The Press Association; q. 3,979 to 3,986.

107 *Report from the Select Committee on the Post Office* (*Telegraph Department*), 1876; q. 5,122 to 5,129.

108 *Report from the Select Committee on the Post Office* (*Telegraph Department*), 1876; q. 5,278.

109 *Report from the Select Committee on the Post Office* (*Telegraph Department*), 1876; q. 3,385 and following, 4,926, 4,927, 3,371, and 3,372.

Receipts from messages sent to individual newspapers, and not duplicated to any extent:

	$
1870	29,000
1871	41,000
1872	60,000
1873	78,000
1874	85,000
1875	91,000

110 Questions 2,007 and 2,167.

111 *Hansard's Parliamentary Debates*, August 30, 1888, p. 305.

112 *Hansard's Parliamentary Debates*, November 27, 1893, p. 1,789. Compare also June 19, 1893, p. 1,316.

113 *Hansard's Parliamentary Debates*, April 4, 1895, p. 919.

114 *Hansard's Parliamentary Debates*, April 27, 1900, p. 136.

115 *Report from the Select Committee on the Post Office* (*Telegraph Department*), 1876; q. 3,360 to 3,370, 3,423, 4,917 to 4,923, and 5,147 to 5,149.

116 *Report by Mr. Scudamore on the Re-organization of the Telegraph System of the United Kingdom*, 1871, pp. 31 and 32; and *Report from the Select Committee on Revenue Departments Estimates*, 1888; Mr. C. H. B. Patey, Third Secretary to the Post Office, in Appendix No. 14.

	Towns	News-papers	News-rooms and Clubs (pool-rooms)	Messages Delivered	Words Delivered
1869	144	173	133	?	?

1871	365	467	639	?	21,702,000
1881	326	525	278	2,735,042	327,707,400
1885	371	578	397	3,616,653	421,362,579
1887	286	499	289	4,289,986	481,796,400

117 *Report from the Select Committee on the Post Office* (*Telegraph Department*), 1876; q. 4,047 to 4,051, 4,889, 4,890 and 3,343.

118 *Parliamentary Paper*, No. 196, Session of 1877; Copy *of the Regulations Relating to Press Telegraph Messages issued by the Postmaster General* in 1876.

119 *Hansard's Parliamentary Debates*, March 12, 1906, p. 867.

CHAPTER IX
THE POST OFFICE EMPLOYEES PRESS THE HOUSE OF COMMONS FOR INCREASES OF WAGES AND SALARIES

British Government's policy as to wages and salaries for routine work, as distinguished from work requiring a high order of intelligence. The Fawcett revision of wages, 1881. Lord Frederick Cavendish, Financial Secretary to the Treasury, on pressure exerted on Members of Parliament by the telegraph employees. Sir S. A. Blackwood, Permanent Secretary to the Post Office, on the Fawcett revision of 1881. Evidence as to civil servants' pressure on Members of Parliament presented to the Royal Commission on Civil Establishments, 1888. The Raikes revision of 1890-91; based largely on the Report of the Committee on the Indoor Staff, which Committee had recommended increases in order "to end agitation." The Earl Compton, M. P., champions the cause of the postal employees in 1890; and moves for a Select Committee in 1891. Sir James Fergusson, Postmaster General in the Salisbury Ministry, issues an order against Post Office servants "endeavoring to extract promises from any candidate for election to the House of Commons with reference to their pay or duties." The Gladstone Ministry rescinds Sir James Fergusson's order. Mr. Macdonald's Motion, in 1893, for a House of Commons Select Committee. Mr. Kearley's Motion, in 1895. The Government compromises, and appoints the so-called Tweedmouth Inter-Departmental Committee.

At the time of the transfer of the telegraphs to the State, February, 1870, the average weekly wages paid by the telegraph companies to the telegraphists in the seven largest cities of the United Kingdom, was $5.14 for the male staff, and $3.56 for the female staff. That average for the male staff includes the salaries of the supervisors; if the latter be excluded, the average for the rank and file of the male employees will fall to $4.80.[120] In 1872, two years after the transfer, the average wage of the male telegraphists in the offices of Metropolitan London was $6.56, while the average wage of the female clerks was $4.30. For the United Kingdom exclusive of London, the average wage of the telegraphists was $5.46 for the male employees, and $4.50 for the female employees.[121] The latter averages record a larger increase of wages in the period 1870 to 1872, than would appear at first blush upon comparison with the average of 1870, namely: $4.80 for men telegraphists and $3.56 for women telegraphists. For while the figures for 1872 record the averages for the whole United Kingdom exclusive of London, those for 1870 record the averages of the seven largest cities only.

The increases in wages and salaries in the years 1870 to 1872 were due mainly to the all round rise in wages and salaries that occurred in the United Kingdom in the period from 1868 to 1872. In the case of the telegraphists the rise in wages was postponed until 1870 to 1872, for the reason that the telegraph companies, as much as possible, adhered to the past scale of wages and salaries on account of the pending transfer of their properties to the State.[122] The companies were able to pursue the policy in question by refraining from increasing their forces materially, working their old staff overtime. In part, however, the increase in the wages of the telegraphists after the transfer of the telegraphs to the Post Office was due to the fact that the Government was obliged to pay the employees in the Telegraph Department something more than the rates of wages prevailing in the open market. For, previous to the acquisition of the telegraphs, the Government had established the policy of paying its employees more than the open market rate for work requiring only fidelity and diligence in the performances of routine duty, as distinguished from work requiring a high order of intelligence and discretion. Shortly after the Post Office had acquired the telegraphs, it was compelled to extend the aforesaid policy to the new body of State employees. As a matter of everyday politics, it proved impossible for the Government to discriminate between the several classes of public servants, paying one part of them "fancy" wages, and the rest of them wages determined by demand and supply.[123]

An episode from the reorganization of the Civil Service in 1876, in accordance with the recommendation of the so-called Playfair Commission, affords insight into the British practice of paying the public servants something more than the market rate of wages and salaries. The Playfair Commission had recommended that the pay of the lower division of Government clerks begin with $325, and rise by annual increments to $1,000, for seven hours' work a day. Thereupon the Government had fixed the rate at $400, to rise by annual increments to $1,000. The Playfair Commission had stated that if it had been guided by the "voluminous" evidence which it had taken, it would have fixed at $750, the maximum to which should rise the salaries of the lower division clerks. But it had desired to attract "the elite" of the classes that the Government could draw from, and therefore it had fixed the maximum at $1,000.[124]

Fawcett Revision of Wages, 1881

In August, 1881, the House of Commons accepted the proposal of Mr. Fawcett, Postmaster General, to increase the pay of the telegraph operators, to count seven hours of night attendance a day's work, and to grant various other minor concessions.[125] Those several changes raised the average sum spent for salaries and wages in the transmission of a telegraphic message, from 11.70 cents in 1880-81, to 13.72 cents in 1884-85.[126] Mr. Fawcett stated in the House of Commons that inquiry of "leading employees of labor, such as bankers, railway companies, manufacturers, and others" had led him to conclude that the telegraph operators were underpaid. He also mentioned the fact that while he was considering the arguments that the telegraphists had made before him in support of the proposition that their pay was inadequate, "outside influence" was brought to bear repeatedly upon the telegraphists, and that the aforesaid outside influence "went so far as to recommend the employees to resort to the last extremity of a strike."[127]

Mr. MacIver replied that "he wished to say a word with regard to the imputation contained in the statement of the Right Honorable Gentleman, that he [Mr. MacIver] had exercised outside influence upon the telegraphists. In common with other members of the House, he had heard[128] the complaints of the telegraphists, and had thought it his duty to bring complaints before the House and the Right Honorable Gentleman, the Postmaster General, so that, if he had erred, he had erred in common with many others."

The Treasury on Civil Service Pressure

In the course of the debate in the House of Commons, Lord Frederick Cavendish, Financial Secretary to the Treasury, said: "With respect to the telegraph clerks, since they had received the franchise, they had used it to apply pressure to Members of Parliament for the furtherance of their own objects.... If, instead of the Executive being responsible, Members of the House were to conduct the administration of the departments, there would be an end of all responsibility whatever. In the same way, if the Treasury was not to have control over expenditure, and Members of the House were to become promoters of it, the system [of administering the national finances] which had worked so admirably in the past would be at an end.... With regard to the position of the telegraphists in the Government Service as compared with their former position under private companies, what had taken place would be a warning to the Government to be careful against unduly extending the sphere of their operations by entering every day upon some new field, and placing themselves at a disadvantage by undertaking the work of private persons. He pointed out that the Government Service was always more highly paid than that of the companies and private persons, and in the particular case of the telegraph clerks [operators] the men themselves received higher pay than they had before."[129]

Before the Postmaster General had introduced into Parliament his scheme for improving the positions of the telegraphists, sorting clerks and postmen,[130] Lord Frederick Cavendish, in his position as Financial Secretary of the Treasury,[131] had written the Postmaster General as follows: "... Admitting, as my Lords [of the Treasury] do, that when discontent is shown to prevail extensively in any branch of the Public Service, it calls for attention and inquiry, and, so far as it is proved to be well founded, for redress, they are not prepared to acquiesce in any organized agitation which openly seeks to bring its extensive voting power to bear on the House of Commons against the Executive Government responsible for conducting in detail the administration of the country. The persons who are affected by the change now proposed are, as you observe, no fewer than 10,000, and the entire postal service numbers nearly five times as many. Other branches of the Civil Service employed and voting in various parts of the United Kingdom, are at least as numerous in the aggregate as the servants of the Post Office. All this vast number of persons, not living like soldiers and sailors outside ordinary civil life are individually and collectively interested in using their votes to increase, in their own favor, the public expenditure, which the rest of the community, who have to gain their living in the unrestricted competition of the open market, must provide by taxation, if it is provided at all. My Lords therefore reserve to themselves the power of directing that the execution of the terms agreed to in the preceding part of the letter be suspended in any post office of which the members are henceforth known to be taking part in extra-official agitation. They understand that you are inquiring whether the law, as declared in the existing Post Office Acts, does not afford to the public similar protection in respect of postal communication, including telegraphs, as is afforded by the Act 38 and 39 Victoria, c. 86, s. 4, to municipal authorities and other contractors, against breaches of contracts of service in respect of gas or water, the wilful interruption to the use of which [by means of a strike] is hardly of more serious import to the local community than is that of postal communications to the national community. If the existing Post Office Acts do not meet this case, it will be for my Lords to consider whether the circumstances continue to be such as to make it their duty to propose to Parliament an extension to the Post Office of provisions similar to those cited above from the Act 38 and 39 Victoria, c. 86, s. 4."[132]

In June, 1882, Mr. Fawcett, Postmaster General, said in the House of Commons: "The House would remember how, last session, he was pressed by honorable Members on both sides of the House to increase the pay of the telegraph employees ... in spite of all that was done for the telegraph employees, he noticed that they were constantly saying that what they received was worse than nothing. All he could say was that if $400,000[133] a year out of public funds was worse than nothing, he, for one, deeply regretted that that sacrifice of public money was ever made."[134] In March, 1883, Mr. Fawcett, Postmaster General, said: "The salaries of the telegraph employees have—I will not say by the pressure of the House, but certainly with the approval of the House—been increased [in 1881]. I do not regret that increase; I think the extra pay they receive was due to them, and if I had not thought so, no number of memorials would have induced me to recommend the Treasury to make such a large sacrifice of revenue."[135] In April, 1884, Mr. Fawcett, Postmaster General, said: "$750,000 a year has been spent [of late] in improving the position of the telegraphists and letter sorters, and I say there never was an expenditure of public money which was more justifiable than that. If we had yielded to mere popular demands and thrown away the money we should deserve the severest censure; but I believe that if an increase of wages had not been conceded, it would have been impossible to carry on the administration of the Department; and I think there is no economy so unwise as refusing to increase remuneration when you are convinced that the circumstances of the case demand the increase."[136]

In July, 1888, the following questions and answers passed between the Chairman of the Select Committee on Revenue Departments Estimates, and Sir S. A. Blackwood, Secretary to the Post Office. "With respect to the increase of salaries at the time when Mr. Fawcett was Postmaster General, I presume that those recommendations of his were founded upon recommendations addressed to him by the [permanent officers of the] Department?" "I can hardly say that they were. Mr. Fawcett held very strong views himself as to the propriety of making an increase to the pay of the lower ranks of the Department, and he carried out that arrangement." "But the Department, I take for granted, was not excluded from expressing an opinion upon the subject?" "Certainly not. I became Secretary at the time [1880] when Mr. Fawcett became Postmaster General.[137] I never should have initiated such a movement, but I saw great force in many of the reasons which Mr. Fawcett urged in favor of such an increase; and, at any rate, the Department, as represented by me, saw no reason to raise a serious opposition, if it were at liberty to do so, to the Postmaster General's views and determinations."[138]

Before the Tweedmouth Committee, 1897, Mr. E. B. L. Hill, "practically commander-in-chief of the provincial postmen," testified as follows upon that part of the Fawcett revision of 1882 that applied to the postal service proper. He said that previous to 1882 all the revisions of the wages of the postmen had been made on the basis of demand and supply; but that the Fawcett revision had departed from that policy.[139]

Evidence, in 1888, as to Civil Service Pressure

The Royal Commission on Civil Establishments, 1888, took up at some length, the question of the pressure brought by the civil servants upon the House of Commons for increases of wages and salaries. Before that Commission, Sir Reginald E. Welby, who had entered the Treasury in 1856, had become Assistant Financial Secretary in 1880, and had been made Permanent Secretary to the Treasury in 1885, testified that many Members of the House of Commons had recently attended meetings of the civil servants for the purpose of endorsing the claims of the civil servants for increases of pay; and that they had taken that action without having made a close examination of the grounds upon which the civil servants had put forward their claims. He added: "It is utterly impossible for us [the Treasury] to ignore these symptoms that make it very difficult to keep within reasonable bounds the remuneration of such a body." Thereupon one of the members of the Royal Commission said to Sir R. Welby: "…but are you not aware that there is a general feeling throughout the country among the people who are employed by private individuals and public bodies [other than the State], that Government servants receive higher pay than they do, and that when these persons are called upon to exercise the franchise they bring pressure to bear upon their Members just the other way [i. e., against the increase of government wages and salaries]?" Sir R. Welby replied: "Of course, I have no means of testing that. I am very glad to hear that Parliamentary influence is not all in one direction. We do not see the proof of it at the Treasury."[140]

Sir Algernon E. West, Chairman Inland Revenue Commissioners,[141] said he wished for a greater spirit of economy, "not in the offices so much as outside." Thereupon the Chairman of the Royal Commission said: "I do not quite understand what you mean by outside." Sir Algernon E. West replied: "I say it with all possible deference, particularly Parliament." To the further query: "Has there been on the part of Members of Parliament, an increase of intervention on behalf either of the individual officers of the Inland Revenue or on behalf of classes of the Inland Revenue since the enfranchisement in 1869?" Sir A. West replied: "A large increase on behalf of classes, not of individuals.... I should like to add ... that I think last year the Lower Division clerks succeeded in getting two hundred Members of Parliament to attend a meeting which was held to protest against their grievances."[142]

Sir Lyon Playfair, who had been Chairman of the Royal Commission on the Civil Service, 1874 to 1876, and the author of the Playfair Reorganization of the Civil Service, 1876, testified as follows before the Royal Commission of 1888. "Unfortunately Members of Parliament yield to pressure a great deal too much in that direction, and they are certainly pressing the Exchequer to increase the wages and salaries of the employees of the Crown.... In a private establishment a man looks after his own interests, and if a person came to him and said: 'Now you must increase the salaries of these men by $100 or $250 all round,' he would say: 'You are an impertinent man, you have no business to interfere,' but you cannot say that to Members of Parliament, and there is continual pressure from Members of Parliament to augment the salaries of the civil servants."[143]

With the increase of the number of telegraphic messages transmitted, from 33,278,000 in 1884-85, to 62,403,000 in 1889-90, the average sum spent on wages and salaries per message transmitted, fell from 13.72 cents in 1884-85, to 10.62 cents in 1889-90. In the following year, 1890-91, Mr. Raikes, Postmaster General, inaugurated an extensive scheme of increases in wages, reductions in the hours of work, and other "improvements in the condition" of the telegraph employees, that again raised to 12.28 cents per message in 1894-95, the average sum spent on wages and salaries. Mr. Raikes, Postmaster General, raised the wages of the supervising staff, as well as the wages of the rank and file;[144] he granted payment at one and one-quarter rates for over time, granted payment at double rates for all work done on Sunday, gave extra pay for work done on Bank Holidays, and increased from half pay to full pay the sick-leave allowance. The annual cost of those concessions Mr. Raikes estimated at $500,000 a year. The cost of the concessions granted at the same time to the employees in the postal branch of the Post Office Department, he estimated at $535,000 a year.[145]

Mr. Raikes' schemes were based largely upon the *Report of Committee of the Indoor Staff*. That Report has not been published; but in 1896, Mr. Lewin Hill, Assistant Secretary General Post Office, London, stated before the so-called Tweedmouth Committee,[146] that the majority of the committee on the Indoor Staff had signed the Report because they believed that if the concessions recommended in the Report were granted, "that would be the end of all agitation." Mr. Hill added: "I remember myself saying [to the Committee] whatever else happens, that will not happen. Do not delude yourselves with the notion that the men will cease to ask." He continued: "Mr. Raikes' improvements were received with the greatest gratitude, and there were any number of letters of thanks from the staff; but the ink was scarcely dry when the demands began again, and they have been going on ever since, and will go on.... There is, unfortunately, a growing habit among the main body of Post Office servants to use their voting power at elections to get higher pay for themselves, and it is well known that in constituencies in which political parties are at all evenly balanced, the Post Office servants can turn the election."

The Committee on the Indoor Staff appointed by Mr. Raikes in March, 1890, had not had the approval of the rank and file of the civil servants, nor had it had the approval of the representatives of the civil servants in the House of Commons, on the ground that it consisted of government officials, who were not responsible directly to the voters. Therefore one of the leading representatives in the House of Commons of the Post Office employees, Earl Compton,[147] on April 15, 1890, had moved: "That, in the opinion of the House, the present position of the telegraphists in London and elsewhere is unsatisfactory, and their just grievances require redress."[148] In the course of his argument, Earl Compton said: "Perhaps the Right Honorable Gentleman [the Postmaster General] has been cramped [in the administration of his department] by what is called officialism. In that case, if the present motion is passed, the Right Honorable Gentleman's hands will be strengthened [against his permanent officials], and he will be able to redress the grievances which have been brought under his attention."

Baron F. de Rothschild followed Earl Compton, with the statement: "The Postmaster General may well say it is no business of ours to interfere between the civil servants and himself, but here I would venture to ask him whether the civil servants are not quite as much our [*i. e.*, the public's] servants as they are those of the Postmaster General?" Baron de Rothschild went on to say that through an error made in the course of the transmission of a telegram his betting agent had placed his money on the wrong horse, causing him to lose a considerable sum of money. Such mistakes would not occur if the telegraphists were better paid.

Sir A. Borthwick regretted "the increasing tendency to invoke the direct interposition of Parliament between the Executive Government and the Civil Service."

The Postmaster General concluded his statement with the words: "I hope that after the statement which I have been able to make, the House will recognize the claim of every Government that the House shall not interfere with matters of Departmental administration, except where it thinks fit to censure the Minister in charge. So long as a Minister occupies his position at the head of a department, he ought to be allowed to occupy it in his own way. I venture to hope that the House will leave questions of this sort in the hands of those who are directly and primarily responsible for them, in the belief that grievances of the servants of any department are not likely to lack careful consideration, and, I believe, just and fair treatment."

A few months later, the Postmaster General made this statement in the House of Commons: "I wish to correct one misapprehension. It is supposed that the position of the Government is that only the market value should be paid for labor of this sort [the nonestablished post office servants]. Those who sat in the Committee [of Supply] will remember that I laid down a different doctrine the other day. My own view is, that while the market value must be the governing consideration, because we are not dealing with our own money, but with the money of the taxpayers, the taxpayers would wish that, in applying that standard to those in the Public Service, we should always bear in mind that a great Government should treat its employees liberally."[149]

Earl Compton failed to carry his motion in 1890; and in the following year he made another unsuccessful attempt, moving: "That, in the opinion of this House, it is desirable that a Select Committee be appointed to inquire into the Administration of the Post Office."[150]

Mr. Ambrose, speaking against the motion, said: "Questions between capital and labor and between the Government and its employees should not be influenced by motions in the House. We are all subjected as Members of this House to all manner of whips from employees of the Civil Service and the Post Office, and I know that when the *status* of the Civil Service clerks was being settled some time ago, there was, among Members generally, a feeling of disgust at the telegrams and letters being received almost very minute from people seeking to influence our votes on some particular question of interest to them."

Mr. Raikes, Postmaster General, enumerated in detail the concessions made to the telegraphists and letter sorters in 1890 and 1891, at a cost of $1,035,000 a year, and added: "and to all this, not one single reference has escaped those who have spoken." He concluded with the words: "It would never do if, in order to encourage the vaporings of three or four of those gutter journals which disfigure the Metropolitan Press, Members of this House were to make the grave mistake of throwing discredit upon a body of men like the permanent officials [Executive Officers] of the Post Office, of whom any country might be proud, with whom, I believe, any Minister would be delighted to work, and of diminishing the authority in his own Department of a Minister, who, whatever may be his personal deficiencies, at heart believes that he has done nothing to forfeit the confidence of this House."

A few months later, when the House was considering the Estimates of the Post Office Department, the Postmaster General said: "Economists [advocates of economy] of former days would have been interested and surprised by the general tenor of the debate to which we have just listened. The great point used to be, as I understand, to show a large balance of revenue to the State [from the Post Office], and to make a defense against charges of extravagance in the past. But we have now arrived at a time when the opposite course is to be taken, and the only chance a Minister has of enjoying the confidence of this House is to point to a diminished balance of revenue and to a greater expenditure on the part of the department...." In 1891-92 our telegraph expenditure will increase by $3,000,000, while our revenue will increase by $1,700,000; "the reason is to be found in the very comprehensive measures framed in the course of the last year for the improvement of the position of the staff."[151]

Civil Servants circularize Members of Parliament

Mr. Raikes died in August, 1891; and in June, 1892, Sir James Fergusson, his successor, asked the House of Commons to permit him to call attention to a circular addressed to Candidates at the [impending] General Election, and also sent to Members of the [present] House. The circular had been issued by "The Provincial Postal Telegraph Male Clerks" to "Candidates at the General Election," and contained the following statement: "We have, in addition, to ask you whether you will, if elected, vote for the appointment of a

Parliamentary Committee to inquire into the working of the Telegraph Service, as we believe such an investigation would be of great utility, and could not but tend to the improvement of the service, the state of which is causing great public dissatisfaction, as will be seen from the subjoined newspaper extracts. In conclusion, we beg to state that we await your reply to these few questions of vital importance with considerable anxiety, and trust that you will give them your careful consideration."

Sir James Fergusson added that another branch of the Post Office servants was issuing similar circulars.[152] He said, "I think that there would be an end to the discipline which should characterize members of the Public Service if encouragement were given to such attempts to bring pressure to bear on Members of the House and Candidates on the eve of a General Election.... I have to say that the leading Members of the Opposition, including the right honorable Member for Midlothian [Mr. W. E. Gladstone], and the right honorable Member for Derby [Sir Wm. Harcourt], fully concur in the observations I have made."[153]

A few days later, the Postmaster General issued the following notice: "The Postmaster General at the same time warns Post Office servants that it would be improper for them, in combination or individually, to endeavor to extract promises from any candidate for election to the House of Commons with reference to their pay or duties."

In the House of Commons Sir James Fergusson defended this notice in these words: "I in no way deny the right of Members of the Public Service to appeal to Members of this House to get their case represented here, but there is all the difference between Members being asked to represent a *prima facie* case, and candidates being asked to pledge themselves upon an ex-parte statement to support a revision [of wages and salaries] or a commission of inquiry—in fact, to prejudge the case. To ask for such a promise as a condition of giving a vote does seem to me inconsistent with the duties of a public servant, and to go beyond his constitutional privileges. In that view the warning has been issued. By what law or right has this been done, the honorable Member asks? By the right and duty which belongs to the head of a Department to preserve proper discipline."[154]

In August, 1892, the Salisbury Government was succeeded by the Gladstone Government, and Mr. Arnold Morley became Postmaster General. On August 28, 1893, Mr. W. E. Gladstone, First Lord of the Treasury, in reply to a question from Mr. Macdonald, said: "Questions may be raised, on which I have no judgment to give on the part of the Government, as to how far, for example, it is desirable for the public functionaries to make use of their position as voters for the purpose of obtaining from candidates promises or engagements tending directly to the advantage of public servants in respect of pay and promotion. These are matters which we deem not undeserving of consideration; but still they do not form the subject of any decision on the part of Her Majesty's Government in the nature of a restraint."[155] In accordance with the policy thus announced, the Gladstone Ministry rescinded Sir James Fergusson's order of June 17, 1892.[156]

Mr. Macdonald demands a Select Committee

In September, 1893, while the House was in Committee of Supply, Mr. Macdonald[157] moved "a reduction of $500 in respect of the Salary of the Postmaster General", in order to bring before the committee the demand of the Post Office employees for "an independent inquiry by a Parliamentary Committee." He stated "that in 1891 the present Postmaster General [Mr. Arnold Morley] voted in favor of an inquiry such as that for which he [Mr. Macdonald] now asked, and he wished to know whether anything had occurred to cause the Right Honorable Gentleman to change his view since that time."[158]

The Postmaster General, Mr. Morley, replied: "He was asked how he could account for his vote in 1891 when he had supported the Motion of the noble Earl, the Member for Barnsley [Earl Compton]? He accounted for it on two grounds: He had supported the proposal, which was an unprecedented one, because there was an unprecedented condition of discontent prevailing throughout the Postal and Telegraph Service—or, he confessed, he was under that impression at the time. The condition of things in various branches of the Service was serious. There had been an *émeute* in the Savings Bank Department, and whether with reason or without reason, the whole of the Services were discontented with their position. The condition of things at present, however, did not bear out the idea that there was anything like general discontent prevailing. He accounted for his action on another ground. Since 1891 large concessions had been made, with enormous additional expense to the country, and that made the state of things very different to what it was when he supported the noble Earl's Motion."

Earl Compton said: "He had several times in past years stood up and spoken for the telegraph clerks, and as the Amendment before the committee related practically to them, it would be dishonest and mean on his part, if, having taken a strong course [while sitting] in opposition, he did not take the same course now his friends were in power."

Mr. Macdonald's Motion was lost.

Mr. Kearley demands a Select Committee

In May, 1895, Mr. Kearley[159] moved: "That in the opinion of this House, it is highly desirable that the terms and conditions of employment in the Post Office should be made the subject of competent and immediate inquiry, with a view to the removal of any reasonable cause of complaint which may be found to exist."[160] The Motion was seconded by Sir Albert K. Rollit.[161] Mr. Kearley stated at the outset, that his remarks would be directed to the advisability of granting some inquiry. He was not in a position to assert that any particular alleged grievance really existed as stated by the employees; but there could be no doubt that there was general discontent. Mr. Kearley next stated that the most serious grievance alleged by the Post Office employees was inadequacy of pay arising from stagnation of promotion. It was true that at the time the blocking extended only to the more highly paid portions of the rank and file, but it must soon extend to the general body of employees unless relief were afforded. In 1880, and in 1890, Parliament had sanctioned respectively the Fawcett revision of wages, and the Raikes revision, for the purpose of correcting inadequacies of pay arising from stagnation of promotion. The employees now demanded the abolition of the classes into which were divided the various grades of the rank and file of the Post Office employees; they demanded assured promotion to a definite maximum wage or salary.

That demand rested on the assumption that the employees had a vested right to the rate of promotion that had obtained under the extraordinary increase of telegraphic business that had followed the transfer of the telegraphs to the State in 1870, and had followed the adoption of the 12 cent tariff in October, 1885.[162]

Mr. Kearley supported his argument by reference to the telegraphists, who enter the service between the ages of fourteen and eighteen, as second class telegraphists, and in the course of fourteen years rise by annual increments from the wage of $3 a week to $10 a week. At the latter wage they remain, unless they are promoted to be first class telegraphists, whose wages rise by annual increments, from $10 a week to $14 a week—payment for over-time, and so forth, being excluded in all cases. Mr. Kearley argued that promotion from the second class to the first class was blocked, stating that in Birmingham, in the last 4¾ years, only 11 men in 168 had been promoted from second class telegraphists to first class telegraphists; and that in Belfast and Edinburgh the annual rate of promotion had been respectively 1.14 per cent. and 2 per cent. Those instances, said the speaker, were typical of the larger cities; the conditions in the smaller cities and in the towns being still worse.

Mr. Arnold Morley, Postmaster General, replied to this part of Mr. Kearley's argument with the statement that there were in London and in the Provinces 3,308 second class male telegraphists, and that out of that number only 65 were both eligible for promotion and in receipt of the maximum wage of the second class, namely $10 a week. He added that the average wage of the men telegraphists who had been promoted from the second class to the first in 1894 had been $8.46. That meant that, on an average, the men in question had been promoted three years before they had reached the maximum wage of the second class. The Postmaster General characterized as "extraordinarily misleading" the source from which Mr. Kearley had taken his statements of fact, namely, a table in a pamphlet issued by the telegraphists in support of their contention that promotion was blocked. The compilers of the table had left out promotions "due to causes other than what were termed ordinary causes, namely promotions due to appointments to postmasterships and chief clerkships, to transfers from provincial offices to the central office in London, and to reductions of officers on account of misconduct." Thus at Birmingham there had been, not 11 promotions, but 16; at Liverpool, not 8, but 37; at Belfast, not 4, but 14; at Newcastle, not 5, but 24; at Bristol, not 6, but 13; at Southampton, not 2, but 8.

The second alleged grievance brought forward by Mr. Kearley related to the so-called auxiliary staff, which consisted of men who supplemented their earnings in private employment by working for the Post Office in the mail branch. It was stated that the Post Office was paying the auxiliary staff from $3.75 to $4.00 a week, whereas it should pay at least $6.00 a week. The third grievance related to the so-called split duties, which involved in the course of the 24 hours of the day more than one attendance at the office. The abolition of those duties was demanded. The fourth grievance was that some of the younger employees were obliged to take their annual three weeks' vacation [on full pay] in the months of November to February.

Sir Albert Rollit,[163] in seconding the motion, termed "reasonable" the demand of the telegraphists that the wages of the London telegraphists should rise automatically to $1,150 a year; and those of the provincial telegraphists to $1,000 a year. At the time the maximum wage attainable in London was $950, while the maximum attainable in the provinces was $800. Sir Albert Rollit added that the recent order of the Post Office that first class telegraphists must pass certain technical examinations or forego further promotion and further increments in pay, "amounted almost to tyranny," and he further reflected that "where law ended, tyranny began." Sir Albert Rollit, an eminent merchant and capitalist, contended that when the existing body of telegraphists had entered the service, no knowledge of the technics of telegraphy had been required, and that therefore it would be a breach of contract to require the present staff to acquire such knowledge unless it were specifically paid for going to the trouble of acquiring such knowledge. That contention of Sir Albert Rollit was but one of many instances of the extraordinary doctrine of "vested rights" developed by the British Civil Service, and recognized by the British Government, namely, that the State may make no changes in the terms and conditions of employment, unless it shall indemnify by money payments the persons affected by the changes. If the State shall be unwilling to make such indemnification, the changes in the terms and conditions of employment must be made to apply only to persons who shall enter the service in the future; they may not be made to apply to those already in the service. This doctrine is supported in the House of Commons by eminent merchants, manufacturers and capitalists. Sir Albert K. Rollit, for instance, is a steamship owner at Hull, Newcastle and London; a Director of the National Telephone Company, and he has held for six years and five years respectively the positions of President of the Associated Chambers of Commerce of the United Kingdom and President of the London Chamber of Commerce.

When Sir Albert Rollit argued that the Government had broken faith with the telegraphers, those public servants, acting under instructions from their leaders, were neglecting to avail themselves of their opportunities to learn the elementary scientific principles underlying telegraphy, and were even repudiating the obligation to acquire knowledge of those principles. The state of affairs was such that the Engineer-in-Chief of the Telegraphs, Mr. W. H. Preece, began to fear that before long he would be unable to fill the positions requiring an elementary knowledge of the technics of telegraphy.[164]

Mr. Arnold Morley, Postmaster General, began his reply to Mr. Kearley's Motion with the statement that "he understood the mover of the Motion spoke on behalf of those in the Post Office service who had taken an active part in the promoting what he might call an agitation, and that his [Mr. Kearley's] position was that, in the condition of feeling in the service, some steps ought to be taken which would enable the real facts to be brought not only before the public, but before Parliament...." He [Mr. Morley] had made a careful examination of most of the alleged grievances during the three years he had been at the Post Office, and though he had satisfied himself that in the main they were not well founded, he recognized that a very strong feeling existed not only among a portion of the staff, but also among the public, and among Members of the House.

The Civil Servants' Campaign of Education

The feeling in question the Postmaster General attributed largely to the manner in which the case of the telegraphists had been presented by the telegraphists in the House of Commons, and in the newspaper press. He spoke of the "extraordinarily misleading" table of promotions published by the telegraphists. He then went on to state that recently the Postmaster at Bristol had reorganized the local telegraph office. By reducing the amount of over-time work, and by abolishing four junior offices, he had effected a saving of $3,000 to $3,500 a year. Thereupon a local newspaper had come out with the heading: "A Premium on Sweating;" and had made the statement, which was not true, that the local Postmaster had received a premium of $500 for effecting a saving of $3,800 at the expense of the staff.[165] Mr. Morley continued with the statement that in June, 1894, a deputation from the London Trades Council had complained to the Postmaster General that skilled electric light men were often employed by the Post Office at laborer's wages at its factory at Holloway, citing the case of one Turner. Upon inquiry the Postmaster General had learned that Turner had been employed as a wireman, had been "discharged from slackness of work," and, upon his own request in writing, had been taken back "out of kindness" as a laborer. The same deputation had mentioned the case of one Harrison, alleged to be earning on piece work, at the Holloway Factory, $1.75, $2.25, and $3.75 a week. On inquiry the Postmaster had ascertained that Harrison was able to earn $10 a week and more, but that "for the purpose of agitation, he had deliberately lowered the amount of his wages by abstaining from doing full work." After the Postmaster General had informed the London Trades Council of the facts of the case, that body had passed resolutions denouncing the postal authorities at the Holloway Factories. Again, Mr. Churchfield, Secretary of the Postmen's Federation, in an interview with the representative of a London newspaper had stated that the shortest time worked by the men on split duties was 12¾ hours, while the longest was 22 hours [in the course of one day and night]. A duty of seven hours lasting from 8 p. m. to 10 p. m., and from 12 p. m. to 5 a. m., Mr. Churchfield had called a continuous duty of twenty-two hours, lasting from 12 p. m. to 10 p. m. The public also was "grossly misled" as to the condition of the auxiliary postmen. For example, one Mears was alleged to earn, after 27 years' service, only $3 a week. Inquiry showed that Mears worked in a warehouse during the day, and received from the Post Office $3 a week for duties performed between the hours of 6 p. m. and 10 p.

m. Other cases had been reported, but in not one instance had the figures been correct. One man in receipt of $3.94 a week, had been put down at $2.62. The London auxiliary postmen received from 12 cents to 18 cents an hour; they were mainly small tradesmen, shop assistants, and private watchmen. In the country, the auxiliary postmen received from 8 cents to 10 cents an hour.

The Postmaster General continued with the statement that the increases in wages and the concessions granted by Mr. Fawcett and Mr. Raikes had augmented the combined expenditures of the postal branch and telegraph branch by $3,750,000 a year.[166] "In 1881, the wages formed 48.7 per cent. of the gross expenditure, whereas now they formed 59.9 per cent.... He did not think that he need add to those figures, except to say that in addition to salaries there were a large number of allowances for special duties. In the circulation office in London were 4,000 sorters, of whom 250 had each an allowance of $2.50 a week, while a very large number had allowances of $1.25, $0.75 and $0.50, of which never a word was said when complaints were made about salaries." The demands made by the telegraphists would increase the State's expenditures by $3,250,000 a year, "taking into account the consequential advances which other classes in the Public Service, treated on the same footing, would naturally receive." Similarly, the letter sorters made an application involving a direct increase of $635,000, and an indirect increase of another $2,500,000.

Mr. Morley next recited some statistics to show, "first of all, the desire among people outside to come into the Post Office Service, and secondly, the disinclination of those inside to go out." The Post Office recently had called for 650 male letter sorters, and had received 1,506 applications. A call for 188 "telegraph learners," had brought out 2,486 candidates. In London, in 1894, there had been no resignations among 1,261 first class sorters, and 23 resignations among 2,958 second class sorters. Out of 5,000 London postmen, 19 had resigned in 1894; and in the 5 years ending with 1894, a total of 5,700 telegraphists had furnished 348 resignations, including the resignations of women who left the service in order to marry.[167] "He could not help thinking that when the working men got to know to the full extent the terms and prospects of Postal Service, the sympathy which they had so freely bestowed on Post Office employees would be largely withdrawn."

Mr. Morley, Postmaster General, summed up with the statement that "he should be the last to deny that change and amelioration might be required in certain respects, but, having examined all the cases, he believed the men of the Postal Service, the Telegraph Staff as well as the Postal Staff, were better treated than people from the same class in private employment. But that opinion was not altogether shared by the public, or by certain Members of the House of Commons, and therefore the Government was prepared to appoint a strong Committee, composed of men who would have special and practical knowledge and experience of administration, and who would, he hoped, be assisted by a Member of the Labor Department of the Board of Trade.... There must be upon the Committee one official of the Post Office in order to assist the Committee, but apart from that one appointment, he proposed that the Committee should be appointed from executive officers of the Government not connected with the Post Office."

Sir James Fergusson, who had preceded Mr. Morley as Postmaster General, said: "He could not shut his eyes to the fact that there was no difficulty whatever in finding candidates for employment in the Post Office. In fact, it was impossible to meet the wishes of many of those who desired to enter the Department. In those circumstances he thought it could hardly be contended seriously that the remuneration offered was grossly inadequate, or that the conditions of service were unduly onerous."

The House of Commons accepted the compromise offered by the Government. Lord Tweedmouth, Lord Privy Seal and a Member of the Cabinet, was made Chairman of the Committee, which consisted, in addition, of Sir F. Mowatt, Permanent Secretary of the Treasury; Sir A. Godley, Under Secretary of State for India; Mr. Spencer Walpole, Permanent Secretary to the Post Office; and Mr. Llewellyn Smith, of the Labor Department of the Board of Trade.[168]

FOOTNOTES:

120 *Report of the Inter-Departmental Committee on Post Office Establishments*, 1897; q. 15,119; Mr. Lewin Hill, Assistant Secretary, General Post Office, London.

121 *Return to an Order of the Honorable, The House of Commons*, dated March 16th, 1898.

122 *Parliamentary Paper*, No. 34, Session of 1876, Lord John Manners, Postmaster General; and *Report of the Inter-Departmental Committee on Post Office Establishments*, 1897, Mr. L. Hill, Assistant Secretary, General Post Office, London; Appendix, pp. 1,095 and 1,099.

123 *Report of a Committee Appointed by the Treasury to investigate the Causes of the Increased Cost of the Telegraph Service since the Acquisition of the Telegraphs by the State*, 1875, p. 5; *First Report of the Civil Service Inquiry Commission*, 1875, p. 9; and *Report from the Select Committee on Post Office (Telegraph Department)*, 1876; Mr. E. Graves, Divisional Engineer; q. 1,566 and following.

124 *Second Report of the Royal Commission on Civil Establishments*, 1888; Sir Lyon Playfair; q. 20,124 to 20,194; Sir Reginald E. Welby, Permanent Secretary to the Treasury, 10,557 to 10,560; and Appendix, p. 570 and following.

125 *Parliamentary Paper*, No. 286, Session of 1881.

126 *Report from the Select Committee on Revenue Departments Estimates*, 1888; Appendix No. 12, Mr. C. H. B. Patey, Third Secretary to the Post Office.

127 *Hansard's Parliamentary Debates*, August 16, 1881, p. 128.

128 That is, he had given the telegraphists an interview.

129 *Hansard's Parliamentary Debates*, August 16, 1881, p. 141.

130 *The narrative ignores the parts of the scheme affecting the* letter carriers and letter sorters.

131 For an account of the organization and the duties of the Treasury, as well as of the position and the duties of the Financial Secretary to the Treasury, see Chapter XVII.

132 *Parliamentary Paper*, No. 286, Session of 1881.

133 In consequence of the fact that wages and salaries rise by annual increments from the minimum to the maximum, some years must elapse before the full effect of the increase in pay granted in 1881 would be felt. It was assumed that in the first year the total increase in expenditure would be $85,000, and that ultimately it would be $700,000. In that connection it was common to speak of a mean increase of $450,000.

134 *Hansard's Parliamentary Debates*, June 26, 1882, p. 429 and 431.

135 *Hansard's Parliamentary Debates*, March 29, 1883, p. 1,016.

136 *Hansard's Parliamentary Debates*, April 24, 1884, p. 572.

137 From 1874 to 1880 Sir S. A. Blackwood had been Financial Secretary to the Post Office.

138 *Report from the Select Committee on Revenue Departments Estimates*; q. 403 and 404.

139 *Report of the Inter-Departmental Committee on Post Office Establishments*, 1897; q. 11,641 to 11,648.

114

140 *Second Report of the Royal Commission on Civil Establishments*, 1888; q. 10,562-3, 10,742 to 10,749, and 10,772 to 10,783.

141 *Who's Who*, 1903, West, Sir Algernon E.; Was a clerk in the Admiralty: Assistant Secretary to Sir C. Wood and Duke of Somerset; Secretary to Sir C. Wood at India Office, and to Mr. Gladstone when Prime Minister; Chairman of Board of Inland Revenue.

142 *Second Report of the Royal Commission on Civil Establishments*, 1888; q. 17,438 to 17,447.

143 *Second Report of the Royal Commission on Civil Establishments*, 1888; q. 20,238.

144 *Report of the Inter-Departmental Committee on Post Office Establishments*, 1897, Mr. Lewin Hill, Assistant Secretary, General Post Office, London; q. 15,123 and 15,119.

The subjoined table shows the changes made in the wages of the second class provincial telegraphists, who enter the service as boys and girls, from fourteen years upward, and are taught telegraphy at the cost of the Department.

Age of the Telegraphist	Wage Under the Fawcett Scheme	Wage Under the Raikes Scheme
Years	$	$
16	4.00	3.50
17	4.37	4.50
18	4.75	5.00
19	5.12	5.50
20	5.50	6.00
21	5.87	6.50
22	6.25	7.00
23	6.62	7.50
24	7.00	8.00
25	7.37	8.50
26	7.75	9.00
27	8.12	9.50
28	8.50	10.00
29	8.87	10.00
30	9.25	10.00

145 *Hansard's Parliamentary Debates*, August 1, 1890, p. 1,623 and following; April 17, 1891, p. 883; and August 1, 1891, p. 1,059 and following.

146 *Report of the Inter-Departmental Committee on Post Office Establishments*, 1897; q. 11,706.

147 *Who's Who*, 1903, Compton, family name of Marquis of Northampton.

Northampton, 5th Marquis of, Wm. Geo. Spencer Scott Compton; was in Diplomatic Service; Private Secretary to Lord Lieutenant of Ireland (Earl Cowper), 1880 to 1882; Member of Parliament (G. L.) 1889 to 1897; owns about 23,600 acres.

148 *Hansard's Parliamentary Debates*, April 15, 1890, p. 581 and following.

149 *Hansard's Parliamentary Debates*, July 31, 1890, p. 1,441.

150 *Hansard's Parliamentary Debates*, April 17, 1891, p. 851 and following.

151 *Hansard's Parliamentary Debates*, August 1, 1891, p. 1,059 and following.

152 *Hansard's Parliamentary Debates*, February 18, 1898, p. 1,109. S. Woods quotes as follows from the circular issued by the Fawcett Association in June, 1892: "Will you, in the event of being elected a Member of Parliament, support a motion for the appointment of a Parliamentary Committee of Inquiry into the Post Office Service, such as was advocated by Earl Compton, and largely supported during the recent Session of the House of Commons?"

153 *Hansard's Parliamentary Debates*, June 14, 1892, p. 1,123 and following.

154 *Hansard's Parliamentary Debates*, June 20, 1892, p. 1,565 and following.

155 *Hansard's Parliamentary Debates*, August 28, 1893, p. 1,218.

156 *Hansard's Parliamentary Debates*, May 17, 1895, p. 1,455, Sir A. K. Rollit, one of the most aggressive champions of the demands of the civil servants.

157 *Who's Who*, 1903. Macdonald, J. A. M.; Member of Parliament for Bow and Bromley, 1892 to 1895; Member of the London School Board for Marylebone since 1897; Education: Edinburgh and Glasgow Universities.

158 *Hansard's Parliamentary Debates*, September 16, 1893, p. 1,453 and following.

159 *Who's Who*, 1905, Kearley, H. E., J. P., D. L., Member of Parliament (G. L.), Devenport, since 1892. Director of Kearley and Tonge, L't'd., tea importers and merchants; owns 1,200 acres. In 1906 Mr. Kearley became Political Secretary of the Board of Trade in the Campbell-Bannerman Ministry.

160 *Hansard's Parliamentary Debates*, May 17, 1895, p. 1,446 and following.

161 *Who's Who*, 1905, Rollit, Sir Albert Kaye, J. P., LL. D., D. C. L., D. L., Member of Parliament, South Islington, since 1886. Partner in Bailey and Leatham, steamship owners at Hull, Newcastle and London; Director of National Telephone Co.; Mayor of Hull, 1883 to 1885; President Associated Chambers of Commerce of the United Kingdom, 1890 to 1896; President London Chamber of Commerce, 1893 to 1898; Chairman Inspection

Committee Trustee Savings Bank since 1890; President of Association of Municipal Corporations.

162 In 1891-92 to 1894-95 the number of telegrams transmitted had remained practically stationary.

Number of Telegrams

1890-91	66,409,000
1891-92	69,685,000
1892-93	69,908,000
1893-94	70,899,000
1894-95	71,589,000

163 *Who's Who*, 1905, Rollit, Sir Albert Kaye, J. P., LL. D., D. C. L., D. L., M. P., South Islington, since 1886. Partner in Bailey and Leetham, steamship owners at Hull, Newcastle and London; Director of National Telephone Co.; Mayor of Hull, 1883 to 1885; President Associated Chambers of Commerce of the United Kingdom, 1890 to 1896; President London Chamber of Commerce, 1893 to 1898; Chairman Inspection Committee Trustee Savings Bank since 1890; President of Association of Municipal Corporations.

164 *Report of Bradford Committee on Post Office Wages*, 1904; q. 1,024; Mr. E. Trenam, Controller London Central Telegraph Office; and q. 1,048, Mr. W. G. Kirkwood, a principal clerk in Secretary's department, General Post Office.

165 Compare also, *Hansard's Parliamentary Debates*, March 4, 1890, p. 1,774. Mr. Cunninghame-Grahame: "I beg to ask the Postmaster General whether it is the custom of the Post Office to give bonuses to Inspectors or other officials for cutting down working expenses, and whether continual complaints are being made of the arbitrary stoppage of payment for over-time?" "No," was answered to both questions.

166 In April, 1896, Mr. Lewin Hill, Assistant Secretary to General Post Office, stated that on the basis of the staff of 1896, the Fawcett and Raikes schemes were costing the Post Office Department $6,000,000 a year in increased expenditure. The Postmaster General's statement of an increase of $3,750,000 in the expenditure had been made on the basis of the members actually employed in 1881 and 1891 respectively. *Report of the Inter-Departmental Committee on Post Office Establishments*, 1897; q. 12,382 and 15,123.

167 Compare *Report of Inter Departmental Committee on Post Office Establishments*, 1897; Mr. Lewin Hill, Assistant Secretary to General Post Office; q. 15,272.

On April 1, 1891, there were employed at 57 of the largest post offices in the United Kingdom, 2,614 first class and second class male letter sorters. In the next 5 years there resigned, in all, 95 sorters. Twelve of that number resigned in order to avoid dismissal.

On April 1, 1891, there were employed at 96 of the largest telegraph offices, 4,211 first class and second class male telegraphists. In the next 5 years there were 235 resignations. Of the men who resigned, 12 avoided dismissal, 23 left because of ill health, 38 went to

South Africa, 28 obtained superior appointments in the Civil Service, by open competition, 11 enlisted with the Royal Engineers, 1 entered the service of an electric light company, 1 became a bank clerk, 2 became commercial travelers, 3 went to sea, 4 emigrated to the United States, and 48 entered the service of the British Cable companies, which pay higher salaries than the Post Office, but work their men much harder and demand greater efficiency than does the Post Office.

168 *Report of the Inter-Departmental Committee on Post Office Establishments*, 1897, is the official title of the Committee's Report.

CHAPTER X
THE TWEEDMOUTH COMMITTEE REPORT

The Government accepts all recommendations made by the
Committee. Sir Albert K. Rollit, one of the principal
champions in the House of Commons of the postal employees,
immediately follows with a motion "intended to reflect upon
the Report of the Tweedmouth Committee." Mr. Hanbury,
Financial Secretary to the Treasury, intimates that it may
become necessary to disfranchise the civil servants. The
Treasury accepts the recommendations of the so-called
Norfolk-Hanbury Committee. The average of expenses on
account of wages and salaries rises from 11.54 cents per
telegram in 1895-96, to 13.02 cents in 1902-03, concomitantly
with an increase in the number of telegrams from 79,423,000
to 92,471,000.

In the preceding chapter the narrative was brought down to the appointment
in 1895, of the so-called Tweedmouth Committee.[169] That Committee
consisted of Lord Tweedmouth, Lord Privy Seal and a Member of the
Cabinet; Sir F. Mowatt, Permanent Secretary of the Treasury; Sir A. Godley,
Under Secretary of State for India; Mr. Spence Walpole, Permanent Secretary
of the Post Office; and Mr. Llewellyn Smith, of the Labor Department of the
Board of Trade.

In the "Terms of Reference to the Committee on Post Office
Establishments," the Postmaster General included this paragraph: "In
conducting this inquiry, I can have no doubt you will recollect that the Post
Office is a great Revenue Department; and that, in the words of the *Select
Committee on Revenue Departments Estimates* in 1888, it 'is most likely to
continue to be conducted satisfactorily, if it should also continue to be
conducted with a view to profit, as one of the Revenue yielding Departments
of the State.'"[170]

No Service like the Public Service

Before the Tweedmouth Committee Mr. Lewin Hill, who, as Assistant
Secretary General Post Office, was the executive officer who had general

119

charge of all the postal and telegraph employees outside of London, testified as follows: "My own view is that the time has come for telling the postmen, in common with the members of the rest of the manipulative staff [the telegraphists] in answer to their demand for a general rise of wages, that the Post Office Department is satisfied that the wages already paid are in excess of the market value of their services; that this being so, no general addition to pay will be given, and that if the staff are dissatisfied, and can do better for themselves outside the Post Office, they are, as they know, at perfect liberty to seek employment elsewhere." The Chairman, Lord Tweedmouth, asked Mr. Hill: "Do you think there is any other particular class of employment which is comparable with that of the postmen [and telegraphists]?" Mr. Hill replied: "I thoughtof railway servants, whose work in many ways resembles the work of our employees. If they have not the same permanence [of tenure] as our own people have, they have continuous employment so long as they are efficient, but our people have continuous employment whether they are efficient or not.... In that respect all of us in the Postal Service stand in a unique position, from top to bottom our men are certain as long as they conduct themselves reasonably well to retain their maximum pay down to the last day they remain in the Service, and whatever their class may be, whether postmen, or sorting clerks, or telegraphists, or officers of higher grade, they continue, failing misconduct, to rise to the maximum pay of their class, quite regardless of whether they are worth the higher pay that they get from year to year." The only concession that Mr. Hill was willing to recommend was, that in the larger towns the time required for postmen and telegraphists to rise from the minimum scale of pay to the maximum be reduced from 13 years to 6 years.[171]

Mr. J. C. Badcock, Controller of the Metropolitan Postal Service other than the Service in the London Central Post Office, and Mr. H. C. Fischer, Controller of the London Central Post Office, joined in Mr. Lewin Hill's recommendation. Mr. Fischer added that the London telegraphists should be given better chances of passing from the second class to the first class than they had enjoyed in the last three or four years,[172] and that the pay of the London senior telegraphists, who were a kind of assistants to the assistant superintendents, ought to be raised above the existing scale of $950.

Mr. C. H. Kerry, Postmaster at Stoke-on-Trent, stated that if the Post Office Department "was willing to act, not only the part of the model employer, but of an exceptionally liberal employer; and it was thought after all that had been done for the staff so recently, that still a little further should be done," the Department might reduce from 13 years to 5 years the period that it took the rank and file to pass from the minimum salary of their class to the maximum salary. But there was no necessity of doing anything for any one, "on a general consideration of the pay given elsewhere to persons performing duties requiring about the same amount of intelligence." There was "absolutely no justification" for increasing the existing maximum of pay.

Mr. Kerry had entered the Post Office telegraph service in 1870, after having served with the Electric and International Company from 1854 to 1870. He said: "The speed at which the telegraphists had to work present, that is the speed per man,[173] because the telegraph companies kept only enough force for the minimum work, and when the work increased you had to catch that up by increased effort.... As a previous witness said, one of the laws of the service is that there must be no delay, but I think there is a well understood law, also, that there must be no confusion, and the arrangements made are now such that the maximum of work, as a rule, can be dealt with without undue pressure.... From 1870 to 1889, I was constantly in the Telegraph branch and witnessing from day to day, and almost from hour to hour, the work which the telegraphists performed...."[174]

This testimony from Mr. Kerry must be borne in mind when reading the complaints of the Post Office telegraphists that the salaries paid by the Eastern Telegraph [Cable] Company rise to $1,020 a year, whereas the salaries of first class telegraphists in London rise only to $950. The employees of the Eastern Telegraph Company have to work under so much greater pressure than the State telegraphists, that Mr. Fischer, Controller of the London Central Telegraph Office, was able to state: "I have never known a telegraphist in the first class to leave our service for that of any of the [Cable] companies. The cable companies draw very few men from us, and those drawn away as a rule, are young men in the second class who are receiving about $250 or $300, and are attracted by the prospect of an immediate increase of some $150 upon entrance into the service of the cable companies."[175]

The Tweedmouth Committee's Recommendations

Those telegraph offices which are not sufficiently important to justify the employment of telegraphists of the first class, are divided into four groups: B, C, D and E. The Tweedmouth Committee recommended that the maximum salary of the telegraphists in the offices of Group E be raised from $8 a week to $8.50: in offices of group D from $8.75 to $9; in offices of group C from $9.50 to $10; and in offices of group B from $10 to $11. It recommended furthermore that all provincial telegraphists should rise automatically and without regard to efficiency, to a salary of not less than $10 a week. Beyond $10 they should not go, unless fully competent. The Committee added that it placed "the efficiency bar at the high figure of $10 a week,[176] for the special reason that it may be rigorously enforced, and that all inducements to treat it as a matter of form, liable to be abrogated for the reason of compassion, may be removed."

As for the telegraphists employed in Metropolitan London, the Tweedmouth Committee recommended that all telegraphists should rise at least to "the efficiency bar" of $560 a year; and that those who could pass the efficiency bar, should rise automatically to $800, the maximum salary of first class telegraphists. In the past, telegraphists in London had been promoted from the second class to the first class, only upon the occurrence of vacancies. In this case, also, the Committee added to its recommendation the words: "This efficiency bar has been placed at the high figure of $560 for the special reason that it may be rigorously enforced, and that all inducements to treat it as a matter of form, liable to be abrogated for reasons of compassion, may be removed."[177]

These recommendations the Tweedmouth Committee made in order to meet the complaints advanced by the Post Office employees that the falling off in the rate of increase of the business of the telegraph branch had caused a slackening in the flow of promotion.

The remaining recommendations of the Tweedmouth Committee it is not necessary to enumerate; suffice it to say, that the Postmaster General, the Duke of Norfolk, advised the Government to accept all of the Committee's recommendations, with the statement that, on the basis of the staff of 1897, the cost of carrying out the recommendations would begin with $695,000 a year, and would rise ultimately to $1,375,000. That estimate related to both branches of the Post Office, the postal branch and the telegraph; no separate estimates were made for the several branches.

The Government accepts the Committee's Recommendations

The Lords Commissioners of Her Majesty's Treasury accepted the Postmaster General's recommendations, and directed the Financial Secretary of the Treasury, Mr. R. W. Hanbury, to write as follows to the Postmaster General.

"It has, of course, been necessary for my Lords to consider very carefully proposals involving so large an increase of expenditure in a single Department at one time, and they have duly weighed the reasons which the Committee adduces in support of its conclusions. While many of the proposals appear to be abundantly justified by the considerations put forward, there are others which my Lords would have hesitated to accept on any authority less entitled to respect than that by which they are supported. But, my Lords readily acknowledge the exceptional competence of the Committee to pronounce a judgment on the question which came before it, and the great care with which the inquiry has been conducted. They also note that the conclusions represent the unanimous opinion of the Committee, and that they are, in all cases, endorsed by your Grace. They have therefore decided, in view of the weight of authority by which your recommendations are supported, to accept them as they stand, and they authorize you to give effect to them as from the first of April next. They have adopted this course from a strong desire to do full justice to one of the largest and most important services of the State, and because they feel that the settlement now effected must be accepted as permanently satisfying all reasonable claims on the part of the classes included in its terms. The only condition which my Lords desire to attach to their acceptance of your proposals is that the annual increments of pay should, in all cases, be dependent on the certificate of a superior officer, that the conduct of the recipient during the preceding year has been satisfactory."

The recommendations of the Tweedmouth Committee went into effect on April 1, 1897. On July 16, 1897, while the House of Commons was in Committee of Supply, Sir Albert K. Rollit moved the reduction of the salary of the Postmaster General by $5,000.[178] Sir Albert Rollit said: "The Amendment was intended to reflect upon the report of the Tweedmouth Committee, rather than upon either the Government or the Post Office Department, for he thought more might be done to remedy the abuses which were known [shown?] to exist in the course of the report itself. To speak of the Post Office as a revenue earning machine was, in his opinion, not a full or adequate description. He shared to the full the opinion that its first object was to give facilities to the public rather than merely to earn profits, and also to do justice to its employees.... There were grievances which had not been redressed by the report, and the House had a great deal more to do in that direction. It was no answer to say that the Treasury had appropriated a large sum of $695,000 for that very purpose, for after all, what did the appropriation amount to? It only amounted to a rectification of the inadequacies of the past. It was not in London alone, but throughout the United Kingdom, that something like chronic discontent existed. The complaints were loud and widespread. He did not at all agree as to the propriety of the course intimated [by the telegraphists] by way of notice to the Postmaster General, that if the grievances were not redressed, over-time work at night would be suspended [*i. e.* the telegraphists would refuse to work over-time in order to compel the Government to redress their grievances]. That was an extreme remedy in cases where the public convenience and service were concerned; but, after all, every man's labor was his own right, and if there were no disposition to remedy present grievances, even that extreme way of trying to bring about a remedy might possibly have to be resorted to. The Treasury was, of course, a barrier to a good deal. He did not say the heads of a

Department did not value as much as he might do pecuniarily the services of those who contributed to the joint effect which he and they made for the public advantage, and if we had a splendid Civil Service in this country, he thought it had one great defect, and that was too glaring disproportion between the salaries of the highest officials and those of the lower, and this proportion might well be redressed."

Sir Albert Rollit said he could not enumerate all the grievances, he would have to confine himself to the enumeration of the worst ones. He began by endorsing the contention of the telegraphists that everybody should rise automatically to a salary of $1,000 a year. The establishment of the "efficiency bars" he said, "was really a violation of the contract with the telegraph operators, and was a grave and gross injustice to them." He maintained, also, that the Committee's recommendation that the payment for Sunday labor be reduced from double rates to a rate and a half was "a material alteration of the contract under which servants entered the Department." He supported the contention of the State employees that it was a grievance that some of the employees had to take their annual vacation in the winter months. "The postmen had asked that the Christmas boxes [contributions from the public] be abolished, $26 a year being added to the wages as a compromise. Evidence had been given that $1.25 a year was the real value of the Christmas boxes, but the Committee said there should be no solicitation for Christmas boxes, and no compensation for their loss." "He hoped that a statement of grievances, which were provoking the strongest possible feeling, with disadvantage to the efficiency of the Post Office, would be listened to. He was extremely glad to recognize that the Postmaster General had been willing to receive two deputations—one on June 15, which had not yet been replied to, and one yesterday. But he would urge upon the Department and the Government that the real remedy for this strong and wide discontent was the appointment of an independent Committee, because the decision of such a tribunal composed not of officials, but of practical business men, who would perhaps have more sympathy with men in the lower grades of the service, would be loyally accepted, and thus the public would be advantaged and contentment restored to a service which was of great value to the country." ["Hear, hear."]

Mr. R. W. Hanbury, who, as Financial Secretary to the Treasury, represented in the House of Commons the Postmaster General, the Duke of Norfolk, replied: "that throughout the discussion some facts had been more or less left out of sight. Honorable Members ought to recollect, in the first place, that the Tweedmouth Committee gave universal satisfaction when it was appointed. It was then agreed that it was the right kind of Committee; and that the right kind of men were appointed to serve upon it. There was no preponderance of Treasury opinion upon the Committee. In fact, the only Treasury official sitting upon it was Sir Francis Mowatt. There was on it a high representative of the Post Office, and the officials of a Department were not as a rule anxious to cut down the salaries of their subordinates. Their tendency would rather be to recommend an increase in salaries. There was also on the Committee a representative of the Labor Department of the Board of Trade, who was particularly well qualified to give an opinion as to the proportion which the wages of the postal and telegraph employees bore to the wages of persons doing corresponding work outside the Post Office. Therefore the Committee was a very efficient body, and through its recommendations the salaries of the officials had already been increased by $700,000 a year, and the increase would amount to something like $1,250,000 a year in the next few years. The Treasury had accepted every recommendation of the Committee, whose suggestions had been adopted wholesale. There was no ground for complaint, therefore, in that direction."

Disfranchisement of Civil Servants Suggested

"Another fact which Members ought not to overlook was the political pressure which was far too frequently exercised by Civil Servants upon those who also represented them." ["Hear, hear."] "That was a great and growing danger. It was chiefly in London that this pressure was brought to bear.... He would give an instance of the way in which these Civil Servants spoke of the expediency of political pressure. At one of the great meetings which had been held, a speaker said there were 8,000 postmen in London, and that he hoped every one would have his name upon the register [of voters], so that at election times they could exercise their influence upon candidates and advocate the cause of higher wages. He was of the opinion that political pressure ought not to be brought to bear in that way." ["Hear, hear."]

"Ordinary workmen could not exercise the same power, but Civil Servants could, and, whether their agitation succeeded or not, their position was secure, so that it was a case of 'Heads, I win; tails, I don't lose'.... Before the Royal Commission [of 1888], which had inquired into the Civil Service establishments, evidence was given with regard to the way in which pressure was brought to bear in certain constituencies upon Members, and he thought that the almost unanimous feeling of the Commission was that, if this state of things continued, it would be necessary to disfranchise the Civil Service." ["Hear, hear."][179]

Sir Albert Rollit replied: "They had to acknowledge a very sympathetic speech from the Secretary to the Treasury. Perhaps if some honorable Members went to the Treasury in regard to this matter, accompanied by one person who might represent practically the views which were entertained by those concerned, the matter might be further gone into. He begged leave to withdraw his Amendment."

The Secretary to the Treasury replied: "There was no objection on the part of the Treasury to hearing communications from Members of Parliament on the subject, but with regard to officials of the Post Office coming to the Treasury, he should not like to give any pledge without first consulting with the Postmaster General."

| The Norfolk-Hanbury Committee |

Shortly afterward the Postmaster General, the Duke of Norfolk, and the Financial Secretary to the Treasury, Mr. Hanbury, constituted themselves a Committee to investigate the grievances that the Tweedmouth Committee had left unredressed. All Members of the House of Commons were invited to attend the meetings of the Norfolk-Hanbury Committee, and to take part in examining the witnesses. Sir Albert Rollit presented the case of the Post Office employees. The Norfolk-Hanbury Committee recommended further concessions involving an additional outlay of $400,000 a year; and the Treasury accepted the recommendations.

The Report of the Postmaster General for the year 1897-98 stated that the concessions granted would entail a total increase of expenditure of $1,940,000 a year. The Duke of Norfolk concluded his reference to the foregoing episodes with the words: "Since that time I have declined, and I shall continue to decline, to allow decisions which have been considered by the Tweedmouth Committee, and which have been revised by Mr. Hanbury and myself, to be reopened. It is my belief that those decisions have been liberal, but whether they are liberal or not, it is for the interest of all parties that it should be understood that they are final."

In April, 1900, Mr. R. W. Hanbury, Financial Secretary to the Treasury, stated the concessions granted by the Tweedmouth and Norfolk-Hanbury Committees were costing $2,200,000 a year. In April, 1901, Mr. Austen Chamberlain, Financial Secretary to the Treasury, said they were costing $2,500,000 a year; and in April, 1903, he stated that they were costing $3,000,000 a year.[180] Those figures related to the combined postal and telegraph service. So far as the latter service alone is concerned, the average expenses on account of wages and salaries rose steadily from 11.54 cents per telegram in 1895-96, to 13.02 cents in 1902-03, under an increase in the number of messages from 79,423,000 in 1895-96, to 92,471,000 in 1902-03. In 1905-06, the average in question rose to 14.29 cents, partly in consequence of the increases in wages made in response to the demands of the Civil Servants, partly in consequence of the drop in the number of telegrams to 89,478,000—as a result of the growing competition from the telephone.

In 1895-96 the receipts of the Telegraph Department proper exceeded the operating expenses by $646,000; in 1900-01, the operating expenses exceeded the receipts by $34,000; in 1903-04 the deficit rose to $1,505,000, and in 1904-05 it was $917,000. In 1905-06, the gross revenue exceeded the operating expenses by $63,500.[181]

FOOTNOTES:

169 *Report of the Inter-Departmental Committee on Post Office Establishments*, 1897, is the official title of the Committee's Report.

170 *Report of the Inter-Departmental Committee on Post Office Establishments*, 1897, p. 4.

171 *Report of the Inter-Departmental Committee on Post Office Establishments*, 1897; q. 15,119 and following, 11,706, 11,694, 15,123, 11,642 to 11,648, 11,680 to 11,697, 11,774 and 11,805.

172 *Report of the Inter-Departmental Committee on Post Office Establishments*, 1897; q.

4,183 to 4,185, 3,907 to 3,912, 3,868 to 3,879 and 4,140 to 4,149.

173 Mr. Kerry probably meant that the employees of the companies worked under greater pressure.

174 *Report of the Inter-Departmental Committee on Post Office Establishments*, 1897; q. 6,747 and following, and 6,691 to 6,694.

175 *Report of the Inter-Departmental Committee on Post Office Establishments*, 1897; q. 3,863 and 3,853.

176 Compare: *Second Report of the Royal Commission appointed to inquire into the Civil Establishments*, 1888, p. xvi. In 1888 the salaries of the Lower Division Clerks of the Civil Service ranged from $475 to $1,250. The Royal Commission recommended that in the future the salaries in question should range from $350 to $1,750, with an efficiency bar at $500 at the end of seven years' service, and a second efficiency bar at $950 at the end of nineteen years' service.

177 *Report of the Inter-Departmental Committee on Post Office Establishments*, 1897, pp. 9, 11 and 1,088; and q. 4,256 and following, 4,161 to 4,162, 15,126 to 15,134, and 3,913 to 3,937.

178 *Hansard's Parliamentary Debates*, July 16, 1897, p. 323 and following.

179 Compare also *Hansard's Parliamentary Debates*, April 9, 1896, p. 597, Mr. R. W. Hanbury: "He had sat for some years as a member of the Royal Commission upon Civil Service Establishments, and the Members of that Commission had been greatly struck by the enormous pressure that civil servants in particular constituencies were able to bring to bear upon candidates, and in his view the House ought not to adopt any line of action that would encourage that pressure being brought into operation. So great, indeed, had been the abuses that it had even been suggested that civil servants ought to be disfranchised altogether.... Another great danger that had to be provided against was that in certain London constituencies, and in some of the large towns, it was quite possible that the civil servants might, by combining together, succeed in turning the balance at an election in the event of one of the candidates refusing to pledge himself with regard to raising the scale of wage, or an increase in the amount of pensions, or similar advantages which the civil servants might desire to obtain."

180 *Hansard's Parliamentary Debates*, April 27, 1900, p. 135; April 25, 1901, p. 1,325; and April 30, 1903, p. 1,022.

181 *Report of the Postmaster General*, 1906.

CHAPTER XI

THE POST OFFICE EMPLOYEES CONTINUE TO PRESS THE HOUSE OF COMMONS FOR INCREASES OF WAGES AND SALARIES

The Post Office employees demand "a new judgment on the old facts." Mr. S. Woods' Motion, in February, 1898. Mr. Steadman's Motions in February and June, 1899. Mr. Hanbury, Financial Secretary to the Treasury, points out that the postal employees are demanding a House of Commons Select Committee because under such a Committee "the agitation and pressure, now distributed over the whole House, would be focussed and concentrated upon the unfortunate members of the Select Committee." Mr. Steadman's Motion, in April, 1900. Mr. Bayley's Motion, in June, 1901. Mr. Balfour, Prime Minister, confesses that the debate has filled him "with considerable anxiety as to the future of the public service if pressure of the kind which has been put upon the Government to-night is persisted in by the House." Captain Norton's Motion, in April, 1902. The Government compromises by appointing the Bradford Committee of business men. Mr. Austen Chamberlain, Postmaster General, states that members from both sides of the House "seek from him, in his position as Postmaster General, protection for them in the discharge of their public duties against the pressure sought to be put upon them by employees of the Post Office." He adds: "Even if the machinery by which our Select Committees are appointed were such as would enable us to secure a Select Committee composed of thoroughly impartial men who had committed themselves by no expression of opinion, I still think that it would not be fair to pick out fifteen members of this House and make them marked men for the purpose of such pressure as is now distributed more or less over the whole Assembly."

On February 18, 1898, in the House of Commons, Mr. S. Woods[182] moved: "And we humbly represent to Your Majesty that your servants in the Post Office are not permitted to exercise the franchise, generally allowed to other Departments in the State; nor to serve on electoral committees; nor to take part in political agitation; and are otherwise deprived of the privileges of citizenship in defiance of the letter and spirit of the law; that the officials of the Post Office refuse to recognize the Postmen's Trade Union; their officials are illegally and unjustly dismissed for circularizing Parliamentary Candidates; and we humbly beg Your Majesty to instruct the Postmaster General to remedy these grievances."[183]

Sir James Fergusson, a former Postmaster General, said Mr. Woods' motion had been brought "by the direction of the central Committee of the Postal Union, or some such party." He continued with the statement that the motion was the outcome of the agitation carried on since he, Sir James Fergusson, had dismissed from the Post Office service Messrs. Clery and Cheeseman, the ringleaders of a political campaign carried on in violation of Sir James Fergusson's order of June 17, 1892. He said the employees in the Revenue Departments had been disfranchised in 1782 by the Marquis of Rockingham, Prime Minister, but that the franchise had been restored to them in 1868. That in that year both Mr. Disraeli and Mr. Gladstone had approved the policy of enfranchising the employees of the Revenue Departments, subject to the limitation that the ministerial heads of the Departments were to have the power to determine the limits within which the employees were to take an active part in politics. That an attempt had been made in 1874 to remove that limitation, but that the House had supported the Government of the day in resisting the attempt.[184]

Mr. R. W. Hanbury, Financial Secretary to the Treasury, and representative in the House of Commons of the Postmaster General, the Duke of Norfolk, said, in the course of his reply to Mr. Woods: "We must recognize the fact that in this House of Commons, public servants have a Court of Appeal such as exists with regard to no private employee whatever. It is a Court of Appeal which not only exists with regard to the grievances of classes, and even of individuals, but it is a Court of Appeal which applies even to the wages and duties of classes and individuals, and its functions in that respect are only limited by the common sense of Members, who should exercise caution in bringing forward cases of individuals, because, if political influence is brought to bear in favor of one individual, the chances are that injury is done to some other individual…. I think it is only reasonable to expect that, as both [political] parties in the State have dropped party politics with regard to their employees, the employees should in turn recognize that fact, and drop party politics with regard to their employers." Mr. Hanbury enforced this point by stating that, upon the request of the Civil Servants themselves, Lord Rockingham, Prime Minister, in 1782 had disfranchised the Civil Servants in the Revenue Departments. At that time the party in power, through the Public Service, controlled 70 seats in Parliament. Lord North, who had been in power twelve years, had sent out notices to certain constituencies where the Civil Servants were able to turn the scale, saying, that unless the Civil Servants supported the Government, it would go hard with them. Thereupon the Opposition had sent out counter notices, and thus had put the Civil Service in an awkward position. The result had been that the Civil Servants themselves had requested Lord Rockingham to disfranchise them.

Mr. Hanbury continued with the statement that, in 1892, Sir James Fergusson had dismissed Mr. Clery for ignoring his order forbidding Civil Servants to "circularize" parliamentary candidates. Thereupon Mr. Clery, at Newcastle-on-Tyne, had said to a political meeting of postmen: "They must approach the House of Commons on its weak side; they must influence Members through their susceptibilities as opportunity presents itself when candidates appeal to their respective constituencies. A man is never more amenable to reason than when making a request." Mr. Hanbury continued: "What private employee is able to say: 'I am the permanent servant of my employer; I have a share in declaring who that employer shall be; I will attack him on his weak side when he comes up for re-election, and then I will use my power? I will bring organized pressure to bear throughout the constituencies, and I will make this bargain: that if he will not vote for an increase in my pay, or diminish my duties, then I will not give him my vote.' We have done away with personal and individual bribery, but there is still a worse form of bribery, and that is when a man asks a candidate to buy his vote out of the public purse. There are three great things which distinguish our permanent public service. There is, in the first place, the remarkable loyalty with which they serve both parties in the State. Then there is the permanency of their employment. Again, a great feature of that service is that no longer is it a question of favoritism, but promotion by merit is the rule. Those three great features have been slowly built upon this foundation—the elimination altogether of the element of political partisanship from the service. I hope nothing will be done to break down those foundations, on which alone the public service can rest—a service which, for its efficiency, its loyalty, and its high sense of public duty, I do not think is surpassed. I doubt whether it is equalled or even approached."

Mr. Woods' Motion was lost by a vote of 163 to 86. It was supported almost exclusively by the Opposition, only three Government supporters voting for it.[185]

Mr. Steadman demands a Select Committee

In the House of Commons, on February 20, 1899, Mr. Steadman[186] moved: "And we humbly represent to Your Majesty that, in view of the great discontent existing among employees of the Postal and Telegraph Services, immediate inquiry should be made into the causes of complaint."[187] Mr. Steadman had been elected to the House of Commons by a majority of twenty votes.

Parliament not competent to judge

Mr. R. W. Hanbury, Financial Secretary to the Treasury, replied that no new facts had been brought to light since the Tweedmouth Committee and the Norfolk-Hanbury Committee had made concessions entailing an annual expenditure of $1,900,000 a year. The Post Office servants were demanding "a new judgment on the old facts." He continued: "I confess, I am not quite sure that we did not go too far [in 1897], because by increasing these salaries we are bringing into this service an entirely new social class; you are bringing in men who perhaps are socially a little above their work, and these men naturally have a standard of living and requirements which are not essential to men doing this kind of work. If we are going to raise the salaries more and more, you will get a higher social class into the service, and there will be no limit to the demands made upon us." Mr. Hanbury continued: "You have got to trust the heads of the Departments, or get new heads; it is quite impossible for the House of Commons to go into all these technicalities, and I know no Department where the work is more technical and more complicated than the Post Office. The Treasury work is supposed to be hard to learn [by the Members of the House of Commons working for promotion to the Ministry], but the technicalities of the Post Office is about the most difficult job I ever had, and I do not think a Select Committee would be really able to get to the bottom of this matter. But, after all, we must recollect another fact, and it is this: that the Civil Service is a great deal too much inclined to attempt to put pressure upon Members of Parliament. That is a very bad system, upon which we ought to put our foot. It is bad enough when it is brought to bear upon the House as a whole, but what would happen with a Select Committee of this House? You would have the resentment of the Civil Service focussed and concentrated upon the unfortunate Members of the Committee, and I do not think it would act more independently or more impartially than those two bodies which have sat already."

Mr. Steadman's Motion was lost by a vote of 159 to 91. Eighty-six members of the Opposition and two Government supporters voted for the Motion.[188]

***

Civil Servants have "Friends" in the Commons

On June 1, 1899, Mr. Steadman moved the reduction of the Postmaster General's salary by $500, by way of asking the House of Commons to instruct the Government to appoint a Select Committee of the House of Commons to investigate the grievances of the Post Office employees.[189] He said: "It stands to reason that a Departmental Committee [Tweedmouth Committee] composed of officials, which contained only one impartial member—a Member of the House of Lords—could not be satisfactory to the 160,000 male and female employees in the Post Office service…. Every department of the Post Office service now has its organization. All these organizations right through the departments have their coaches and organizers; true, they are not yet directly represented here in this House, but they have friends here who are prepared to take up their quarrels."

Captain Norton[190] seconded the Motion. He spoke of the fact that any telegraphist could obtain $30 a year extra pay by making himself competent to discharge the duties of a letter sorter, and another $30 by passing an examination on the technical questions of telegraphy. He asserted that it was a grievance that the men had to acquire, in their leisure hours, the additional proficiency in question; and that only 46 per cent. of the men were able to pass the examinations on the technical questions involved in telegraphy.

Mr. Maddison[191] supported Mr. Steadman's Motion with the words: "For my part, I have always had some hesitation in taking up the cases of men employed by the State, because undoubtedly there is a sort of notion that, because they are employed by the State, they can make such demands as they like, because they are paid out of a very full Treasury. I know that every half penny of that money comes out of the general taxation of the country, and I agree that we are here as the guardians of the public purse. The Right Honorable Gentleman has never denied that we are here as the guardians of these men's interest, and it has not been shown that the public interest is of greater importance than the interest of these men, who do so much for the prosperity of the Country…. In this case we want a non-official committee, although I confess that I do not think such an inquiry will put an end to disputes in the future."

Mr. Hanbury, Financial Secretary to the Treasury, said that if the Government yielded to the demand for a House of Commons Committee in this case, there would be a House of Commons Committee sitting practically every session of Parliament. The points now under discussion had been under agitation for four, five, or six years. Before the Tweedmouth Committee entered upon its duties, and before the Norfolk-Hanbury Conference with Members of the House of Commons, the Government had a distinct understanding with Members of the House that the decisions come to should be accepted. Mr. Hanbury continued: "It is somewhat difficult, no doubt, to draw a comparison between what the Post Office pays and what is paid by private firms. But I will give one comparison, at any rate, and I think it is the only one possible. A few years ago we took over from the National Telephone Company the employees, principally women, who were engaged on the [long-distance] trunk wires, and I venture to say that, counting in the pensions we pay, these people are receiving from 30 per cent. to 40 per cent. larger salaries than when they were in the employment of the company. Honorable Members who draw comparisons between servants of the State and others, are too apt to forget the great facilities Post Office servants get, such as constant employment, large pensions, good holidays, for which they are paid, and large sick-pay and sick-leave. If these are added together, it will be found that the Post Office is paying wages considerably above the level of those paid by outside employers. I should like to say one further word with regard to this application for a Committee of this House. Why should we have it at all? Let me speak with perfect frankness about this thing. We have already had two Committees; we have also had a great deal of pressure brought to bear upon Members; that pressure is becoming almost intolerable. The honorable Member for Newington posed as the just judge and said: 'I am weary of all this agitation; let us try to put an end to it.' Well I am not weary of the agitation; so long as I am satisfied, as I am now, that everything has been done that ought to be done for the men, I will not yield to agitation. I say at once that I do myself believe that, considering everything, and that full inquiry has already been held, the only advantage these men could derive from a House of Commons Committee would be that the agitation and pressure, now distributed over the whole House, would be focussed and concentrated upon the Select Committee. I, for one, am not prepared to grant a Committee of that kind."

Mr. Steadman's Motion was lost by a vote of 157 to 107; ninety-seven members of the Opposition and nine Government supporters voting for the Motion.[192]

On April 27, 1900, Mr. Steadman moved the reduction of the Postmaster General's salary by $2,500.[193] He said: "I rise for the purpose of advocating the claims of the 160,000 persons employed in the Post Office for a fair and impartial Committee of Inquiry to be elected by this House to look into their grievances."

The contention that there were grievances, Mr. Steadman supported with the following arguments. From 1881 to 1891, the Civil Service Commissioners, in issuing notices that they would hold competitive examinations for intending entrants into the telegraph service, had stated that in London telegraphists had "a prospect of obtaining [ultimately] $950 a year." That, argued Mr. Steadman, was a contract between the Government and the telegraphists who entered the London service between 1881 and 1891, that every such telegraphist should rise to $950. The Government therefore had committed a breach of contract when, in 1892, it had announced that good character and good skill as an operator would not secure a telegraphist promotion to the senior class, in which the salary rose from $800 a year to $950. To be eligible for promotion to the senior class, a man must be not only an excellent telegraphist, but must, in addition, possess such executive ability as would enable him to act as an overseer, or as assistant to the Assistant Superintendent.

Mr. Steadman continued: "Now I come to the question of the postmen. Goodness knows where all that $1,950,000 a year has gone to. You cannot get away from the fact that the postman to-day in London commences [at the age of 16 years to 18 years] with a minimum wage of $4.50 a week.... Fancy that, Mr. Chairman, a man commencing on $4.50 a week, and employed by the State in a Department that has a clean profit of between $15,000,000 and $20,000,000." Mr. Steadman next contended that a good conduct stripe— worth $13 a year—should be given every three years; that the present period of five years was too long. Moreover, the Department was altogether too rigorous in withholding good conduct stripes for breaches of discipline. Mr. Steadman cited the following instances to prove the necessity of an inquiry by Members of the House of Commons into the discipline enforced by the

Department. A man who had served nine years as an auxiliary postman had been arrested on the charge of stealing a postal money order. Though found not guilty by the Court, he had been dismissed, without a certificate of good character. Postman Taylor, of Stirling, after suffering an accident, was unable to cover his route in the time fixed by the Post Office. Thereupon the local postmaster had asked Taylor to retire on a pension. "The latest information that I have in regard to that case is that the man who is now doing Taylor's duties, in order to get through his round in the time allotted, has his son to help him." Again, the annual increment had been withheld from one Lacon, a telegraphist at Birmingham, and the local Secretary of the Postal Telegraph Clerks' Association. The Secretary to the Treasury, Mr. Hanbury, had told Mr. Steadman that the Superintendent at Birmingham reported that Lacon's increment had been withheld because Lacon had been insubordinate while on duty. Lacon had told Mr. Steadman that he had been disciplined because of his connection with the union. Mr. Steadman added: "I will not for one moment attempt to stand up in the House and attack permanent officials who are not able to defend themselves; it would be unmanly for me to do so. But I do say that I have as much right to believe the statement of Lacon, as the Right Honorable Gentleman [the Secretary to the Treasury] has to believe the statement of the Birmingham Superintendent. There is only one way of proving these cases, and that is for a Committee of impartial Members of this House to be appointed before which the permanent official can state his case and the men theirs. If that is done, the Members, if their minds are unbiased, will very soon be able to judge as to who is telling the truth."

Commons reminded of Civil Servants' votes

Sir Albert Rollit seconded Mr. Steadman's Motion, saying: "and we ought not to overlook the fact, that, rightly or wrongly, these men now have votes, and if they cannot obtain redress for their grievances here in the House of Commons, they will try to obtain it from our masters, the electorate."

Mr. R. W. Hanbury, Financial Secretary to the Treasury, and representative in the House of Commons of the Postmaster General, the Duke of Norfolk, "on principle" opposed the request for a Select Committee. "Well, I say that the House of Commons is the last body which ought to interfere in these questions of the payment of our public servants. It is the last body which ought to be appealed to as regularly as it is by civil servants to raise their salaries, because that, after all, is the real object of this proposed committee. Already I think the pressure brought to bear on individual Members, and especially on Members who have a large number of civil servants in their constituencies, has become perfectly intolerable, and civil servants may depend upon it that it is the general opinion in this House, although they may have their cause advocated by Members upon whom they may be able to bring particular pressure, because large numbers of them happen to live in the constituencies of those Members; I repeat that they may depend upon it that in the opinion of the great body of the Members of this House they are taking a highly irregular course, and are in no way making their position more favorable in the minds of the great majority of Members. Nothing will induce me personally to agree to any committee such as has been suggested. And while I object on principle, I object also because absolutely no necessity has been shown for the committee.... The Duke of Norfolk and I, because we were so desirous that no case of the slightest grievance should be left untouched, inquired into every grievance which was said to have been left unredressed by the Tweedmouth Committee.... Every Member of the House had a right to attend our [Norfolk-Hanbury Committee] meetings, and to cross-examine the witnesses.... It is the intention of the Post Office and of the Treasury to carry out the recommendations of the Tweedmouth Committee to the very fullest extent, and if the honorable Member [Mr. Steadman] is able to show me any case whatever in which that has not been done, even in the case of an individual postman, or sorter, or telegraphist, I will go into it myself, and I will do more: I will promise that the grievance shall be redressed."

Mr. Steadman's Motion was lost by a vote of 66 to 46. It was supported by forty-one members of the Opposition and by four supporters of the Government.[194]

On June 7, 1901, while the House of Commons was in Committee of Supply, Mr. Thomas Bayley[195] asked for a Select Committee of the House of Commons to investigate the grievance of the Post Office servants.[196] He said:

"This House shows a want of moral courage by throwing the responsibility for redressing the grievance of the Post Office servants on the other House [Lord Tweedmouth] or the permanent officials of any Department whatsoever." Mr. Bayley had begun his political career as a Town Councillor in Nottingham.

The Prime Minister's Anxiety

After many Members had supported the request for a Select Committee, the Prime Minister, Mr. A. J. Balfour, said: "I have listened with great interest to this debate, and, I confess frankly, with considerable anxiety as to the future of the public service if pressure of the kind which has been put upon the Government to-night is persisted in by this House. This House is omnipotent. It can make and unmake Governments. It can decide what, when, and how public money is to be spent. But with that omnipotence I would venture to urge upon Members their great responsibility with a subject like this. Everyone knows that a great organized body like the Post Office Service has in its power to put great pressure upon Members, but I earnestly urge upon honorable Gentlemen that unless we take our courage in both hands, and say that, although most desirous that all legitimate grievances shall be dealt with, we cannot permit the Government as a great employer of labor to have this kind of pressure put upon it, I think the future of the public service is in peril. I assure the committee that I speak with a great sense of responsibility. In this very case the Post Office employees have brought forward their grievances year after year. Two Commissions have been appointed, and no one ever ventured to impugn the ability or impartiality of the members of those Commissions. These Commissions made the fullest examination into the case put before them, and reported at length, and as a consequence of that report the British taxpayers are now paying $2,500,000 more of money than they paid before.... In none of the speeches has any specific complaint been brought forward, or any point urged which suggests the necessity for further inquiry, but only the statement that there is a feeling of uneasiness, and a desire for further examination, and that when such a desire is expressed, the House should listen to it. We cannot keep the Civil Service in a sound and healthy condition if we are going to examine into it by a committee every five years. If the House of Commons were to yield to the very natural temptation of granting a committee such as had been asked for, though we might escape an inconvenient division, we should be unworthy, in my opinion, of bearing any longer the great responsibility of being the enormous employer of labor that we are. We should not be carrying out our duty to the public, and, worst of all, we should aim a blow at the Civil Service, which is the boast of this country and the envy of the civilized world, because we should become the parliamentary creatures of every organized body of public servants who chose to use the great power which the Constitution gives, for ends which I am sure they believe to be right, but which this House could not yield to in the manner now suggested without derogating from the high functions and spirit of pure impartiality which the House must maintain if Members are to do their duty by their constituents."

Mr. Bayley's Motion was lost by a vote of 148 to 103; it being supported by ninety-one members of the Opposition and nine Government supporters.[197]

| Captain Norton demands a Select Committee

On April 18, 1902, while the House of Commons was in Committee of Supply, Captain Norton[198] moved the reduction by $500 of the item: Salaries and Working Expenses of the Post Office Telegraph Service: $12,056,250.[199] He said: "The case briefly was this, that the Government had been guilty of a distinct breach of faith in connection with a certain number of worthy Government officials. He knew that to make this statement of breach of faith was what must be called a strong order, but he was prepared to prove that he was not exaggerating in the smallest degree." He went on to state that the telegraphists who entered the service in London in 1881 to 1891, when the Civil Service Commissioners had advertised that entrants had "a prospect of obtaining $950," had a contract with the Government that the possession of "ordinary manipulative ability, with regular attendance and good conduct" would insure advancement to a position paying $950. The Government had broken that contract by prescribing, in 1892, that men "must be equal to supervising duties" in order to be promoted to the positions carrying $950.

Sir Albert Rollit[200] supported Captain Norton with the words: "For a long time past there had been a very strong and general feeling in the service that many of the men had been the victims of something amounting almost to an imposition, however unintentional, on the part of a public Department. Strong terms had been used in the course of the debate, but he should endeavor to deal with the matter on the basis of what he believed to have been a contract between those employees and the Post Office. It was not difficult to show that that implied—or, he might even say, express—contract had induced many to enter the service, only to find that the contract was afterward departed from by one of the contracting parties, the State."

Mr. Keir Hardie supported Captain Norton's Motion with the argument that the concessions made by the Tweedmouth Committee had imposed no additional burdens upon the taxpayers, for that committee merely had allocated a small portion of the extra profit made by the Post Office to the Post Office servants who made that profit. Mr. Keir Hardie at one time has held the office of Chairman of the Independent Labor Party,[201] an organization that brings to bear upon the British municipal governments a pressure similar to that here shown to be brought upon the House of Commons.

Members of Parliament coerced

Mr. Gibson Bowles said: "He was aware that many honorable Members who brought forward the position of servants of the State, did so against their own desires, because of the almost irresistible pressure placed upon them by the servants of the State, who were at the same time electors…. He supported the Secretary to the Treasury in resisting this particular amendment, because it was one of many which tended to illustrate a form of tyranny that was becoming unbearable, and which tended seriously to injure the character of this House as making its Members the advocates of classes, sections, and little communities, instead of being trustees not for them alone, but for the whole community."

Mr. Austen Chamberlain, Financial Secretary to the Treasury, and representative in the House of Commons of the Postmaster General, the Marquis of Londonderry, said he "supposed it would not be unfair to say that an officer joining the British Army had a prospect of becoming a field marshal." As to the telegraphists, "all that the Government ever had held out to them was a prospect of a certain number of them attaining something beyond the ordinary maximum" of $800, to which any man could rise by the display of ordinary manipulative ability and the observance of good conduct. Under Mr. Fawcett, in 1881 to 1884, one telegraphist out of every 6.3 telegraphists had risen beyond $800. In 1890 the proportion in question had been exactly the same. In 1902, the proportion was one in six, or, "practically the same."

Mr. Austen Chamberlain continued: "When I consider the great concessions that were made [by the Tweedmouth Committee], and the great burden that was placed upon the taxpayers, the care that was given to that inquiry, and the opportunity that was afforded to every one to have their grievances heard, I cannot pretend to think that a case has been made out for trying, not fresh matters, but for retrying the same matters and changing the tribunal, merely because all its decisions [i. e., some of its decisions] were not agreeable to one of the parties concerned. I hope the House will not do anything so fatal to the efficiency and the organization of our Civil Service, as to allow any large body of civil servants to think that they have only to be importunate enough to secure in this House repeated inquiries into their grievances, no matter what previous care has been given to their consideration. I trust this House will have confidence in the desire of the Postmaster General to deal fairly with all his employees, and believe me when I say that there is nothing easier for us to do than to give way; and that it is only because we believe it to be our duty to the taxpayers that we find it necessary to refuse these recurring and increasing demands."

Captain Norton's Motion was lost by a vote of 164 to 134. It was supported by one hundred and twenty-three Opposition members, and by seven Government supporters.[202]

A few hours later, Mr. Thomas Bayley[203] moved a reduction of $500 on the salary of the Postmaster General, in order to call attention to the grievances of the officials of the Post Office.[204] He said there should be a Court of Appeal for the civil servants, and that Court should be the House of Commons alone;

whenever a dispute arose between the Government of the day and its servants, the House should constitute itself the Court of Appeal. Mr. Bayley added: "It had been distinctly laid down that it was no part of the duty of the Post Office to make a profit, but it should be worked for the future convenience of the public and not reduced to the level of a mere profit making machine. It was this desire on the part of the Post Office officials to make profit which lay at the root of all the troubles which the House had been discussing in the debate that evening."

Mr. Austen Chamberlain, Financial Secretary to the Treasury, and representative, in the House of Commons, of the Postmaster General, replied: "I refuse to resign one particle of my responsibility, or to accept the suggestion that the Government should wash their hands of their responsibility, and throw the subject, as an open question, before the House of Commons, and ask a Committee of this House, without aid or guidance from responsible Ministers, to judge upon the multitude of conflicting interests and details incident to the administration of so great a service as the Post Office. I, for one, will not be party to putting off that responsibility on to the House of Commons.... But we consider that it would be a grave dereliction of duty on our part to throw this great service into the turmoil and confusion of a Parliamentary inquiry, with the knowledge that such an inquiry would not be final—honorable Gentlemen who have supported this Amendment have declared that to talk about finality in this matter is absurd—with the knowledge that what is done to-day for the Post Office, must be done to-morrow for every other Department employing a large number of Government servants, until elections to this House will depend more and more on the willingness of Members to purchase the support of those who are in public employment by promises of concessions at the public expense, instead of securing their support, like that of other citizens, on public grounds and national interests."

The Government's Compromise

On April 30, 1903, while the House was in Committee of Supply, Mr. Austen Chamberlain, Postmaster General, prefaced the discussion by the

Committee of the Post Office Vote, with the following statement:[205].... "The demand is that a Select Committee of this House should be appointed to examine into the grievances of the Post Office staff. I have made it my business since I have been at the post office to see that every memorial from the staff dealing with their grievances, addressed to me, should come before me personally.... Even though I have felt that many of the matters thus brought to my notice were very small details of administration. I am determined that an official [employee] of the Post Office, going to the head of his service, should receive as fair and careful consideration of his appeal, if he applies to me direct, as if he sought Parliamentary influence to urge his claim. And I venture to think that nothing has occurred during the time that I have been responsible which can justify any servant of the Post Office in saying that he is unable, except by Parliamentary influence, or by Parliamentary exposure, to obtain the attention of the head of the Department. The other day at the request of several Members on both sides of the House, I met the Members themselves, and consented that if they wished, they should be accompanied by members of the Post Office Staff, who should make before them, and in my presence, a statement of the grounds on which they asked for this inquiry by a Select Committee, in order that then and there I might discuss it with my honorable friends. The Vote comes on to-night, and I intend to take this opportunity of making a few observations on the grounds for this Parliamentary inquiry as put forth by the Staff. There are three main grounds alleged by the spokesman for the staff for a Parliamentary inquiry— wages, sanitation [i. e., the sanitary condition of certain offices], and meal reliefs, or the time allowed out of working hours for taking refreshment. If a person does eight hours' continuous work he is allowed half an hour out of that time for a meal, reducing his actual working hours to seven and a half hours.... I only wish to draw the attention of the committee to what was described to me as a typical grievance by the spokesman of a deputation which waited on me shortly before Christmas. Certain men are on duty from 10 a. m. to 2 p. m., and from 4 p. m. to 8 p. m., and complain because they are not allowed 20 minutes for tea. In the judgment of any impartial person, was that a reasonable grievance...? I myself have come to the conclusion, ... that while a great number of the complaints made have no foundation in justice, and that a great number of the men who think themselves aggrieved would find it difficult to get, elsewhere than in the public service, such good employment as they have now, there are other cases which are open to improvement and for which further inquiry is needed to fix exactly what should be done. The Government is unalterably opposed to a Select Committee of the House of Commons for the decision of this question. Honorable Members know, and it is no use blinking it, the kind of pressure which is brought to bear, or is attempted to be brought to bear, upon Members in all parts of the House by the public servants, servants of the Post Office, I am afraid, especially, though not entirely [exclusively], at election times. I have had Members come to me, not from one side of the House alone, to seek from me, in my position as Postmaster General, protection for them in the discharge of their public duties against the pressure sought to be put upon them by the employees of the Post Office. Even if the machinery by which our Select Committees are appointed were such as would enable us to secure a Select Committee composed of thoroughly impartial men who had committed themselves by no expression of opinion, I still think that it would not be fair to pick out fifteen Members of this House and make them marked men for the purposes of such pressure as is now distributed more or less over the whole Assembly. But if I am opposed to the appointment of a House of Commons Committee for fixing wages in the Post Office, I am still more opposed to thrusting upon it, or, indeed, on any Committee, the duty of regulating in all its details the daily administration and work of the Post Office. The wages paid are not in all respects satisfactory, some are too low, others are too high. Advice from men of practical and business experience would help me, the Minister in this matter. Therefore, I propose to take such advice—of men as free from any kind of political and electoral pressure, as they should be free from any departmental influence. I should suggest a body of five to report for my advice and information on the wages paid in the Post Office Department to the four great classes of employees, the letter sorters and the telegraphists in London, and the letter sorters and the telegraphists in the provinces."

After reiterating that he proposed to get the advice of business men only on the question of the scale of wages paid in the Post Office Department, and that he in no way proposed to surrender to any Committee of any sort the general duties of the Postmaster General, Mr. Austen Chamberlain closed with the words: "I ask the Committee [of Supply] to give me all the confidence it can, and when it is unable to give me that confidence, I say that that is no reason for granting a Select Committee to do my work, but only a reason for transferring the office of Postmaster General to someone who is more competent."

Mr. Thomas Bayley replied that "he was not willing to give up the rights and privileges of the House of Commons, whose duty it was to remedy the grievances of the public service.... And although he had been assured by those whom he represented [*i. e.*, post office servants] that the Post Office officials would loyally abide by the decision of a Committee of the House of Commons, the Right Honorable Gentleman [the Postmaster General] could not expect the same loyalty with regard to the decision of the Committee he proposed to appoint."

Sir Albert Rollit said: "The Tweedmouth Committee was a one-sided tribunal; the officials were represented on it, but the men not at all...."

Captain Norton replied: "The Right Honorable Gentleman had also referred to the question of Members on both sides of the House coming to him for protection. That was very startling, because the reason they were there at all was that they might represent every section of their constituents,[206] ... but presuming the Post Office servants were organized, he submitted they were within their rights to appeal to their Members.... If the postal officials were such terrible tyrants he hoped they would take note that they could never hope for fair play from the present Government. The Right Honorable Gentleman had appointed a packed jury of five individuals to deal with a fraction of the question.... In other words, he was going to take shelter behind this bogus committee.... He was going to appoint five Members, possibly sweaters, to determine the rate of wages.... It would be astounding if the postal officials accepted any such bogus arbitration. If it was to be a Board of Arbitration, why should not they have five postal servants added to the five employers of labor?" Captain Norton is a Junior Lord of the Treasury in the present Sir Henry Campbell-Bannerman Ministry.

On May 17, 1903, the National Joint Committee of the Postal Association unanimously resolved: "That this National Joint Committee views with extreme dissatisfaction the appointment of a Court of Inquiry which is not composed of members of Parliament, but is an altogether irresponsible body, and protests against the scope of the inquiry being limited to a single grievance and to a minority of the Staff. It pledges itself to continue to use every legitimate endeavor to obtain an impartial Parliamentary Committee of Inquiry into the causes of discontent in the postal and telegraph service.[207]

In August, 1903, the Postmaster General appointed a "Committee to inquire into the adequacy of the wages paid to certain classes of the postal servants." The Committee consisted of: Sir Edward Bradford, until lately Chief Commissioner of the Metropolitan Police; Mr. Charles Booth, a Liverpool Merchant, and the author of "The Life and Labor of the People in London;" Mr. Samuel Fay, General Manager of the Great Central Railway; Mr. Thomas Brodrick, Secretary of the Co-operative Wholesale Society, Manchester; and Mr. R. Burbridge, Managing Director of Harrod's Stores.[208]

FOOTNOTES:

[182] *Who's Who*, 1903, Woods, Sam'l., M. P. for S. W. Lancashire, 1892 to 1895; M. P. (R.) for Walthamstow, Essex, 1897 to 1900; President of Lancashire Miners' Federation; Vice-President of Miners' Federation of Great Britain; Secretary of Trade Union Congress since 1894.

[183] *Hansard's Parliamentary Debates*, February 18, 1898, p. 1,107 and following.

[184] Compare also *Hansard's Parliamentary Debates*, April 22, 1874, p. 958 and following, and June 1, 1874, p. 797 and following. *Parliamentary Papers*, 1874, vol. IV: A Bill to Relieve Revenue Officers from remaining Electoral Disabilities; and 37 and 38 Victoriæ, c. 22: An Act to Relieve Revenue Officers from remaining Electoral Disabilities.

[185]

		Ayes	Noes
Conservatives	Government Supporters	2	132
Liberal Unionists		1	27
Liberals	The Opposition	48	3
Nationalists		32	0

148

Various factions		3	1
		86	163

186 *Who's Who*, 1903, Steadman, W. C., M. P. (R.) Stepney, Tower Hamlets, 1898 to 1900 —returned by a majority of twenty, defeated 1900; stood for Parliament, Mid-Kent, defeated, 1892; Hammersmith, defeated, 1895. Is Secretary Barge Builders' Trade Union.

187 *Hansard's Parliamentary Debates*, February 20, 1899; p. 1,523 and following.

188

		Ayes	Noes
Conservatives	Government Supporters	1	129
Liberal Unionists		1	28
Liberals	The Opposition	67	2
Nationalists		19	0
Various factions		3	0
		91	159

189 *Hansard's Parliamentary Debates*, June 1, 1899, p. 99 and following.

190 *Who's Who*, 1903, Norton, C. W., M. P. (L.) W. Newington, London, since 1892. Late Captain 5th Royal Irish Lancers, … some years in India; selected to report upon Italian Cavalry, 1880; Brigade-Major of Cavalry, Aldershot, 1881-82. In 1906 Captain Norton was made a Junior Lord of the Treasury in the Campbell-Bannerman Liberal Government.

191 *Who's Who*, 1903, Maddison, F., M. P., Sheffield, Brightside Division, 1897 to 1900. Three years Chairman of the Hull Branch of Typographical Association; first Labor Member of the Hull Corporation; offered post of Labor Correspondent to the Board of Trade in 1893; Editor of the *Railway Review*, official organ of the Amalgamated Society of Railway Servants (resigned, 1897); Ex-President of the Labor Association for Promoting Co-operative Production.

192

		Ayes	Noes
Conservatives	Government Supporters	5	133
Liberal Unionists		4	21
Liberals	The Opposition	83	2

Nationalists		14	0
Various factions		1	1
		107	157

193 *Hansard's Parliamentary Debates*, April 27, 1900, p. 199 and following.

194

		Ayes	Noes
Conservatives	Government Supporters	4	55
Liberal Unionists		0	9
Liberals	The Opposition	40	0
Nationalists		1	0
Various factions		1	2
		46	66

195 *Who's Who*, 1903, Bayley, Thos., J. P., M. P. (L) Chesterfield Division, Derbyshire, since 1892. Many years on Nottingham Town Council; Alderman, Nottingham County Council; contested Barkston Ash Division of Yorkshire, 1885; Chesterfield, 1886.

196 *Hansard's Parliamentary Debates*, June 7, 1901, p. 1,358 and following.

197

		Ayes	Noes
Conservatives	Government Supporters	8	120
Liberal Unionists		1	25
Liberals	The Opposition	57	0
Nationalists		34	0
Various factions		3	3
		103	148

198 *Who's Who*, 1905, Norton, C. W., M. P. (L.) West Newington (London), since 1892; late Captain 5th Royal Irish Lancers; selected to report upon Italian Cavalry, 1880; Brigade-Major of Cavalry, Aldershot, 1881-82. In 1906 Captain Norton was made a Junior Lord of the Treasury in the Campbell-Bannerman Liberal Government.

199 *Hansard's Parliamentary Debates*, April 18, 1902, p. 660 and following.

200 *Who's Who*, 1904. Rollit, Sir Albert Kaye, J. P., LL. D., D. C. L., D. L., M. P., Islington, since 1886. Partner in Bailey and Leetham, steamship owners; Director of National Telephone Co.; Mayor of Hull 1883 to 1885; President of Associated Chambers of Commerce of the United Kingdom, 1890 to 1896; President London Chambers of Commerce 1893 to 1898; Chairman Inspection Committee, Trustee Savings Bank since 1890; President Municipal Corporations' Association.

201 *Who's Who*, 1905.

202

		Ayes	Noes
Conservatives	Government Supporters	6	127
Liberal Unionists		1	31
Liberals	The Opposition	72	4
Nationalists		51	0
Various factions		4	2
		134	164

203 *Who's Who*, 1905, Bayley, Thos., J. P., M. P. (L.), Chesterfield Division Derbyshire since 1892; many years on Nottingham Town Council.

204 *Hansard's Parliamentary Debates*, April 18, 1902, p. 706 and following.

205 *Hansard's Parliamentary Debates*, April 30, 1903, p. 1,015 and following, and May 11, p. 313 and following.

206 According to *The Times*, May 11, 1903, Captain Norton said: "The Right Honorable Gentleman had told a startling story of how Members on both sides of the House had appealed to him to protect them from the postal servants. Members of the House represented all sections in their constituencies and surely postal servants as voters had the right to approach their representatives, and apply the same kind of pressure that other organized bodies applied."

207 *The Times*, May 18, 1903.

208 *The Times*, August 14, 1903.

CHAPTER XII
THE BRADFORD COMMITTEE REPORT

> The Bradford Committee ignores its reference. It recommends
> measures that would cost $6,500,000 a year, in the hope of
> satisfying the postal employees, who had asked for
> $12,500,000 a year. Lord Stanley, Postmaster General, rejects
> the Bradford Committee's Report; but grants increases in
> wages and salaries aggregating $1,861,500 a year.

In the preceding chapter it was stated that the Government in August, 1903, appointed Sir Edward Bradford, Mr. Charles Booth, Mr. Thomas Brodrick, Mr. R. Burbidge, and Mr. Samuel Fay a Committee "to inquire into the scales of pay received by the undermentioned classes of Established Post Office Servants, and to report whether, having regard to the conditions of their employment and to the rates current in other occupations, the remuneration of (a) Postmen, (b) Sorters (London), (c) Telegraphists (London), (d) Sorting Clerks and Telegraphists (Provincial) is adequate." No further question was submitted to the Committee.

The Committee, in May, 1904, reported: "We have not seen our way to obtain any specific evidence as to the comparative rates of wages current in other occupations. So far as regards this portion of the reference to us,[209] we came to the conclusion that no really useful purpose would be served by asking employers of labor to furnish precise details of the wages paid by them. Certain official information is already available, being obtained and published from time to time by the Board of Trade. This information, supplemented by our own experience, affords more reliable data than any particulars we could hope to obtain in the way of evidence within the limits of an inquiry of reasonable duration.

"Moreover, it is difficult to make any valid comparison between a National Postal Service and any form of private industrial employment, the entire conditions being necessarily so different; payment by results and promotion or dismissal according to the will of the employer being inapplicable if not impossible under the State."[210]

The Committee's report covers nineteen pages, but only these two paragraphs are in answer to the reference given to the Committee. In them the Committee reports its failure; and with that report of failure the Committee should have contented itself, under all of the rules of procedure governing Committees and Commissions appointed by the British Government. But the Committee ignored the established rules of procedure, roamed about at will, and reopened many of the questions settled by the Tweedmouth Committee, which had sat two years, and had taken upward of a thousand closely printed folio pages of evidence. The Bradford Committee did this in violation of the established usage of the country, as well as in spite of the fact that Mr. Austen Chamberlain, Postmaster General, had closed the speech in which he announced his resolve to appoint the Committee, with the words that he wanted advice on the question of comparative wages only and that he refused to transfer to "any Committee the duty of regulating in all its details the daily administration and work of the Post Office."

Upon the Report of the Committee, *The Economist*[211] (London) commented as follows: "This Committee was asked to compare the wages of Post Office servants with those paid for corresponding work outside. Their answer was, in effect, that no such comparison could be instituted. Why, when postal servants are taken from various ascertained classes [of society], it should be impossible to compare their pay with that ordinarily received by the same classes in other employments is not obvious. What is obvious is that the Committee either mistook the inquiry entrusted to them, or did not choose to enter upon it."

The Times[212] said: "The reference here is explicit, ... The specific question they were asked was the question to which, as our Correspondent says, the taxpayer really wants an answer—namely, are postal servants fairly paid...?

This question the Committee has neither answered nor attempted to answer. Passing by the terms of reference altogether, the Report declares that 'it is difficult'.... But, as an answer to the specific question addressed to the Committee; it is, in our judgment, in the literal sense of the word, impertinent. However, having rejected the criterion propounded to them by the Postmaster General, the Committee proposed to apply a criterion of their own...." The Committee made some general statements as to the rates of wages that should prevail in the public service. They were: "We think that Postal employees are justified in resting their claims to remuneration on the responsible and exacting[213] character of the duties performed and on the social position they fill as servants of the State. The State, for its part, does right in taking an independent course guided by principles of its own, irrespective of what others may do; neither following an example nor pretending to set one. It must always be remembered that in the working of a monopoly by the State, the interest of the public as a whole is the paramount consideration, and every economy consistent with efficiency must be adopted. The terms offered by the State should, however, be such as to secure men and women of the requisite character and capacity and ought to be such as will insure the response of hearty service." If one seeks to find in the foregoing statements an answer to the very matter-of-fact question whether the postal servants' wages are too high or too low, compared with wages in outside employment, he will have to conclude, with *Alice in Wonderland*, that "it seems very pretty, but it's rather hard to understand; somehow it seems to fill my head with ideas, only I don't know exactly what they are."

The Committee concluded with the statement that the adequacy of the wages obtaining among the postal employees could be tested by the numbers and character of those who offered themselves; by the capacity they showed on trial; and finally, by their contentment. It found that there was no lack of suitable candidates; that there was no complaint as to their capacity; but that there was widespread discontent. It added that the Tweedmouth and Norfolk-Hanbury settlements did not give satisfaction at the time; and that that dissatisfaction had been "aggravated by the general rise in wages and prices and in the standard of life which took place to some extent even during the two years occupied by the Tweedmouth inquiry (1895 and 1896) and had continued since, culminating, however, in 1900, since when there has been some slight reaction. The same period has seen a great development of Postal and Telegraph business, causing greater pressure of work. This has been combined with lower charges to the public and a considerable increase in Postal Revenue. We therefore consider there is a just claim for revision."

Taking these statements in their order, one finds, first of all, that the Committee took no evidence on the question how Post Office wages had compared with wages in outside employment previous to the rise in wages and prices in the period from 1895 to 1900, nor on the question of the rise in wages in the Post Office Service in 1896 to 1900, compared with the rise in wages in outside employment and in prices in 1895 to 1900. The first statement of the Committee, therefore, was supported by no evidence, it was a mere assertion. The second statement, namely, that the growth of the Postal and Telegraph business had caused greater pressure of work, also was not supported by evidence. On the other hand, it was absolutely essential that such a statement should be supported by evidence, because it is a fact that in both branches of the Postal Service the policy obtains of having so large a body of employees "that the maximum of work, as a rule, can be dealt with without undue pressure."[214] As to the Post Office having lowered its charges to the public in the period from 1895 to 1900, it is to be said, first, that it does not follow therefrom that wages should be raised; and second, that the penny rate on domestic letters was not lowered, and that the carriage of penny letters is the only work upon which the Post Office makes a profit.[215] Finally, as to the statement that there had been, in 1895 to 1904, "a considerable increase in Postal Revenue," the facts are, first, that the net revenue of the Post Office as a whole increased from $14,640,000 in 1895, to $18,166,000 in 1896, and to $18,781,000 in 1897; but that in the subsequent years, 1898 to 1904, it did not again reach the high-water mark of 1897, and averaged $17,642,000. Second, that in the period, from 1895 to 1904, the Telegraph Branch did not earn operating expenses, the expenses on account of wages and salaries having risen from 11.9 cents per telegram in 1897, to 13.7 cents in 1904. That is a matter of importance, for the recommendations of the Committee extended to the Telegraph Branch as well as to the Postal Branch proper. Again, the

Committee had stated that "in the working of a monopoly by the State, the interest of the public as a whole is the paramount consideration, and every economy consistent with efficiency must be adopted." In the 20 years ending with 1903, the proportion of the Post Office's gross revenue available for defraying the general expenses of the State had declined steadily from 33 per cent. to 20 per cent.[216] Still, again, in the year 1903, the expenses of the Post Office had been increased by $3,000,000 through the Tweedmouth and Norfolk-Hanbury settlements.[217] In the face of those facts, the Bradford Committee made recommendations that Lord Stanley, Postmaster General, said would cost $6,500,000 a year.[218] The Bradford Committee sought to justify its recommendations with the simple statement that there was "widespread discontent" among the Postal employees. The Postal employees themselves had made demands before the Committee that would have called for the expenditure of an additional $12,500,000 a year. Their attitude to the Committee's amiable proposal to conciliate them by giving them $6,500,000 a year, is shown in the subjoined extract from the official organ of the telegraph staff. "It is perfectly plain, … that the recommendations of the Committee, well-meaning as we frankly admit them to be, cannot be accepted as a full settlement of the case of the Post Office workers, or as one carrying with it the character of finality. They can only be accepted as an instalment of a long overdue account; and Postal Telegraphists, even if they have to fight alone for their own hand in the future as they did for many long years in the past, will combine for the payment of the balance."[219]

That a body of five men, of whom four were respectively a Liverpool merchant and ship owner, a general manager of a railway, a manager of a large wholesale coöperative society, and a manager of a large department store, could make a Report such as the foregoing one, affords a melancholy illustration of the fact that no matter how far popular governments may go in assuming the conduct of great business enterprises, they never will succeed in creating a public opinion that will sustain them in their efforts to conduct their business ventures on the commonly accepted principles of the business world.

In the House of Commons, Lord Stanley, the Postmaster General, said: "As to the Committee's Report, it did not comply with the reference, because no comparison was made with the rates of pay in other occupations ... but they conclude that as there was discontent there ought to be an increase of wages. That was a direct premium on discontent, a direct encouragement to the employees to say among themselves that if they were to be discontented and to agitate, they would get more in the future. The Committee, on the other hand, went outside the reference, because they proposed a complete reorganization of the Post Office, including overseers, who were not referred to in the reference. On this particular subject they took no evidence.... Since the employees of the Post Office had said in a circular: 'We wish to make it perfectly clear that we do not regard the Committee as in any sense an arbitration board,' that was rather against the argument that the Report ought to be accepted as an arbitration award. He did not complain of the ordinary circulars of the employees [sent to Members of Parliament], but he did object to one circular [sent to every Member of the House of Commons], at the bottom of which was a paragraph, which could be torn off, for Members to sign [and mail to the Postmaster General], informing him [the Postmaster General] that he ought to do this or that.[220] That [circular] he [Lord Stanley] would not receive.... Coming to the main question, he thought it was obvious that it was impossible for either side when in power to go on for long being swayed in all these questions of increases of wages by any pressure, political or otherwise, that might be put upon them. [Cheers.] The Post Office was not the only party concerned. There was not a class employed by the Government, who, if it saw another class getting an increase of wages by agitation, would not try the same method. He supported cordially the suggestion which had been made in the debate that all questions of pay of employees of the Government should not be referred to the House, but referred to some judicial body on whom no outside influence could be brought to bear, who would look at the matter in dispute as between employer and employee with the object of giving to the employee the wages which in the open market a good employer would give, while at the same time protecting the master—in this case the State—from any outside influence."[221] In conclusion, Lord Stanley made the statement that the adoption of the Committee's Report would cost "well over $5,000,000 a year."

Sir Albert Rollit acted as the spokesman of the Postal employees. He is a Solicitor in Mincing Lane and at Hull; a steamship owner at Hull, Newcastle and London; and a Director in the National Telephone Company, which pays its employees materially less than the Post Office pays the employees of the Post Office Telephone system.[222] He has been President of the Associated Chambers of Commerce of the United Kingdom, as well as of the London and Hull Chambers of Commerce. He was Mayor of Hull from 1883 to 1885; and for several years past he has been the President of the Association of Municipal Corporations. Sir Albert K. Rollit was not re-elected to Parliament in the General Election of January, 1906; and in the following March, the Postal Telegraph Clerks' Association passed a resolution "expressing appreciation of the services rendered to the Postal movement in and out of Parliament by Sir Albert K. Rollit, and regret that they were no longer able to command his championship in the House of Commons."[223]

After the Balfour Government had rejected the Report of the Bradford Committee, in the interest of the taxpayers, Lord Stanley, Postmaster General, instituted "a careful comparison between Post Office wages and those current in other employments; and, as the result of the comparison, he felt justified in recommending to the Lords Commissioners of His Majesty's Treasury certain improvements of pay" aggregating $1,861,500 a year.[224] The improvements of pay were granted to sorters, telegraphists, sorting clerks and telegraphists, postmen, assistant and auxiliary postmen, and various smaller classes throughout the United Kingdom.

FOOTNOTES:

[209] There was no reference but that one.

[210] *Report and Appendices of the Committee appointed to inquire into Post Office Wages,* 1904.

[211] September 17,1904.

[212] September 12,1904.

[213] *Report of the Bradford Committee on Post Office Wages,* 1904, p. 198.

Dr. A. H. Wilson, Chief Medical Officer of the Post Office, testified: "When cases of breakdown have been brought to my notice I have invariably found the primary origin of the illness to have been due to causes outside Post Office life. These causes are generally drink, financial worry, domestic troubles, etc."

214 Compare Chapter XI, testimony of Mr. Kerry.

215 *Hansard's Parliamentary Debates*, April 27, 1900, pp. 229 and 136; Mr. R. W. Hanbury, Financial Secretary to the Treasury.

216 *Hansard's Parliamentary Debates*, May 11, p. 342; Mr. Austen Chamberlain, Postmaster General.

217 *Hansard's Parliamentary Debates*, April 20, 1903, p. 1,022; Mr. Austen Chamberlain, Postmaster General.

218 *Hansard's Parliamentary Debates*, July 6, 1905, p. 1,390; Lord Stanley.

219 *The Times*, September 17, 1904: Correspondence.

220 *The Times*, September 12, 1904, denominated this episode "a melancholy and even ominous illustration of the process of democratic degeneration." In the same issue Mr. S. W. Belderson writes that 130 Members of the House signed the paragraph in question.

221 *The Times*, August 10, 1904.

222 *Report of the Inter-Departmental Committee on Post Office Establishments*, 1897; q. 13,804; Mr. S. Walpole, Permanent Secretary of the Post Office.

223 *The Times*, March 17, 1906; and *Who's Who*, 1905.

224 *Fifty-first Report of the Postmaster General*, 1905.

CHAPTER XIII
THE HOUSE OF COMMONS SELECT COMMITTEE ON POST OFFICE SERVANTS, 1906

The Post Office Civil Servants' Unions demand the adoption of the Bradford Committee Report. Lord Stanley, Postmaster General, applies the words "blackmail" and "blood-sucking" to the postal employees' methods. Captain Norton moves for a House of Commons Select Committee. Mr. Austen Chamberlain, Chancellor of the Exchequer, in vain asks the Opposition Party's support for a Select Committee to which shall be referred the question of the feasibility of establishing a permanent, non-political Commission which shall establish general principles for settling disputes between the Civil Servants and the Government of the day. Captain Norton's Motion is lost, nine Ministerial supporters voting for it, and only two Opposition members voting against it. Mr. J. Henniker Heaton's appeal to the British public for "An End to Political Patronage." The Post Office employees, in the campaign preceding the General Election of January, 1906, induce nearly 450 of the 670 parliamentary candidates who succeeded in being elected, to pledge themselves to vote for a House of Commons Select Committee on Post Office Wages. Immediately upon the opening of Parliament, the Sir H. Campbell-Bannerman Liberal Ministry gives the Post Office employees a House of Commons Select Committee.

On September 17, 1904, the Postal Telegraph Clerks' Association unanimously resolved: "That this Conference expresses its indignation that the Postmaster General, having appointed a Committee of his own choosing to inquire into the Post Office wages ... now, for no good reason, has rejected the Report. This Conference, therefore, calls upon the Postmaster General to adopt immediately, as dated from May 9, 1904, the whole of the ameliorative recommendations contained in the Bradford Committee's Report; but the Postal Telegraph Clerks' Association reserves to itself the right to object to, and protest against, any recommendations which may be considered by this Association to be of a restrictive and retrograde character."[225]

In the evening of the same day a mass meeting was addressed by Mr. W. W. Rutherford, M. P., the head of the firm of Miller, Peel, Hughes and Rutherford, Liverpool. Mr. Rutherford had been Lord Mayor of Liverpool in 1902. He said: "He ventured to think that the great Postal and Telegraph Service was suffering because its position and its grievances had not been made thoroughly intelligible to the general public…. That was not a matter touching a few hundreds of people in a hole and corner of the country, but was one of extreme importance affecting no less than 185,000 people…. The real foes of the employees were the highly paid officials at the head of the Department, who were quite content to draw their salaries and show that the Government was making four or five million pounds sterling[226] out of the public and the Postal Service."

Mr. Rutherford's speech recalls to mind the fact that the Australian cousins of the British civil servants have learned to deal with their "foes" by compelling the popular branches of the Australian Parliaments to reduce the salaries of offensive officials, or to drive them out of the Service by means of "fishing" Parliamentary Committees, appointed to report on—and to condemn —the offending officials.

On August 14, 1904, the London Branch of the Postal Telegraph Clerks' Association held a meeting, at which Mr. C. H. Garland,[227] the Secretary, spoke of Mr. Thomas Baylcy, M. P., as one who "had rendered valuable service to their cause in the House of Commons." The presiding officer, Mr. R. H. Davis, said: "In burking the recommendations of the Committee they could not help feeling that the Post Office authorities had been guilty of a breach of faith. Were they going to take the rebuff lying down? The London Committee were determined to fight the matter harder than ever. By the time Parliament assembled next year, they would have an effective organization at their disposal, and the enemy would feel their pressure very considerably."[228]

The Special Conference of the Postal Telegraph Clerks' Association held on September 17, 1904, resolved to hold mass meetings in all the district centres between then and next February [opening of Parliament] to protest against the action of the Postmaster General. The series to conclude with a "monster" demonstration in London immediately before the opening of Parliament.[229]

On July 6, 1905, while the House of Commons was in Committee of Supply, and was considering the vote upon the Post Office, there was a long and instructive debate upon the Report of the Bradford Committee.[230] Lord Stanley, Postmaster General, opened the debate with a quotation from *The Post*,[231] the Post Office employees' organ. The statement quoted read: "Not only do we object to the composition of the [Bradford] Committee, but we take the strongest exception to its terms of reference. The inquiry as to whether our wages are adequate or otherwise becomes a farce if their adequacy is to be judged by the standard of wages of the open labor market. No such comparison would be reasonable or fair. There is no other employer who fixes his own prices or makes an annual profit of $20,000,000. There is no other class of work which can be compared to the Post Office work, neither any other employee who can be compared with the Post Office servants.... Surely Mr. Chamberlain does not think we should regard such an inquiry as final. If he does, the sooner his mind is disabused the better." Lord Stanley next discussed the manner in which the Bradford Committee had made recommendations which were based on no evidence whatever. For instance, in order to improve the chances of promotion, the Committee had recommended the creation of additional higher posts—"for which there was no work." In one Department of the Post Office that recommendation would mean the increase in the number of overseers from 250 to 900. Lord Stanley next made lengthy comparisons between the wages received by letter sorters and telegraphists on the one hand, and employees of equal intelligence and attainments in the service of private companies on the other hand. He showed that in London the maximum wage of the sorters and telegraphists was equal to the salary of the "non-college-trained certified teacher," and that in such provincial cities as Hull, Swansea and Exeter it was larger. "The only comparison which was not entirely upon his [the Postmaster General's] side was that with the clerks in the cable companies, who were paid more than the Post Office cable room operators. But the work of the cable companies' operators was more arduous, and there was liability to be sent abroad at any moment. But he had granted the Post Office cable room operators an increase of pay." He added that the ultimate aggregate cost of the increases in pay made since the publication of the Bradford Committee's Report would be $642,000 a year.[232]

The Postmaster General applies the Terms "Blackmail" and "Blood-sucking"

Lord Stanley, Postmaster General, concluded as follows: "But he would ask the House just to consider what was going to be the end of all these demands. This was really a question worthy of consideration on both sides of the House. What were the demands on the public purse for this particular office? It would be within the recollection of the Committee of Supply that at a deputation to his Right Honorable Friend and himself, one of the men stated that he thought the whole of the $20,000,000 profit, as he regarded it, made by the Post Office employees, ought to be devoted to the payment of those employees … that man made a deliberate statement, not on his own account, but as representing a particular section or organization in the Department. It was repudiated by others present…." Lord Stanley next stated that the demands made by the Post Office employees before the Bradford Committee would have called for $12,500,000 a year. He continued: "Honorable Members knew better than he how they were being bombarded with applications from Post Office employees and other classes of Civil Servants for increases of wages. This had taken a form which was not illegal, but which he could not help thinking was an abuse of their rights, to wit, the form of a political threat. They had circulated an appeal in which they expressed very clearly and very frankly their intention, and it was one of which the Committee would have to take note now, or it would be much worse in the future. They said: 'Two-thirds at least of one political party are in great fear of losing their seats. The swing of the pendulum is against them, and any Member who receives 40 or 50 such letters will under present circumstances have to consider very seriously whether on this question he can afford to go into the wrong lobby. This is taking advantage of the political situation.' It was indeed, but it was abusing, as it seemed to him, their rights as voters. It was nothing more nor less than blackmail. It was nothing more nor less than asking Members to purchase votes for themselves at the General Election[233] at the expense of the Public Exchequer. Both sides would have to make up their minds that some means should be devised by which there should not be this continual blood-sucking on the part of the public servants."

A permanent non-political Tribunal suggested

"How it was to be done, was not for him to say, but he had suggested, and he still thought that there would have to be some organization outside party politics altogether, and unconnected with and unmoved by Parliament and political considerations, to whom such questions should be referred and by whom an impartial opinion should be given.... He wanted now rather to anticipate a request that would probably be made by Honorable Members opposite—that he should appoint a Parliamentary Committee. To that request he would have to give a negative reply, and he would say why. First, too great political pressure would be brought to bear on the Committee; second, the whole case of the Post Office employees was before the House in the evidence taken by the Bradford Committee, and everybody could make up his mind as well as he would be able to if appointed to a Select Committee. Third, he would not throw the responsibility on to a Committee; it was his place to bear it himself."

On July 18, Lord Stanley, Postmaster General, stated that he would neither withdraw nor modify the epithets "blackmail" and "blood-sucking" which he had used. He stated that those epithets applied "only to those who by speeches, letters or circulars, attempt unduly to influence the votes of Honorable Members with regard to the questions affecting Post Office wages, and to those who associate themselves with such action."[234]

Captain Norton on Civil Service Agitation

After the Postmaster General had spoken, Captain Norton moved a reduction of the Post Office Vote, for the purpose of drawing attention to the grievances of long standing of the Post Office employees. He said: "As regarded what had been said about undue influence, his contention was that so long as the Postal officials, or should he say the members of the Civil Service, and for that matter the members of the fighting services were allowed to maintain a vote, they had precisely the same rights as all other voters in the country to exercise their fullest influence in the defense of their rights, privileges and interests. He might mention that all classes of all communities, all professions, all trades, all combinations of individuals, such as anti-vaccinationists and so forth, had invariably used their utmost pressure in defense of their interests and views upon Members of the House...."[235]

Sir Albert K. Rollit supported Captain Norton's motion.

Chancellor of the Exchequer asks for non-Party Vote

The Chancellor of the Exchequer, Mr. Austen Chamberlain, spoke as follows: "The question at issue was not one between the two political parties. It was above parties. It was whether there was to be good economical government in the country at all, or whether the Civil Servants in the employment of the Crown could make such use of their votes, as citizens, for the purely selfish purpose of forcing the public to pay more for their services and so increase the expenditure of a great Department of State. He did not know how long they could go on in the position they had now reached, under which pressure was brought to bear on Honorable Members of all parties by their constituents. He was certain that if any scheme could be devised ... so that they might take this question altogether out of the region of political life —not merely out of party life, but out of Parliamentary life—it would be a great advantage. It would tend to preserve the Civil Service free from that political influence and independent of the changing fortunes of party which had been their great boast and security in the past. If there were a general feeling in the House that an object of that kind was one on which all parties might well coöperate, then His Majesty's Government, while maintaining as resolutely as they had in past years their objection to referring these specific grievances to a Select Committee appointed in the ordinary way for that particular purpose, would be prepared to assent to the appointment of a Committee of this House to consider the state of affairs which had arisen; to see if they could devise some remedy for it; to lay down the principles by which they should be governed in these matters; and to advise whether it would be possible to establish some permanent body or Commission, outside the sphere of electoral pressure and above and beyond any of our party conflicts, which might advise the Government in applying those principles to particular cases. Such a Committee could, of course, only be successfully conceded with the good will of all parties in the House, and if the whole House were animated by a desire, if possible, to set this question at rest. With that good-will, he thought, it might serve a useful purpose. The object to be attained was of such vast importance that he, for one, would not refuse any method by which they might hope successfully to compass it and to maintain the Civil Service in that high position of which, with its great traditions, they had such just cause to be proud and such good reason to be grateful for."[236]

Captain Norton's motion was lost by a vote of 249 to 205. The House divided on party lines, only two Members of the Opposition voting with the Government, and only nine supporters of the Government voting with the Opposition.[237] Of the Members of the Opposition who voted in support of Captain Norton's motion, two shortly afterward became members of the Cabinet in Sir Henry Campbell-Bannerman's Liberal Ministry, and fifteen others became members of the Ministry, but not of the Cabinet, or inner circle.[238]

Captain Norton himself became one of the four Junior Lords of the Treasury. The latter functionaries "are expected to gather the greatest number of their own party into every division [of the House of Commons], and by persuasion, promises, explanation, and every available expedient, to bring their men from all quarters to the aid of the Government upon any emergency. It is also their business to conciliate the discontented and doubtful among the ministerial supporters, and to keep every one, as far as possible, in good humor."[239]

In *The Nineteenth Century and After*, for April, 1906, Mr. J. H. Heaton, in an article entitled: *Wanted! An End to Political Patronage*, discussed at length some of the after effects of the memorable debate of July 6, 1905. Mr. Heaton had been returned to Parliament from Canterbury in 1885, 1886, 1892, 1895, and 1900; the last four occasions as an unopposed candidate. He had carried the Imperial Penny Postage Scheme in 1888; he had introduced telegraph money orders in England; the parcel post to France, etc.; and the freedom of the City of London in a gold casket had been conferred on him in 1899.

A Prime Minister on the Civil Service

Mr. Heaton opened his article with the statement: "Many years ago a great Prime Minister wrote to me as follows: 'There can be no doubt that the organized attempts of servants of the State to use their political influence at the cost of the taxpayer is likely to become a serious danger. I agree with you in thinking that it can only be effectually met by agreement between the two sides of the House.'" Mr. Heaton continued: "The Civil Servants of the Crown are, taken as a whole, an admirable and efficient body of workers, of whom England is justifiably proud, and whom—as was held, I think, by the late Mr. Gladstone—she rewards on a generous scale.... It is the more to be regretted that large classes of them should have fallen into the hands of agitators, who incite to the systematic intimidation of Members of Parliament with a view to the extortion of larger and larger votes [appropriations] for salaries. This evil is rapidly becoming formidable.... Any official raising the cry of 'higher wages' is sure of popularity among his fellows, who instantly regard him as a born leader. The pleasant prospect of an increase of income without working for it is a bait that never fails to appeal most strongly to the least energetic and deserving. A postman or dockyard hand finds that he can win promotion and increased pay only by strenuous hard work, just as if he were a mere artisan or shop assistant. But the agitators point out that he can attain an equivalent result by bullying the local M. P., and so he joins the league or union formed for the purpose."

Sir William Harcourt on Post Office Employees

"Where is this to stop? The late Sir W. Harcourt[240] wrote (to me) that the demands of the Postal employees reached a depth, or abyss, which no plummet would fathom. We know now that they claim the Postal surplus, which amounts to nearly five millions [sterling].... There are 192,000 of them, and of these probably 100,000 have votes. Adding these to the dockyard, arsenal, and stores factory hands, and other Government employees, we have a political force that may turn the scale at a General Election. Candidates are tempted to bid against one another with the taxpayer's money. 'Let us be charitable!' said Sydney Smith, and put his hand into a bystander's pocket. Our legislators were proof against the hectoring of the Tudors, the violence of the Stuarts, and the blandishments of the Georges; surely they will never yield to the menaces of demagogues."

Thirty M. P.'s threatened with Loss of Seat

"At this point I would like to state briefly my own experience.... Last year great pressure was brought to bear in the House of Commons on Members of Parliament, and, with thirty other Members, I was threatened with the loss of my seat unless I voted to meet the demands of the Postal servants. It was further intimated to me that the Postal servants' vote, 100,000 strong, would turn out any Government. A few minutes afterwards it fell to my lot to address the House on the question of increase of postmen's wages.... I ended my speech by declaring that civil servants who threatened Members of Parliament for refusing to vote them increased salaries ought to be disfranchised. Result—a meeting called in my constituency, my opponent placed in the chair, and a vote of censure passed on me. The London postmen came to Canterbury and addressed my constituents at the meeting. It is not surprising, therefore, that at the recent election my agents informed me that 46 postmen voted solid against me.[241] I do not blame the postmen; they were perfectly justified in using their power; but if I had not had at my back one of the most intelligent bodies of electors in the United Kingdom, I should have been defeated through the postmen's action.

"It was some consolation to me to receive in the House of Commons, after my speech, hearty, though private, congratulations from hard-working, earnest workingmen representatives, who expressed their entire approval of what they were pleased to call my courage. But something ought to be done to prevent a recurrence of such a scandal."

In view of Mr. Heaton's closing remarks, it is interesting to note that four of the eight[242] Labor Members voted, and that all of them favored the appointment of a House of Commons Select Committee.

In the campaign preceding the General Election of January, 1906, the several associations of Postal and Telegraph employees addressed letters to the candidates for Parliament, asking those candidates whether they would "support the claims of the Postal and Telegraph employees and vote for the appointment of a Select Committee of the House of Commons for the purpose of inquiring into their conditions of pay and service; and stating that on their part the workers pledged themselves to accept as final the decision of such a tribunal." At the annual conference of the Postal Telegraph Clerks' Association, held in March, 1906, the President of the Association said that nearly 450 of the 670 Members of the House of Commons[243] had pledged themselves to support a motion for a Parliamentary Inquiry into the position of the Post Office employees.[244]

In the third sitting of the new Parliament, held on February 20, the Postmaster General, Mr. Sydney Buxton, announced that the Government had decided to appoint a Select Committee of the House of Commons.[245] And on March 6, the Postmaster General introduced a motion for a Committee of seven to be nominated by the Committee of Selection. In response to the wishes of the House, the Postmaster General subsequently changed his motion to one calling for a Committee of nine, to be appointed by the whips of the several parties in the House.[246]

The Prime Minister on Election Pledges

The motion was carried without debate upon the question whether a Committee should be appointed. In the course of the debate whether the Committee should be appointed by the Committee of Selection, or by the Party Whips, Lord Balcarres, who had been a Junior Lord of the Treasury in the Balfour Government, used these words: "As regards those Honorable Gentlemen who had entered Parliament for the first time,[247] he thought he was fairly accurate when he said that they had given pretty specific pledges upon the matter [of the appointment of a Select Committee] to those who had sent them to the House." Sir A. Acland-Hood, who had been Chief Whip and Patronage Secretary to the Treasury in the late Balfour Government, said:

"There was a debate and a division [upon this question, last year,] and nearly the whole of the supporters of the Government voted against the appointment of the Committee. No doubt many of them suffered for it at the General Election; they either lost their seats or had their majorities reduced in consequence of the vote." And, finally, Sir Henry Campbell-Bannerman, the new Prime Minister, expressed himself as follows in the course of an argument in favor of a Committee appointed by the Committee of Selection rather than by the House itself through the agency of the Party Whips. The Prime Minister said: "There was a great deal of force in what the Right Honorable Gentleman [Sir A. Acland-Hood] had said as to the fears that were entertained in many quarters of the effect on the Committee if appointed under pressure and insistence, and the retroactive effect of old promises extracted in moments of agony from candidates at the General Election."[248]

The Select Committee on Post Office Servants consists of: 4 Liberals, Messrs. Barker, Edwards, Hobhouse and Sutherland; 2 Conservatives, the Honorable Claude Hay and Sir Clement Hill; 2 Liberal and Labor Members, Messrs. John Ward and G. J. Wardle; and 1 Nationalist, Mr. P. A. Meechan.[249]

The reference to the Committee is: "to inquire into the wages and position of the principal classes of Post Office servants, and also of the unestablished postmasters. To examine, so far as may be necessary for the purpose of their Report, the conditions of employment of these classes. To report, whether, having regard to the conditions and prospects of their employment, and, as far as may be, to the standard rate of wages and the position of other classes of workers, the remuneration they receive is adequate or otherwise."

In the spring of 1907, the Committee reported that it had not had time to perform its task, and asked for reappointment. The evidence thus far taken by the Committee had not been published at the date of this writing, March 20, 1907.

Lord Stanley Congratulated

Lord Stanley was one of the many Conservative candidates defeated in the General Election of January, 1906. When his defeat became known, hundreds

170

of telegrams were showered upon him by postal and telegraph employees located in all parts of the United Kingdom. The telegram sent by Liverpool postal and telegraph employees was typical of the lot. It congratulated Lord Stanley upon his retirement to private life, and assured him that the senders at all times would do all in their power to make the retirement a permanent one.

FOOTNOTES:

225 *The Times*, September 19, 1904.

226 The apparent net profits of the Post Office Department average about $18,500,000 a year. Those profits are subject to the correction that the Post Office does not charge itself with interest and depreciation upon its capital investment, which cannot be ascertained, but must be very large.

227 *Hansard's Parliamentary Debates*, March 10, 1890, p. 342. Mr. McCartan asks the Postmaster General "on what grounds Messrs. C. Hughes and C. H. Garland were recently punished." ... The intervention was repeated on March 14, p. 865.

228 *The Times*, August 25, 1904.

229 *The Times*, September 19, 1904.

230 *Hansard's Parliamentary Debates*, July 6, 1905, p. 1,350 and following.

231 August 29, 1903.

232 In his annual *Report*, dated July 28, 1905, Lord Stanley stated that the ultimate cost would be $1,861,500 a year.

233 To be held in January, 1906.

234 *Hansard's Parliamentary Debates*, July 18, 1905, p. 1,062.

235 *Hansard's Parliamentary Debates*, July 6, 1905, p. 1,367.

236 *Hansard's Parliamentary Debates*, July 6, 1905, p. 1,401.

237

		Ayes	Noes
Conservatives	Government Supporters	9	210
Liberal Unionists		0	37
Liberals	The Opposition	138	2
Nationalists		49	0
Various factions		9	0
		205	249

Name	Office
Mr. Herbert Gladstone	Home Secretary
Mr. Lloyd George	President of Board of Trade
Mr. Thos. Lough	Parliamentary Sec'y of Board of Education
Mr. R. McKenna	Financial Secretary to Treasury
Mr. J. A. Pease	Junior Lord of Treasury
Mr. J. Herbert Lewis	Junior Lord of Treasury
Captain Cecil Norton	Junior Lord of Treasury
Mr. F. Freman-Thomas	Junior Lord of Treasury
Mr. J. M. Fuller	Junior Lord of Treasury
Mr. R. K. Causton	Paymaster General
Mr. Geo. Lambert	Civil Lord of Admiralty
Mr. Edward Robertson	Secretary to Admiralty
Mr. Herbert Samuel	Under Home Secretary
Mr. J. E. Ellis	Under Secretary for India
Mr. H. E. Kearley	Secretary of Board of Trade
Sir Jno. L. Walton	Attorney-General
Mr. Thos. Shaw	Lord Advocate

239 A. Todd: *On Parliamentary Government in England.*

240 Chancellor of the Exchequer, 1886 and 1892-95.

241 At the election of 1906 Mr. Heaton received 2,210 votes, while his opponent received 1,262.

242 *The House of Commons Poll Book*, 1885-1906, issued by The Liberal Publication Department.

243 Composition of the House: Liberal and Labor Members, 428; Conservatives, 130; Liberal Unionists, 28; and Nationalists, 80.

244 *The Times*, March 17, 1906.

245 *Hansard's Parliamentary Debates*.

246 *Hansard's Parliamentary Debates*, March 6, 1906, p. 323 and following.

247 281 in number.

248 *Hansard's Parliamentary Debates*, March 6, 1906.

249 *Hansard's Parliamentary Debates*, March 9, 1906, p. 847.

CHAPTER XIV

THE HOUSE OF COMMONS, UNDER PRESSURE FROM THE CIVIL SERVICE UNIONS, CURTAILS THE EXECUTIVE'S POWER TO DISMISS INCOMPETENT AND REDUNDANT EMPLOYEES

The old practice of intervention by Members of Parliament on behalf of individual civil servants with political influence has given way to the new practice of intervention on behalf of the individual civil servant because he is a member of a civil service union. The new practice is the more insidious and dangerous one, for it means class bribery. The doctrine that entrance upon the State's service means "something very nearly approaching to a freehold provision for life." Official testimony of various prominent civil servants, especially of Mr. (now Lord) Welby, Permanent Secretary to the Treasury from 1885 to 1894; and Mr. T. H. Farrer, Permanent Secretary to Board of Trade from 1867 to 1886. The costly practice of giving pensions no solution of the problem of getting rid of unsatisfactory public servants. The difficulty of dismissing incompetent persons extends even to probationers. The cost of "reorganizing" incompetent persons out of the public service.

Personal Bribery replaced by Class Bribery

The intervention of the House of Commons in the details of the administration of the Post Office Department and the other State Departments, is by no means confined to the raising of salaries and wages. It extends to practically every kind of question that arises out of the conflicts of the interests of the State servants and the interests of the public Treasury. The intervention is due to the organized action of the "civil service unions;" and it is exercised primarily on behalf of classes of employees, but not exclusively. The latter day spirit of the civil service unions is to make the cause of the individual the cause of the class, and that brings about much intervention through the House of Commons, by the organized civil service, on behalf of individual State servants. The ancient form of intervention on behalf of the individual who had claims that were based on personal influence or family influence, on family ties, or on friendship, has been abolished. In its place has been developed intervention on behalf of the individual, prompted by the fact that the individual in question is a member of a civil service union that seeks to enforce certain ideals as to the terms and conditions that shall prevail in the public service. Of the two forms of intervention, the latter is the more pernicious and demoralizing, partly because it is—or will become—more pervasive, partly because it rests on class bribery and class corruption, as distinguished from the individual bribery and the individual corruption upon which rested the old form of intervention. Of those two forms of corruption, the bribery of classes is the more difficult to eradicate.

State Employment means Life Employment

One of the most important results of this intervention on behalf of individuals has been the establishment of the doctrine that once a man has landed in the employ of the State, he has "something very nearly approaching to a freehold of provision for life," to employ the words of the Chairman of the Select Committee on the Civil Services Expenditure, 1873.[250]

Before that committee, Sir Wm. H. Stephenson, Chairman of the Inland Revenue Commissioners, said: "…if a man was reported to be hopelessly inefficient, I should dismiss him; but even then you must act with a great deal of forbearance. For the simple reason that you are amenable to many opinions beside your own. You cannot act absolutely upon your own judgment without being liable to be compelled to give your reasons for that judgment; and these reasons, though perfectly clear in your own mind, may not always be easy to give to the satisfaction of another man…. I am afraid we should have a very bad time of it out of doors if we exercised a little more freedom in dismissing incompetent clerks and promoting deserving ones; I judge very much by what I see; as it is, there is a great disposition, I think, to exclaim against anything like an act of tyranny, and the exercise of such freedom would be called tyranny…. I have no doubt that if a public department had the power of absolute dismissal, it would have a considerable effect in increasing efficiency; but what I say is, that you cannot give them that power in the same way that it is held by a man in private employment. You have too many critics; you have the public newspaper press; you have Members of the House of Commons who are personally interested in these people; and you would be surprised, I am sure, if you knew the numerous instances in which, for the smallest thing [inflictions of punishment], applications are made, pressing that this man is an excellent man, a good brother, a kind father, and all that kind of thing which influences men individually, but which cannot [does, but should not] influence the judgment of the heads of a public office." Sir William H. Stephenson was asked: "Do you not think that it might be made a rule in your office, as in the Customs, that any interference through a Member of Parliament should lead to dismissal?" He replied: "Yes; but you must prove that a man knows it. You cannot dismiss a man if some injudicious friend takes up his case; and if a man has a friend, it is always an injudicious one under these circumstances."[251]

Before this same committee of 1873, Mr. Stanfeld, M. P., Third Lord of the Treasury, who, in 1869 to 1871 had been Financial Secretary to the Treasury, said: "...the great difference between the public establishment and the private establishment is this: that practically speaking, in a public establishment, you have a large proportion of established clerks who can do no more than a moderate amount of service.... Because you have not the faculty which men in private business have, without any particular fault, of saying to a man: 'On the whole, you do not suit me, and I mean to get somebody else.' When you get a clerk on a public establishment, he remains on that establishment with very rare exceptions, and you have to make the best of your bargain; the result naturally is that, with the exception of men of ability and energy, you have not so much stimulus for their effort as you have in private employment, and you have not by any means the same power of dealing with them...."[252]

In 1888, before the Royal Commission appointed to inquire into the Civil Establishments, this question of the great difficulty of getting rid of incompetent or undesirable men, was threshed out at great length. Sir Charles DuCane, Chairman of the Commissioners of Customs, said: "But it is an invidious thing, I do not mean to say as regards myself, but invidious rather as regards the [political] head of a department [the Minister], to come and make complaints against men whom one cannot perhaps accuse of any overt act of negligence or carelessness, but who are merely rather below the level of ordinary efficiency…. I think it would be a most desirable thing that we should have the power of getting rid of incapable and inefficient men who have yet managed to keep themselves out of any positive scrape or offence, for which they would be charged before a Member of the Board of Commissioners of Customs."[253]

To Sir S. A. Blackwood, Secretary to the Post Office since 1880, the Chairman of the Royal Commission put the question: "Do you think it is a real evil in the public service that there should not be the same power to remove inefficient men as exists outside the public service, of course I mean within certain limits, because the public service must be different from private service, but in your experience, have you found it to be a real evil in the way of efficiency as well as of wise economy to be obliged to keep men whom you would be glad to get rid of if you could have sent them away with something in their pocket, [i. e., a pension]?" The answer was: "Yes, it is a serious objection." Sir S. A. Blackwood even asserted that the Act of 1887, giving the Treasury discretionary power to pension men unable to discharge efficiently the duties of their office,[254] would not help much. "We should always be asking an officer to relinquish his full pay, and to retire upon a lesser pension than he would be entitled to if he served his full time, and there is always a disinclination on the part of heads of departments to do that."[255]

Sir Reginald E. Welby, who had entered the Treasury service in 1856, and had been made Permanent Secretary in 1885, said there was full power to dismiss idle or incompetent persons without granting pensions or allowances of any sort. Thereupon, Mr. F. Mitford, one of the Members of the Royal Commission, asked: "Is not really the sole difficulty that public departments have to contend with in exercising that full power, the fact that Parliament is behind them, and a Member of Parliament always asks questions [in the House] and brings interest [pressure] to bear upon the head of the department, which practically annuls that power? The difficulty lies not with the public

177

officer, but practically with the difficulties that are thrown in his way outside his department by individual Members of Parliament?" The Permanent Secretary of the Treasury answered: "There is always before the heads of departments the fact that pressure may be brought to bear by Members of Parliament, and it requires, therefore, that a case must be very strong, that it must be a very good case before you would dismiss. Probably you would be much more long-suffering in a Government department, than you would be in a private establishment." Sir Reginald Welby just previously had said: "I have known men dismissed from the Treasury.... Perhaps I had better say, I have heard of men being dismissed from the Treasury for simple idleness, but it was before my time." Thereupon the Chairman had queried: "It is the fact, speaking generally, is it not, that mere idleness and mere incompetence, without very gross negligence of duty or gross misbehavior, does not bring about dismissal from the service, either in the Treasury or anywhere else that you are aware of?" The reply was: "I would rather put it in this way: I think that Government offices are very long-suffering in that matter. If the man was reported as distinctly very idle and not doing his work he would be warned, and I think if it was repeated after that (I am speaking of any fairly managed Government department), he would be dismissed. But I think that a Government department is, for one reason or another, more long-suffering than a private establishment would be.... While I am admitting the possibility of there being bad officers, I should like to add that both in the Upper and Lower Division Clerks, we have got, on the whole, a very satisfactory set of men under the present regulations of the Treasury, and that they do their work well. I am happy to say that very few cases of complaint come before me."

The House of Commons is Master

Mr. Lawson, a member of the Royal Commission, asked Sir Reginald Welby: "But you would hardly plead the interference of Members of Parliament as a justification for not getting rid of an unworthy servant, would you?" Sir Reginald Welby replied: "It is not a good reason, but as a matter of fact it is powerful. The House of Commons are our masters."[256]

Sir T. H. Farrer, who had been Permanent Secretary of the Board of Trade from 1867 to 1886, and had been a Member of the so-called Playfair

Commission, of 1876, on the Civil Service, was asked by Mr. R. W. Hanbury, a Member of the Royal Commission of 1888, whether the failure to dismiss incompetent men could not be attributed to "soft heartedness" on the part of heads of departments? Sir T. H. Farrer replied: "Yes, that is another aspect of the case, and it is no doubt theoretically perfectly true; but I think it overlooks what is the real difficulty of getting rid of useless men. There is a certain difficulty in the soft heartedness of heads of departments and of Ministers. But there is a very much greater difficulty in the pressure which is put upon them by Members of the House of Commons. That is the real difficulty; the real difficulty of the public service is getting rid of bad men; and the real difficulty of getting rid of bad men is that no Minister will face the pressure which is put upon him from outside.... I have had much personal experience of the matter; I have been plagued all my life at the Board of Trade with inefficient men that I wanted to get rid of, but have been unable to do so.... Parliamentary pressure is the main difficulty.... Members are economical in general [protestations]; but in particular cases they think more of their constituents than of the public service. No doubt with a little thinking I could recall a very great number of instances, but two or three occur to me."

You may dismiss but you must not

"Not very many years ago there was a clerk of whom perpetual complaints were made to me. He was in a hard-worked department, and the heads of it told me repeatedly: 'We can do nothing with him.' At last we got it arranged that he should go [with a large pension, on the theory that his office was abolished, because no longer required]. My back was turned—I was away on a holiday—and when I came back, I found that Parliamentary pressure, by which I mean applications from Members, had been put on, and in spite of us all, the man was back in the place to the detriment of our credit. Let me mention another case. I was engaged upon a reorganization of the department under one of the strongest men [Ministers] I have ever served. What the President of the Board of Trade said to me, in effect was: 'We must have new blood; we are getting crowded up with effete men; I will back you in anything you do, only you must undertake not to get me into a difficulty in the House of Commons. I cannot afford it; the Government cannot afford time for it; they cannot afford strength to fight battles of that kind.' We set to work about the reorganization with our hands tied, and we were obliged to say to these men: 'Well, if you stay here, we will make it very uncomfortable for you; we will put you in the very worst places in the office,' The Treasury offered good terms of retirement [pensions], and in that way, after a good deal of fighting, we got rid of most of them.... We had to give them very high terms [that is, very liberal pensions]. I may mention a case which happened even since then. I refer to the official Receivers in Bankruptcy. They were men who were appointed only a few years ago, under the most stringent conditions imposed by the Treasury and the Board of Trade, and without the slightest reference to personal considerations or to politics. They were told that they were appointed on trial, that they might be removed at any moment if the Board of Trade desired it for the good of the service. Fortunately, most of them have turned out extremely well. One, perhaps more, turned out bad, but one certainly turned out very bad. Perpetual complaints were made to me by the head of that department that he could do nothing with this man, and that the business was being badly conducted. After a good deal of trouble, after I left, it was determined to remove this man. The Members of Parliament for the county, as I am told, came and put pressure upon the President of the Board of Trade [the Minister], till he was obliged to say: 'I cannot remove him; he must stay.'"

Pension System no Remedy

To the foregoing testimony from the Permanent Secretary of the Board of Trade, the Chairman of the Royal Commission replied: "I gather from what you say, that, supposing it was possible, under this new system of pensions and allowances, to give a man who was sent away from the service the money which he had himself contributed toward his ultimate pension, either with or without the addition of a Government grant, you do not think that would get over the difficulty in getting rid of incompetent men?" Sir T. H. Farrer replied: "No, I do not think it would, unless the House of Commons passes a self-denying ordinance, and refuses to interfere with the Ministers in the management of their departments."[257]

Later in the examination, Lord Lingen, who had been Permanent Secretary of the Treasury from 1869 to 1885, said to Sir T. H. Farrer: "You have given a good deal of evidence as to the difficulties which the relation of the public departments to Parliament creates. I think we might hold there is nothing in private service analogous to what you may call the triennial change of Government, that [when] everybody who has been passed over [not promoted], who thinks he has any grievance, considers that he has a fresh chance on a change of Ministry?" The Secretary of the Board of Trade replied: "Yes, I remember distinctly one particular case in which on every change of Government a fresh appeal was made to the new Ministers on behalf of men who had been retired for good reasons." Lord Lingen continued: "It revived questions which had been supposed to be settled?" "Yes, it does, not infrequently."

On August 1, 1890, in the House of Commons, the Postmaster General, Mr. Raikes, in speaking of a Post Office employee who had been disciplined, said: "The case is one to which I have given a great deal of personal attention; indeed, I may say that in cases of dismissal or punishment I have always endeavored to satisfy myself thoroughly as to the facts, and to mitigate, if I can, the effect of the regulations of the Department." On that same day the Postmaster General stated—in reply to Mr. Conybeare,[258] who was intervening on behalf of one Cornwell, dismissed from the postal service— that Cornwell had been dismissed for the second time. After the first dismissal, the Postmaster General himself had reinstated Cornwell. The second dismissal had been necessary "in the interest of the Service at large, but especially in that of the other men employed on the same duty, his case should be dealt with in an exemplary manner."[259]

In March, 1896, the Chairman of the Inter-Departmental Committee on Post Office Establishments, asked Mr. Lewin Hill, Assistant Secretary General Post Office: "Do you think there is any other particular class of employment which is comparable with that of the postmen?" Mr. Hill replied: "I thought of railway servants, whose work in many ways resembles the work of our employees. If they have not the same permanence as our people have, they have continuous employment so long as they are efficient, but our people have continuous employment whether they are efficient or not."[260] Several months later, Mr. Hill testified as follows before this same Committee: "Our

181

inquiries have proved that the telegraph staff at Liverpool is excessive, and it has been decided, on vacancies [occurring], to abolish the ten appointments."[261] The meaning of this statement is, that if a mistake is made, and too many men are appointed to a certain office; or, if the business of an office falls off, the Government cannot correct the redundancy of employees by dismissing, or by transferring to some other office, the redundant employees. It must wait until promotion, retirement on account of old age, or death shall remove the redundant employees. Before this same committee, Mr. J. C. Badcock, Controller London Postal Service, testified that in theory there were no first class letter sorters in the foreign newspaper department of the London Post Office, since there had been, since 1886, no work that called for first class newspaper sorters. But as a matter of fact there were thirty-seven "redundant first class sorters, who, upon resignation, or pensioning, or death, would be replaced by second class sorters."[262]

In 1902, Sir Edgar Vincent,[263] a Member of the Select Committee on National Expenditure, 1902, asked Lord Welby, who had been Permanent Secretary to the Treasury from 1885 to 1894: "It is, I presume, extremely difficult for the Minister at the head of a Department to dismiss, or place on the retired list incompetent officers?" Lord Welby replied: "It is very difficult. Of course there are different degrees of incompetency. It is not so difficult in the case of a notoriously incompetent officer, but there are many people, as the honorable Member is aware, against whom nothing whatever can be said, who are still the very reverse of competent." Sir Edgar Vincent continued: "Can you suggest any means of substituting for a Minister whom it is almost impossible to expect to perform the duty, some authority who should revise Establishments and exclude the bad bargains?" Lord Welby, of course, replied that the remedy suggested would be inconsistent with the principles of

parliamentary government,[264] in that it would substitute for the Minister, who holds office at the pleasure of the House of Commons, some permanent officer or officers appointed by the Ministry.

Difficult to dismiss Probationers

182

Oftentimes the difficulty experienced in dismissing unsatisfactory public servants, extends even to persons appointed on probation.

In April, 1875, the Chancellor of the Exchequer, in the course of the Financial Statement, said: "We now appoint young men upon probation, and the understanding of that probationary employment is that if the person is found after six months or a year to be unfit, he is told that he must look elsewhere. This is a very invidious duty for the head of an office to perform, and it is very often not performed."[265]

In 1888, Mr. Harvey, a Member of the Royal Commission on the Civil Establishments, said: "The tendency in a Government office is for the man to regard his probationary period as practically a '*nominis umbra*' [the mere shadow of a name], nothing else."[266]

The Chairman of the Royal Commission of 1888 asked Sir Reginald Welby, the Permanent Secretary to the Treasury: "Is there anything like a real probation in any one of the divisions of the clerks at the Treasury, so that you can find out [whether they are likely to prove competent]?" "Yes, I think so. The principal clerk of the division to which the probationer is attached makes a report at the end of six months; and I have known a principal clerk to make a doubtful report. In that case, if I remember rightly, the term of probation was extended."[267]

The boys employed by the Post Office Department for the delivery of telegrams, are, in a way, on continuous probation. If they serve satisfactorily, they are, at the age of 16, taken in training for the position of postmen. In 1897, Mr. Lewin Hill, Assistant Secretary General Post Office, said: "...in London, in the past, the weeding out of messenger boys at 16 years has not been carried out so far, I think, owing to the paternal feelings of the Department. Every effort seems to have been made to keep in the service anybody who could possibly scrape through. But the country postmasters were, as a rule, careful to weed out unsatisfactory lads." He continued: "...We could have got better postmen [in London], if we had had a free hand."[268]

In 1857 the opposition made in Parliament to the system of pensions, led to the appointment of a Committee to inquire into the operation of the Superannuation Act, 1834. That Committee stated as follows the argument "from the public point of view" in favor of pensions. "Though it is strictly the duty of heads of departments to remove from the public service all those who have become unfit to discharge their duties, yet experience shows that this duty cannot be enforced. It is felt to be hard—and even unjust—and inefficient men are, therefore, retained in the Service to the detriment of efficiency. They, therefore, were unhesitatingly of opinion that the public interest would be best consulted by maintaining a system of superannuation allowances."[269]

In accordance with the foregoing recommendation Parliament, in 1859, enacted that the Treasury might give "abolition terms" to persons whose offices should be abolished in consequence of the "reorganization" of their department, or branch of service. Under that Act, inefficient persons who are "reorganized out of the service" are given "pro rata" pensions, plus an allowance for "abolition of their office." For example, a man aged 50, with 30 years of service, who would become entitled to a pension at the age of 60, will be retired at 50 years, with a pro rata pension on the basis of 30 years' service, plus an allowance of 7 or 10 years' service for abolition of his office.[270]

Cost of Pensions to the Incompetent

In 1873, before the Select Committee on Civil Services Expenditure, Sir William H. Stephenson, Chairman of the Commissioners of Inland Revenue, illustrated the working of this system with the statement that in 1873-74, the salaries paid in the Inland Revenue Department would aggregate $4,808,580. An additional $683,160 would be required for pensions; and a further $234,175 would be required on account of the abolition terms given to men who had been reorganized out of the Inland Revenue Department. Thus the "non-effective," or non-revenue producing, charges of the department were equivalent to 19 per cent. of the effective, or revenue producing, charges.[271]

In 1888 the Royal Commission appointed to inquire into the Civil Establishments reported that the burden on the State for pensions was equivalent to 12 per cent. to 15 per cent. of the working salaries, and that the payment of the abolition terms raised the percentage in question to 20 per cent. of the working salaries. Sir Reginald E. Welby, Secretary to the Treasury, stated before the Commission, that even the past liberal expenditure on account of pro rata pensions with abolition terms, had not enabled the State to get rid of "inefficient and incapable men." The Chairman of the Royal Commission spoke of the abolition terms as amounting "almost to a scandal." Sir R. E. Welby and Lord Lingen, a former Secretary to the Treasury, contrasted the State's system of pensions with the system of the London and North Western Railway. The Railway's pension system was maintained out of a fund raised by a 2.5 per cent. reduction from the salaries of the employees, and a 2.5 per cent. contribution from the treasury of the railway.

Sir R. E. Welby, Secretary to the Treasury, and other witnesses, spoke of the abolition terms often acting as a premium on inefficiency. Mr. Robert Giffen, the eminent statistician and political economist, who also was an officer of the Board of Trade, said: "When a man is reorganized out of the service, as a rule he gets so many years' service added [to his actual service], that is to say, at 50 years, if he has served 30 years, he may have 7 or 10 years' service added, and thus get two-thirds of his salary as a pension; and he begins to get his pension at once, instead of waiting until he is 60 years of age. A man who thus gets a pension at 50 years, really gets more than double what he would get if he waited until 60 years of age. The present value of $100 a year, beginning at once at the age of 50 years, is a good deal more than double the present value of $100 a year to be paid to a man when he reaches 60 years. The difference in favor of the man who is reorganized out of the service, as against the man who remains until he is 60 years of age, is simply overwhelming to my mind."

Sir Algernon E. West, Chairman of the Inland Revenue Commissioners, illustrated the working of the practice of getting rid of inefficient men by reorganizing an office, by citing the following instance of "successful" reorganization. Sir Algernon West had retired 39 upper division clerks, permanently reducing the number of the staff by 39. He had thus effected a saving in salaries of $70,000 a year. But he had incurred an annual expenditure of $44,160 on account of pensions, and an annual expenditure of $10,000 on account of abolition terms. Therefore his net saving was not $70,000 but only $15,840. Yet Sir Algernon West denominated his reorganization successful.

In the course of this reorganization, Sir Algernon West had increased the hours of work from 6 hours to 7 hours. The reorganization, also, had necessitated certain promotions. Sir Algernon had made it a condition of promotion, that the man promoted should consent to work 7 hours a day. Men not promoted he gave $150 a year "as a personal allowance in consideration of the extra hour they were called to serve." One man, aged 34 years, declined to work more than 6 hours on any terms, saying that the Government had made a contract with him for six hours' work a day. In order to get rid of this man, Sir Algernon West gave him a pension on the basis of 10 years' service. Legally, of course, the man had no claim to any pension or abolition allowance whatever, for he was in reality dismissed for refusing to perform the duties demanded of him.[272]

FOOTNOTES:

250 *Third Report from the Select Committee on Civil Services Expenditure*, 1873; q. 4,283 to 4,288.

251 *Third Report from the Select Committee on Civil Services Expenditure*, 1873; q. 4,270 to 4,282, 4,146 and following, and 4,198 to 4,210.

252 *Third Report from the Select Committee on Civil Services Expenditure*, 1873; q. 4,937.

253 *Second Report of the Royal Commission appointed to inquire into the Civil Establishments*, 1888; q. 17,559, 17,572, and 17,564.

254 The Act of 1887 reads: "Where a civil servant is removed from office on the ground of his inability to discharge efficiently the duties of his office, and a superannuation allowance cannot lawfully be granted to him under the Superannuation Acts of 1834 and 1859, and the Treasury thinks that the special circumstances of the case justify the grant to him of a retiring allowance, they may grant to him such retiring allowance as they think just and proper...."

255 *Second Report of the Royal Commission appointed to inquire into the Civil Establishments*, 1888; q. 17,774 to 17,776, and 17,942a.

256 *Second Report of the Royal Commission appointed to inquire into the Civil Establishments*, 1888; q. 10,532 to 10,544.

257 *Second Report of the Royal Commission appointed to inquire into the Civil Establishments*, 1888; q. 19,980, 20,011 to 20,020, and 20,082.

258 *Who's Who*, 1905, Conybeare, C. A. V., M. P., N. W. Div. of Cornwall, 1885 to 1895; Member London School Board, 1888 to 1890; Education: Christ Church, Oxford; Publications: *Treatise on the Corrupt and Illegal Practices Acts*, 1892.

259 *Hansard's Parliamentary Debates*, August 1, 1890, p. 1,647.

260 *Report of the Inter-Departmental Committee on Post Office Establishments*, 1897; q. 11,694.

261 *Report of the Inter-Departmental Committee on Post Office Establishments*, 1897; q. 15,166 to 15,171.

262 *Report of the Inter-Departmental Committee on Post Office Establishments*, 1897; q. 1,881 to 1,883; and q. 1,270, Mr. G. E. Rably.

263 *Who's Who*, 1904, Vincent, Sir Edgar; M. P. since 1899; President of Council of Ottoman Public Debt, 1883; Financial Adviser to Egyptian Government, 1883 to 1889; Governor of Imperial Ottoman Bank, Constantinople, 1889 to 1897.

264 *Report from the Select Committee on National Expenditure*, 1902; q. 2,559 and 2,560.

265 *Hansard's Parliamentary Debates*, April 15, 1875, p. 1,033.

266 *Second Report of the Royal Commission appointed to inquire into the Civil Establishments*, 1888; q. 20,084.

267 *Second Report of the Royal Commission appointed to inquire into the Civil Establishments*, 1888; q. 10,535 to 10,536.

268 *Report of the Inter-Departmental Committee on Post Office Establishments*, 1897; q. 11,619 and 11,697.

269 *Second Report of the Royal Commission appointed to inquire into the Civil Establishments*, 1888, p. xx.

270 *Second Report of the Royal Commission appointed to inquire into the Civil Establishments*, 1888; q. 19,229, Mr. Robert Giffen, the eminent statistician and economist, who was also an officer in the Board of Trade.

271 *Third Report from the Select Committee on Civil Services Expenditure*, 1873; q. 4,225.

272 *Second Report of the Royal Commission appointed to inquire into the Civil Establishments*, 1888, pp. xx and xxv, and q. 19,240, 20,434 and 20,435, 20,370, 20,392 to 20,395, 20,412, 20,434 to 20,438, 20,441, 19,229 and following, 17,245 and following, and 20,398 to 20,404.

CHAPTER XV

THE HOUSE OF COMMONS, UNDER PRESSURE FROM THE CIVIL SERVICE UNIONS, CURTAILS THE EXECUTIVE'S POWER TO PROMOTE EMPLOYEES ACCORDING TO MERIT

> The civil service unions oppose promotion by merit, and demand promotion by seniority. Testimony presented before: Select Committee on Civil Services Expenditure, 1873; Select Committee on Post Office, 1876; Royal Commission to inquire into the Civil Establishments, 1888; from statement made in House of Commons, in 1887, by Mr. Raikes, Postmaster General; and before the so-called Tweedmouth Committee, 1897. Instances of intervention by Members of House of Commons on behalf of civil servants who have not been promoted, or are afraid they shall not be promoted.

In the matter of promotion, also, the civil servants' unions compel the Members of Parliament to intervene, on behalf of individual employees, in the details of the administration of the several Departments of State. The organized civil service is not content that every man should have an equal chance of promotion, so far as his industry and capacity shall qualify him for advancement; it evinces a marked tendency to demand equal promotion in fact, that is, the elimination of the effects of the natural inequality among men. The House of Commons, in yielding in this matter to the pressure from the organized civil service, is tending to reduce the public service to a dull level of mediocrity, which action at one and the same time impairs the efficiency of the public service and makes the service of the State unattractive to able and ambitious men.

In this matter of promotion, the permanent heads of the Departments are hampered also by the unbusinesslike attitude toward the conduct of the public business that characterizes large sections of the newspaper press as well the great mass of the voters. That unbusinesslike frame of mind, in turn, is the outgrowth of that untrained sympathy which makes every one tend to sympathize with the individual, whenever the interest of the individual clashes with that of the State. To illustrate, in 1873, before the Select Committee on Civil Services Expenditure, Sir William H. Stephenson, Chairman of the Commissioners of Inland Revenue, stated that in his Department promotion was mainly by seniority in the two lowest classes, to some extent by seniority in the third class, but beyond that entirely by merit. But he hastened to add: "Indeed, if I may judge by the complaints that I have heard out of doors, occasionally in the newspaper press, and elsewhere, the system of promotion by merit is supposed to be carried to rather an excessive extent in the Inland Revenue."[273]

The Glasgow Postmaster's "Mistake"

In 1876, before the Select Committee on Post Office, Mr. Hobson, Postmaster at Glasgow, stated that he could not promote his telegraph operators according to their dexterity, he was obliged to promote according to seniority. Mr. Gower, a member of the Select Committee queried: "Therefore, there is no encouragement whatever to superior dexterity?" Mr. Hobson replied: "I should not recommend a clerk for promotion ... if I were satisfied that he was not doing all he could to improve himself ... and was only an indifferent operator. I should mention that in submitting the report, and recommend him to be passed over." Mr. Gower continued: "But suppose he took every sort of pains to improve himself, but did not improve?" The answer came: "I would then recommend him to go forward [*i. e.* for promotion]." Mr. Gower then asked: "Have you any power to exchange a clerk who is a slow operator for another quicker operator in a district where it would not signify?" The Postmaster at Glasgow replied: "None whatever."[274] The reader will recall that there are numerous telegraph stations in Glasgow.

In April, 1877, the Postmaster General, Lord John Manners, replied to the Report of the Select Committee of 1876, in a letter to the Lords Commissioners of the Treasury. He concluded the letter with the statement: "In conclusion, I beg leave to say that it is, I think, hardly worth while to attempt to contradict the mistakes as to promotion into which the postmaster of Glasgow was accidentally betrayed in giving his evidence before the

Committee of last Session, and to which no reference is made in their Report."[275]

Before the same Committee, Mr. Edward Graves, Divisional Engineer, recommended that the head of the Post Office establish the rule, "that, other things being equal as to seniority and general business capacity, preference for promotion shall always be given to the telegraph clerk who has shown himself possessed of technical knowledge, and who is desirous of obtaining technical information."[276]

Passing over a period of 28 years, that is, from the year 1876 to the year 1904, we find Mr. E. Trenam, Controller London Central Telegraph Office, testifying that because of danger that in the immediate future there would be a lack of telegraph clerks who had a knowledge of the technics of telegraphy, Mr. W. H. Preece, Engineer-in-Chief, had caused a special increase in pay— $26 a year—to be offered to men who should acquire such knowledge. The witness added that "unfortunately many of the men who have [acquired] this knowledge are comparative juniors, and we are compelled to put them to work which those receiving higher pay are incompetent to perform. It will take some years to adjust the anomaly … [that is, before the incompetent men receiving higher pay shall have been pensioned or shall have died]".[277]

Promotion by Seniority, not Jobbery, the Public Service's weak Point

Before the Royal Commission of 1888, appointed to inquire into the Civil Establishments, Sir Thomas H. Farrer, who had been a Member of the Playfair Royal Commission of 1876, and had been Permanent Secretary of the Board of Trade from 1867 to 1886, said: "I should like to say that in the discussion which led [in 1872] to the adoption of Mr. Lowe's [Chancellor of the Exchequer] scheme[278] [for the reform of the civil service] a mistake was often made, and is still made, in supposing that the great evil of the service is jobbery. That is not the case, and I say so with great confidence, having regard to what has been done by Ministers whom I have served of both parties. The real evil of the service is promotion by routine, and not jobbing in the selection for superior places.[279] But make your regulations what you will, the *sine qua non*, to make any regulations work well, is that the men at the head of the different offices shall have discretion, honesty, and courage, and shall not be afraid to put up the good men and to keep the inferior men in their place. I am quite confident from my own experience that it can be done, but I am certain that it can be done only if the men at the head of the offices will take a good deal of trouble about it." Lord Lingen, a Member of the Royal Commission, and a former Permanent Secretary to the Treasury, interpolated: "A good deal of trouble and a good deal of disagreeable interference." Mr. Farrer continued: "It requires tact, because of course you must not put a man up for mere merit. You cannot take a lad of 19 and put him over a man of 30 without a very strong reason; but taking the different sub-heads of the department into counsel; by a little give and take; by care, discretion, and confidence in the perfect honesty with which the thing is done, I believe it can be perfectly well managed…. The key of the whole thing is to put the proper men at the top of the offices."

Lord Lingen and Mr. Farrer then went on to state that with every change of the Government of the day, some civil servants who had been passed over, or had some other grievance, made the attempt to have their cases reopened.[280]

Sir Charles DuCane, Chairman of the Commissioners of Customs, said: "We promote strictly by merit; we never allow seniority to weigh with us."[281]

Sir Algernon E. West, Chairman of the Commissioners of Inland Revenue, said that he promoted by merit within the limits allowed him by the Treasury ruling that no clerk could pass out of the second class into the first class without 10 years' service in the second class. Subsequent testimony established the fact that the Treasury had made that ruling in order to prevent the second class clerks from bringing pressure on Members of Parliament with the view to securing automatic promotion from the second class into the first.[282] Just before making the foregoing statement, Sir Algernon West had said: "If you take the whole Civil Service, I think you will find a general concord of opinion that the man receiving from $2,500 to $3,000 a year is the weakest part of the Civil Service. I am not speaking of a young man who is in process of going higher, but of an elderly man who has risen to that kind of high salary, and has no prospect of getting anything more…. An ordinary middle aged man, who has got to $2,500 or $3,000 or $3,500, generally is far too highly paid." Mr. R. W. Hanbury, a Member of the Royal Commission, queried: "How would he get such a position?" The answer came: "By natural progression," *i. e.* promotion by routine.[283]

Sir Lyon Playfair, a man of vast experience in the administration of the British Civil Service, said: "Promotions by merit hardly take place in most offices, I think; at all events, there are very few instances brought before us."[284]

Promotion by Seniority the Great Evil

The Royal Commission itself reported: "We think that promotion by seniority is the great evil of the Service, and that it is indispensable to proceed throughout every branch of it strictly on the principle of promotion by merit, that is to say, by selecting always the fittest man, instead of considering claims in order of seniority, and rejecting only the unfit. It is no doubt true that objections on the score of favoritism may arise in the application of such a rule in public departments, and the intervention of Members of Parliament also presents an obvious difficulty, but we think that such constant vigilance, tact, and resolution as may fairly be expected on the part of heads of branches and of offices, will meet these objections, and we believe that the certain advantages of promotion by merit to the most deserving men, and therefore to the public service, are so great as to be sure, in the long run, to command public support."

Able Men must "wait their Turn"

Shortly before the Royal Commission had made this recommendation, in words which seemed to place the responsibility for past failure to promote by merit, on the permanent officers of the Departments, as distinguished from the political heads of the Departments, the Ministers, Mr. Raikes, the Postmaster General, and the representative in the House of Commons of the University of Cambridge, had refused to accept the advice of the Permanent Secretary of the Post Office, Mr. S. A. Blackwood, in filling a post of some importance in the Secretary's office. On March 1, 1887, the Postmaster General, Mr. Raikes, in reply to questions put to him in the House of Commons, said: "...It is also the fact that I have recently declined to adopt the Secretary's recommendation to promote to the first class [in the Secretary's office] one of the junior officers in the second class over the heads of several clerks of much longer standing. The gentleman whom I have promoted was, in my judgment, fully qualified for promotion, and was senior clerk in the class, with the exception of one officer who, on the Secretary's recommendation, has been passed over on sixteen occasions…. What was I asked to do? I was asked to promote a gentleman who was much lower down in the class, a gentleman who was third or fourth in the class, and to place him over the heads of his colleagues. This I declined to do. I made inquiries in the office, and I found that the gentleman who was promoted was a meritorious officer who had discharged his duties with adequate ability, and therefore I thought there was no reason for promoting over his head and over the heads of one or two other competent officers, a junior officer who could well afford to wait his turn. I acted in the interests of the Public Service, and especially in the interests of the Department itself."[285]

No Post Office official in the United Kingdom has power to make a promotion. No one has power to do more than recommend for promotion. Each recommendation for promotion is examined by the surveyor, and is then sent to headquarters, where "a most vigilant check is always exercised, not from the suspicion that there has been favoritism, but in order to secure that favoritism shall not be practised."[286] Ultimately the Postmaster General passes upon every recommendation. Sometimes the action of the Postmaster General is merely formal, and is limited to the mere affixing of the Postmaster General's signature to the recommendation made by the permanent officers of the Department; at other times it is independent, and is preceded by careful consideration of the case by the Postmaster General himself. Whether or not the Postmaster General shall give his personal attention to a recommendation for promotion, is determined largely by the presence or absence of the political element, that is, the temper of the House of Commons. The Postmaster General is not a mere executive officer with a single aim: the efficient administration of his Department. He is first of all an important Minister, that is, one of the aids of the Prime Minister in keeping intact the party following. He must know to a nicety how any given administrative act in the Post Office will affect his party's standing, first in Parliament, and then among the constituents of the Members of Parliament. It is true that no British Postmaster General would convert the Post Office into a political engine for promoting the interests of his party; but it is equally true that no British Postmaster General would for a moment lose sight of the fact that Governments have not their being in either a vacuum or a Utopia, but that they live in a medium constituted of Members of Parliament and the constituents of Members of Parliament.

In the course of a protest against the Postmaster General being a Member of the House of Lords, Sir H. H. Fowler[287] recently said: "No man who has sat in the House of Commons for 10 years can be ignorant of the fact that there is a tone in the House; that there are occasions in the House when, in dealing with votes [of Supply] and administrative questions, a Minister is required, who, with his finger on the pulse of the House, can sweep away the red tape limits and deal with the questions at once on broad general public grounds." To make the statement complete, Sir H. H. Fowler should have added the words: "and grounds of political expediency." In the course of his reply to Sir H. H. Fowler, Mr. R. W. Hanbury, Financial Secretary to the Treasury and representative in the House of Commons of the Postmaster General, said: "When I undertook the representation of the Post Office in the House of Commons, the first rule I laid down was that [in replying to questions put by Members as to the administrative acts of the Post Office] I would take no answer from a permanent official, and that all answers [framed in the first instance by permanent officials] should be seen and approved by the Postmaster General [a Member of the House of Lords]. I also reserved to myself full discretion to alter the answers if I saw any necessity so to do."[288]

The Anxieties of Postmasters General

In 1896, before the Tweedmouth Committee, Mr. H. Joyce, Third Secretary to General Post Office, London, said: "I well remember Mr. Fawcett's[289] address to the head of a large Department [of the Post Office] who, ... having a large number of promotions to recommend, had told the officers concerned whom he had recommended, and whom he had not, and what made the matters worse, he had in his recommendations taken little account of seniority, whereas Mr. Fawcett, like Mr. Arnold Morley,[290] had a perfect horror of passing anyone over. I only saw Mr. Fawcett angry on two occasions, and that was one of them."[291] A moment before giving this testimony, Mr. Joyce had said: "It is always a matter of deep regret to the Postmaster General—every Postmaster General under whom I have served—when he is constrained to pass anyone over. I have seen Mr. Arnold Morley in the greatest distress on such occasions."[292] Again, in defending the action of the Post Office in promoting one Bocking, a second class sorting clerk at Norwich, over the heads of 15 men in his own class, and 8 men in the first class, to a full clerkship, Mr. Joyce said: "It is a matter of the greatest regret to the Postmaster General to feel constrained to pass over so many officers, all of whom were thoroughly respectable and zealous, and performed the duties on which they were employed very well, but the lamentable fact remains that they were not fit for a higher position; every endeavor was made at headquarters to what I might call squeeze them through, but it was no use." Mr. Badcock, Controller London Postal Service, corroborated this testimony with the words: "The statement is absolutely correct. The reports on which it was based can be produced."[293] In passing it may be added that in February, 1895, Mr. R. J. Price, M. P., for Norfolk, East, sought to intervene from the floor of the House of Commons in this case of promotion. In 1892 and 1895, Mr. Price had been returned to Parliament from Norfolk, East, with majorities of respectively 440 votes and 198 votes.

Still, again, at the Barry Dock Post Office, a branch office in Cardiff, one Arnold had been promoted from position number 9, by seniority, among the second class telegraph clerks, to a full clerkship, skipping class 1 of the telegraphists. Of this action, Mr. Joyce said: "It was a matter of great regret to the Postmaster General, as expressed at the time, to pass so many officers, many of them most deserving men, but above Mr. Arnold there was actually no one competent to fill this important post. Some had a knowledge of postal work, and some a knowledge of telegraph work, but none [beside Mr. Arnold] were conversant with work of both kinds, and some were otherwise objectionable. Barry Dock had suddenly shot into existence as a large town, which has now a population of about 13,000, and so painful was it to the

Postmaster General to pass over all these deserving officers, that, rather than do so, he seriously contemplated raising Barry Dock to the level of a post town, and giving it a separate establishment of its own."[294] Again, one Robinson was transferred from the Post Office at Pontefract to a clerkship in the office of Blackpool, being made to pass over the heads of two young men at Blackpool, by name of Eaton and Butcher. Mr. Joyce said: "The case was specially put before the Postmaster General, and with all his horror of passing people over, he decided that the two young men Eaton and Butcher were not qualified for promotion."[295]

<hr>

"A Strong Order"

In 1885, one Robinson, a postman at Liverpool, and number 210 in his class, was jumped to the position of assistant inspector. "He had, when a young postman, been selected by his inspector as a superior and promising officer. He had been temporarily employed [by way of tests] as assistant inspector, and had discharged the duties so efficiently that, on a vacancy occurring, he had been promoted to it." This case, as well as those previously mentioned, were cited as "grievances," before the Tweedmouth Committee, by the men selected by the Post Office employees to act as their spokesmen before the Committee. Lord Tweedmouth, chairman of the Committee, commenting on the case, said to Mr. Joyce: "Still, it seems to have been rather a strong order to appoint an assistant postman to such an office and to give him such a great promotion." Mr. Joyce replied: "Yes, it certainly does seem so; but for the position of inspector or assistant inspector of postmen there is no doubt that qualifications are required which are not ordinarily to be found in postmen.... For the positions of inspectors and assistant inspectors, I think I may say that the local authorities, and also headquarters, are more particular than they are about any other promotion, and they are most anxious to select actually the best man. In almost every other promotion, very great allowance is made for seniority; but in the case of inspectors it is not so, on account of the somewhat rare qualities required of inspectors, and because the post is a most invidious one."[296]

The reader will note that in 1896 the Post Office employees were complaining of a promotion made in 1885.

| The Ablest Man in the Sheffield Office

It was established before the Tweedmouth Committee that in instances the Post Office employees, with the aid of Members of the House of Commons, have succeeded in forcing the Post Office to revoke promotions, or to promote men that have been passed over. For example, Mr. Joyce, Third Secretary, General Post Office, said: "Wykes is unquestionably a very able man—probably the ablest man in the Sheffield office—and it is quite true that he was promoted [from a second class sortership] to be an assistant superintendent; but for reasons quite unconnected with his ability and qualifications, that promotion has been cancelled. Having said that, I trust the Committee will not press me further upon the point, inasmuch as it is very undesirable that I should say more." Mr. Spencer Walpole, a Member of the Committee and the Secretary of the Post Office, added: "Except, perhaps, that the cancelling of that promotion had nothing to do with the evidence that has been quoted?" Mr. Joyce replied: "It had nothing to do with that; the matter is still in a certain sense *subjudice*."[297]

| An M. P. promotes Eleven Men

In 1887, one M'Dougall, a second class sorter in Liverpool, was made a first class sorter, being promoted over the heads of 14 men whom the Liverpool postmaster had reported to be "not qualified for the duties of the higher class." On March 31, 1887, Mr. Bradlaugh brought the matter up in the House of Commons, by means of a question addressed to the Postmaster General. He was not satisfied with the answer that the men passed over had been reported "not qualified for promotion."[298] Therefore, on June 6, 1887, in Committee of Supply, on the Post Office Vote, Mr. Bradlaugh again brought up the case of the 14 Liverpool sorters who had been passed over. He said he had personally investigated the qualifications of the men, and had found "that none of them warranted the answer given by the Postmaster General" [on March 31].[299] Mr. Bradlaugh also brought up the case of one Hegnett, who had been made assistant superintendent over the heads of 19 persons "who were his seniors by many years." Also the case of one Helsby, promoted over the heads of 11 persons. Also the case of one Miller, promoted over one

Richardson, "who had been acting as assistant superintendent for years with the salary of a Supervising Clerk only." Mr. Bradlaugh spoke of the Committee of Supply as "the only tribunal that can overrule the Postmaster General." On June 17, Mr. Bradlaugh again intervened on behalf of the 14 men who had been passed over.

Before the Tweedmouth Committee, Mr. F. T. Crosse, a sorting clerk at Bristol, and one of the spokesmen of the Post Office employees, said: "Macdougall, Liverpool, a second class sorting clerk, was promoted to the first class over the heads of 14 men, his seniors. Mr. Bradlaugh, M. P., brought the matter up in Parliament during the discussion on the Estimates. The result of Mr. Bradlaugh's intervention was that 11 of the 14 men passed over were promoted in a batch six months later."

Mr. Joyce, Third Secretary to General Post Office, London, said it was true that "very soon afterward," 11 of the 14 men were promoted.[300] "A great point was stretched" in favor of 5 of the 11 men. Those 5 men were technically called single duty men, and since 1881 no sorting clerk had been promoted to the first class [at Liverpool] who could not perform dual duty. Although these five men were single duty men, and therefore unable to rotate with others, which was a "great disability," they were promoted by reason of Mr. Bradlaugh's intervention.

In explanation of the Bradlaugh episode, it should be added, that dual duty men are those who are able to act as letter sorters as well as telegraphists; while single duty men are able to act only as sorters, or as telegraphists. In order to reap full advantage from the consolidation of the telegraph business with the Postal business, the Post Office for years has been seeking to induce as many as possible of its employees to make themselves competent to act both as sorters and as telegraphists. At offices where it would be particularly advantageous to have the men able to act both as sorters and as telegraphists, the Post Office has sought to establish the rule that no sorter or telegraphist shall be promoted to the first class, unless able to act both as sorter and as telegraphist.

Mr. Crosse was not the only witness before the Tweedmouth Committee whose testimony illustrated "the stimulus" conveyed by questions in the

House of Commons. Mr. C. J. Ansell, the representative of the second class tracers in London, stated that in 1891 two vacancies among the first class tracers in a London office had been left open for respectively 5 months and 8 months. He added: "In March, 1894, the Postmaster General's attention had to be called to this disgraceful state of affairs [by the tracers' union]. It required, however, the stimulus of a question in the House of Commons. We do not know how far the Postmaster General is responsible for this state of affairs, but it is only fair to state that his attention being drawn to this matter by the question, we were successful in getting those promotions ante-dated."[301]

The limitations upon the Postmaster General's power to promote men in accordance with the advice tendered him by his official advisers by no means is confined to the cases of promotion among the rank and file. For instance, it was established by the testimony given before the Tweedmouth Committee, that the Postmaster cannot freely promote, to offices of more importance, postmasters who show that they have more ability than is required to administer the offices over which they happen to preside. For if a postmaster proves to be not equal to the demands of his office, the Postmaster General cannot always remove him to a smaller office, promoting at the same time the more able man who happens to be in charge of the smaller office. The Department tries to meet the situation by sending to the aid of the relatively incompetent postmaster "a smart chief clerk," taking care, however, that the inefficient postmaster shall receive less than the full salary to which the volume of business of the office would entitle him. If that expedient fails, the Department will transfer the postmaster. Mr. Uren, postmaster at Maidstone, and President of the Postmasters' Association, even asserted that nothing short of misconduct would lead to the transfer of a postmaster.[302] It should be added, however, that Mr. Uren's testimony related to the small and medium sized places only, not to the larger cities.[303]

It must not be inferred, however, that the postmasters of the small and medium sized places appeared before the Tweedmouth Committee to demand unrestricted promotion by merit. On the contrary, with the great bulk of the public service of all descriptions,[304] they held that promotion is "slow and uncertain" and that the system of promotion by merit "is thoroughly uncertain in its practical working." They protested also against the uncertainty and inequality inseparable from the system of making postmasters' salaries dependent upon the volume of business done by the several and individual Post Offices. They held that no postmaster should be made to suffer by reason of the fact that he happened to be stationed in a town or city that was not growing, or was not growing so rapidly as were other cities. By way of relief from the foregoing "uncertainties" and "inequalities" they demanded a reorganization of the postal service which should secure to the postmasters regular annual increments of pay, and should "regularize" promotion.[305]

Rank and File Oppose Promotion by Merit

It will be remembered that the Royal Commission appointed to inquire into the Civil Establishments, 1888, expressed the belief: "that the certain advantages of promotion by merit to the most deserving men, and therefore to the public service, are so great as to be sure, in the long run, to command public support." But the fact remains that a large part of the rank and file of the British civil service is growing more and more intolerant of promotion by merit, and demands promotion by seniority. It will not accept as a fact the natural inequality of men; it asserts, with its cousins at the Antipodes, the Australasian civil servants, that it is the opportunity that makes the man, not the man that makes the opportunity. This impatience of the rank and file of the civil servants of promotion by merit was brought out in striking manner by many of the "grievances" cited by the men who appeared before the Tweedmouth Committee as the accredited representatives of the Post Office employees. Some of those allegations of grievance have just been recorded, but this matter is of sufficient importance to warrant the recording of still others.

Mr. Joseph Shephard, Chairman of the Metropolitan Districts Board of the Postal Telegraph Clerks' Association, complained before the Tweedmouth Committee that one West, who had entered the telegraph service as a learner in 1881, one month after one Ward had entered as a learner, in 1896 was receiving $640, whereas Ward was receiving only $550. It was true that Ward had "had the misfortune to fail in the needle examination," the first time he had tried to qualify as a telegraphist, but "that little failure" ought not to have made the difference which existed in 1896. Mr. Shephard also complained that one Morgan, after 14 years and 11 months of service, was receiving only $550, whereas one Kensington, after 14 years and 5 months of service, was receiving $670. He brushed aside as of no consequence, the fact that Kensington had "qualified" in four months, whereas Ward had taken twelve months to "qualify."[306]

One Richardson, a telegraphist, at his own request had been transferred from Horsham to East Grinstead, and thence to Redhill, because of the small chances of vacancies at the first two places. But the staff at Redhill was weak and therefore the Post Office could not follow its usual practice of promoting a man, "not because he is a good man, but because he is not a bad one," to use the words of Mr. J. C. Badcock, Controller London Postal Service.[307] The authorities had to promote the best man at Redhill, and thus Richardson was passed over. Mr. James Green, who appeared as the representative of the Postal Telegraph Clerks' Association, referred to Richardson's case as "the case of a learner who with some 5 years' service is, according to my information, sent here and there relieving, presumably as a sort of recompense, though what his future will be remains a mystery. What surprises me in this matter is the spirit of indifference displayed by the heads of our Department regarding the hopelessness of these learners' positions."[308] One J. R. Walker was an indoor messenger until October, 1893, when he was apprenticed a paid learner. Shortly before October, two lads had been brought in as paid learners; and, after a short service, they were appointed sorting clerks and telegraphists. They were promoted over Walker, because of their superior education and intelligence. Mr. Green, the representative of the Postal Telegraph Clerks' Association, admitted the superior education of the lads in question, but complained that they had been preferred to Walker.[309]

One Crompton, a letter sorting clerk at Liverpool, in his leisure moments had made himself a telegraph instrument, had taught himself to telegraph, and had acquired a considerable technical knowledge of electricity. He had attracted the attention of the superintending engineer at Liverpool; had been promoted, in 1886, to the office of the superintending engineer; and, by 1896, he had become one of the best engineers in the service. In 1896, Mr. Tipping, the accredited spokesman of the Postal Telegraphists' Association as well as of the Telegraph Clerks' Association, complained of the promotion of Crompton, which had occurred in 1886. He said: "It seems most unreasonable that men who have, in some cases, not the slightest acquaintance with telegraphic apparatus and methods of working, should be preferred to those whose whole period of service has been passed in immediate connection therewith. It is apparent that such an absence of method is open to very serious objections, and allows great freedom of choice to those upon whose recommendations the appointments are made. In order, therefore, to safeguard, on the one hand, the interests of the department, and, on the other, to encourage those members of the telegraph staff who desire, by energy and ability, to improve their official *status*, the following suggestions are humbly submitted: That vacancies for junior clerkships in the offices of the superintending engineers, and for clerks at relay stations, should be filled by open competitive examination, held under the control of the Civil Service Commissioners, and that telegraphists only be eligible."[310]

The Crompton episode shows what minute supervision over the administration of the Post Office the civil service unions seek to exercise. The same minute supervision was attempted as recently as 1903-04 by Mr. Nannetti, M. P. for the College Division of Dublin, and also a Member of the Corporation of Dublin, as well as a member of the Dublin Port and Docks Board.[311] On March 23, 1903, Mr. Nannetti spoke as follows, in the House of Commons: "I beg to ask the Postmaster General whether his attention has been directed to the fact that two female technical officers, appointed in connection with the recently introduced intercommunication switch system in London, were selected over the heads of seniors possessing equal qualifications, and whether, seeing that in one case the official selected was taught switching duties by a telegraphist who is now passed over, he will state the reason for the selection of these officers?" The Postmaster General, Mr. Austen Chamberlain, replied: "The honorable Member has been misinformed. There is no question of promoting or passing over any officer. All that has been done is to assign to particular duties, carrying no special rank or pay, two officers who were believed to be competent to perform them." On May 7, 1903, Mr. Nannetti followed up the question with another one, namely: "I beg to ask the Postmaster General whether his attention has been called to the fact that two women telegraphists were selected to perform technical duties in reference to the intercommunication switch in London, who were juniors in service and possessed of less technical qualifications than other women telegraphists who were passed over; and whether, seeing that, although official information was given that such selection was not a question of promotion and no special rank or pay would result, one of the two officers concerned has been appointed to a superior grade on account of her experience gained by being selected for these duties, he will explain why the more senior and experienced women were passed over in the first place?" The Postmaster General replied: "I have nothing to add to the answer I gave on March 23, beyond stating that the officer to whom he is supposed to refer has not been appointed to any superior grade. She has merely been lent temporarily to assist at the Central Telephone Exchange in work for which she has special qualifications."[312]

On April 19 and May 12, 1904, Mr. Nannetti again protested against the promotion of the woman in question to the position of first class assistant supervisor, saying: "This girl was appointed because she had strong friends at Court...." On the latter date Mr. Nannetti also intervened on behalf of a telegraphist at North Wall, whose salary had been reduced from $6 a week to $5, as well as on behalf of one Wood, who had been retired on a reduced pension, by way of punishment. The case of Wood, Mr. Nannetti had brought up in 1903, when the Post Office Vote was under discussion. For the purpose of bringing these several matters before the House, he now moved the reduction of the salary of the Postmaster General by $500.[313]

On March 16, 1903, Mr. Nannetti asked whether the statement of the Controller that there was not a man qualified for promotion in the [Dublin letter sorting] branch had had any influence "with the Department in the filling of a certain vacancy in the Dublin Post Office."[314] That question illustrated a type of intervention that suggests the possibility of Great Britain reaching the stage that has been reached in Australia, where Members of Parliament have been known to move reductions in the salaries of officers who had offended the rank and file by attempting to introduce businesslike methods and practices. If that stage ever is reached, there will be a great multiplication of cases like the following one. Before the Tweedmouth Committee appeared Mr. J. Shephard, Chairman Metropolitan Districts Board of Postal Clerks' Association, to champion the cause of Mr.——. Said Mr. Shephard: "I have it here on his word that his postmaster has recommended him for a vacant clerkship at the District Office. Mr.—— has served for many years under the eyes of this postmaster who recommends him for promotion, and I take it that that is full and sufficient evidence of Mr.——'s fitness to perform the duties of the clerk." Mr. J. C. Badcock, Controller London Postal Service, testified in reply that he had summoned the postmaster in question, who had admitted that Mr.—— had discharged "minor clerical duties" in a perfectly satisfactory manner, but that his recommendation that Mr.—— should be promoted to a clerkship, "was made more out of sympathy with the man than with any hope that he would be qualified to undertake the higher duties which he would have to succeed to if appointed to a clerkship."[315]

M. P.'s act in Advance

In March, 1887, Mr. Bradlaugh, M. P., intervened in the House of Commons on behalf of two telegraph clerks at Liverpool who feared they were about to be passed over in favor "of a young man who entered the Engineering Department nine months ago as a temporary foreman."[316]

In April, 1902, Captain Norton intervened on behalf of two letter sorters, R. H. Brown and H. Johnson, who feared they were going to be passed over in the filling of certain vacancies among the overseers.[317] In 1906, Captain

Norton was made a Junior Lord of the Treasury in the Campbell-Bannerman Liberal Government.

In March, 1903, Mr. M. Joyce, M. P. for Limerick as well as an Alderman, asked the Postmaster General:

"Whether it is his intention to promote a local official to the assistant superintendentship now vacant at the Limerick Post Office, and, if not, will he assign the reason…? May I ask whether the duties of this office have not been performed in the most satisfactory manner by a local officer during the absence of the assistant superintendent, and will he give this matter due consideration, as every class of the community would be pleased at such an appointment."[318]

In April, 1903, Mr. Shehan asked the Postmaster General: "Whether his attention has been directed to an application from Dennis Murphy, at present acting as auxiliary postman, for appointment to the vacant position of rural postman from Mill Street to Culler, County Cork; and whether, in view of the man's character and qualifications, he will consider the advisability of appointing him to the vacancy?"[319]

In February, 1903, Mr. Nannetti asked the Postmaster General "whether he is aware that a telegraphist named Mercer, of the Bristol Post Office, has applied for 160 vacant postmaster ships since 1894; whether, seeing that during these periods clerks of less service, experience, ability and salary have been the recipients of these positions, he will make inquiry into the case?"[320]

In July, 1899, Mr. O'Brien,[321] M. P. for Kilkenny, asked the Secretary to the Treasury, as representing the Postmaster General, "whether he is aware that a postman named Jackson, in Kilkenny, has been in the Post Office service over 20 years and that his wages at present are only 12s. per week; and whether Jackson was given the increment of 1s. 6d. per week fixed by the new wages scale which came into operation in April, 1897; and if not, whether he will cause inquiry to be made into the case, with the view of giving Jackson the wages to which he is entitled by the rules of the service?" Mr. R. W. Hanbury, Financial Secretary to the Treasury, replied: "The rural postman at Kilkenny to whom the Honorable Member refers was transferred, on June 19, to another walk at that place, carrying wages of 16s. a week. His previous duty was not sufficient to warrant higher wages than 12s. a week."[322]

In April, 1901, Sir George Newnes, M. P. for Swansea, protested against the promotion out of order, according to seniority, of one A. E. Samuel, a sorter and telegraphist at Swansea.[323] Sir George Newnes is the founder of George Newnes, Limited, proprietors *Strand Magazine*, *Tit-Bits*, etc.; and proprietor of the *Westminster Gazette*, the London evening newspaper of the Liberal Party.

In February and March, 1903, Mr. C. E. Schwann, M. P. for Manchester, protested against the promotion out of order of two men at Manchester, who had been respectively numbers 99 and 133 in their class.[324] Mr. Schwann is President of the Manchester Reform Club, and has been nine years President of the National Reform Union. He has held successively the offices of Secretary, Treasurer and President of the Manchester Liberal Association. In 1900 he was elected to Parliament by a majority of twenty-six votes.

In July, 1902, Mr. Keir Hardie asked the Financial Secretary to the Treasury: "Whether the overseer's vacancy in the South Eastern Metropolitan district, created by the death of Mr. Feldwick, and recently filled by a suburban officer, will now be restored to the town establishment, seeing that the appointment properly belongs to this establishment?" Mr. Austen Chamberlain replied: "The vacancy in question has been filled by the transfer of an overseer from a suburban office in the same postal district, but the vacancy thus created in the suburbs has been filled by the promotion of an officer in the town district office." In August, 1902, Mr. Keir Hardie asked the Financial Secretary to the Treasury: "Whether he is aware that the overseer's vacancy which occurred in the town establishment of the South Eastern Metropolitan District by the promotion of Mr. May to an inspectorship at another office, has been filled by the transfer of an officer in the suburban establishment, thus diverting a town vacancy to the suburbs; and whether, in view of the fact that the chances of promotion in the suburban establishments are 75 per cent. better than in the town establishment, he will cause the vacancy to be restored to the establishment in which it originally occurred?"

Mr. Austen Chamberlain replied: "The Postmaster General is aware of the effect of the promotion in question, and has already arranged that the balance of promotion shall be readjusted on an early opportunity by the transfer of a town [officer] to a suburban vacancy."[325]

A Member of the Select Committee on Post Office Servants, 1906

On March 24, 1905, Mr. Charles Hobhouse, M. P. for Bristol, asked the Postmaster General "why a number of men with unblemished character and with service ranging from 15 to 25 years have, in the recent promotions in the Bristol Post Office, been passed over in favor of a junior postman?" In 1906, Mr. Hobhouse was made a member of the Select Committee on Post Office Servants.[326]

On March 15, 1906,[327] Mr. Sloan, M. P. for Belfast, intervened on behalf of the men who had recently been passed over in the selection of three men to act as "provincial clerks" in the Post Office at Belfast.

On the same day, Mr. Sloan asked the Postmaster General "under what circumstances the junior head postman at Belfast is retained permanently on a regular duty while his seniors, equally capable men, are compelled to rotate on irregular duties with irregular hours."

On August 2, 1906, the Postmaster General, Mr. Sydney Buxton, replied to Mr. Sloan: "I cannot review cases of promotion decided by my predecessor eighteen months ago."

In 1905 Mr. Sloan had voted for a Select Committee on Postal Servants' Grievances.

The foregoing quotations could be extended indefinitely, but they illustrate sufficiently the several kinds of intervention in matters of mere administrative detail, as well as the high political and social standing of some of the Members of Parliament who lend themselves to those several kinds of intervention. But these quotations may not be brought to an end without mention of the qualifying fact that Lord Stanley, Postmaster General from 1903 to 1905, repeatedly stated in the House of Commons that he did "not select the senior men unless they were best qualified to do the work."[328]

FOOTNOTES:

273 *Third Report from the Select Committee on Civil Services Expenditure*, 1873; q. 4,193 to 4,206, and 4,267.

274 *Report from the Select Committee on Post Office (Telegraph Department)*, 1876; q. 3,122 to 3,125.

275 *Correspondence Relating to the Post Office Telegraph Department*: Letter of April 12, 1877, Postmaster General, Lord John Manners, to the Lords Commissioners of the Treasury.

276 *Report from the Select Committee on Post Office (Telegraph Department)*, 1876; q. 1,259.

277 *Report of the Bradford Committee on Post Office Wages*, 1904; q. 1,024 and 1,048.

278 Mr. Lowe, Chancellor of the Exchequer, divided the service into three classes, in such a way that it was difficult, if not impossible, to pass from one class to the other. That was done with the object of preventing individuals from bringing pressure on Members of Parliament for promotion from class to class.

279 Compare also: *Third Report from the Select Committee on Civil Services Expenditure*, 1873; q. 3,703 to 3,705, Mr. T. H. Farrer, Permanent Secretary of the Board of Trade. "The salt of the service is the staff appointments.... Since I have been in the Board of Trade there have been almost forty higher staff appointments, and on not more than four could I put my finger and say they had been made from any other motive than the desire to get the best man. On some occasions the good appointments have been made in the teeth of strong political motives to the contrary."

280 *Second Report of the Royal Commission appointed to inquire into the Civil Establishments*, 1888; q. 19,980, and 20,079 to 20,083.

281 *Second Report of the Royal Commission appointed to inquire into the Civil Establishments*, 1888; q. 17,564.

282 *Second Report of the Royal Commission appointed to inquire into the Civil Establishments*, 1888; q. 17,500, 20,141 to 20,149, 20,260, 20,262 and 20,338; and *First Report of the Royal Commission appointed to inquire into the Civil Establishments*, 1887, p. 424.

283 *Second Report of the Royal Commission appointed to inquire into the Civil Establishments*, 1888; q. 17,250 to 17,253.

284 *Second Report of the Royal Commission appointed to inquire into the Civil Establishments*, 1888; q. 20,253.

285 *Hansard's Parliamentary Debates*, March 1, 1887, p. 890; March 7, p. 1,400; May 12, p. 1,723; and April 4, p. 456.

286 *Report of the Inter-Departmental Committee on Post Office Establishments*, 1897; q. 12,152 to 12,154, Mr. H. Joyce, Third Secretary to General Post Office. Compare also: q. 131 and 7,891, and Appendix, p. 1,068.

Extract from the "Postmaster's Book of Instructions," p. 105. "Except to clerkships of first class, all promotions from class to class, whether in the Major or Minor Establishments, are governed by seniority, combined with full competency and good character. Thus, on a vacancy occurring in a higher class, not being the first class of clerks, recommend for promotion that officer of highest standing [according to seniority] in the class next below who is qualified for the efficient performance of the duties of the higher class, and has conducted himself with diligence, propriety and attention in his present class to your satisfaction. If on the other hand you feel it incumbent on you to recommend some officer other than the one of highest standing [according to seniority] in his class, furnish a tabular statement after the following specimens, giving the names and dates of appointment of those you propose to pass over, and your reasons. These reasons must be stated with precision in the column set apart for observations. Such entries as: 'Scarcely qualified,' 'has not given satisfaction,' being insufficient in so important a matter."

287 *Who's Who*, 1905, Fowler, Rt. Hon. Sir H. H., M. P. (L.), Wolverhampton, 1880 to 1900, and since 1900; Under Secretary Home Department, 1884-85; Financial Secretary to Treasury, 1886; President Local Government Board, 1892-94; Secretary of State for India, 1894-95.

288 *Hansard's Parliamentary Debates*, April 27, 1900, p. 128, Sir H. H. Fowler, and Mr. R. W. Hanbury.

289 Mr. Fawcett, Postmaster General.

290 Mr. Arnold Morley, Postmaster General, 1892-95; Chief Liberal Whip, 1886-1892.

291 *Report of the Inter-Departmental Committee on Post Office Establishments*, 1897; q. 12,220.

292 *Report of the Inter-Departmental Committee on Post Office Establishments*, 1897; q. 12,158. Compare, for example, *Hansard's Parliamentary Debates*, September 18, 1893. Mr. A. Morley, Postmaster General, states that 10 men had been passed over, after having been found wanting upon a trial on higher duties. He added: "I am, however, making further inquiries."

293 *Report of the Inter-Departmental Committee on Post Office Establishments*, 1897; q. 12,180, and Appendix, p. 1,110.

294 *Report of the Inter-Departmental Committee on Post Office Establishments*, 1897; q. 12,205.

295 *Report of the Inter-Departmental Committee on Post Office Establishments*, 1897; q. 12,184 and 12,185.

296 *Report of the Inter-Departmental Committee on Post Office Establishments*, 1897; q. 12,230 and 12,239.

297 *Report of the Inter-Departmental Committee on Post Office Establishments*, 1897; q. 12,182 and 5,629.

298 *Hansard's Parliamentary Debates*, March 31, 1883, p. 55.

299 *Hansard's Parliamentary Debates*, June 6, 1887, p. 1,081 and following.

300 *Report of the Inter-Departmental Committee on Post Office Establishments*, 1897; q. 5,603 and 12,160 to 12,162.

301 *Report of the Inter-Departmental Committee on the Post Office Establishments*, 1897; q. 6,983.

302 *Report of the Inter-Departmental Committee on the Post Office Establishments*, 1897; Mr. J. G. Uren, President Postmasters' Association; q. 12,493 and following; and Mr. E. B. L. Hill, Assistant Secretary General Post Office; q. 15,450.

303 "But I do not think I ought to conceal the fact that the majority of our members are the postmasters of small and medium sized places who have very likely got, according to our ideas, more grounds for grievance than the postmasters of larger towns."

304 That the peculiar demands and ideals described in these chapters are by no means confined to the Post Office employees, is shown by the subjoined quotation from a Treasury Minute of March, 1891, relative to an Inquiry by the Chancellor of the Exchequer, and the Financial Secretary to the Treasury into the Administration of the Outdoor Department of the Customs Revenue Department, to wit: "Besides the alleged loss of promotion through a reduction in the higher appointments, and the various arrangements by which they considered that they were injured in their emoluments or as to the hours of working, the officers of all grades complained of the existing system of promotion. They contended that it was unfair and fortuitous in its operation, and did not pay sufficient regard to seniority."—*Report of the Inter-Departmental Committee on the Post Office Establishments*, 1897; q. 12,577.

305 *Report of the Inter-Departmental Committee on the Post Office Establishments*, 1897. Testimony of the representatives of the Postmasters' Association: Mr. J. G. Uren, Mr. W. E. Carrette (Queenstown), Mr. John Macmaster; and Appendix, p. 1,127.

306 *Report of the Inter-Departmental Committee on Post Office Establishments*, 1897, Mr. Joseph Shephard; q. 3,117 to 3,126, and testimony of Mr. J. C. Badcock, Controller London Postal Service.

307 *Report of the Inter-Departmental Committee on Post Office Establishments*, 1897; q. 1,614.

308 *Report of the Inter-Departmental Committee on Post Office Establishments*, 1897; q. 15,219, Mr. Lewin Hill, Assistant Secretary General Post Office, London; and 5,290, Mr. Jas. Green.

309 *Report of the Inter-Departmental Committee on Post Office Establishments*, 1897; q. 15,217, Mr. Lewin Hill, Assistant Secretary General Post Office, London; and 5,282 to 5,284, Mr. Jas. Green.

310 *Report of the Inter-Departmental Committee on Post Office Establishments*, 1897; q. 15,097, Mr. W. H. Preece, Engineer-in-Chief at the Post Office; and 4,876, Mr. E. J. Tipping.

311 *Who's Who*, 1905.

312 *Hansard's Parliamentary Debates*, March 23, 1903, p. 1,464; and May 7, 1903, p. 27.

313 *Hansard's Parliamentary Debates*, April 9, and May 12, 1904, p. 1,239 and 1,246 to 1,268.

314 *Hansard's Parliamentary Debates*, March 16, 1903, p. 856.

315 *Report of the Inter-Departmental Committee on the Post Office Establishments*, 1897; q. 3,214 and 4,206.

316 *Hansard's Parliamentary Debates*, March 10, 1887, p. 1,733.

317 *Hansard's Parliamentary Debates*, April 24, 1902, p. 1,189.

318 *Hansard's Parliamentary Debates*, March 9, 1903, p. 113.

319 *Hansard's Parliamentary Debates*, April 7, 1903, p. 1,242.

320 *Hansard's Parliamentary Debates*, February 24, 1903, p. 670.

321 *Who's Who*, 1905, O'Brien, P., M. P. since 1886; mechanical and marine engineer. In 1895 Mr. O'Brien had been elected to Parliament by a majority of fourteen votes.

322*Hansard's Parliamentary Debates*, July 3, 1899.

323 *Hansard's Parliamentary Debates*, April 22, 1901, p. 919.

324 *Hansard's Parliamentary Debates*, February 25, 1903, p. 803; and March 9, 1903, p. 108.

325 *Hansard's Parliamentary Debates*, July 10, 1902, p. 1,359; and August 8, 1902, p. 1,102.

326 *Who's Who*, 1905, Hobhouse, C. E. H., M. P. (R.), East Bristol since 1900; Recorder of Wills since 1901. Education: Eton; Christ Church, Oxford. M. P. (L), East Wilts, 1892-95; private secretary at Colonial Office, 1892-95; County Alderman, Wilts, 1893 to present time. Clubs: Brooks', Naval and Military.

327 *Hansard's Parliamentary Debates*, March 15, 1906.

328 *Hansard's Parliamentary Debates*, April 28, 1904, p. 1,428; April 14, and May 12, 1904, p. 1,253.

CHAPTER XVI
MEMBERS OF THE HOUSE OF COMMONS INTERVENE ON BEHALF OF PUBLIC SERVANTS WHO HAVE BEEN DISCIPLINED

Evidence presented before: The Royal Commission appointed
to inquire into the Civil Establishments, 1888; and the
Tweedmouth Committee, 1897. Instances of intervention by
Members of Parliament. Mr. Austen Chamberlain, Financial
Secretary to the Treasury, in April, 1902, states that at a low
estimate one-third of the time of the highest officials in the
Post Office is occupied with petty questions of discipline and
administrative detail, because of the intervention of Members
of Parliament. He adds that it is "absolutely deplorable" that
time and energy that should be given to the consideration of
large questions must be given to matters that "in any private
business would be dealt with by the officer on the spot." Sir
John Eldon Gorst's testimony before the Committee on
National Expenditure, 1902.

M. P.'s and the Rank and File

In 1888, Mr. Harvey, a Member of the Royal Commission appointed to
inquire into the Civil Establishments, asked Sir S. A. Blackwood, Secretary to
the Post Office since 1880: "Now I should like to ask you ... whether you
consider there is a distinct tendency among the clerical establishments [*i. e.*,
the clerks above the rank and file], especially the lower division clerks, to
develop what for want of a better term I will call trades union spirit?" "Yes, I
believe there is a good deal of evidence of that." "Have you, yourself, found it
difficult to deal with that; is it a factor in your administration [of the Post
Office]?" "Not with regard to the lower division clerks [above the rank and
file]; it is with regard to the subordinate ranks of the service, the rank and file;
amongst them there is a very strong tendency in that direction." "A growing

tendency?" "It is certainly growing." "A growing tendency then we may say to introduce the coöperation of Members of Parliament to deal with individual grievances?" "A very strongly growing tendency." At this point Mr. Lawson interrupted: "Individual or class grievances?" "Class grievances, but there are a great many instances in which individual grievances are brought forward [by Members of Parliament]." "The point of the question was whether this spirit of trades unionism was evoked for the sake of bringing forward individual grievances, and you said yes; and then I asked whether it was class grievances or individual grievances?" "I mean class grievances, but it is made use of in respect of individual grievances." Mr. Harvey resumed: "And you think it is growing?" "I think it is strongly growing." "So we may say, to repeat the question I put just now, that it makes a factor in your administration of the Post Office, and you have always to be prepared to meet this growing tendency?" "It is continuously raising difficulties, and very serious ones."

Mr. Lawson queried: "You said something about trades unionism; do you think it is possible by any regulation to stop trades unionism of a great class such as the senior division, or the classes which are the subordinate part of your establishment?" "I think it would be very difficult." "You would have to reckon with that as a permanent factor?" "Yes."[329]

This intervention on behalf of individual employees is managed as follows. Members of Parliament first interview the Postmaster General; if they fail to obtain satisfaction, they bring the grievance of their constituent before the House of Commons, by means of a question addressed in the House to the Postmaster General. It will be remembered that Mr. Hanbury, Financial Secretary to the Treasury, in 1900 stated that he had agreed to represent the Postmaster General in the House of Commons only on condition that he should be given full freedom to answer such questions in any way he saw fit, and that he should not be bound by any answers furnished him either by the permanent officers of the Post Office or by the Postmaster General. And that Sir H. H. Fowler protested against the Postmaster General sitting in the House of Lords, on the ground that the questions asked by Members of the House of Commons often demanded to be answered by a man who had his finger on the pulse of the House, and was able to cut through the red tape of officialism on public grounds, which meant, to set aside the rules of the Department in response to the exigencies of political expediency.

If the answer given by the Postmaster General is unsatisfactory, the Member of Parliament gives notice that he will bring the matter up again on the discussion of the Estimates of Expenditure. In the meantime he brings to bear, behind the scenes, what pressure he can command. And he often learns to appreciate the grim humor of the reply once given by a former Minister of Railways in Victoria, Australia, to a Victorian Royal Commission, to the query whether political influence was exercised in the administration of the State railways of Victoria. The reply had been: "I should like to know how you can have a politician without political influence?"

Of course not all cases of intervention by Members of Parliament are as successful as was the intervention of Mr. Bradlaugh, which resulted in the promotion of eleven men out of fourteen who had been passed over as "not qualified for promotion," or, as was the intervention of the Member of Parliament whose name was not revealed, which brought about the revocation of the promotion of the ablest man in the Post Office at Sheffield. Indeed, the principal effect of these interventions is not to force the Post Office to retrace steps already taken, it is to prevent the Post Office from taking certain steps. These interventions modify the entire administration of the British Post Office. They compel the Postmaster General and his leading officers to consider the political aspect of every proposal coming from the local postmasters, and other intermediate officers, be it a proposal to promote, to pass over, to discipline, or to dismiss. It was this possibility of intervention by Members of Parliament, acting under pressure from civil servants' unions, that gave the late Mr. Fawcett "a perfect horror of passing over," that caused Mr. Arnold Morley "the greatest distress" whenever he had to pass anyone over, and that led Mr. Raikes to state in the House of Commons, that, "in the interests of the Public Service, and especially in the interests of the Post Office itself," he had declined to follow the advice of his officers that he promote a certain clerk in the Secretary's Office; as well as that he made it his practice to try to mitigate the rules of the Department governing punishment and dismissal. It was with the thought of Parliamentary intervention in mind, that Mr. Austen Chamberlain,[330] Postmaster General, said, in February, 1903: "The selection of officers for promotion is always an invidious task."

The testimony given before the Tweedmouth Committee, 1897, contains a number of incidents which show how leniently the Post Office Department is obliged to deal with men who violate the rules. These incidents were brought before the Committee by the representatives of the employees of the Post Office, for the purpose of proving by individual cases, that the Department's rulings were unduly severe, and afforded just cause for grievance.

One Webster, a letter carrier at Liverpool, in July, 1883, failed to cover his whole walk, and brought back to the office, letters which he should have delivered. These letters he surreptitiously inserted among the letters of other carriers. Mr. Herbert Joyce, Third Secretary to General Post Office, said dismissal would not have been harsh punishment for the offence; but Webster was merely deprived of one good conduct stripe, worth 25 cents a week. In 1884 and 1885 Webster's increment of salary was arrested for unsatisfactory conduct. In July, 1886, Webster was removed from his walk, and reduced to the "junior men" on the "relief force," for having been under the influence of drink while on duty. In 1890, Webster complained to headquarters of harsh treatment, stating that though he had served 15 years, he had not received three good conduct stripes. And in 1896, Mr. J. S. Smith, the official representative of the provincial postmen, deemed it expedient to cite the case to the Tweedmouth Committee in the course of an argument to the effect that there was too great a difference "between the punishment meted out to postmen and the punishment meted out to sorters; not that I say the punishment is too slight for sorters, but it is, I might say, too severe for postmen," It may be added that, in 1896, Webster was recommended for three good conduct stripes, though the regulation says that a good conduct stripe shall be awarded only for five clear and consecutive years of good conduct. Non-observance of that regulation led the Tweedmouth Committee to report: "The practice which has grown up in the Department of awarding two stripes at the same time to a man whose service exceeds 10 years, but whose unblemished service extends over only 5 years, is, we think, a bad one, and should be discontinued."[331]

The foregoing recommendation of the Tweedmouth Committee was not endorsed by the Government. On March 13, 1906, the Postmaster General, Mr. Sydney Buxton, in reply to Mr. Thomas Smyth, M. P., who was intervening on behalf of one Thomas Reilly, said: "I find that Thomas Reilly would have been entitled to an increase of one shilling and six pence a week in his wages as from April 1, 1905, if his conduct during the preceding twelve months had been satisfactory. Unfortunately the necessary certificate to that effect could not be given, but the question of granting the increase to Reilly will come up again for consideration shortly.... It will be necessary to postpone for a time the award of a second stripe."[332]

In October, 1895, one Roberts, an auxiliary postman was warned that he would be dismissed unless his conduct improved. He had been reported for "treating parcel receptacles in a rough and reckless manner, and smashing the parcels." In November, 1895, he altered the address on a parcel in order to save himself the trouble of delivering the parcel on the day on which he made the alteration. The parcel was given to a carrier on another route, who returned it as not deliverable. After some delay the parcel finally was delivered by Roberts. When Mr. S. Walpole, Secretary of the Post Office, heard this testimony, he exclaimed: "And was Roberts dismissed on the spot?" Mr. Badcock, Controller London Postal Service, replied: "No. The overseer described him as totally unreliable, and he was warned for the last time." Mr. Walpole continued: "Why was he not dismissed?" Mr. Badcock replied: "Well, he ought to have been." In January, 1896, Roberts was again cautioned; on February 24, 1896, he failed to attend his morning duty; and he was seriously cautioned again. In March, 1896, he was guilty of "gross carelessness," and was told to look for other employment. Thereupon Roberts wrote his postmaster that he was a member of the Postmen's Federation. Shortly afterward, Mr. Churchfield, Secretary of the Postmen's Federation, brought Roberts' case before the Tweedmouth Committee, alleging that the Post Office Department had dismissed Roberts because he had supplied evidence to the representatives of the postal employees who had appeared before the Tweedmouth Committee.[333]

In 1878, one Woodhouse, a postman at Norwich, was suspended for two days for irregular attendance, having been late 42 times in three months. In

1880, he was suspended for three days, having been late 173 times during the year. Woodhouse also had been very troublesome to the inspector, setting a bad example to the younger men. In 1882, he was absent from duty because of intoxication, was grossly insubordinate to the local postmaster, whom he set at defiance, and also grossly insubordinate to the surveyor. The local postmaster recommended that he be dismissed. "At headquarters, however, with a large, and some people think a very undue, leniency, it was decided to give him one more trial." In 1889, Woodhouse was cautioned by the postmaster for insubordinate conduct to the inspector. In 1891 and 1892, the postmaster refused to recommend him for good conduct stripes. In 1894 there was a marked improvement in Woodhouse's conduct. The improvement was maintained, and in 1896, Woodhouse was recommended for good conduct stripes. Of this man, Mr. J. S. Smith, the official representative of the provincial postmen, said, in 1896, before the Tweedmouth Committee: "The last 17 or 18 years of Woodhouse's career have been of a most exemplary description, a good time-keeper and zealous in the discharge of his duties, and yet, though he had been a postman for 25 years, he has never been the recipient of a good conduct stripe. By this means he has been deprived of about $450, truly a great loss for a postman to suffer through having this vast sum deducted from his wages. It needs no words of mine to point out the great injustice that has been inflicted upon Woodhouse. Any little irregularity that may have occurred (such as bad time-keeping, which is admitted) in the first 7 or 8 years of his service, has been amply atoned for by 17 or 18 years' punctuality and excellent behavior."[334]

In November, 1895, a letter carrier at Manchester came "under the influence of drink," and reached at 3.50 p. m. a point in his walk which he should have reached at 2.30 p. m. "On the following day he was again under the influence of drink and unfit to make his delivery." The punishment was the deprivation of one good conduct stripe.[335]

In December, 1895, a postman at Newcastle, while off duty, but in uniform, "was reeling along [one of the principal streets] intoxicated at 3 p. m." The case was sent up to the Postmaster General, who decided that the man should lose one good conduct stripe. Mr. Spencer Walpole, a member of the

Tweedmouth Committee, and the Permanent Secretary to the Post Office, said dismissal would not have been too severe a punishment; and Mr. H. Joyce, Third Secretary General Post Office, London, assented to the statement.[336]

Mr. Badcock, Controller London Postal Service, in replying to the testimony of Mr. A. F. Harris, the official representative of the London postmen, said that it was true that while one Worth for some years past had off and on been made an acting head postman, he had not been recommended for promotion to the position of head postman, because his postmaster had reported that he was "shifty, unreliable, and careless." Mr. Walpole, Secretary of the Post Office, thereupon queried: "Is that not a reason for not employing him to act as head postman?" Mr. Badcock replied: "It was thought better to give him a chance, instead of letting him have the grievance of complaining that he had not had an opportunity of showing whether he was qualified." Mr. Walpole continued: "But if he showed himself shifty, unreliable, and careless for several years, ought not his trial as a head postman to cease?" Mr. Badcock replied: "I must confess that I think so."[337]

In February, 1887, Mr. Marum intervened in the House of Commons on behalf of one Ward, a telegraphist, who had been dismissed in 1876 because he had discharged his duties unsatisfactorily.[338]

In February, 1888, Mr. Lawson, a Member of the Royal Commission appointed to inquire into the Civil Establishments, intervened on behalf of one Harvey, a letter carrier who had been dismissed in 1882.[339]

In March, 1901, Mr. Bartley[340] intervened on behalf of one Canless, who had been dismissed because the Postmaster General "was of the opinion that Mr. Canless was not a fit person to be retained in the service." On dismissing the man, the Post Office had deducted from his pay the value of a postal money order—$2.25—alleged to have been stolen by him.[341] Canless' case was brought up again in August, 1904, upon the occasion of the debate upon the Report of the Bradford Committee.

In July, 1897, Mr. C. Seale-Hayne intervened on behalf of one J. C. Kinsman, dismissed for insubordination and delegation of his duties to unauthorized persons.[342]

In August, 1903, Mr. Sloan, M. P. for Belfast, intervened on behalf of one Templeton, of the Belfast Post Office, dismissed for emptying ink on the head of a workman engaged in the Post Office.[343]

In March, 1905, Mr. John Campbell, M. P., tried to induce the Postmaster General to reopen the case of one M'Cusker, who had been disciplined in 1897.[344]

In April, 1899, Mr. Lenty asked for a pension for one Wright, whose "conduct had been such as to render him unfit for further employment in the public service."[345]

In August, 1902, Mr. Crean asked for a pension for W. H. Allshire, "Who was reported for certain irregularities for which he would probably have been dismissed. While the matter was under consideration he sent in his resignation, which was accepted."[346]

In August, 1903, Mr. L. Sinclair intervened on behalf of B. J. Foreman, "who was not qualified for the award of a pension, as he was neither 60 years of age nor incapacitated from the performance of his duty" when his service was terminated.[347]

In March, 1891, Earl Compton intervened on behalf of a first class sorter who had been reduced to the second class after having been sentenced to a fine by a Police Magistrate.[348]

In December, 1893, Mr. Keir Hardie asked the Postmaster General to modify the rules governing fines for being late at duty. In February, 1899, Mr. Maddison made a similar request.[349]

In October, 1902, Mr. Palmer intervened on behalf of some "learners" at Reading, who had been punished "for careless performance of their duties, leading to serious delay in the delivery of telegrams."[350] Mr. Palmer, a biscuit manufacturer, was the Member for Reading. In the past he had been an Alderman as well as the Mayor of Reading.

In July, 1901, Mr. Groves intervened on behalf of a postman at Manchester from whom annual increments of pay had been withheld under the rules governing irregular attendance.[351] Mr. Groves is Chairman of the South Salford Conservative Association.

In April, 1900, Mr. Steadman said: "I honestly admit that this question business might be overdone; but at the same time, if anyone, postman or anyone else, thinks I can do his case any good by putting down a question, I shall always do so as long as I am a Member of this House." Mr. Steadman proved as good as his boast; and in July, 1900, he intervened on behalf of a man from whom the Post Office Department had withheld two good conduct stripes "because he had absented himself frequently on insufficient plea of illness." Mr. Steadman stood ready to shield any malingerer who might apply to him, though malingering is a serious evil in the Post Office service. For example, in 1901 the average number of days' absence on sick-leave was 7.6 days for the men in that part of the staff that receives full pay during sick-leave, as against 5.2 days for the men in that part of the staff that receives only half-pay during sick-leave.[352] Mr. Steadman had been elected to Parliament by a majority of 20 votes. He is at present a Member of the London County Council.[353]

In June, 1906, Mr. Sydney Buxton, who had become Postmaster General, upon the formation of the Sir Henry Campbell-Bannerman Ministry, in December, 1905, expressed himself as follows:[354] "He was informed a little while ago by his private secretary that in the ordinary way 60 or 70 applications of various sorts were made by honorable Members in the course of a calendar month, but that for some months past, in consequence perhaps of there being a new Government, a new Parliament, new Members, and a new Postmaster General, the number of applications of all sorts had amounted to between 300 and 400 per month."

A Member of the Select Committee on Post Office Servants, 1906

In May, 1906, Mr. J. Ward, a Member of the Select Committee on Post Office Servants, 1906, asked the Postmaster General "whether his attention had been called to the dismissal of E. C. Feasey, of Walsall, who had been an efficient officer in the postal service for 17 years … and whether he will reconsider the question of the man's reinstatement?" Mr. Buxton replied: "I have looked into the circumstances connected with the dismissal by my predecessor of E. C. Feasey, formerly a town postman at Walsall. I find that Feasey had a most unsatisfactory record…. I am not prepared to consider the question of reinstatement."[355]

In March, 1906, the Postmaster General, in reply to Mr. Nannetti, M. P., said: "The Reports and statements in the Corcoran case were fully considered at the time [1901], and I can see no good purpose in reopening the matter after a lapse of five years."[356]

In April, 1906, Mr. Wiles,[357] M. P., intervened on behalf of the head messenger in the Secretary's Office at the General Post Office, London. Under the administration of Lord Stanley, Postmaster General, an allowance of 4 shillings a week given the head messenger at the time of his appointment, had been withheld from October, 1900, to October, 1905. Mr. Sydney Buxton replied: "I have already had this case under my consideration. The allowance of 4 shillings a week is being granted, but unfortunately the allowance cannot be made retrospective."

Mr. Wiles had been elected to Parliament in January, 1906, having defeated Sir Albert K. Rollit, who, for many years, had made a specialty of championing the cause of Post Office employees who had a grievance.

Deplorable Waste of Executive Ability

In April, 1902, Mr. Austen Chamberlain, Financial Secretary to the Treasury, and representative in the House of Commons of the Postmaster General, the Marquis of Londonderry, said: "In a great administration like this there must be decentralization, and how difficult it is to decentralize, either in the Post Office or in the Army, when working under constant examination by question and answer in this House, no honorable Member who has not had experience of official life can easily realize. But there must be decentralization, because every little petty matter cannot be dealt with by the Postmaster General or the Permanent Secretary to the Post Office. Their attention should be reserved in the main for large questions, and I think it is deplorable, absolutely deplorable, that so much of their time should be occupied, as under the present circumstances it necessarily is occupied, with matters of very small detail, because these matters of detail are asked by honorable Members, and because we do not feel an honorable Member will accept an answer from anyone but the highest authority. I think a third of the time—I am putting it at a low estimate—of the highest officials in the Post Office is occupied in answering questions raised by Members of this House, and in providing me with information in order that I may be in a position to answer the inquiries addressed to me" concerning matters which, "in any private business, would be dealt with by the officer on the spot, without appeal or consideration unless grievous cause were shown."[358]

In March, 1903, Mr. Austen Chamberlain, Postmaster General, read the following Post Office Rule: "A postmaster is to address to his surveyor, and a subordinate officer is to address to the postmaster (who will forward it to his surveyor), any application from himself having reference to his duties or pay, or any communications he may desire to make relating to official matters; and if the applicant is dissatisfied with the result he may appeal direct to the Postmaster General. But it is strictly forbidden to make any such application or other communication through the public, or to procure one to be made by Members of Parliament, or others; and should an irregular application be received, the officer on whose behalf it is made will be subject to censure or punishment proportionate to the extent of his participation in the violation of the rule." Mr. Chamberlain added: "But it has been my practice [as well as that of Mr. Chamberlain's predecessors] to treat the rule as applying only to applications so made in the first instance, and I have raised no objection to an officer who had appealed to me, and was dissatisfied with my decision, applying subsequently to a Member of Parliament."[359]

The Post Office is not the only British Department of State which is obliged to consider with care how far it may go counter to individual interests in enforcing rules and standards adopted for the preservation of the public interest.

Before the Select Committee on National Expenditure, 1902, Sir John Eldon Gorst, M. P., and Vice-President of the Committee of Council on Education, 1895 to 1902, said: "What I want to impress upon the Committee is that Parliament has never an influence which goes for economy of any kind in the expenditure of public money on education [about $40,000,000 a year]. Then I hope I have now shown the Committee that the only security the public has that what it spends will be efficiently spent is the system of inspection. Earlier in my evidence I also pointed out the two systems which are in vogue for inspection, namely the South Kensington system and the Whitehall system. The Whitehall system, which deals with the larger amount of public money, is extremely inefficient. The Elementary Education Inspectors have before their eyes the fear, first of all, of the managers of the schools which they visit. The managers of the schools are often important School Boards like the School Board of London, which is not a body to be trifled with, which has very great influence, both in Parliament and in the Education Department, and which the Inspectors are very much afraid of offending. But it is not only powerful School Boards, but any managers [of schools] can take the matter up. If an Inspector goes into a school and sees [reports] that the children are dirty, or that the school is dirty, or that the teacher is inefficient, the manager is up in arms at once, and writes a letter to the Board of Education, and comes up and sees the Secretary, and protests against the Inspector for having dared to make an unfavorable report of his or her school. Besides that, the Inspectors have before their eyes the fear of the National Union of Teachers. Almost every teacher now is a member of the National Union of Teachers, and if an Inspector is supposed to be severe, a teacher complains at once to the National Union, and the case is taken up, possibly even in Parliament, by some of the officials of the National Union of Teachers in Parliament, and it is made very uncomfortable for the Inspector. Then, lastly, they [*i. e.*, the Inspectors] have the office—that is not, say, their own Chief Inspector, but the officials of the office, who do not like an Inspector who makes trouble. The great art of an Inspector is to get on well with the managers [of schools] and teachers, and to make no trouble at all. I have known cases of adverse reports which were not liked at the office being sent back to the Inspector to alter," not by the Chief Inspector, or Senior

Inspector of the District, but by some other person in the office.[360]

Sir John Eldon Gorst was Solicitor-General in 1885-86, Under Secretary for India in 1886 to 1891, Financial Secretary to the Treasury in 1891-92, Deputy Chairman of Committees of the House of Commons in 1888 to 1891, and Vice-President of Council on Education in 1885 to 1902. He was a Member of the House of Commons in 1866 to 1868, and has been a member continuously since 1875. Since 1892 he has sat as representative of the University of Cambridge.

Sir John Eldon Gorst was by no means unwilling to take his share of blame for the mismanagement in the various Departments of State arising out of the intervention of the House of Commons—under pressure from the constituencies, or organized groups in the constituencies—in the administrative details of the Departments of State. He said: "I have been as great a sinner as anyone in the days when I represented Chatham,[361] before I was a Member of the Government; I was perpetually urging the Secretary of the Admiralty for the time being to increase the expenditures at the dockyards"[362] [in the interest of the laborers in the dockyards and of the merchants and manufacturers who have raw materials to sell to the dockyards].

FOOTNOTES:

329 *Second Report of the Royal Commission appointed to inquire into the Civil Establishments*, 1888; Sir S. A. Blackwood, Secretary to the Post Office since 1880; q. 17,821 to 17,827.

330 *Hansard's Parliamentary Debates*, February 25, 1903, p. 803.

331 *Report of the Inter-Departmental Committee on Post Office Establishments*, 1897, p. 19; q. 9,132 and following, Mr. J. S. Smith; and q. 12,366, Mr. H. Joyce, Third Secretary to the General Post Office.

332 *Hansard's Parliamentary Debates*, March 13, 1906.

333 *Report of the Inter-Departmental Committee on Post Office Establishments*, 1897; Mr. Churchfield, Secretary Postmen's Federation; q. 10,994 and following; and Mr. J. C. Badcock, Controller London Postal Service; q. 11,585 to 11,589.

334 *Report of the Inter-Departmental Committee on Post Office Establishments*, 1897; Mr. H. Joyce, Third Secretary to General Post Office; q. 12,316; and Mr. J. S. Smith; q. 9,063.

335 *Report of the Inter-Departmental Committee on Post Office Establishments*, 1897; Mr. H. Joyce, Third Secretary General Post Office; q. 12,374; and Mr. J. S. Smith; q. 9,115.

336 *Report of the Inter-Departmental Committee on Post Office Establishments*, 1897; Mr. H. Joyce, Third Secretary General Post Office; q. 12,356 to 12,360; and Mr. J. S. Smith, representative of the provincial postmen; q. 9,108.

337 *Report of the Inter-Departmental Committee on Post Office Establishments*, 1897; q. 11,485 and following, and 9,187 and following.

338 *Hansard's Parliamentary Debates*, February 14, 1887, p. 1,399.

339 *Hansard's Parliamentary Debates*, February 24, 1888, p. 1,375.

340 *Who's Who*, 1905, Bartley, Sir G. C. T., K. C. B., cr. 1902; M. P. North Islington since 1885; Assistant Director of Science Division of Science and Art Department till 1880; resigned to stand for Parliament; established National Penny Bank to promote thrift, 1875.

341 *Hansard's Parliamentary Debates*, March 15, 1901, p. 84.

342 *Hansard's Parliamentary Debates*, July 27, 1897, p. 1,221.

343 *Hansard's Parliamentary Debates*, August 13, 1903, p. 1,160.

344 *Hansard's Parliamentary Debates*, March 9, 1905, p. 397.

345 *Hansard's Parliamentary Debates*, April 27, 1899, p. 711.

346 *Hansard's Parliamentary Debates*, August 1, 1902, p. 395.

347 *Hansard's Parliamentary Debates*, August 5, 1903, p. 1,528.

348 *Hansard's Parliamentary Debates*, March 13, 1891.

349 *Hansard's Parliamentary Debates*, December 7, 1893, p. 633; and February 24, 1899, p. 443.

350 *Hansard's Parliamentary Debates*, October 27, 1902, p. 797.

351 *Hansard's Parliamentary Debates*, July 18, 1901, p. 840.

352 *Hansard's Parliamentary Debates*, April 27, 1900, p. 206; July 23, p. 1,468; and Mr. Austen Chamberlain, Postmaster General, April 30, 1903, pp. 1,024 and 1,035.

353 *Who's Who*, 1905.

354 *Hansard's Parliamentary Debates*, June 21, 1906, p. 397.

355 *Hansard's Parliamentary Debates*, May 21, 1906, p. 938.

356 *Hansard's Parliamentary Debates*, March 20, 1906, p. 198.

357 *Hansard's Parliamentary Debates*, April 5, 1906, p. 705.

358 *Hansard's Parliamentary Debates*, April 2, 1902.

359 *Hansard's Parliamentary Debates*, March 12, 1903, p. 564.

360 *Report from the Select Committee on National Expenditure*, 1902; q. 2,430 *et passim.*

361 1875 to 1885.

362 *Report from the Select Committee on National Expenditure*, 1902; q. 2,502.

CHAPTER XVII
THE SPIRIT OF THE CIVIL SERVICE

The doctrine of an "implied contract" between the State and each civil servant, to the effect that the State may make no change in the manner of administering its great trading departments without compensating every civil servant however remotely or indirectly affected. The hours of work may not be increased without compensating every one affected. Administrative "mistakes" may not be corrected without compensating the past beneficiaries of such mistakes. Violation of the order that promotion must not be mechanical, or by seniority alone, may not be corrected without compensating those civil servants who would have been benefitted by the continued violation of the aforesaid order. The State may not demand increased efficiency of its servants without compensating every one affected. Persons filling positions for which there is no further need, must be compensated. Each civil servant has a "vested right" to the maintenance of such rate of promotion as obtains when he enters the service, irrespective of the volume of business or of any diminution in the number of higher posts consequent upon administrative reforms. The telegraph clerks demand that their chances of promotion be made as good as those of the postal clerks proper, but they refuse to avail themselves of the opportunity to pass over to the postal side proper of the service, on the ground that the postal duties proper are more irksome than the telegraph duties. Members of Parliament support recalcitrant telegraph clerks whom the Government is attempting to force to learn to perform postal duties, in order that it may reap advantage from having combined the postal service and the telegraph service in 1870. Special allowances may not be discontinued; and vacations may not be shortened, without safeguarding all "vested interests." Further illustrations of the hopelessly unbusinesslike spirit of the rank and file of the public servants.

Upon a preceding page has been mentioned the contention of the civil servants that there is an implied contract between the State and the Civil Service that the conditions of employment obtaining at any moment shall not be changed to the disadvantage of the civil servants, except upon payment of compensation to all persons disadvantageously affected; and that unless such compensation is paid, any change in the conditions and terms of employment must be limited to future entrants upon the service of the State, or to persons who shall accept promotion on the express condition of becoming subject to the altered terms of employment.

Implied Contract for Six Hour Day

Before the Select Committee on Civil Services Expenditure, 1873, Mr. W. E. Baxter, Financial Secretary to the Treasury, said: "I am not an advocate for long hours; and in the mercantile business with which I am connected, I have years ago reduced the hours both of the clerks and of the workmen, but I am inclined to think the six hours given to their work by the Government officials [that is, Upper and Lower Division clerks], rather too short a period, and that it might with advantage be somewhat lengthened. At the same time we must always keep in mind that the effect of lengthening the hours would be to cause an immediate demand for an increase of pay. However I have a very strong impression that in most of the Government offices there are too many clerks, and that there might be considerable economy in a reduction of numbers and an increase of hours."

The Chancellor of the Exchequer stated to the Committee that it would be inexpedient to try to raise the hours of clerks from 6 hours to, say, 7 hours. He said: "I suspect that my one-seventh more time would be more than compensated by my having to pay them a great deal more than one-seventh more salary; and I think it would be very perilous to take up the floodgates in that way."[363]

Before the Royal Commission appointed to inquire into the Civil

Establishments, 1888, Sir Reginald E. Welby, Permanent Secretary to the Treasury, stated that he was in favor of extending the hours of the Upper and Lower Division clerks from 6 hours to 7. The Chairman queried: "But can it be done with existing clerks without a breach of faith?" Sir R. E. Welby replied: "With regard to Lower Division clerks, it is provided that in consideration of an extra payment, which is according to the regulation, a 6 hour office can be turned into a 7 hour office.... There is no provision of that kind for the Upper Division, and, of course, any change would have to be made a matter of consideration.... The arrangement made between the authorities of the Inland Revenue and the Treasury, in those departments of the Inland Revenue which have adopted the 7 hours system, has been that the clerks who were under no stipulation to do 7 hours' work, should have an extra allowance until promotion. As soon as they are promoted to another class, we have assumed that we have the right to put our conditions upon the promotion, and, therefore, from that time they fall into the ordinary scale of salary without addition." At this point Mr. H. H. Fowler, a Member of the Commission, queried: "I understand you to say there is no provision made for altering the period of service of an Upper Division clerk from 6 hours to 7 hours. I want to know where is the document by which the State binds itself over to accept 6 hours' work ...?" "Nowhere. The only thing is that when he enters the office he is told that the hours are from 10 to 4, or from 11 to 5." Mr. Fowler continued: "I consider this is a question of vital importance, and I want to have it very distinctly from you: I want to know where is the contract between the State and any Upper Division clerk in any department, that he is only to work 6 hours a day?" "There is no such document that I know of, and no such understanding further than the statement upon his entering the office that the hours are such and such." "But I want to ascertain whether there would be even an approach to a breach of faith (if such a term may be used) if the State says: 'We insist upon our servants working for us 7 hours a day?'" "None in my mind, and I may add that it is generally known that the hours are so and so, but longer hours when required" [on exceptionally busy days].

To Sir T. H. Farrer, Permanent Secretary to the Board of Trade, 1867 to 1886, the Chairman of the Royal commission said: "What is your view with reference to its being fair or necessary to increase the pay if seven hours' work be asked from an Upper Division clerk. Do you think there is any contract to do only 6 hours' work?" "No, there is no contract whatever; theoretically the rule is that civil servants are to do the business that is required of them. The practical difficulty remains that if you do it you may have a great uproar. You may cause discontent, and you may have, as I said before, pressure in the House of Commons; but theoretically, and as a matter of right, I can see no reason why every officer should not be obliged to give 7 hours for the existing pay." "Have you not to some extent recognized it[364] by creating a different scale of pay in the Lower Division for 7 hours than for 6 hours?" "Yes, you have, and I am very sorry for it; when I say you have, I was a party to it,[365] but I am sorry that we did it." "But you are of course of opinion that when you announce that the office hours are from 10 to 4, it means that these are the hours of public attendance, but that it does not in any way prevent the head of the office from asking the clerks to stop until the work is done?" "No; but the larger your class of Lower Division clerks, the more you will find that the hours become fixed hours, and if they are asked to attend beyond them [because of unusual pressure of work], they will ask for extra pay for attendance."[366]

In 1881, Mr. Fawcett, Postmaster General, created for the provincial towns the class of "telegraph clerks," who are recruited from the first class of telegraphists, and act as assistants to the assistant superintendents. Since the men in question were styled clerks, they immediately contended that their hours of work should be reduced from 8 hours a day to 39 hours a week, the hours of the clerks proper. The Department always has refused to recognize that claim. But Mr. Beaufort, Postmaster at Manchester, acting on a misreading of the rules, from 1884 to 1890 granted the telegraph clerks at Manchester the 39 hours a week. In 1892 the hours were raised to the correct number, namely 8 hours a day, with half an hour for a meal. In 1896, 9 telegraph clerks from Manchester sent a spokesman to the Tweedmouth Committee to state that they had become telegraph clerks in 1890, when the hours were 35 a week, and that they deemed it a "hardship" to be compelled to work 8 hours a day.[367]

In November, 1902, Mr. Austen Chamberlain, Financial Secretary to the Treasury, stated in the House of Commons: "The town postmen at Newton Abbot were formerly paid on too high a scale [in consequence of an error of judgment made by a departmental officer]. The wages were accordingly reduced some years ago, but the postmen then in the service were allowed to retain their old scale of payment so long as they should remain in the service, and the new scale was applied only to postmen who entered the service subsequently. This will account for there being temporarily two scales for postmen at Newton Abbott."[368]

In 1881, Mr. Fawcett, Postmaster General, established for Metropolitan London the class of "senior telegraphists," with a salary rising by annual increments of $40, from $800 to $950. He intended that this class should be filled by the promotion of men from the first class of telegraphists who possessed exceptional manipulative efficiency as well as sufficient executive ability to act as assistants to the assistant superintendents. But as a matter of fact many men were promoted to this class by mere seniority and without reference to their qualifications. In 1890, however, under Mr. Raikes,

Postmaster General, the Department resolved to promote to the senior class no more men who were not fully qualified.[369] And in 1894, the Department imposed a technical examination[370] between the first class of telegraphists and the senior class, in order to insure that all men promoted to the senior class should have the qualifications required of them. Mr. H. C. Fischer, Controller of the London Central Telegraph Office, said of this examination: "It is not considered unjust that this should have been enforced in the case of men who had always been employed on instrument duties, and who had only themselves to blame if they neglected to acquire some knowledge of technical matters, which all skilled telegraphists are expected to possess…. Even before the institution of the examination it was always held that the possession of technical knowledge gave the man an additional claim to promotion to the senior class."[371]

Before the Tweedmouth Committee the representatives of the first class telegraphists complained of the technical examination as a "grievance." They said: "The regulation came into operation at once, an act which is regarded as exceptionally unjust toward men of more than 20 years' service, who, up to that time had understood from the general practice of the Department, that, other things being equal, good conduct and manipulative efficiency would secure promotion. Now, however, the possession of technical knowledge is added as a necessary qualification before promotion to the senior class, and this without a coincident rise in the maximum [salary] of the first class as compensation for the additional demand upon the capacity of the staff." As the alternative to the raising of the maximum salary of the first class [$800], "it was earnestly contended that the scale to which the officer is raised on passing the examination should be materially enhanced [beyond the present maximum of $950] in recompense for the further additional demand upon his time, and for his pecuniary outlay in preparing himself for the requirements of the Department."[372]

Prior to November, 1886, special intelligence was required of the sorters of foreign letters in the London Central Post Office, who were correspondingly well paid. The wages of the first class of sorters of foreign letters began at $13.75 a week, and rose to $17.50, by triennial increments of $1.25 a week.

Those of the second class began at $11.25, and rose to $13.75, by annual increments of $0.50 a week. But in consequence of a material simplification of the duties of the foreign letter sorters, consequent upon the changes in the international postage charges, the Department resolved, in November, 1886, to replace the two classes of sorters of foreign letters by one class, with wages ranging from $12.50 a week to $15.[373] It was provided, however, that the existing sorters of the first class should retain the old scale of wages; and that the existing sorters of the second class should have the option of immediate promotion to the new class, with wages rising from $12.50 to $15, or, "of being advanced to the $13.75 to $17.50 scale, in the order in which they would have attained to that scale if the old first class scale had not been abolished." In other words, the men who, prior to November, 1886, had been in line for ultimate promotion to a class carrying wages of $13.75 to $17.50, were offered the option "of being regarded as having a vested interest to rise to $17.50 a week, as vacancies should occur."[374]

Claim of Exemption from Vicissitudes of Life

In 1895, Mr. H. B. Irons, a second class sorter in London, appeared before the Tweedmouth Committee to present the grievance of himself and colleagues, who, prior to 1886, had given up the position of first class letter carriers to become second class letter sorters in order to improve their prospects of promotion. The grievance was that the prospects of promotion of letter sorters had been curtailed by the abolition of the sorterships of foreign letters in 1886, and the abolition of the sortership of the first class of inland and foreign newspapers in 1890. Mr. Irons alleged that he would have remained a letter carrier had he foreseen the changes in question.[375] His argument was that the civil servant must be exempt from the ordinary chances and vicissitudes of life.

In 1890 some senior telegraphists protested that they ought to be made assistant superintendents, alleging that they were performing the duties of assistant superintendents. Mr. Raikes, Postmaster General, found that some of the duties of the complainants were of the nature alleged, but not all of them. Therefore, he made the complainants, forty-nine in number, second class assistant superintendents. By 1896, this new class had come to number sixty-five.

From 1881 to 1890, the proportion borne by the senior telegraphists to the first class and second class telegraphists had ranged between 1 to 6.6 and 1 to 7.7. The promotion of forty-nine senior telegraphists in 1890, and of the others in subsequent years, raised the proportion in question to 1 to 10, in 1895. But counting senior telegraphists and second class assistant superintendents, there was, in 1895, one of these superior officers to each 6.5 of first class and second class telegraphists. In other words, the rate of promotion of first class and second class telegraphists to appointments superior to the first class of telegraphists, but inferior to the position of assistant superintendent, had been more rapid in 1891 to 1895, than it had been in 1881 to 1890.

In 1895, Mr. Nicholson, Chairman London Branch of the Postal Telegraph Clerks' Association, appeared before the Tweedmouth Committee to voice the grievance of the first class and second class telegraphists, which was, that the rate of promotion from the second class and first class had decreased, as shown by the fact that there was only one senior telegraphist to each ten first class and second class telegraphists. Mr. Nicholson contended that the increase of telegraphic messages consequent upon the introduction of the charge of 12 cents for 12 words had necessitated the creation of a new class, the second class superintendents; and that the first class and second class telegraphists had a right to demand that they should derive benefit from that increase of traffic and that necessity of creating a new class of officers. That the Department's failure to fill the vacancies created in the senior class of telegraphists by promotions to the class of second class superintendents, had deprived the first class and second class telegraphists of all advantage arising out of the creation of a new class of officers, the second class assistant superintendents.[376]

Right to Fixed Rate of Promotion

The nature of the claim made by the Chairman London Branch of the Postal Telegraph Clerks' Association is forcibly illustrated by the following incident from the proceedings of the Royal Commission on Civil

Establishments, 1888. Mr. H. A. Davies, the official representative of the clerks in the Receiver and Accountant General's Office of the General Post Office, had made a similar demand on behalf of the men whom he represented. The Chairman asked him: "Does a man enter the public service on the assumption that all the upper places are to remain the same as when he enters.... If you and I enter the public service finding a certain Department, the Post Office or any other, with twenty posts above to which we had a reasonable hope, if we behaved well, and showed merit; if administrative reform takes away five of these posts, are we entitled to compensation, because that is what it [your allegation of grievance] comes to? Can you say, there being no contract whatever between me and the State when I entered the office as a clerk, no contract whatever that I should attain to a higher post, except when there is a vacancy, that I have a claim [to compensation] when administrative reform takes away some of the other places?" The spokesman of the Post Office clerks replied: "If I were defending that [position] to Parliament, I think I should say that the country has a certain duty toward men who, when they entered the service, had, judging by the precedents of their office, a fair prospect of reasonable promotion, and that if any economy is effected by subsequent administrative reforms, the sufferers deserve some consideration."[377]

From 1885 to 1888 Mr. Lawson, M. P.,[378] was a Member of the Royal Commission appointed to inquire into the Civil Establishments. In March, 1889, he intervened in the administration of the Post Office by asking the Postmaster General how many vacancies there were in the first class of telegraphists at the Central Telegraph Office, London; how long those vacancies had been open, and whether the Postmaster General had received a petition from the second class telegraphists for their promotion; and whether there was anything to prevent him from complying with the request. The Postmaster General replied that on January 1, 1889, there had been 53 vacancies. "To thirty-four of those vacancies I have made promotions within the last few days; and this, practically, is an answer to the petition of December, 1888."[379] The reader will recall that in February, 1888, Mr.

Lawson had intervened on behalf of a letter carrier who had been dismissed in 1882. In 1889 to 1892, and 1897 to 1904, Mr. Lawson was a Member of the London County Council.

In June, 1902, Mr. Hay, M. P.,[380] asked the Postmaster General, through the Financial Secretary to the Treasury: "With reference to the fact that the proportion of appointments above $800 a year in the Central Telegraph Office, London, now bears the same relation to the staff below that salary as during the period when the circular [1881 to 1891] was issued promising a prospect of $950, whether he is aware that during the years 1882 to 1892 the proportion was one appointment above $800 to 5.5 below [that salary], and that the proportion at the present time is one appointment above $800 to 6.4 below; and, seeing that this difference of proportion represents nearly forty appointments, above $800, whether he will take steps to readjust that proportion on the basis of 1 to 5.5?"[381] In 1906, Mr. Hay was made a member of the Select Committee on Post Office Servants.

In April and in August, 1902, Captain Norton asked the Postmaster General, through the Financial Secretary to the Treasury, to appoint so many additional senior telegraphists that it should no longer be necessary to call on men in the class below to act as substitutes for the senior telegraphists who were taking their annual leave of one month.[382] In 1906, Captain Norton became a Junior Lord of the Treasury in the Sir Campbell-Bannerman Ministry.

In February, 1902, Mr. Plummer[383] stated that at Newcastle-on-Tyne thirty-eight telegraphists, who had, on an average, served 27 years each, were waiting for promotion. "Will the Postmaster General facilitate promotion by enforcing in the future the Civil Service Regulation with reference to retirement[384] at the age of sixty years?" Mr. Austen Chamberlain, Financial Secretary to the Treasury, replied: "The Postmaster General would not feel justified in enforcing the retirement of any efficient officers for the purpose of accelerating the promotion of others." On August 1, 1902, Captain Norton repeated the request.[385]

On November 24, 1902, Mr. O'Brien asked the Postmaster to create more rapid promotion at Liverpool by retiring all men who had qualified for the maximum pension [two-thirds of salary], irrespective of the fitness of such men to continue to serve.[386]

On June 19, 1902, Mr. Keir Hardie asked the Secretary to the Treasury, as representing the Postmaster General: "Whether he will state the special qualifications which necessitate the retention in the Postal service of the assistant superintendent, Mr. Napper, and the inspector, Mr. Graham, at the West Central District Office, after reaching 60 years of age; and if the probable date of retirement can be given?" On July 28, 1902, Mr. Keir Hardie asked: "If he will state what are the special qualifications which necessitate the retention of the inspector, Mr. E. Stamp, at the North Western District Office, after attaining the age of 60 years; and if he can give the probable date of this officer's retirement?"[387]

Any officer who is retired with a pension, on account of ill health, before he is sixty years of age, may, if he recovers his health, be recalled to duty at the discretion of the head of his Department or of the Treasury. Under such circumstances the officer receives the salary of his new office and so much of his pension as shall be sufficient to make his total income equal to the original pension. Under the foregoing rule two officers were made respectively postmaster at Bristol and postmaster at Hastings.

Before the Tweedmouth Committee, Mr. Uren, President of the Postmasters' Association, protested against such "blocking of some of the best offices by pensioners.... Here are two good offices, one with $4,000 a year, and the other with $2,750, which are taken up by pensioners who recover their health, and so block a line of promotion.... I only mention these as the two most recent cases with which this sort of thing has happened, but they are not the only occasions by a good many, which I am instructed to bring before your Committee as a fair subject for consideration." Mr. Crosse, another witness, added: "The Postal Clerks' Association also desire to endorse the evidence put forward by the Postmasters' Association as to the anomaly and injustice of certain postmasters being retained in the service who are in the receipt of pension and salary from the Department."[388]

Mechanical Equality Demanded

Prior to August, 1891, the postmen of metropolitan London were divided into two classes: the second class, with wages rising from $4.50 a week to $6, by annual increments of $0.25 a week; and the first class, with wages rising from $6 a week, to $7.50, by annual increments of $0.25 a week. In consequence of the rapid growth of the postal business, however, the postmen frequently passed through the second class into the first class, not in six years, but in from two to five years. But the rate of promotion from the second class into the first differed materially in the several metropolitan branch offices, because of the unequal growth of business at those several offices. That inequality of promotion violated the ideal[389] of the civil servants, which is, that all should fare alike; and therefore, the postmen demanded that the division into two classes be abolished, and that every postman should rise, by stated annual increments, from the initial wage of $4.50 to the final wage of $7.50. But the abolition of classification would put an end to the possibility of those rapid passings through the stages between $4.50 and $6 that had been of frequent occurrence in the past in some of the metropolitan branch offices. By way of compensation for the loss of that chance the postmen demanded that the annual increment be increased beyond $0.25 a week.

The Department, in August, 1891, abolished the classification of the postmen, but it refused to raise the annual increment. It said that the rapid promotion from $4.50 to $6 that had characterized the past had been an accident, that it had not been foreseen, and that the men who had entered the service while it had obtained had not acquired a vested right to it. In 1896 the men who had been postmen prior to the abolition of classification appeared before the Tweedmouth Committee with the statement that they "were under the impression that it was an official principle that no individual should suffer by the introduction of a new scale of promotion or wages." They demanded compensation for the fact that they had lost, in 1891, the possibility of passing in less than the regular time from the wage of $4.50 to that of $6. They stated that they were prepared to show that "they had suffered material pecuniary loss ... amounting in some cases to about $500."[390] All of which goes to show that in the British Post Office service the abolition of a grievance can in turn become a grievance.

Before the Tweedmouth Committee appeared also the representatives of the telegraphers, to demand the abolition of the division of the telegraphers into classes, with promotion by merit between the classes. They demanded amalgamation into a single class, in which each one should pass automatically from the minimum pay to the maximum, provided he was not arrested by the efficiency bar, to be placed at $800 a year. Mr. E. B. L. Hill, Assistant Secretary, General Post Office, London, began his discussion of this demand by quoting with approval the conclusion of the Telegraph Committee of 1893, which was: "We have taken great pains to investigate this matter. Almost without exception the provincial postmasters and telegraph superintendents were opposed to an amalgamation of the classes, and gave the strongest testimony to the value of the present division [into classes] as a means of discouraging indifference, and encouraging zeal and efficiency. We think … that for purposes of discipline it is desirable to maintain the division of the establishment into two classes." Mr. Hill continued by saying that in the course of the last three or four years he had changed his opinion, and had come to the conclusion that amalgamation into one class must come. "The staff seems to desire, first of all, equality, and the abolition of classification seems to insure the fulfillment of that wish. At the same time classification is a valuable incentive to exertion and efficiency…."[391]

Opportunities Rejected; Increased Pay Demanded

In 1896 the proportion borne by the supervising officers above the rank of first class sorting clerks to the total staff of sorting clerks was 18.85 per cent., whereas the proportion borne by the officers above the rank of first class telegraphists to the total staff was 12.59 per cent. At the same time the proportion borne by the first class clerks to the total of first and second class clerks was 20.17 per cent. on the postal side of the service, and 24.64 per cent. on the telegraph side. In other words, the chances of promotion to a supervising position are much better in the postal branch than in the telegraph branch; so much so, that to an able and energetic man, the postal branch is more attractive than the telegraph branch, even though the chances of reaching a first class clerkship are somewhat better in the telegraph branch than in the postal branch. But the letter sorting clerk's work is more irksome than the work of the telegraphist, and therefore "the telegraphists are usually reluctant, notwithstanding the better prospects of promotion, to accept work on the postal side." For example, in the four years ending with 1896, only ten telegraphists at Birmingham had themselves transferred to the postal side, and three of those ten had themselves re-transferred to the instrument room, because the work on the postal side proved too hard for them. Again, on March 6, 1896, Mr. Harley, the postmaster at Manchester, issued the following notice: "I should like to afford an opportunity to telegraphists in this office of becoming acquainted with letter sorting duties, and, with this view, if a sufficient number of officers apply, I will arrange an evening duty of from 2 to 3 hours in the sorting office for a month in every three, such duty to form a portion of their 8 hours' duty. About 50 officers would be required to enable me to carry this suggestion into effect, and I shall be glad if all officers who are disposed to avail themselves of this opportunity of acquiring postal knowledge will submit their names." At the end of three weeks Mr. Harley had not had a single response, though he had in person explained to a number of "representative telegraphists the advantage which a knowledge of postal work would give them."

The telegraphists, as a body, decline to avail themselves of the opportunities offered them to improve their chances of promotion; none the less they allege they have a grievance in the fact that their chances of promotion are not so good as are the chances of the sorting clerks. They demand that the Post Office redress their grievance, either by increasing the number of telegraph supervising officers, or by raising the salaries of the first and second class telegraphists sufficiently to compensate the telegraphists for their smaller chance of becoming supervising officers.[392]

Parliamentary Intervention

The telegraphists even try to bring pressure on the Government to stop the Post Office from forcing them to learn letter sorting. For example, in 1896, the Post Office required the telegraphists and sorters employed in the Oxford Central Post Office to work at the pleasure of the Oxford postmaster at letter sorting or at telegraphing. The Oxford telegraph clerks argued that they had contracts with the Government to work as telegraph operators, and that the

Government had no right to force them either to do sorting, or to suffer transfer to some other office where the convenience of the Government would not be affected by their refusal to act as sorters. The clerks kept up their agitation for years, and in December, 1902, they induced Mr. Samuel,[393] M. P., to champion their cause in the House of Commons.[394] Mr. Samuel, in 1895 and 1900, had contested unsuccessfully South Oxfordshire. He took "First Class Honors" at Oxford, and he has published: *Liberalism, Its Principles and Purposes.* In 1906, Mr. Samuel became Under Home Secretary in the Campbell-Bannerman Ministry.

In June, 1904, Mr. William Jones asked the Postmaster General: "Whether he is aware that for some time past endeavors have been made to compel the telegraph staff at Oxford to perform postal duties, and that they have been informed that they would be removed compulsorily to other offices in the event of the men declining to perform those duties; and whether, in view of the declaration of previous Postmasters General, that telegraphists who had entered the service before 1896 are exempt from the performance of postal work, he will explain the reasons for his action?" Lord Stanley, Postmaster General, replied: "The telegraph work at Oxford has of late considerably fallen off [in consequence of the competition from the telephone], and there is consequently not sufficient work to keep the officers in the telegraph office fully occupied. Their services have therefore been utilized for the benefit of the Department in such manner as the exigencies of the service require. All officers of the Department are expected loyally to perform any work required of them which they are capable of undertaking; and unless some means can be found of utilizing the services of redundant telegraphists at the offices where they are at present employed, a transfer to another office is the only alternative."[395] Mr. Jones had sat in Parliament since 1895. He is a private tutor at Oxford; has been assistant schoolmaster at Anglesey; and has served under the London School Board.[396]

Within ten days of the Jones episode, Mr. Dobbie,[397] who had just been sent to Parliament to represent Ayr Burghs, Scotland, intervened on behalf of the Glasgow Post Office clerks, who objected to being compelled to do dual duties.[398] At about the same time Mr. Henderson, who, before entering Parliament, had been a Member of the Newcastle Town Council, intervened on behalf of one Chandler, a sorting clerk and telegraphist at Middlesbrough, who had been informed that his increment would be withheld because of his ignorance of telegraphy. The Postmaster General replied: "All the circumstances of his case have already been examined more than once both by my predecessor and myself, and I am quite satisfied that he has received proper treatment."[399]

In October, 1906, Mr. Parker, M. P., intervened on behalf of some telegraph clerks at Halifax who were being made to sort letters.[400]

The Bradford Committee on Post Office Wages, 1904, reported: "...it was pointed out that in the larger offices promotion is better on the Postal side.... This is admitted, though we understand that it is open to any telegraphists to acquire a knowledge of Postal business, and so qualify for promotion on either side. It is found that this is not done, however, as the men prefer the Telegraph work to the more irksome Postal duties."

Sundry Vested Rights

The Post Office gives those counter men of London and Dublin who receive or pay money over the counter, a risk allowance, for the purpose of reimbursing them for any errors that they may make in dealing with the public. No such allowance is given to the postal clerks in any other city; nor are such allowances paid by railway companies or other private employers. Upon the provincial Post Office clerks making a demand for equal treatment with the London and Dublin clerks, the Department decided to discontinue the allowances in London and Dublin "as to future entrants to the postal service," and under "the most sacred preservation of all existing interests."[401] The Tweedmouth Committee endorsed this resolution, with the statement that "the rights of existing holders of risk allowances should, of course, in all cases be maintained."

The Tweedmouth Committee suggested a new scale of pay for the several kinds of letter sorters in London. That new scale was suggested for two reasons: for the purpose of discontinuing the complex system of special allowances that had sprung up; and for the purpose of reducing the pay of several classes of sorters, the existing scale of payment being too high. The Committee proposed that all existing rights be safeguarded, saying: "Present holders of allowances should enter the [new] scale of salary at a point equal to their previous salary and allowances combined, and wherever the maximum of the present scale together with the allowances exceeds the maximum of the new scale, that, but no further excess, should be granted."[402]

The Tweedmouth Committee also reported: "We think that the holidays of the Dublin and Edinburgh [telegram] tracers should for the future be 14 week days, the same period as London men performing the same duties, instead of 3 weeks as at present, the change as to holidays of course not applying to present members of the class."[403]

The Tweedmouth Committee concluded that the holidays given to the letter sorters and the telegraphists in London and in the provincial towns were excessive. It proposed that the annual vacation of 21 week days during the first 5 years of service and of one month after 5 years of service, be reduced, to respectively 14 week days and 21 week days. It added: "It is not, however, suggested that this change should apply to those officers already in the service who receive a leave of 3 weeks during the first 5 years, nor is it proposed to curtail the leave granted to those officers who have already served 5 years, and are, therefore, in enjoyment of a month's holiday."[404]

Before the Royal Commission on Civil Establishments, 1888, Sir Reginald E. Welby, Secretary to the Treasury, testified that throughout the Civil Service the Upper Division Clerks had 48 working days' vacation a year, besides the usual holidays. He said that but for custom, which had become "almost common law," there was no reason for giving such a "very liberal" annual vacation. But he added that any change should be made to apply only to future entrants to the public service.[405]

In 1892 the Department increased from 21 week days, to one calendar month, the annual leave of all men in the Central Post Office, London, who were in receipt of $750 a year, or more. In the following year, 1893, the Department gave the same increase to men with $750 a year, or more, in the branch offices of Metropolitan London, and in the offices of the provincial towns. In 1895 the representatives of the men who had not obtained the increase of annual leave until 1893, appeared before the Tweedmouth Committee with the demand for ten days' pay by way of compensation for the fact that, in 1892, they had "lost ten days."[406]

The tenacity with which the civil servants resist any change in the conditions of service that is to their advantage, is further illustrated by the following incidents.

Down to 1880, the overseers in the postal service, who are on their feet all day, had one day a week of relief from duty. In 1880 that allowance was reduced to half a day; and in 1893 it was discontinued altogether. In each case the change was made to apply only to the future entrants upon the office of overseer. In 1896 the new entrants upon the office still were complying under protest only with the requirement of the Department that they sign a paper stating that they were not entitled to any weekly "relief leave of absence."[407]

There are four Monday Bank Holidays in the year; and for several years prior to 1892, the Telegraph Branch, as an act of grace, gave a Saturday holiday to those "news distributors" whose services could be spared on the Saturdays preceding Monday Bank Holidays. In 1892 it ceased to be possible to continue this act of grace without employing men on over-time, and therefore the practice was discontinued. In 1896 the news distributors complained before the Tweedmouth Committee that the withdrawal of "the days of grace was a grievance with which they would like the Committee to grapple." The spokesman of the news distributors said: "After having enjoyed the privilege for [several] years it was withdrawn, an arbitrary course, almost, it is thought, without precedent. To grant a privilege, and then take it away, displayed a lamentable want of that courtesy that we think should be inseparable qualities of power and position."[408]

Intervention by Members of Parliament

In June, 1904, Mr. Shackleton[409] intervened in the House of Commons on behalf of some men in the Liverpool Post Office, whose grievance was that an interval of 15 minutes, given as "an act of grace," had been reduced to 10 minutes.[410]

In July, 1905, Mr. James O'Connor, M. P. for Wicklow, intervened in a similar matter on behalf of the men at the London West Central District Office.[411]

Before the Royal Commission on Civil Establishments, 1888, Sir Lyon Playfair was asked whether it would not be better to replace by boy clerks the "writers" employed in the past. Sir Lyon replied: "I think that would be better for the civil service and better for the boy clerks themselves. Of course, regard should be had to the writers who are employed now, and the change should be made by not taking on more, and not by dispensing with those that are now employed." A moment before, Sir Lyon Playfair had been asked: "The writers are now a very large and very important body in the public service, are they not?" He had replied: "Yes, and they make you feel their largeness and importance by Parliamentary pressure."[412] Sir Lyon Playfair had been Chairman of the Royal Commission on the Civil Service which had sat from 1875 to 1876; and he had been the author of the Playfair Reorganization of the civil service in 1876.

Before the Committee on Civil Services Expenditure, 1873, Mr. W. E. Baxter, Financial Secretary to the Treasury, said: "…but I may say at once in regard to the matter of the travelling expenses of county court judges, that I think the whole thing has hitherto been in such an unsatisfactory state that it would be very difficult to defend the action of the Treasury in various matters connected with it." Thereupon Mr. West, a Member of the Committee, queried: "Acting in accordance with that view last year, the Chancellor of the Exchequer endeavored to reform the system as to existing judges and as to future judges, did he not…? Is that reform being now pursued with regard to the existing judges?" The Financial Secretary to the Treasury replied: "Not in regard to existing judges. I have always been of opinion that it is very difficult to go back upon arrangements which have been made in the past, however injurious to the public service and uneconomical they may have been, and that it would be better for economists [persons desiring to effect economy] to direct their attention to preventing new arrangements of a similar character."[413]

Unbusinesslike Spirit Further Illustrated

The thoroughly unbusinesslike spirit of the postal employees is illustrated still further in the following "grievance" laid before the Tweedmouth Committee by the official representatives of the postal employees, who spoke, not as individuals, but as the instructed representatives of their respective classes of public servants.

Mr. G. McDonald presented the grievance of the "news distributors," who "are the picked men of the Telegraph Service, chosen on the ground of exceptional merit." He complained that there was not sufficient opportunity for promotion, since [the automatic] promotion was limited to postmasterships worth from $1,000 to $1,250 a year, and there were not enough postmasterships of that kind. Mr. McDonald admitted that men under 35 years "by competitive examination," could rise out of the class of News Distributors to surveyors' clerkships; but he argued that since such promotion was attained by competitive examination, "it must be credited to the man himself who wins his position, and I therefore beg to suggest that it cannot count as promotion in the ordinary sense."[414]

Another grievance of the News Distributors was that they were not "treated and classed" as Major Division Clerks, though they were paid on the scale of such clerks. They were compelled to work 48 hours a week, whereas Major Division Clerks worked only 39 hours a week.[415]

Mr. Alfred Boulden presented the telegraphists' grievances as to pensions. He demanded that retirement on pension should be optional at the age of fifty; and that if a man died in harness, such deduction as had been made from his salary toward the pension fund, should be paid to his heir-at-law. Mr. H. C. Fischer, Controller London Central Telegraph Office, replied that "optional retirement at 50 years of age would result in the more healthy members of the staff retiring at that age, and seeking other employment to add to their income, leaving the less healthy and less useful persons to hang on in the service as long as they could."[416]

Mr. A. W. North presented another grievance, namely, that a female telegraph clerk can become a female superintendent in 21 years, whereas a male telegraph clerk can reach the corresponding position only after 27 years of service.[417]

Mr. J R. Lickfold appeared as the representative of the postal employees to demand that in the case of an employee having failed to appear for duty, the Department should accept without any inquiry whatever the medical certificate of any physician. At this time it was the practice of the Department to doubt the genuineness of the illness and the *bona fides* of a medical certificate only in case "the man had a bad record for frequent short sick absences," "though it was a well known fact that private [physicians' as distinguished from departmental physicians'] certificates could be obtained for 12 cents without even the doctor seeing the patient, but on a mere statement of his symptoms from somebody else." In support of this request, Mr. Lickfold, as the instructed representative of the postal employees, could make no better argument than to cite the dismissal, early in 1894, of two railway Post Office sorters, W—— and J——. In the evidence in rebuttal, Mr. J. C. Badcock, Controller London Postal Service, gave the following account of the episode in question. W—— and J—— were absent from duty from January 8 to 11 inclusive. On January 10 they sent in medical certificates dated the 8th, but the date of one of the certificates had apparently been changed from the 9th. W——'s landlady testified that W—— and J—— had returned to W——'s lodgings on the 8th, shortly after the departure of the mail train, saying that they had missed the mail, but saying nothing of illness. She added that both men had been repeatedly at W——'s lodgings on the 8th and 9th. Both W—— and J—— were absent from their lodgings during the greater part of the three days from the 8th to the 10th. The Post Office inspector found J—— in bed on the night of the 10th. J—— told him he had not seen W—— since the 6th, gave evasive answers, and contradicted himself. The inspector also found W—— on the night of the 10th, and gave an equally unfavorable report upon W——'s answers. On the 11th, the Departmental Medical Officer found both men in W——'s room, and reported there was no reason why both men should not have been on duty from the 8th to the 10th.

Mr. Spencer Walpole, Permanent Secretary of the Post Office and a Member of the Committee, said to the witness: "Have you any doubt that the Department would not have taken the extreme course of dismissing any of its servants on the divided opinion of two medical men, if there had been no previous cases against them...? These men are described as deliberate malingerers?" The Chairman of the Committee added: "Do you not think it would be wise that before bringing forward a particular case of this sort, you should inform yourself thoroughly as to the nature of the case, and as to the character of the men to whom you refer?"[418]

A very large portion of the evidence presented before the Tweedmouth Committee, which evidence covered upward of a thousand closely printed folio pages, affords a melancholy comment upon the theory which is rapidly spreading from the German Universities over the English speaking countries, to wit, that the extension of the functions of the State to the inclusion of business enterprises automatically creates a public spirit which strengthens the hands of the political leaders in charge of the State, even to the point of enabling those leaders to reject the improper demands made upon them by organized bodies of voters, and to administer the State's business ventures with an eye single to the welfare of the community as a whole, particularly the long-run interest of the taxpayers. The so-called Norfolk-Hanbury compromise, the appointment and Report of the Bradford Committee, and the appointment, in 1906, of the Select Committee on Post Office Servants—the last act not having the support, by speech or by vote, of a single man of first rate importance in the House of Commons—are melancholy instances of what that most discerning of statesmen, the late Marquis of Salisbury, used to call "the visible helplessness of Governments."

FOOTNOTES:

363 *Third Report from the Select Committee on Civil Services Expenditure*, 1873; q. 4,641 and 4,418.

364 That is, the claim to additional pay for seven hours' work.

365 That is, the Civil Service Inquiry Commission, 1875-76, of which Sir T. H. Farrer was a member.

366 *Second Report of the Royal Commission appointed to inquire into the Civil Establishments*, 1888; q. 10,545 and following, and 20,043 and following.

367 *Report of the Inter-Departmental Committee on Post Office Establishments*, 1897; q. 13,279, 13,301 and following.

368 *Hansard's Parliamentary Debates*, November 21, 1902, p. 147.

369 *Hansard's Parliamentary Debates*, July 16, 1897, p. 352. Mr. R. W. Hanbury, Financial Secretary to the Treasury and representing the Postmaster General: "But there were in the senior class certain men who, owing to the fact that they had been promoted by seniority without passing any examination, were not quite up to the normal average of the senior class."

The reader will note that in 1890 no effort was made to remove the men not up to the standard of the senior class. The Government had to await the retirement or the death of the incompetent men.

370 *Report of the Inter-Departmental Committee on Post Office Establishments*, 1897; Mr. H. C. Fischer, Controller London Central Telegraph Office; q. 2,305.

The examination covers: (1) "Crossing and looping wires with facility and certainty. (2) Tracing and localizing faults in instruments. (3) Tracing and localizing permanent and intermittent earth contact and disconnection faults on wires. (4) Methods of testing the electro-motive force and resistance of batteries, and a general knowledge of the essential features of the various descriptions of batteries. (5) System of morning testing, both as regards sending and receiving currents, with the necessary calculations in connection with the same. (6) Making up special circuits in cases of emergency. (7) Joining up and adjusting single-needle, single-current, and double-current Morse, both simplex and duplex, and Wheatstone apparatus. (8) Fitting a Wheatstone transmitter to an ordinary key-worked circuit. (9) A general knowledge of the principles of quadruplex and multiplex working. (10) Measuring resistance by Wheatstone bridge."

These subjects are the same as those prescribed for superintendents and assistant superintendents, but the examination is less severe.

371 *Report of the Inter-Departmental Committee on Post Office Establishments*, 1897; Appendix, p. 1,083.

372 *Report of the Inter-Departmental Committee on Post Office Establishments*, 1897; Appendix, p. 1,078; and q. 2,320, Mr. Nicholson, Chairman London Branch, Postal Telegraph Clerks Association. See also: q. 3,919, 4,135, 13,333, 13,344, 13,415, 15,142, and Appendix, p. 1,083.

373 The wages of the sorters of inland letters at the time were: $10 to $14 for the first class, and $4.50 to $10 for the second class.

374 *Report of the Inter-Departmental Committee on Post Office Establishments*, 1897; Mr. J. C. Badcock, Controller London Postal Service; q. 2,190 *et passim*, and Appendix, pp. 1,063 and 1,074.

375 *Report of the Inter-Departmental Committee on Post Office Establishments*, 1897; q. 719 and following.

376 *Report of the Inter-Departmental Committee on Post Office Establishments*, 1897; q. 2,292 to 2,366, and 3,945 and following.

377 *Second Report of the Royal Commission on Civil Establishments*, 1888; q. 20,291 to 20,346.

378 *Who's Who*, 1905, Lawson, Hon. H. L. W.; Lieutenant-Colonel and Honorable-Colonel commanding Royal Bucks Hussars; e. s. of 1st Baron Burnham. Education: Eton; Balliol College, Oxford. M. P. (L.) West St. Pancras, 1885-92; East Gloucestershire, 1883-95; L. C. C. West St. Pancras, 1889-92, and Whitechapel, 1897-1904.

379 *Hansard's Parliamentary Debates*, March 28, 1889, p. 1,022.

380 *Who's Who*, 1905, Hay, Honorable C. G. D., M. P. (C.) since 1900; partner in Ramsford & Co., Stock-brokers; founder, manager, and director of the Fine Art and General Insurance Co., Ltd.

381 *Hansard's Parliamentary Debates*, June 2, 1902, p. 1,096.

382 *Hansard's Parliamentary Debates*, April 15, 1902, p. 283; and August 1, 1902, p. 396.

383 *Who's Who*, 1905, Plummer, Sir W. R., Kt. cr. 1904; M. P. (C.) Newcastle-on-Tyne since 1900; merchant; member of City Council; Director of Newcastle and Gateshead Gas Co.

384 *Hansard's Parliamentary Debates*, March 25, 1903; Mr. Austen Chamberlain, Postmaster General: "The regulation is that all pensionable officers of whatever grade whose conduct, capacity, and efficiency fall below a fair standard shall be called upon to retire at sixty; but retirement at sixty is not enforced in the case of officers whose conduct is good, and who are certified by their superior officers to be thoroughly efficient."

385 *Hansard's Parliamentary Debates*, February 4, 1902, and August 1, 1902, p. 396.

386 *Hansard's Parliamentary Debates*, November 24, 1902, p. 231.

387 *Hansard's Parliamentary Debates*, June 19, 1902, p. 1,101; and July 28, 1902, p. 1,346.

388 *Report of the Inter-Departmental Committee on Post Office Establishments*, 1897; q. 12,537 to 12,551; and Appendix, p. 1,108. See also: *Second Report of the Royal Commission on Civil Establishments*, 1888, p. xxiii; and *Third Report from the Select Committee on Civil Services Expenditure*, 1873; Mr. R. E. Welby, Principal Clerk for Financial Business in the Treasury; q. 507 to 515.

389 *Report of the Inter-Departmental Committee on Post Office Establishments*, 1897; Mr. E. B. L. Hill, Assistant Secretary General Post Office, London; q. 15,134.

390 *Report of the Inter-Departmental Committee on Post Office Establishments*, 1897; Mr. H. Symes, representative of the London Postmen; q. 10,115 to 10,197; and Mr. J. C. Badcock, Controller London Postal Service; q. 11,492.

391 *Report of the Inter-Departmental Committee on Post Office Establishments*, 1897; q. 15,134 *et passim*.

392 *Report of the Inter-Departmental Committee on Post Office Establishments*, 1897; Mr. Lewin Hill, Assistant Secretary General Post Office, London; q. 15,135 to 15,142; Mr. T. D. Venables, General Secretary Postal Telegraph Clerks' Association; q. 4,620 *et passim*; and Mr. Jno. Christie, first class telegraphist at Edinburgh; q. 5,117 *et passim*.

393 *Who's Who*, 1904, Samuel, Herbert, (L.) M. P., Cleveland Division of N. Riding,

Yorkshire, since 1902. Contested unsuccessfully, South Oxfordshire, 1895 and 1900. Education: University College School; Balliol College, Oxford. First Class Honors, Oxford, 1893.

394 *Hansard's Parliamentary Debates*, December 10, 1902, p. 658.

395 *Hansard's Parliamentary Debates*, June 6, 1904, p. 780.

396 *Who's Who*, 1905.

397 At the by-election of January 29, 1904, Mr. Dobbie was elected by a majority of 44; at the General Election of January, 1906, he was defeated by 261 votes. The number of electors in the Ayr District is 8,031.

398 *Hansard's Parliamentary Debates*, June 14, 1904.

399 *Hansard's Parliamentary Debates*, June 13, 1904.

400 *Hansard's Parliamentary Debates*, October 29, 1906, p. 669.

401 *Report of the Inter-Departmental Committee on Post Office Establishments*, 1897; Mr. E. B. L. Hill, Assistant Secretary General Post Office, London; q. 15,180; and Mr. S. Walpole, Secretary to the Post Office; q. 15,274.

402 *Report of the Inter-Departmental Committee on Post Office Establishments*, 1897, p. 11.

403 *Report of the Inter-Departmental Committee on Post Office Establishments*, 1897, p. 18.

404 *Report of the Inter-Departmental Committee on Post Office Establishments*, 1897, p. 8.

405 *Second Report of the Royal Commission on Civil Establishments*; q. 10,590 to 10,595.

406 *Report of the Inter-Departmental Committee on Post Office Establishments*, 1897; q. 4,215 and following, and 3,198.

407 *Report of the Inter-Departmental Committee on Post Office Establishments*, 1897; q. 3,631 to 3,636, 3,583, and 4,397 and following.

408 *Report of the Inter-Departmental Committee on Post Office Establishments*, 1897; q. 3,037 to 3,060.

409 *Who's Who*, 1905, Shackleton, D. J., M. P. (Lab.), since 1902. Secretary of Darwen Weavers' Association; Vice-President of the Northern Counties Weavers' Amalgamation; Member of Blackburn Chamber of Commerce.

410 *Hansard's Parliamentary Debates*, June 6, 1904, p. 779.

411 *Hansard's Parliamentary Debates*, July 24, 1905, p. 34.

412 *Second Report of the Royal Commission on Civil Establishments*, 1888; q. 20,114 and 20,115.

413 *Third Report from the Committee on Civil Services Expenditure*, 1873; q. 4,729 to 4,731.

414 *Report of the Inter-Departmental Committee on Post Office Establishments*, 1897; q.

3,035 and 3,065.

415 *Report of the Inter-Departmental Committee on Post Office Establishments*, 1897; q. 2,985 and following, and 3,035 to 3,036.

416 *Report of the Inter-Departmental Committee on Post Office Establishments*, 1897; q. 2,777 and following, and Appendix, pp. 1,079 and 1,084.

417 *Report of the Inter-Departmental Committee on Post Office Establishments*, 1897; q. 2,576.

418 *Report of the Inter-Departmental Committee on Post Office Establishments*, 1897; q. 671, 660 to 663, and 1897 to 1914.

CHAPTER XVIII
THE HOUSE OF COMMONS STANDS FOR EXTRAVAGANCE

> Authoritative character of the evidence tendered by the
> several Secretaries of the Treasury. Testimony, in 1902, of
> Lord Welby, who had been in the Treasury from 1856 to 1894.
> Testimony of Sir George H. Murray, Permanent Secretary to
> the Post Office and sometime Private Secretary to the late
> Prime Minister, Mr. Gladstone. Testimony of Sir Ralph H.
> Knox, in the War Office since 1882. Testimony of Sir Edward
> Hamilton, Assistant Secretary to the Treasury since 1894.
> Testimony of Mr. R. Chalmers, a Principal Clerk in the
> Treasury; and of Sir John Eldon Gorst. Mr. Gladstone's tribute
> to Joseph Hume, the first and last Member of the House of
> Commons competent to criticize effectively the details of
> expenditure of the State. Evidence presented before the Select
> Committee on Civil Services Expenditure, 1873.

Before proceeding to the subject proper of this chapter, it is desirable to say a word about the organization and the work of the Treasury.[419]

The Treasury consists of the First Lord of the Treasury, who is almost invariably the Prime Minister; the Chancellor of the Exchequer; and three Junior Lords of the Treasury. "The Treasury is pre-eminently a superintending and controlling office, and has properly no administrative functions." Its duty is to reduce to, and maintain at, the minimum compatible with efficiency, the expenditures of the several Departments of State.

The Treasury has three Secretaries: the Financial Secretary, the Parliamentary, or Patronage Secretary, and the Permanent Secretary. The Financial Secretary, after the Chancellor of the Exchequer, is the political head and conductor of the Treasury. He is one of the hardest worked officers of the Government. His duties were well described, recently, by Mr. Austen Chamberlain, in the course of a brief sketch of his official career. Said Mr.

Chamberlain: "From the Admiralty he was transferred to the position of Financial Secretary to the Treasury, where, as his chief explained to him, he was in the position of an old poacher promoted to be gamekeeper, and his first duty was to unlearn the habits of five years and save money where previously it had been his pleasure to spend it." The Parliamentary, or Patronage Secretary is the principal Government Whip. "He is a very useful and important functionary. His services are indispensable to the Leader of the House of Commons in the control of the House and the management of public business." "It devolves upon him, under the direction of the Leader of the House, 'to facilitate, by mutual understanding, the conduct of public business,' and 'the management of the House of Commons, a position which requires consummate knowledge of human nature, the most amiable flexibility, and complete self-control.'" As "Whipper-in," the Parliamentary Secretary is generally assisted by two of the Junior Lords of the Treasury, who are, at the same time, Government Whips. "Those useful functionaries are expected to gather the greatest number of their own party into every division [of the House of Commons], and by persuasion, promises, explanation, and every available expedient, to bring their men from all quarters to the aid of the Government upon any emergency. It is also their business to conciliate the discontented and doubtful among the ministerial supporters, and to keep every one, as far as possible, in good humor." "An estimate of the importance of the duties which would naturally devolve upon these functionaries—from the increasing interference of the House of Commons in matters of detail, and the necessity for the continual supervision of some Member of the Government conversant with every description of parliamentary business, in order to make sure that the business is done in conformity to the views entertained by the House—induced Sir Charles Wood,[420] to declare, in 1850, that the reduction of the number of Junior Lords from four to three was a very doubtful advantage."

The Financial Secretary and the Parliamentary Secretary are political officers, that is, they sit in the House of Commons, and they change with every change in the Government. The Permanent Secretary, on the other hand, is a non-political officer, or civil servant, who retains office through the successive changes of Government, and secures the continuity of the office.

He is the official head of the Department, and of the whole civil service.

The foregoing facts make it clear that for the purposes of this present discussion, one can cite no more authoritative personages than the several Secretaries of the Treasury.

The Select Committee on National Expenditure, 1902, took a great deal of evidence on the effect of the intervention of the House of Commons in the administrative details of the several Departments of State, particularly on the impairment of the power of the Treasury to control the expenditure of the several Departments.

Lord Welby on Change in Public Opinion

The most important witness was Lord Welby, who, as Mr. Welby, had entered the Treasury in 1856; had been Head of the Finance Department from 1871 to 1885; and had been Permanent Secretary from 1885 to 1894. Lord Welby said that in theory the Treasury had full power of control over the expenditures of the several Departments, but that in practice that power of control was limited by the state of public opinion as reflected in the House of Commons. As soon as the Treasury became aware that it had not public opinion at its back, that fact "would have a certain influence on many of its decisions." Then again, as soon as the other Departments of State became aware that the Treasury was not supported by public opinion, the authority of the Treasury over those Departments was impaired. "If an idea gets abroad that the House of Commons does not care about economy, you will not find your servants economical." Lord Welby then went on to say that in all the political parties in the House of Commons, "the old spirit of economy had been very much weakened." He put the change of public opinion at about the middle of the seventies, or, perhaps, rather later, say, in the eighties. Previous to that change the influence of the Chancellor of the Exchequer had been "paramount, or very powerful, in the Cabinet." But with the change in public opinion, "the effective power of control in the Chancellor of the Exchequer had been proportionately diminished." Lord Welby concluded: "I constantly hear it said now by people of great weight that economy is impossible, that you cannot get the House of Commons to pay attention [to counsels of economy].... The main object [to be striven after], I think, is that there should be some correlation both in the minds of the Government of the day and in the minds of the House of Commons between resources and expenditure; I think that ought to exist, but I do not think it does exist at present. I see no evidence of it."[421]

Mr. Hayes Fisher,[422] a Member of the Committee, and Financial Secretary to the Treasury, in 1902 to 1903, replied to Lord Welby: "But is not the business of the Treasury, and the main business of the Treasury, to check that expenditure and keep it within reasonable bounds, outside of questions of policy?" Lord Welby replied: "Quite so; but might I venture to ask the honorable Member, who occupies one of the most important posts in the Government, whether he would not be glad of support in the House of Commons?" "Most certainly we should on many occasions," was the answer.

Sir George H. Murray on Change in Public Opinion

Sir George H. Murray,[423] Permanent Secretary to the Post Office, was called as a witness because "in the official posts he had held, particularly as Private Secretary to the late Prime Minister, Mr. Gladstone, he had had frequent opportunities for observation not only of the reasons for expenditure, but of the control exercised over it in Parliament." He said: "...But I think the whole attitude of the House itself toward the public service and toward expenditure generally, has undergone a very material change in the present generation.... Of course, the House to this day, in the abstract and in theory, is very strongly in favor of economy, but I am bound to say that in practice Members, both in their corporate capacity and, still more, in their individual capacity, are more disposed to use their influence with the Executive Government in order to increase expenditure than to reduce it.... That is the policy of the House—to spend more money than it did, to criticize expenditure less closely than it did, and to urge the Executive Government to increase expenditure instead of the reverse."[424]

The Commons the Champion of Class Interests

Sir Ralph H. Knox,[425] who had been in the War Office from 1856 to 1901, and who, for forty years, had listened to the discussions in Parliament of the

Estimates of Expenditure, said: "...The mass of speeches that are made in Supply before the House of Commons, are speeches made on behalf of those who have grievances, their friends or constituents, or those with whom they work, or in whom they are particularly interested. If you take speech after speech, you find they are simply to the effect: 'we want more'—and they get more.... In former days there were more Members who were willing to get up with some pertinence and some knowledge to criticize those proposals. But I cannot say there has been any very great tendency in that direction when details are being discussed.... What I want, is [someone] to nip in the bud, new proposals which are made by Members of Parliament very often on behalf of their constituents. A Member, for instance, represents what I should call a labor borough; he gets up and proposes that the pay of every man employed in certain [Government] factories or dockyards should be increased by so much a week, what I want is somebody to get up and say: 'That is not the view of the country, you must not accept that;' but instead of that the matter goes *sub silentio*, and the Government, which is naturally interested in economy and in keeping the expenditure down, is induced to think if there is any feeling in the House at all, it is in favor of doubling everybody's pay." Sir R. H. Knox said he desired more opposition to unwarranted proposals, "because I know what extreme weight is attached to the speeches in Supply by the Minister in charge of a Department, and by the Department itself; but if they find that there is not a single man interested in economy when the details of the Estimates are discussed, it places them in an exceedingly difficult position."[426]

Commons Debates weaken Treasury's Hands

Sir Edward Hamilton, Assistant Secretary to the Treasury since 1894, said that the Treasury could depend less than formerly upon the support of the House of Commons, and that often-times the tendency of the debates in the House was to weaken the hands of the Treasury.[427] Sir Edward Hamilton had entered the Treasury in 1870; had served as Private Secretary to Mr. Lowe, Chancellor of the Exchequer, in 1872-73; and as Private Secretary to Mr. Gladstone, First Lord of the Treasury, in 1880 to 1885. He had been made successively Principal Clerk of the Finance Division in 1885; Assistant

Financial Secretary in 1892; and Assistant Secretary in 1894. In 1902 he was made Permanent Financial Secretary.

Mr. Austen Chamberlain, a member of the Select Committee, asked Mr. R. Chalmers,[428] a Principal Clerk at the Treasury: "Is it within your experience as an official of the Treasury that Ministers of other Departments not infrequently represent, as the reason for allowing expenditure, the strong pressure that has been put upon them in the House of Commons?" "Yes; I have seen repeated instances of that." "And their inability to resist that pressure for another year?" "Yes."[429]

Sir John Eldon Gorst, M. P., a man of large experience of the Public Service, said he had no doubt that in all offices there were officers who had ceased to have anything to do; and that was particularly true of the Education Department, where there was much reading of newspapers, and much literary composition. He had "even heard of rooms where Ping Pong was played, there being nothing else to do at the moment." Sir John Eldon Gorst continued: "The Treasury has power to make an inquiry into every Office, it could institute an inquiry to see whether the office was or was not economically managed, but so far as I know that power never has been exercised. It would be very difficult indeed for the Parliamentary Head of a Department to call in the Treasury for such an investigation. It would make the Parliamentary head extremely unpopular. The only person who, in my opinion, as things are, can really influence the expenses of an office, is the Civil Service head…. But although the Civil Service head of the office has a very great motive to make his office efficient, because his own credit and his own future depend on the efficiency of his office, he has comparatively little motive for economy. Parliament certainly does not thank him; I do not know whether the Treasury thanks him very much; certainly his colleagues do not thank him; … and the natural disposition of a man to let well enough alone renders him reluctant to take upon himself the extremely ungrateful task of making his office, not only an efficient one, but also an economical one. I think anybody who has any experience of mercantile offices, such as a great insurance office, or anything of that kind, would be struck directly with the different atmosphere which prevails in a mercantile office and a Government office…. I have no hesitation in saying that any large insurance company, or any large commercial office of any kind, is worked far more efficiently and far more economically than the best of the Departments of His Majesty's Government."[430]

Sir John Eldon Gorst's statement that he knew of no instance of the Treasury exercising its power of instituting an inquiry conducted by Treasury officers, into the administration of a Department of State, recalls to mind some testimony given by Sir R. E. Welby, Permanent Secretary to the Treasury, before the Royal Commission on Civil Establishments, 1888. Mr. Cleghorn, a Member of that Commission, asked Sir R. E. Welby: "Is there anybody at the Treasury, for instance, who could say to the Board of Trade, or any other particular Department: 'You have too many clerks, you must reduce them by ten?' Is there anybody at the Treasury with sufficient power and knowledge of the work to be in a position to say that, and to take the responsibility of it?" Sir R. E. Welby replied: "No." Thereupon Mr. R. W. Hanbury, another Member of the Commission, asked: "There is not?" Once more the answer was: "No."[431]

Again, in 1876, before the Select Committee on Post Office Telegraph Departments, Mr. Julian Goldsmid, a Member of the Committee, asked Mr. S. A. Blackwood, Financial Secretary to the Post Office: "You would not like, perhaps, to give the reasons for that enormous overmanning which existed in some of the [telegraph] offices [in 1873 to 1875]?" Mr. Blackwood replied: "I am not acquainted with the reasons myself."[432]

Sir Ralph H. Knox, in the course of his testimony, had quoted Mr. Bagehot's statement: "If you want to raise a certain cheer in the House of Commons, make a general panegyric on economy; if you want to invite a sure defeat, propose a particular saving." He had continued: "I should like to add, 'If you want to lose popularity, oppose the proposals for increase.' There ought to be some Members in the House of Commons who would undertake that line."

Gladstone's Tribute to Hume

This wish of Sir Ralph H. Knox recalls to mind the tribute paid, in 1873, by

Mr. Gladstone, to the memory of Joseph Hume, the first as well as the last Member of the House of Commons to acquire a knowledge of the expenditures of the Government which was sufficient to enable the possessor to criticize with intelligence the details of the expenditures of the Government. Said Mr. Gladstone: "…and in like manner, I believe that Mr. Hume has earned for himself an honorable and a prominent place in the history of this country—not by endeavoring to pledge Parliament to abstract resolutions or general declarations on the subject of economy, but by an indefatigable and unwearied devotion, by the labor of a life, to obtain complete mastery of all the details of public expenditure, and by tracking, and I would almost say hunting, the Minister in every Department through all these details with a knowledge equal or superior to his own. In this manner, I do not scruple to say, Mr. Hume did more, not merely to reduce the public expenditure as a matter of figures, but to introduce principles of economy into the management of the administration of public money, than all the men who have lived in our time put together. This is the kind of labor, which, above all things, we want. I do not know whether my honorable and learned friend [Mr. Vernon Harcourt], considering his distinguished career in his profession, is free to devote himself to the public service in the same way as Mr. Hume did. If, however, he is free to do so, I would say to him: 'By all means apply yourself to this vocation. You will find it extremely disagreeable. You will find that during your lifetime very little distinction is to be gained in it, but in the impartiality of history and of posterity you will be judged very severely in the scales of absolute justice as regards the merits of public men, and you will then obtain your reward.'"[433]

The British public, needless to say, still is waiting for the man, or men, who shall take upon themselves the invidious but honorable task of stemming the tide to extravagant expenditure, which, in Great Britain, as elsewhere, is the besetting sin of popular government. The British people still are waiting, though, since 1870, they have vastly increased the functions of the Government by nationalizing a great branch of industry, and therefore are more than ever in need of persons who shall emulate the late Joseph Hume.

In conclusion, let us compare with the testimony given in 1902, the testimony given in 1873, before the Select Committee on Civil Services Expenditure.

A Member of the Select Committee of 1873 asked Mr. W. E. Baxter, Financial Secretary to the Treasury: "Am I right in thinking that you do not agree with the Chancellor of the Exchequer's declaration with regard to the Treasury? I asked him this question: 'Then it is a popular delusion to believe that the Treasury does exercise a direct control over the expenditure of the Department?' And the Chancellor replied: 'I do not know that it is popular, but it is a delusion; I think that it would be much more popular that the Treasury should exercise no control at all.'" Mr. Baxter replied: "I think that the Chancellor stated it too broadly, and would, probably, if he had been Secretary to the Treasury for two or three years, have found that the Treasury did, in point of fact, go back to some extent over the old expenditure as well as try to stop increases." A moment before, Mr. Baxter had said: "The most unpleasant part, as I find it, of the duty of the Financial Secretary to the Treasury is to resist the constant pressure brought day by day, and almost hour by hour, by Members of Parliament, in order to increase expenditure by increasing the pay of individuals, increasing the pay of classes, and granting large compensations to individuals or to classes." The Chairman of the Committee queried: "And that pressure, which is little known to the public, has given you, and your predecessors in office, I presume, a great deal of thought and a great deal of concern?" Mr. Baxter replied: "As I said before, it is the most unpleasant part of my duties, and it occupies a very great deal of time which probably might be better spent." At this point Mr. Sclater-Booth asked: "You spoke of the constant Parliamentary pressure which has been exercised with a view to increasing salaries or compensations, do you allude to proceedings in Parliament as well as private communications, or only to the latter?" Mr. Baxter replied: "I did in my answer only allude to private communications by letter and conversation in the House, because that was in my mind at the time. But of course my answer might be extended to those motions in the House which are resisted without effect by the Government, and which entail great expenditure upon the country." Mr. Herman queried: "When you speak of the pressure put upon you by Members of Parliament for the increase of pay to classes, and the other points that you named, I suppose that you mean that it is partly party pressure, and that you are more subject to it at the present time than you would be if a Conservative Government were in power?" Mr. Baxter replied: "In my experience it has very little to do with party; men from all quarters of the House are at me from week to week." "Do you mean to say that men opposed to you in political principles apply to you for that sort of thing now?" "Certainly I should wish it to be distinctly understood that they do not ask this as a favor; they do not ask favors of me. They simply wish me to look into the question of the pay of individuals and of classes of individuals, as they put it, with a view of benefitting the public service.... In very few instances since I have been Financial Secretary to the Treasury have I been asked by anyone to advance a friend, or to do anything in the shape of a favor. The representations are of this sort: 'Here are a class of public officers who are underpaid. We wish you to look into the matter, and to consider whether or not it would be advantageous to the public service that their salary should be increased.' I look into it, and I say that I am not at all of that opinion, upon which my friend tells me that he will bring the matter before the House, and show us up." "And the other evil is one which is rapidly diminishing, and, in fact, is very small now, namely, interference in favor of individuals?" "Very small indeed."

To a question from Mr. Rathbone, Mr. Baxter replied: "I do not think that the representations in question have much effect; I only stated that the most unpleasant part of my duties was resisting the pressure brought to bear in that way." Thereupon Mr. Rathbone continued: "They may not have an effect when the Government has a majority of one hundred or so, or when there is no election impending, but do you think they have no effect when, as we have seen in former years for long periods, the Government is carried on, whether by one side or the other, by a very small majority, or when an election is impending?" Mr. Baxter replied: "I have no doubt that they have had the effect in former times in those circumstances." "Do you think they would be liable to have that effect again if either party should be reduced to that condition?" "It may be so." "Can you suggest any mode of abating the Parliamentary pressure to which you have alluded, whether it be exercised by public motions or by private influence?" The Financial Secretary to the

Treasury replied: "No; it is an evil very difficult to remedy. I think the better plan would be to inform the constituencies on the subject and let them know the practice which so widely prevails, in order that, if inclined to take the side of economy, they may look after their Members of Parliament." A moment later, Mr. Sclater-Booth asked: "Do you not think from what you have seen of the public service, that the Treasury, existing particularly for that purpose, is the body which must be permanently relied upon to keep down expenditure?" "Decidedly so." "Even the constituencies can scarcely, as a rule, be appealed to in that sense, can they?" "No; I attach very much more importance to the power of the Treasury than either to the action of the House of Commons, or, I am sorry to say, to the voice of the constituencies."[434]

FOOTNOTES:

419 The subjoined statements, excepting the quotation from Mr. Austen Chamberlain, are taken from A. Todd: *On Parliamentary Government in England.*

420 Sir Charles Wood, first Viscount of Halifax. Private Secretary to Earl Grey, 1830 to 1832; Financial Secretary to the Treasury, 1832 to 1834; Secretary to the Admiralty, 1835 to 1839; Chancellor of the Exchequer, 1846 to 1852; President of the Board of Control, 1852 to 1855; First Lord of the Admiralty, 1855 to 1858; Secretary of State for India, 1859 to 1866; raised to Peerage as Viscount Halifax in 1866; Lord Privy Seal, 1870 to 1874.

421 *Report from the Select Committee on National Expenditure*, 1902; q. 2,516 to 2,605.

422 *Who's Who*, 1905, Fisher, Wm. Hayes, M. P., Financial Secretary to the Treasury, 1902-1903; Junior Lord of the Treasury, and a Ministerial Whip, 1895 to 1902; Hon. Private Secretary to Sir Michael Hicks-Beach, 1886 to 1887; and to Right Honorable A. J. Balfour, 1887 to 1892.

423 *Who's Who*, 1904, Murray, Sir G. H., Joint Permanent Under Secretary to the Treasury since 1903. Entered the Foreign Office, 1873; transferred to Treasury, 1880; Private Secretary to Right Honorable W. E. Gladstone and to Earl of Rosebery, when Prime Minister; Chairman Board of Inland Revenue, 1897 to 1899; Secretary to the Post Office, 1899 to 1903.

424 *Report from the Select Committee on National Expenditure*, 1902; q. 1,631 to 1,673, and 1,730 to 1,732.

425 *Who's Who*, 1904, Knox, Sir Ralph H., entered War Office in 1856; Accountant-General, War Office, 1882 to 1897; Permanent Under Secretary of State for War, 1897 to 1901; a Member of the Committee which worked out Lord Cardwell's Army Reform, and of the Royal Commission on Indian Financial Relations, 1896; Civil Service Superannuations, 1902; and Militia and Volunteers, 1903.

426 *Report from the Select Committee on National Expenditure*, 1902; q. 1,567 to 1,569, and 1,823 to 1,825.

427 *Report from the Select Committee on National Expenditure*, 1902; q. 2,081 to 2,084.

428 In 1905 Mr. Chalmers was made Assistant Secretary to the Treasury.

429 *Report from the Select Committee on National Expenditure*, 1902; q. 615 to 618.

430 *Report from the Select Committee on National Expenditure*, 1892; q. 2,406 to 2,419, and 2,502.

431 *Second Report of the Royal Commission on Civil Establishments*, 1888; q. 10,683 to 10,684.

432 *Report from the Select Committee on Post Office (Telegraph Department)*, 1876; q. 5,397 to 5,600.

433 *Hansard's Parliamentary Debates*, February 18, 1873, p. 632 and following.

434 *Third Report from the Select Committee on Civil Services Expenditure*, 1873; q. 4,672 to 4,768.

CHAPTER XIX
CONCLUSION

A large and ever increasing number of us are adherents of the political theory that the extension of the functions of the State to the inclusion of the conduct of business ventures will purify politics and make the citizen take a more intelligent as well as a more active part in public affairs. The verdict of the experience of Great Britain under the public ownership and operation of the telegraphs is that that doctrine is untenable. Instead of purifying politics, public ownership has corrupted them. It has given a great impetus to class bribery, a form of corruption far more insidious than individual bribery. With one exception, wherever the public ownership of the telegraphs has affected the pocket-book interests of any considerable body of voters, the good-will of those voters has been gained at the expense of the public purse. The only exception has been the policy pursued toward the owners of the telephone patents; and even in that case the policy adopted was not dictated by legitimate motives.

The nationalization of the telegraphs was initiated with class bribery. The telegraph companies had been poor politicians, and had failed to conciliate the newspaper press by allowing the newspapers to organize their own news bureaux. The Government played the game of politics much better; it gave the newspapers a tariff which its own advisor, Mr. Scudamore, said would prove unprofitable. No subsequent Government has attempted to abrogate the bargain, though the annual loss to the State now is upward of $1,500,000.

The promise to extend the telegraphs to every place with a money order issuing Post Office was given in ignorance of what it would cost to carry out that promise. But the adherence to the policy until an anticipated expenditure of $1,500,000 had risen to $8,500,000 was nothing more nor less than the purchase of votes out of the public purse. Not until 1873 did the Government abandon the policy that every place with a money order issuing Post Office was entitled to telegraphic service.

When the House of Commons, in March, 1883, against the protests of the Government passed the resolution which demanded that the tariff on telegrams be cut almost in two, the Government should have resigned rather than carry out the order. The Government's obedience to an order which the Government itself contended would put a heavy burden on the taxpayer for four years, was nothing more nor less than the purchase of Parliamentary support out of the public purse. No serious argument had been advanced that the charge of 24 cents for 20 words was excessive. The argument of the leader of the movement for reduction, Dr. Cameron, of Glasgow, was a worthy complement to the argument made in 1868 by Mr. Hunt, Chancellor of the Exchequer, to wit, that telegraphing ought to be made so cheap that the illiterate man who could not write a letter would send a telegram. Dr. Cameron argued that "instead of maintaining a price which was prohibitory not only to the working classes but also to the middle classes, they ought to take every means to encourage telegraphy. They ought to educate the rising generation to it; and he would suggest to the Government that the composing of telegrams would form a useful part of the education in our board schools."

Parliament after Parliament, and Government after Government has purchased out of the public purse the good-will of the telegraph employees. Organized in huge civil servants' unions, the telegraph employees have been permitted to establish the policy that wages and salaries shall be fixed in no small degree by the amount of political pressure that the telegraph employees can bring to bear on Members of the House of Commons. With the rest of the Government employees they have been permitted to establish the doctrine that once a man has landed himself on the State's pay-roll, he has "something very nearly approaching to a freehold of provision for life," irrespective of his fitness and his amenableness to discipline, and no matter what labor-saving machines may be invented, or how much business may fall off. To a considerable degree the State employees have established their demand that promotion be made according to seniority rather than merit. In more than one Postmaster General have they instilled "a perfect horror of passing anyone over." Turning to one part of the service, one finds the civil service unions achieving the revocation of the promotion of the man denominated "probably the ablest man in the Sheffield Post Office." Turning to another part of the service, one finds the Postmaster General, Mr. Raikes, "for the good of the service" telling an exceptionally able man that "he can well afford to wait his turn." The civil servants, in the telegraph service and elsewhere, to a considerable degree have secured to themselves exemption from the rigorous discipline to which must submit the people who are in the service of private individuals and of companies. Finally, the civil servants have been permitted to establish to a greater or a lesser degree a whole host of demands that are inconsistent with the economical conduct of business. Among them may be mentioned the demand that the standard of efficiency may not be raised without reimbursement to those who take the trouble to come up to the new standard; that if a man enters the service when the proportion of higher officers to the rank and file is 1 to 10, he has "an implied contract" with the Government that that proportion shall not be altered to his disadvantage though it may be altered to his advantage.

Public opinion has compelled the great Political Parties to drop Party politics with regard to the State employees, and to give them security of tenure of office. But it permits the State employees to engage in Party politics towards Members of Parliament. The civil service unions watch the speeches and votes of Members of the House of Commons, and send speakers and campaign workers into the districts of offending Members. In the election campaigns they ask candidates to pledge themselves to support in Parliament civil servants' demands. Their political activities have led Mr. Hanbury, Financial Secretary to the Treasury in 1895 to 1900, to say: "We must recognize the fact that in this House of Commons, public servants have a Court of Appeal such as exists with regard to no private employee whatever. It is a Court of Appeal which exists not only with regard to the grievances of classes, and even of individuals, but it is a Court of Appeal which applies even to the wages and duties of classes and individuals, and its functions in that respect are only limited by the common sense of Members, who should exercise caution in bringing forward cases of individuals, because, if political influence is brought to bear in favor of one individual, the chances are that injury is done to some other individual.... We have done away with personal and individual bribery, but there is still a worse form of bribery, and that is when a man asks a candidate [for Parliament] to buy his vote out of the public purse." The tactics employed by civil servants have led the late Postmaster General, Lord Stanley, to apply the terms "blackmail" and "blood-sucking." The conduct of the House of Commons under civil service pressure has led Mr. A. J. Balfour, the late Premier, to express grave anxiety concerning the future of Great Britain's civil service. It has led Mr. Austen Chamberlain, Representative of the Postmaster General, to say that Members of both Parties had come to him seeking protection from the demands made upon them by the civil servants. On another occasion it has led Mr. Chamberlain to say: "In a great administration like this there must be decentralization, and how difficult it is to decentralize, either in the Post Office or in the Army, when working under constant examination by question and answer in this House, no Honorable Member who has not had experience of official life can easily realize. But there must be decentralization, because every little petty matter cannot be dealt with by the Postmaster General or the Permanent Secretary to the Post Office. Their attention should be reserved in the main for large questions, and I think it is deplorable, absolutely deplorable, that so much of their time should be occupied, as under the present circumstances it necessarily is occupied, with matters of very small detail because these matters of detail are asked by Honorable Members and because we do not feel an Honorable Member will accept an answer from anyone but the highest authority. I think a third of the time—I am putting it at a low estimate—of the highest officials in the Post Office is occupied in answering questions raised by Members of this House, and in providing me with information in order that I may be in a position to answer the inquiries addressed to me" about matters which "in any private business would be dealt with by the officer on the spot, without appeal or consideration unless grievous cause were shown."

The questions of which Mr. Austen Chamberlain spoke, at one end of the scale are put on behalf of a man discharged for theft, at the other end of the scale on behalf of the man who fears he will not be promoted. The practice of putting such questions not only leads to deplorable waste of executive ability, it also modifies profoundly the entire administration of the public service. Lord Welby, the highest authority in Great Britain, in 1902 testified that it was the function of the Treasury to hold the various Departments up to efficient and economical administration. But that the debates in the Commons not only weakened the Treasury's control over the several Departments, but also made the Treasury lower its standards of efficiency and economy. He added that in the last twenty or twenty-five years both Parties had lost a great deal of "the old spirit of economy," and that at the same time "the effective power of control in the Chancellor of the Exchequer had been proportionately diminished." In former times the Chancellor of the Exchequer had been "paramount, or very powerful in the Cabinet." Upon the same occasion, Sir George H. Murray was called to testify, because "in the official posts he had held, particularly as Private Secretary to the late Prime Minister, Mr. Gladstone, he had had frequent opportunities for observation not only of the reasons for expenditure, but of the control exercised over it in Parliament." Sir George H. Murray said: "But I think the whole attitude of the House itself toward the public service and toward expenditure generally, has undergone a very material change in the present generation.... Of course, the House to this day, in the abstract and in theory, is very strongly in favor of economy, but I am bound to say that in practice Members, both in their corporate capacity and, still more, in their individual capacity, are more disposed to use their influence with the Executive Government in order to increase expenditure than to reduce it." Sir John Eldon Gorst testified in 1902: "But although the Civil Service head of the office has a very great motive to make his office efficient, because his own credit and his future depend on the efficiency of his office, he has comparatively little motive for economy. Parliament certainly does not thank him; and I do not know whether the Treasury thanks him very much; certainly his colleagues do not thank him.... I think anybody who has any experience of mercantile offices, such as a great insurance office, or anything of that kind, would be struck directly with the different atmosphere which prevails in a mercantile office and a Government office.... I have no hesitation in saying that any large insurance company, or any large commercial office of any kind is worked far more efficiently and far more economically than the best of the Departments of His Majesty's Government."

Sir John Eldon Gorst might have added that the Civil Service head of a Department really had only rather moderate power to enforce economy. Before the Royal Commission of 1888, Lord Welby [then Sir Welby],

Permanent Secretary to the Treasury, was asked: "But you would hardly plead the interference of Members of Parliament as a justification for not getting rid of an unworthy servant, would you?" Lord Welby, who had been in the Treasury since 1856, replied: "It is not a good reason, but as a matter of fact it is powerful. The House of Commons are our masters."

In the hands of a commercial company, the telegraphs in the United Kingdom would yield a handsome return even upon their present cost to the Government. That is proven beyond the possibility of controversy by the figures presented in the preceding chapters. In the hands of the State, in the period from 1892-93 to 1905-06, the operating expenses alone have exceeded the gross receipts by $1,435,000. If one excludes, as not earned by the telegraphs, the $8,552,000 paid the Government by the National Telephone Company in the form of royalties for the privilege of conducting the telephone business in competition with the State's telegraphs, the excess of operating expenses over gross receipts will become $9,987,000. That sum, of course, takes no account of the large sums required annually to pay the interest and depreciation charges upon the capital invested in the telegraph plant.

On March 31, 1906, the capital invested in the telegraphs was $84,812,000. To raise that capital, the Government had sold $54,300,000 of 3 per cent. securities, at an average price of about 92.3; and for the rest the Government had drawn upon the current revenue raised by taxation. On March 31, 1906, the unearned interest which the Government had paid upon the aforesaid $54,300,000 of securities had aggregated $22,530,000, the equivalent of 26.5 per cent. of the capital invested in the telegraphs. Upon the $30,500,000 taken from the current revenue, the Government never has had any return whatever.

The nationalization of the telegraphs has corrupted British politics by giving a great impetus to the insidious practice of class bribery. It also has placed heavy burdens upon the taxpayers. But that is not all. The public ownership of the telegraphs has resulted in the State deliberately hampering the development of the telephone industry. That industry, had the Government let it alone, would have grown to enormous proportions, promoting the convenience and the prosperity of the business community, as well as giving employment to tens of thousands of people. In the year 1906, only one person in each 105 persons in the United Kingdom was a subscriber to the telephone; and the total of persons employed in the telephone industry was only some 20,000. On January 1, 1907, one person in each 20 persons in the United States was a subscriber to the telephone.

Under the telephone policy pursued by the Government, the National Telephone Company down to the close of the year 1896 for all practical purposes had no right to erect a pole in a street or lay a wire under a street. As late as 1898, not less than 120,000 miles of the company's total of 140,000 miles of wire were strung from house-top to house-top, under private way-leaves which the owners of the houses had the right to terminate on six months' notice. Inadequate as it was, the progress made by the National Telephone Company down to 1898 was a splendid tribute to British enterprise.

The necessarily unsatisfactory service given by the National Telephone Company, down to the close of 1898, created a prejudice against the use of the telephone which to this day has not been completely overcome. Again, the Government to this day has left the National Telephone Company in such a position of weakness, that the Company has been unable to brave public opinion to the extent of abolishing the unlimited user tariff and establishing the measured service tariff exclusively. On the other hand, it is an admitted fact that the telephone cannot be brought into very extensive use except on the basis of the measured service exclusively.

The British Government embarked in the telegraph business, thus putting itself in the position of a trader. But it refused subsequently to assume one of the commonest risks to which every trader is exposed, the liability to have his property impaired in value, if not destroyed, by inventions and new ways of doing things. In that respect the British Government has pursued the same policy that the British Municipalities have pursued. The latter bodies first hampered the spread of the electric light, in large part for the purpose of protecting the municipal gas plants; and subsequently they hampered the spread of the so-called electricity-in-bulk generating companies, which threatened to drive out of the field the local municipal electric light plants.

Very recently the British Government has taken measures to protect its telegraphs and its long distance telephone service from competition from wireless telegraphy. It has refused an application for a license made by a company that proposed to establish a wireless telegraphy service between certain English cities. The refusal was made "on the ground that the installations are designed for the purpose of establishing exchanges which would be in contravention of the Postmaster General's ordinary telegraphic monopoly." In order to protect its property in the submarine cables to France, Belgium, Holland and Germany, the Government has inserted in the "model wireless telegraphy license" a prohibition of the sending or receiving of international telegrams, "either directly or by means of any intermediate station or stations, whether on shore or on a ship at sea." In short, the commercial use of wireless telegraphy apparatus the Government has limited to communication with vessels.

In one respect the nationalization of the telegraphs has fulfilled the promises made by the advocates of nationalization. It has increased enormously the use of the telegraphs. But when the eminent economist, Mr. W. S. Jevons, came to consider what the popularization of the telegraphs had cost the taxpayers, he could not refrain from adding that a large part of the increased use made of the telegraphs was of such a nature that the State could have no motive for encouraging it. "Men have been known to telegraph for a pocket handkerchief," was his closing comment. Mr. Jevons had been an ardent advocate of nationalization. Had he lived to witness the corruption of politics produced by the public ownership of the telegraphs, his disillusionment would have been even more complete.

From whatever viewpoint one examines the outcome of the nationalization of the telegraphs, one finds invariably that experience proves the unsoundness of the doctrine that the extension of the functions of the State to the inclusion of the conduct of business ventures will purify politics and make the citizen take a more intelligent as well as a more active part in public affairs. Class bribery has been the outcome, wherever the State as the owner of the telegraphs has come in conflict with the pocket-book interest of the citizen. One reason has been that the citizen has not learned to act on the principle of subordinating his personal interest to the interest of the community as a whole. Another reason has been that the community as a whole has not learned to take the pains to ascertain its interests, and to protect them against the illegitimate demands made by classes or sections of the community. There is no body of intelligent and disinterested public opinion to which can appeal for support the Member of Parliament who is pressed to violate the public interest, but wishes to resist the pressure. The policy of State intervention and State ownership does not create automatically that eternal vigilance which is the price not only of liberty but also of good government. One may go further, and say that the verdict of British experience is that it is more difficult to safeguard and promote the public interest under the policy of State intervention than under the policy of *laissez-faire*. Under the degree of political intelligence and public and private virtue that have existed in Great Britain since 1868, no public service company could have violated the permanent interests of the people in the way in which the National Government and the Municipalities have violated them since they have become the respective owners of the telegraphs and the municipal public service industries. No public service company could have blocked the progress of a rival in the way in which the Government has blocked the progress of the telephone. No combination of capital could have exercised such control over Parliament and Government as the Association of Municipal Corporations has exercised. Finally, no combination of capital could have violated the public interest in such manner as the civil service unions have done.

CPSIA information can be obtained
at www.ICGtesting.com
Printed in the USA
LVHW090048010920
664725LV00010B/345